The Rise
Part I

Marcus Rex

Published by

Melrose Books

An Imprint of Melrose Press Limited
St Thomas Place, Ely
Cambridgeshire
CB7 4GG, UK
www.melrosebooks.co.uk

FIRST EDITION

Copyright © Marcus Rex 2018

The Author asserts his moral right to
be identified as the author of this work

Cover by Melrose Books

ISBN   **978-1-912640-18-8 Paperback**
             978-1-912640-19-5 ePub
             978-1-912640-20-1 **Mobi**

All rights reserved. No part of this publication may be reproduced, stored in a retrieval system, or transmitted, in any form or by any means electronic, mechanical, photocopying, recording or otherwise, without the prior permission of the publishers.

This book is sold subject to the condition that it shall not, by way of trade or otherwise, be lent, re-sold, hired out or otherwise circulated without the publisher's prior consent in any form of binding or cover other than that in which it is published and without a similar condition including this condition being imposed on the subsequent purchaser.

Printed and bound in Great Britain by:
CMP (UK) Ltd, G3 The Fulcrum, Vantage Way
Poole, Dorset, BH12 4NU

For Carol

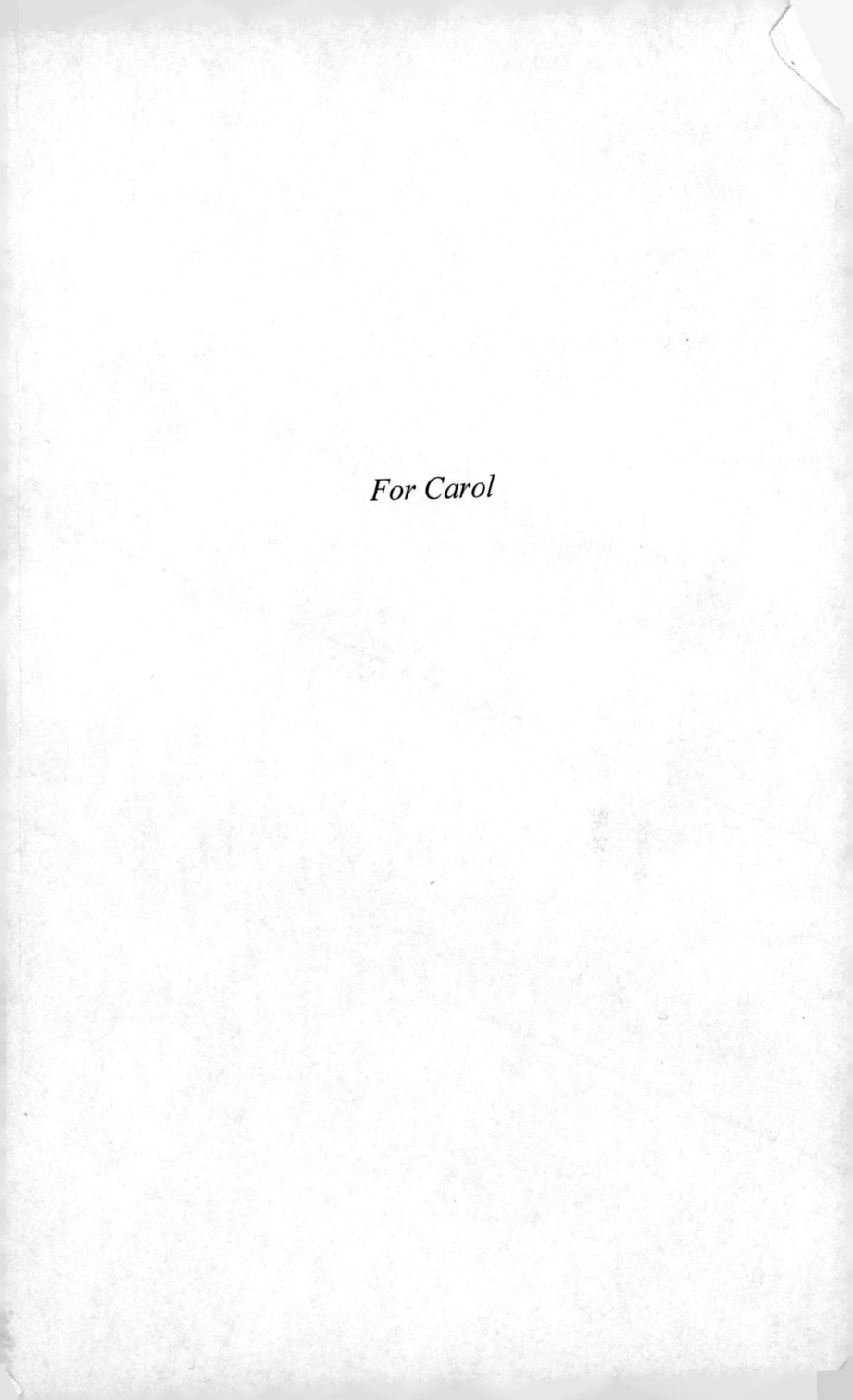

Anyone who has not witnessed a strange event in their life is very strange indeed.

Derek Mills 10.10.2010

Acknowledgements

I am very grateful to those who have helped with contributions, both factual and theoretical, during this process. A very special mention must go to Mark Lynn whose endless enthusiasm gave me the confidence to produce books two and three in this series.

Research came from a multitude of sources, but a special mention must be made for the inspirational writings of Dolores Cannon, Kenneth Hite and Robert Sepehr.

For further information on all things related to *The Rise* series please check out
www.marcusrex.co.uk

MAP OF DULCE BASE

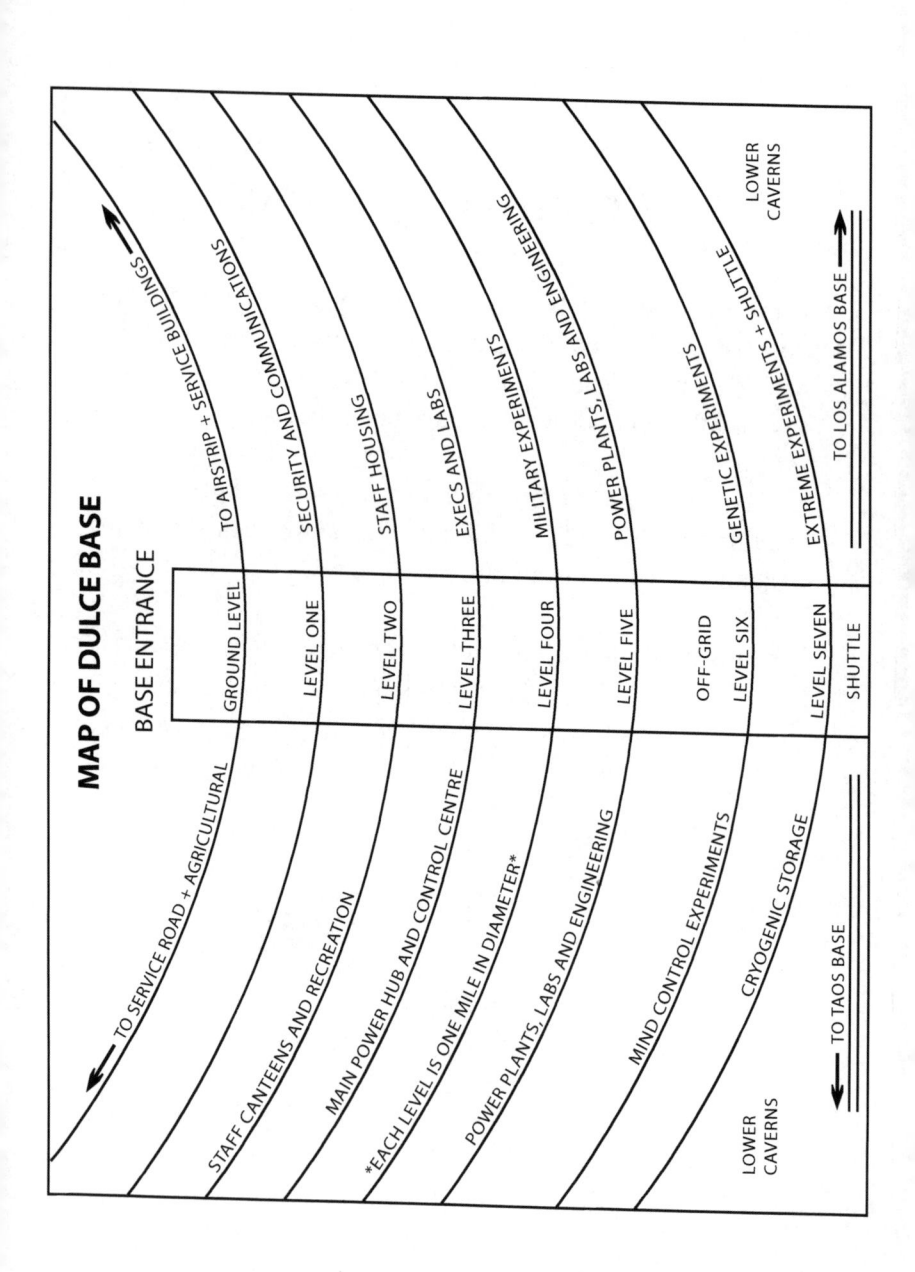

BASE ENTRANCE

TO SERVICE ROAD + AGRICULTURAL	GROUND LEVEL — TO AIRSTRIP + SERVICE BUILDINGS
STAFF CANTEENS AND RECREATION	LEVEL ONE — SECURITY AND COMMUNICATIONS
MAIN POWER HUB AND CONTROL CENTRE	LEVEL TWO — STAFF HOUSING
EACH LEVEL IS ONE MILE IN DIAMETER	LEVEL THREE — EXECS AND LABS
POWER PLANTS, LABS AND ENGINEERING	LEVEL FOUR — MILITARY EXPERIMENTS
MIND CONTROL EXPERIMENTS	LEVEL FIVE — POWER PLANTS, LABS AND ENGINEERING
	OFF-GRID
CRYOGENIC STORAGE	LEVEL SIX — GENETIC EXPERIMENTS
	LEVEL SEVEN — EXTREME EXPERIMENTS + SHUTTLE
LOWER CAVERNS	SHUTTLE — LOWER CAVERNS
← TO TAOS BASE	TO LOS ALAMOS BASE →

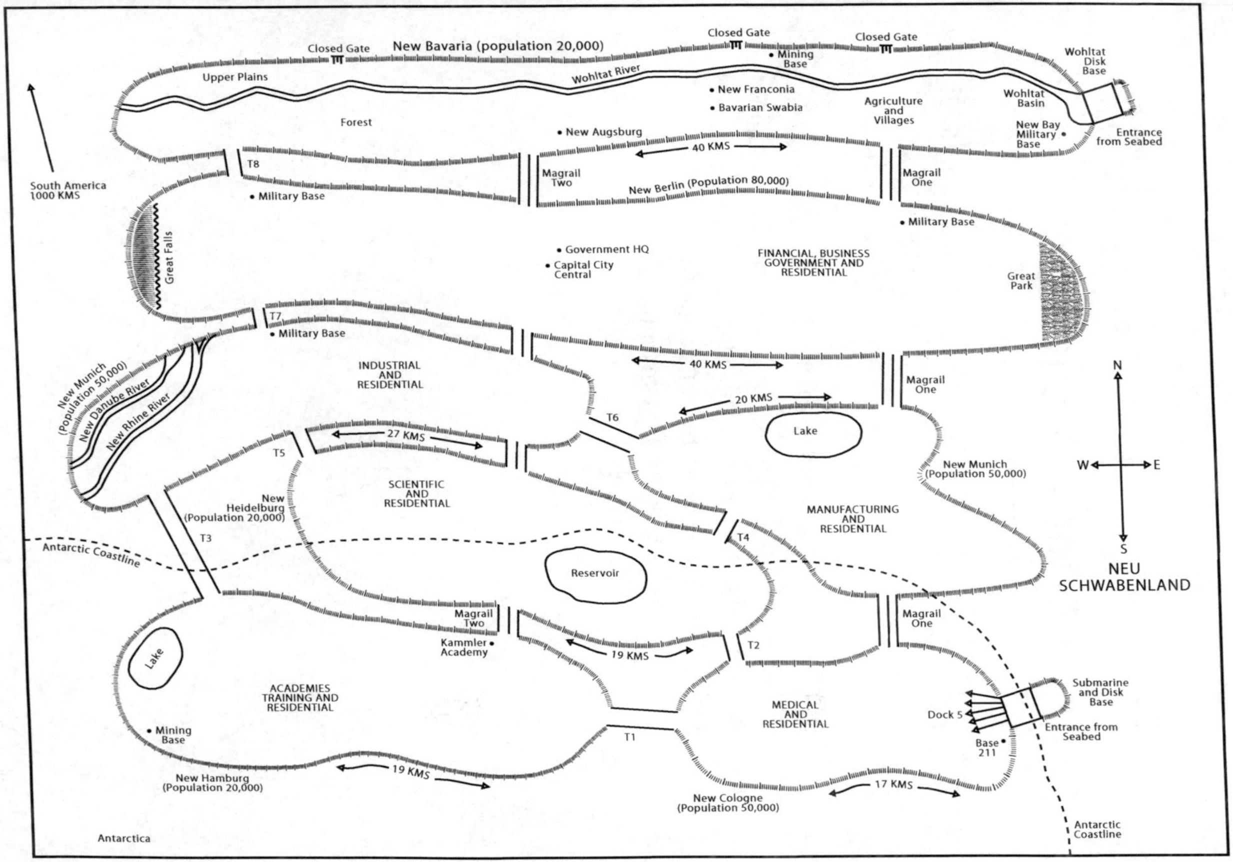

New Bavaria (population 20,000)
Closed Gate
Closed Gate
Closed Gate
Mining Base
Wohltat Disk Base
Upper Plains
Wohltat River
New Franconia
Bavarian Swabia
Agriculture and Villages
Wohltat Basin
Forest
New Augsburg
New Bay Military Base
Entrance from Seabed
40 KMS
T8
Magrail Two
Magrail One
South America 1000 KMS
New Berlin (Population 80,000)
Military Base
Military Base
Government HQ
Capital City Central
FINANCIAL, BUSINESS GOVERNMENT AND RESIDENTIAL
Great Falls
Great Park
T7
Military Base
40 KMS
INDUSTRIAL AND RESIDENTIAL
Magrail One
New Munich (Population 50,000)
New Danube River
New Rhine River
20 KMS
T6
Lake
27 KMS
T5
N
W
E
S
New Munich (Population 50,000)
SCIENTIFIC AND RESIDENTIAL
New Heidelburg (Population 20,000)
MANUFACTURING AND RESIDENTIAL
T3
T4
Antarctic Coastline
Reservoir
NEU SCHWABENLAND
Magrail Two
Magrail One
Kammler Academy
T2
19 KMS
Lake
ACADEMIES TRAINING AND RESIDENTIAL
Submarine and Disk Base
MEDICAL AND RESIDENTIAL
Dock 5
Entrance from Seabed
Mining Base
T1
Base 211
19 KMS
New Hamburg (Population 20,000)
17 KMS
New Cologne (Population 50,000)
Antarctic Coastline
Antarctica

About Marcus Rex

Marcus Rex was born in Dry Drayton, Cambridgeshire in 1965.

He has lived in the area for most of his life and currently resides only a few miles from this location with his wife and two Dobermann dogs.

Before becoming a full time writer, Marcus was involved with property development and ran a successful antiques business. He has been fronting bands since the age of sixteen and is still actively involved in the music industry.

His novel, *The Rise*, is the first instalment in a trilogy of novels.

Glossary

2 i/c	Second In Command
ARF	Airborne Reaction Force
APC	Armoured Personnel Carrier
ATO	Ammunitions Technical Officer
BG	Bodyguard
Comms	Communication
DOP	Drop Off Point
Infil	Infiltration
LS	Landing Site
MOE	Method Of Entry
Net	Communications Network
NVG	Night Vision Goggles
OC	Officer In Command
DPM	Disruptive Pattern Material (Camouflage)
EandE	Escape And Evasion
ERV	Emergency Rendezvous
Exfil	Exfiltration
FOB	Forward Operations Base
QRF	Quick Reaction Force
RPG	Rocket Propelled Grenade
RV	Rendezvous Point
Tacbe	Tactical Beacon (Sends Out Distress Signal)

Prologue

Germany, April 1945

Kessler wrestled with the wheel of the truck, using all his skill to avoid potholes and craters created by the relentless shelling by the advancing allied forces. In addition to shelling the cities, they were attacking the bridges and main roadways, trying to cut off the route network to prevent supplies and reinforcements shoring up the breaches.

Smoke billowed from nearby twisted buildings, the bombers high above covering the airspace like a swarm of green locusts, the ever decreasing German resistance making it all the more easy to line up the high explosives, followed by consignments of incendiaries reducing large swathes of the city nearby to a wasteland. Pockets of soldiers and civilians alike could be seen breaking cover to find safety, running aimlessly, disorientated by the deafening sound of gunfire, screaming and explosions. Life was evaporating from the city; even the birds had disappeared, the only fluttering to witness was the propaganda leaflets as they tumbled out of the sky.

A child, face blackened by smoke, clothes in tatters, was wandering by the side of the road, trying to find parents that were almost certainly dead. The man behind the wheel, grateful to avoid the melee of confusion, momentarily caught the child glancing up, looking directly at him, the black accusing eyes recognising the officer's uniform in the vehicle, and revealing their message; those eyes, that battle-hardened face matured by encapsulated warfare, already witnessing more than his short life on Earth should have permitted, the eyes transmitting words.

"It's your fault. Look around you. You and your comrades are responsible for all this. How dare you do this to us?"

Kessler could see the hatred building. It would probably stay with him, long after the war was over, should the boy survive at all.

Another explosion nearby took the side off a deserted factory building. Their gaze broken momentarily, the boy disappeared behind some ruins.

Kessler had seen that look many times before. He had become immune to fitting the blame around himself; after all, he was only acting on orders. He rubbed the bridge of his nose, clearing the boy from his mind, and floored the accelerator.

The Russians could have Dresden, and the rest of the charred rubble. Like many, the only reason he was here was the push on Russia. Kessler had always thought the move a trifle over-ambitious.

The same thing had been Napoleon's undoing. Splitting the forces was always going to be a strategic risk, and this time the risk had not paid off with good men, some of them close friends taken by the harsh Siberian winter, Kessler reminisced.

The 1941 push into Russia had been quite straightforward. With orders executed to perfection, Kessler and his unit had advanced, reaching the Catherine Palace at Tsarskoye Selo near Saint Petersburg. He remembered storming the building with ruthless efficiency, hardly losing a man in the process, the SS troops securing the area enabling Kessler to begin the hunt to find the wing that housed the room fitted out with panelled walls of amber, gold leaf, and precious stones. After a short search, the intelligence sources were fully vindicated and the gamble had paid off. Kessler allowed himself a brief moment to marvel at the magnificent decoration, of a value that was almost inconceivable. The Führer would be very pleased.

They dismantled the gold room and word of their conquest was sent ahead. The sections were shipped back to their destination as instructed and one of Hitler's many obsessions was ticked off the list. Kessler was expecting a rewarding position for his achievements, and deservedly so in his opinion, an opinion which, unfortunately, was not shared by the Führer.

Almost immediately, Kessler was sent back to repeatedly plunder as much artwork and other valuable treasures as he and his men could find.

It was at this point on sortie number four, deep into Russian territory, that Kessler began to feel somewhat undervalued. While most of the comrades of his stature wined and dined themselves in large chateaux in Belgium and France, he found himself up to his waist in snow, battling the elements rather than the Russian enemy who had the good sense to wait the winter out. Kessler's resentment had now reached breaking point.

Four years later, and with all plans now well and truly abandoned, the Reich retreated to regroup, with Kessler ordered back to Berlin by Hitler for a new assignment.

But with defeat staring them in the face, Kessler had other ideas.

He drove on as fast as he dared, the daylight fading fast, the headlights of the truck masked out to avoid the enemy aircraft, making progress even more difficult, rendering them almost useless. He had to make his destination by nightfall. All was lost now, and it was everyone for themselves.

In the new order, Kessler felt of worth. He had been given a sense of purpose, a meaning amidst all of this madness. Hitler had indeed lost his grip on power, and now he would pay the price for his ingratitude. At least someone had seen the potential in *him*, his sharp intellect, his vast scientific knowledge, his loyalty to the new cause.

A lot of men had welcomed the war. They could not wait to pledge their allegiance, displaying themselves in acts of courage, obeying commands without pausing to question the directive.

Kessler found the war an irritating distraction, preventing him from sticking to his agenda. He knew a lot of Americans felt the same way, the two countries working together on secret projects long before 1939. This was the reason that Kessler had withheld so much information for the last two years. He was sick and tired of Hitler's henchmen hijacking his facilities for their own gains, and then taking credit for the scientific breakthroughs.

Well, now the war was lost, and it was time to reacquaint himself with the original agenda.

As the built-up area of the city dwindled into random surviving residential dwellings, the bombing eased off; the Allies were more interested in the intensive destruction of the infrastructure, smashing the heart of the opposing war machine that had been so dominant only months earlier.

Kessler rounded a bend and saw the entrance.

To the casual observer, the country barn looked like many in the local area that farmers would use to store grain and hay for the winter months, but Kessler knew that this one was very different.

The wooden building with a reinforced steel interior was locked from the inside. Kessler brought the truck to a halt. He climbed from the cabin, giving the breast pocket adorned with an iron cross a reassuring pat. Now was not the time for some snivelling guard to refuse him entry.

It would have been far more straightforward had it not been for an allied aircraft jettisoning the last of its bombs before turning for home, catching the evacuating convoy of three vehicles, one of which was commanding officer Kessler's staff car.

With the driver dead and his beloved Mercedes a wreck, Kessler had been thrown clear by the bomb blast. When he came to, he could see the only other surviving soldier lying on the bonnet of a truck. The young driver had gone through the windscreen, suffering multiple lacerations to the face and body. The chances were that he probably would have survived, but it was a problem Kessler could do without. A swift head shot with his Luger soon solved the dilemma. He pulled the soldier from the engine hood and the lifeless body slumped off the vehicle into the roadside brush.

Kessler climbed aboard the Opel Blitz, smashing loose glass away from his vision with the warm barrel of his pistol. He checked behind him, breathing a sigh of relief; the truck was still roadworthy. It was a pre-war commercial model, six cylinders with twin rear wheels, one of the better ones, converted to meet the demands of the war. Unfortunately, because of the lack of a split screen, he would have to endure the rest of the journey with a stiff breeze in the entire cabin area. No matter, though; a small price to pay ... all things considered.

Apart from a few narrow misses from Allied bombing, and a sore head, Kessler had arrived at the barn relatively unscathed. The war had been full of twists and turns, where the fate of both sides could have been determined by one small detail. Kessler cursed as he fished out the identification from his pocket. Lucky to be alive he certainly was, as were so many others, but they were so tantalisingly close. The end goal, far more important than even the war itself, had been taken from them in such a cruel manner.

It would all have to wait for a while. Right now, Kessler's main objective was self-preservation.

He knocked on the door with the sequence instructed. For what seemed far too long, nothing happened. He was just about to knock again when a small opening appeared. A voice barked, "Papers?"

Kessler pushed his documents through the opening. There was a pause for a few moments and the door opened. He was greeted by a fawning junior officer.

"Obergruppenführer, it is a great honour, sir."

Even in his current dishevelled state, Kessler's uniform still commanded the respect it deserved from the lower ranks, the black Allgemeine SS insignia clearly visible, as was the hash mark on the right arm indicating length of service before 1933, the Ahnenerbe cuff band indicating runic training, and also a ceremonial Athame ritual dagger scabbarded over his right breast. In addition to Kessler's rank were tabs revealing special training outside the regular chain of command.

"Please, sir, follow me." The young soldier ushered him with a leading hand.

They walked across the barn to a trapdoor. The soldier opened the hatch and led the way down a ladder secured to the wall face. Once down the ladder, they walked along an illuminated corridor for the best part of five minutes before reaching a security door. The soldier, who Kessler found out was called Verden, used a coded sequence to knock on the door. They heard the various locks disengage and the heavy door slowly swung open. Standing on the other side was a familiar face.

Kessler grinned broadly for the first time in an age, nodding his head, with arms outstretched, the other officer reciprocating.

"Heinz, thank God you made it."

"Karl, my friend, are the others all here?" Kessler enquired.

Karl Beiger gestured for Kessler to follow him, while Verden closed the door and made his way to his post above ground.

"They are all here ready and waiting. Germany's finest."

The two men were standing in a dome shaped room sparsely decorated with campaign furniture. A large table occupied the centre of the room, research documents being hurriedly collected up by two other men. They exchanged brief pleasantries with Kessler and then all made their way through another door that led into a much bigger space. This time, the walls were racked out with equipment. Below them were workbenches full of abandoned tools, the work now completed. A gantry with a rail encircled a strangely shaped object in the middle of the spotlessly clean floor. Everything was black apart from a tell-tale German insignia on the centre of the object. Leaning on the gantry was another familiar face. He came down a series of steps, greeting Kessler with a warm, low-register voice.

"Herr Kessler, welcome to Das Glocke." He pointed to the object over his shoulder.

It was the first time Kessler had seen The Bell fully assembled. It was simply magnificent with its subtle lines, the understated craftsmanship and the attention to detail in stark contrast to cold, industrial, mass-produced products. There was no expense spared here, the finish to the highest standard. The craft was nicknamed The Bell because of its resemblance to one and was the latest in a long programme of secret projects that, despite the very odd shape, was allegedly capable of incredible speeds, and was also supposed to be invisible to radar. Kessler noticed the unusual writing that encircled the base. He was not familiar with the language, but it looked ancient, maybe cuneiform.

He shook the hand of Kurt Hister, Commander of the High Order, the most super-secret of all German units. To be in his company meant you were regarded as very important to the cause. Indeed, many were not even privy to his existence so as to protect the organisation. Even fewer knew of The Bell or its whereabouts. There were two of them, actually, the other located safely deep in the Bavarian forests. The instructions were to escape to a safe destination in South America and to rendezvous there along with another secret aircraft, a Junkers JU 390 capable of flying long distances. Also involved in the evacuation were a number of warships and submarines that were to head for an undisclosed base in the southern hemisphere.

"Come, gentleman, time waits for no one," Beiger urged, dressed in ceremonial khaki uniform complete with medals and braiding, clearly ready to be welcomed officially on their arrival.

According to Beiger, safe passage had been assured in Argentina by Juan Peron for hundreds of Germans, where, on arrival under the guidance of Hister, they would hatch their own plans for world domination. But for the time being, the most important thing was escape.

With the controls already set, the five men entered, took their places, and strapped themselves in. Kessler observed the simple layout; there was very little in the way of controls or instruments. One of the scientists, Baumann, nodded to them all, and engaged the propulsion system. The lighting took on a warm blue glow that seemed to emanate from the walls. Below the men's feet, the red mercury fuel system engaged the two rotating discs that moved in opposite directions at incredible speed. The Bell hummed and shook a little. Kessler gripped the sides of his seat as the vibrating increased. He had always hated flying; in fact, had he known about their mode of transport, he would probably have requested a place on one of the evacuating warships. But Hister had insisted, and he was not a person to antagonise. Before he could think any more about his personal discomfort, the hum dramatically increased followed by a deafening whoosh. Kessler blacked out.

Chapter 1

Hertfordshire

Caroline was aware of her surroundings. She could sense her own consciousness; and yet the world around her was unrecognisable. The sumptuous chaise longue that she occupied supported her head and cocooned her shoulders. Her arms rested together on her abdomen, calm and at ease.

Marius looked up at the clock and then down at the woman. She had been under for seven minutes now.

Having performed the procedure many times before, he waited patiently, leaning back in his Rizzo chair, elbows on the arms, fingers steeped together, observing, offering simple straightforward commands, coaxing out the right responses.

He knew practically nothing about her, the background information not required in abundance to achieve the end result. Sometimes he would require more details from an individual, but even he was surprised at how effective his methods were. The objective in this instance was a common one: yet another patient trying to kick a smoking addiction.

Slowly, her eyelids moved.

Even though he knew that she was perfectly safe, it was always a relief to see the recovery process take hold. He could see her eyes flickering busily, returning from deep sleep to a realm of awakening. A smile broke onto her face, a sigh, followed by a slight murmur, her brow furrowing.

Marius smiled at the odd incoherent babbling as she approached consciousness.

From her desk in the corner of the room, Helen Moser had broken off from her work, intrigued as to how this would play out.

"Can you hear me now, Caroline?"

"Much better now … I can see them much more clearly … much better."

"Who's with you, Caroline?" Marius asked curiously.

"There are several of them … but I … I can't make out their features … It's a blur … I am … so tired."

That was enough. Time to stop the indulgence. Marius implemented a more stringent wake-up sequence.

Caroline responded, but not as fast as he would have liked. She was perspiring and muttering to herself. Her body trembled slightly.

Helen looked on with interest. In the short time in her employer's service, she had never seen a patient do this.

Caroline continued. "I see one of them, small, like a child … staring at me … the lights are bright … my head hurts. They don't want me to tell … not to tell …"

She started to stir, muttering incoherently.

"How do you feel?" he asked.

She did not reply, not quite ready yet.

With considerable furtiveness, Marius coaxed the woman from the remainder of her trance, making sure that she was fully compliant. The colour began to return to her face, but a look of concern remained.

Marius could feel a strange pressure on his temples, followed by a slight ringing in his ears. The air around him felt chilly.

Her eyes opened. Her faculties returning, she smiled at him.

"That was the last consultation and should enable you to resist the urge now," he said.

"So that's it? I'm cured?"

Marius smiled reassuringly. He was used to the scepticism.

"You should be free from smoking now, and will no longer desire a cigarette like you used to. I have conditioned your mind subliminally and have eliminated the craving. This will not last forever, but will allow you enough time to be able to overcome the addiction."

Slightly dramatic, he thought, but accurate nonetheless.

The woman rose from the chaise, straightened herself up and took a few deep breaths. "And what about the other matter?" she asked expectantly.

"Well, sometimes your thoughts can become confused while under hypnosis." Marius was surprised at her recollection. "What exactly do you remember?"

"The whole thing; it was so vivid, so real and very scary. I felt so powerless." Marius noticed her trembling. "I now have more questions than answers."

"Look, I'm sure it's just the exposure to the hypnosis that has expanded your capability to recall dreams in such detail. It can happen." Marius hoped to assuage his patient and put her concern at ease. It didn't seem to help much.

Caroline produced a small black rectangular box from her jacket pocket. "Ever see anything like this before?"

Marius took the object from her. Turning it over in his hand, he was immediately struck by its lightness. There were no markings and no obvious opening. The box seemed to be seamless, but hollow.

"It arrived through the post anonymously." She stared into space, dumbfounded. "I'm sure I have seen this under hypnosis, but I just don't know where …"

"Sorry, never seen anything like it before." Marius was becoming suspicious. There was a lot of scepticism within his industry and he was fully aware of certain groups trying to discredit the profession. Could this be a prime example playing out right before him?

He kept his gaze firmly locked on the box. It felt weird, almost uncomfortable, to be associated with it. And there was that cold feeling. He still felt the chill and it unnerved him.

He brushed the feeling aside. The whole thing was becoming absurd. He handed the object back to the woman and wrapped up proceedings.

"I can't explain it. I'm afraid this kind of thing is outside my field of expertise. I could recommend you to someone who may be able to help if you like?"

"I would prefer to see you again." She seemed genuinely disappointed.

"Okay, I will do some research and let you know what I can find out."

This seemed to satisfy Caroline somewhat and she brightened a little. Marius felt like a heel.

She produced a credit card to settle the bill for the course of treatment. "Thank you for your help, Dr Marius."

"I'm here if you need to talk, but I'm sure you will be fine," he replied as he processed the payment.

They exchanged pleasantries and he let the patient out of the room.

He let out a heavy sigh and opened up the blinds, the sun beaming through the glass. The heat on his face felt good and comforting; cleansing, even.

He could not help the feeling of guilt at brushing off Caroline's problems so hastily. The woman was counting on his honesty at face value to follow this thing up.

He noticed the client emerge from the building into the busy street below before disappearing into the masses. He felt satisfied that he could be of service regarding her addiction to cigarettes, and at the same time came the realisation of his limitations. It was a very personal consultation; although the relationships between Marius and his clients, at the same time, were usually very distant as it was highly likely that he would not see a client again once the sessions had run their course.

In this instance, and for the first time, the recent session had offered up a second issue.

He was sure the incident must be psychological. Regarding the box, he really was not sure. It was possible that she had seen a similar object in her sleep or during one of the hypnosis sessions. But his mind could only work logically, which threw out only one conclusion. Caroline was playing him.

He turned to Helen. "Well, what did you make of her?"

Helen frowned, leaning back in her chair. "Very strange that she should go off subject like that."

"Well, the course of treatment is now complete and I'm not really qualified to deal with her other issues."

"Let me do some research. It might be helpful," Helen offered.

Marius considered this for a moment. At least Helen could check on a few facts, to see if Caroline worked for the press, for instance.

"Alright. What harm can it do?"

Chapter 2

Washington DC

Damian Buchanan wore a look of contemplation as he stared out over the immaculate grounds of his vast estate. Many a decision had been made from the window of his office, but none was as serious as this one. As leader, the others would look to him for guidance and reassurance that everything would be alright, that all their work would be justified.

He could just make out a small part of the Uber Government building, the puppets busy filing motions that would inevitably satisfy a population completely unaware of what was happening under their noses.

He broke his gaze, wheeling around to face the only other person in the vast study. His furrowed brow softened a little as he sauntered around the partner's desk and over to the arrangement of Chesterfield seating, a file clenched in his left hand. Buchanan extended his right arm and gave a hearty handshake to his colleague.

Vice-President Gerald Korzak reciprocated, rising a little. "Mr President, sir, do we still have control?"

Buchanan nestled into the button-down leather sofa and handed over the file.

"Well, Gerry, I really don't know. No one has reported any more incidents, but the trust on both sides is going downhill."

Korzak nodded, always intrigued as to how genuine the Ronald Reagan voice likeness was. He would never ask the question though. Korzak knew his place which had been well mapped out from the time he first entered Yale. It was not long at all before the job offer beyond his wildest dreams was presented in a quiet corner of the campus grounds. Who would have thought, all these years later, that he would now be one of the most powerful men in the world? The combination of status, privilege and access to unlimited knowledge served as an excellent assurance to all members of the order; total discretion on all data revealed to them. There was also the small matter of an uncertain future if they stepped out of line.

Korzak shifted his posture, his slim frame and rugged jawline belying his sixty years. He was in better shape than Buchanan who, over the last five years, had developed a paunch, a jowly neckline, and he certainly did not look like Ronald Reagan. Korzak was sure that, had Buchanan's career taken a commercial direction, he would have been a famous household name. Strange that their world had no accolades, no recognition even, and yet the decisions the order made could literally change the world.

Buchanan continued. "We should never have got into this situation; I need options, Gerry, and I need some now."

Korzak thought for a moment. Buchanan seemed on edge; he had inherited a unique dilemma culminating from decisions made a long time ago. In addition to this was the untimely death of Bailey Scott, who, along with four other colleagues, had been killed in an air crash nine months previously. There had been no preparation with Damian Buchanan suddenly finding himself in the top chair facing a world crisis. Korzak used his reasoning to offer some advice.

"Can I speak frankly, sir?"

"Please, Gerry."

"Well, Damian, I suggest we meet with the leaders and see if we can agree on a peaceful resolution that would benefit all parties. Difficult as this will be under the circumstances, I feel we have no choice."

Buchanan sighed heavily, looking deep into the Axminster carpet. The patterns seemed to spiral out of control.

"We could always go to Op 100."

"We destroy the site?" Korzak looked incredulous.

"Gerry, you know this was always an option if things got too hot. I mean, we don't even know for sure what we are dealing with here." Buchanan spoke as if this would probably be inevitable.

"We're talking hundreds of billions of dollars' worth of work spanning half a century." The colour was draining from Korzak's suntanned face.

"I know. It's not something I would like, but I have been down there to see for myself. It's out of control and people are scared. They don't know lies from fact. We need to know Joe's intentions."

Yes, Joe. This was the nickname for the other parties involved in the business agreement. The Vice-President was only too aware of the mistrust that had grown in recent years. The fact was that there was no one who could brief him on what was going on. At the beginning of the alliance, there had been so much excitement and trepidation at the prospect of technology that would help develop the world order for the better.

But the super-government quite forgot to ask one simple question: What is it YOU actually want?

Now the hostilities had boiled over again, just like in 1979 when they lost sixty-six men.

The two men were both still juniors in those days, but were already privy to information of a top-secret level. A massive firefight occurred at the facility boundary. They had to pull a lot of strings to keep a lid on things, even though a few involved broke their silence and spoke to the press. One individual in particular made a career of touring the country retelling his account of events: how he was injured by an unknown enemy, saved by a green beret who himself was killed, a conspiracy, a cover-up … you name it, it was all in his story.

And that's how they dealt with his claims: a fabrication, a man with gambling debts, a little unstable, not suitable to return to work; but Phil Steiger would not keep quiet. He kept on pushing, attracting more and more unwanted attention. He had a very good run, though, avoiding the order more by luck than judgement.

In the end, though, Steiger was found dead in his hotel room in Colorado. Too bad.

To execute Op 100 could bring an end to the order itself. It would almost certainly set them back decades, send them back into Uber territory. How Korzak despised the seen government, the known President flying around the world with his cronies to another G8 summit to see how much faster they could all ruin the planet. At least Korzak had steered Buchanan to make provisions for this, their subsurface world unknown to most, a wonderfully advanced civilisation to survive against all odds. So … the decision to destroy a large section of this came at a very high price indeed.

The big mistake was allowing the other members of the alliance access to information regarding base locations. Hindsight was indeed marvellous, but now irrelevant.

Buchanan arose from his contemplation.

"Alright, Gerry, call in the Cabinet."

Chapter 3

Hertfordshire

Clarke walked over and sat on the chaise.

Sidney Cross watched his client from the corner of his eye as he gathered his notes. He also noticed the IWC watch on the client's wrist, worth more than a lot of people earn in a year.

He had been given a very detailed background. The guy was a very successful city trader who needed help to kick a smoking habit; nothing unusual at all in that. But Sidney had gone through the patient's notes a few more times just to ascertain what may come out of the session.

Clarke was now lying flat on the chaise, his Trickers shoes parked neatly underneath, an extra button on the shirt neckline undone. He spoke in a soft voice with no discerning accent, seemingly quite relaxed.

Sidney put his coffee to one side and began the hypnotic process.

In no time at all Mr Clarke was under, with Sidney administering the protocol for his addiction. Everything was going to plan with gentle words reaching the motionless body, the unblinking eyes, totally relaxed.

Tranquillity reached, the hypnotherapist leaned back, satisfied that his client was in a place he was comfortable with. He had his notebook propped on his knee at the ready.

"No, no, no, no, no," Clarke screamed as he bolted upright. Sidney nearly jumped out of his skin, eyes wide; Clarke, still assuming the upright position, muttering incoherently.

Stanley adjusted his spectacles, brushing his hair back into place, and retrieving his note book from the floor. He started the questioning, steering Clarke expertly in the direction of his sudden outburst.

"Who's there with you?"

"The light … it's bright in my face … can only see … wait … there are three of them, they're hurting me … they told me I would feel nothing, a spike going into my head, moving about … I can see one of the faces, big, a lightbulb shape, big eyes, too."

"Is there anyone else?" Stanley whispered.

Clarke, his voice full of emotion with an underlying moan, mumbled subtly for a while before settling down, adopting a foetus position on the chaise.

"Yes … to the right … it's horrible, massive, some sort of hybrid machine … I'm not frightened, though; I think it's friendly … it's weird … lots of arms and … and … huge legs. It's the small ones that scare me … They stare and stare …"

Clarke screamed. "Let me go … why are you doing this …? Why …? Leave me alone". His voice was awash with panic, sweat was pouring from him, his face and hair wet, his body trembling.

Sidney, mouth wide with astonishment, considered bringing his client out of the trance. He was then halted by Clarke, his speech now somewhat less frantic.

"They've all gone. I'm here on my own … It's colder now."

"Describe what you can see around you. Can you do that?"

"Yes … It's okay; I'm not scared now … the room, it's a room … it's big, the walls seem alive, like they seem to wobble

...out. The lights are pink, soft white ... there's some blue over there in the corner ..."

"Can you touch anything?"

"No ... I can't move ... I'm not restrained ... I just can't move at all ... It's like, invisible ... I remember walking round the ship, though ... am I allowed to say?"

It was like Clarke was now asking someone or something for permission to speak. There was a pause, before asking the question again. Another pause, then nothing.

Sidney checked his client. His breathing was steady and he had stopped perspiring. Sidney took a chance.

"I think it's okay to tell us, otherwise they would not have let you speak to us at all."

A good gamble, but two minutes passed by without a word. Sidney scribbled some notes down, all the time aware of the unusual circumstances of the session. He checked the left-hand pulse of his client. Nothing too alarming. He let out a deep sigh. Did he have the nerve to continue? Before he had time to contemplate his options, he felt Clarke's right hand gripping his arm tightly.

He spoke again.

"I walked around the room ... it's round, the walls are soft and spongy ... really weird, the lights are in the walls and change colour ... the lights are amazing. There's not much else to see. I'm not allowed out of this room, I can't find the door anyway, and they have to let me out.

"Wait ... I can see someone ... there's a window ... over there." Clarke pointed into the air above the chaise. "I can see a tall person, but they look different from us ... thin, with grey skin ... but they have that same head ... taller though, much taller, and there's a man with him ... it is a man, he has a white coat on, he wants to talk to me."

"Ask him why you're here," Stanley offered.

Clarke's eyes still closed, he tossed and turned looking concerned. "I don't know; I'm not supposed to talk to him ... only the hybrid man ... only him ... I can talk to him." He sounded rather childish.

"I'm sure, as you have been so good, he won't mind." Stanley was probing with great care.

"Uh, okay ... okay." Clarke cleared his throat and lowered his voice to Sidney. "He's here now ... right here with the tall one. I'll ask." His voice still low.

"Hello, how are you today?" Said in a matter-of-fact voice, clearly that of Clarke, but reciting the other person.

"I'm a little confused ... why am I here?" Clarke's voice returning.

"You're having a nice holiday, remember? Just relax. You can go home soon."

"But I don't like it here, I don't want to come here anymore. I don't like the flying ... It makes me feel ill." Clarke was getting upset again.

"Now, don't you worry," said the reassuring voice. "I have something for you. A present."

Clarke was looking left and right still. His eyes remained closed. He held out his hand and then put it into his right jacket pocket. He beckoned Stanley to come closer.

"I have a present," he smiled cheerfully.

"What is it?"

"It's a box, a very special box, all of my own ... you have to be very good to get one of these."

Clarke was pleased with himself. "I have to go now, it's time to go home now ... goodbye, everyone ... thank you ... goodbye ..." Clarke's mood suddenly darkened. "The little ones are back; they can be really mean ... I don't know why ...

I just want it to stop … stop … stop … ." Clarke drifted into a deep sleep.

Stanley decided that was enough and brought him back round, which took longer than was comfortable.

Clarke sat up rubbing his eyes. He seemed to instinctively know what to do, and immediately requested a pen and some paper. He moved to a table nearby, and started scribbling and drawing at an alarming rate. Stanley fetched a glass of water for his patient who took it graciously, gulping the contents down in one, barely pausing before continuing to scribble away.

He immersed himself in his work and would not talk for another ten minutes. While this was going on, Sidney got some air.

What he had witnessed had shaken him to the core. His mind struggled to function, trying to process the massive amount of shock statements which had issued from Clarke's mouth. It was the most astounding thing he had ever witnessed, and undoubtedly real. Or at least, Clarke genuinely believed what he was experiencing was real.

Sidney reappeared, and after taking a few deep breaths sidled up to Clarke who looked up, leaned back, put his pencil down and smiled broadly.

"Mr Cross, I can't thank you enough for all of your help," delivered with a cheerful lilt.

"Mr Clarke, are you sure you are quite alright? Do you recall any of our consultation?"

Sidney was not expecting this. Clarke had a stretch and checked himself, pointing to the paperwork in front of him.

"I think it's all there. You can check your recordings, but I think you will find these notes and drawings correspond with our session." Clarke was incredibly level-headed, which had the adverse effect of Sidney becoming even more uneasy.

Clarke seemed perfectly alright, though; not a hint of concern for the trauma that he had endured recently.

"I really am alright now, Mr Cross. However this came about, I know that they will not bother me again. Oh, and by the way, is my smoking addiction sorted?"

Sidney nearly keeled over. Clarke was busy writing out the cheque.

"Um, I think so. There are no guarantees, but you should be fine. You seem to be able to cope with most other things."

Clarke flashed him a grin and completed the cheque.

"It's double the payment. Please, I insist. I'm so pleased with your help. Many thanks, Mr Cross."

He handed over the cheque and graciously made his exit. Sidney slumped into a club chair, red-faced and exhausted. For a while he did nothing, trying to make sense of it all. The alarming session had created more questions than answers. And now the consultation threw up far too many loose ends.

What interested Sidney the most was why? Something was happening to Clarke, for sure, but who or what was behind it all?

He rose out of the chair and glanced at the sketches on the table. Clarke had made no attempt to take any of the papers.

The notes and drawings included a detailed description of Clarke's experience, the experiments, the strange entities, everything. It was all there. The detailing was extensive; it all made for a compelling read.

Further into the pile, the subject matter changed. There were a lot more sketches; some sort of craft, starting with a crude prototype, each page revealing a more accomplished version than the previous before Clarke had seemed satisfied with the end product. The final draft resembled a stout hexagonal craft with lights in the centre. The craft was grey with the lights pulsating from white to red, the interior of the craft described next to the drawing.

Further on was a sketch of a huge tunnelling machine, then over the page was a map of North America with a series of dots, circles and lines. Next to the map was a code and a listing. Clarke could see the code, and the listing of underground facilities and tunnels. The detailing and recollection was amazing, the records synchronising perfectly.

Sidney marched across the room and picked up the phone.

Chapter 4

Washington DC

With the guests now assembled in the lobby, Damian Buchanan prepared himself for the most difficult of meetings. He scanned the room, making sure the paintings by Antoine Bouvard were straight on the wall, the beverages were all neatly placed, the flowers looked at their best, there were no smears on the polished surface of the rosewood, and that his notes were all in order at the head of the table.

His appearance was met by a nod of approval from his reflection in the full-length cheval mirror before he summoned the other members to join him.

It was unusual to call a meeting in his own home. To be more accurate, it came with the job and was the official residence of the High President, rather like that of the Uber President across the way in the White House. Damian Buchanan, though, had no plans to relinquish power for the foreseeable future. Unlike the two-term maximum the Uber government were restricted to, he could stay in position for as long as he wished, provided he still had the blessing of the other eleven members.

Into the room filed the members of MJ-12, taking up their designated positions around the table, exchanging pleasantries. The finest and most powerful intellects combined, in an unprecedented state of high alert, here to protect and serve the people of the United States of America. It was their job to make the decisions that were above the pay grade of the Uber government.

It had all been so amusing, as Buchanan briefly recalled the visit to Wright-Patterson Airbase by the Uber President, checking over the latest "state-of-the-art" weaponry, shaking hands with some of the personnel, cracking unfunny lines that were met by over-enthusiastic laughter. That finger pointing as he sauntered up the stairs of Air Force One and fucked off back to his meaningless role.

Buchanan appeared from the shadows, and was promptly ushered into an area previously off limits to be met by other high order members and then shown to the real advancements. And what advancements they were. It was now within touching distance; they were so close to their goal. How the world would thank them when they made the great announcement.

Back to matters in hand.

President Buchanan addressed the full contingent with the usual authoritarian delivery.

"Members of Majestic12. We are assembled here today to tackle the delicate matter in New Mexico. Our latest updates from key operatives reveal some alarming security issues that involve our old friend Joe. Since we have no real knowledge of their intentions, and the alliance is built purely on trust, I propose that we meet with the leaders of Joe and see what they have to say for themselves."

President Buchanan eyed the other members from left to right, all the way around the table. They just stared back, their expressions betraying not a hint of emotion. As no questions were forthcoming, not even from Vice President Korzak, Buchanan decided the best tactic for the time being was to continue.

"Numerous reports have reached my desk in the last few weeks that …"

A regular, controlled chirp sounded from the far end of the table, with Buchanan expelling a low cough, wide-eyed with astonishment at being interrupted. At first he thought it could be a phone ring, but who would be so careless, knowing the gravity of such a meeting. His right hand was shaking. Was it fury or had some unexpected nervousness crept in? The President looked at his board members. They were all smiling now; surely they would not dare to mock him.

More chirping. This was all getting too much. He would open a window … no air in here. He fell back into the sumptuous armchair of nappa leather and rose immediately with his back to the other members. Still the chirping; really annoying. He was groaning now. The pen went spinning from his grip … damn that would look bad in front of everyone. He turned to face them once more … and fell.

The man at the other end of the table put the gun down, the silencer on the Makarov still smouldering. He walked past the other members to where Buchanan lay and gave him a kick. There was no response.

"I thought he was never going to die," he said turning his head, much to the amusement of his colleagues.

The man kicked away Buchanan's chair and pulled up another. He took one last look at the dead man's bullet riddled corpse and looked up.

"Right then, where were we?"

Chapter 5

Hertfordshire

Marius arrived with Helen at the country club. They spotted Sidney in a quiet corner; scotch in hand, papers spread over a table in front of him, wearing a studious expression on his face.

He caught the movement and looked up, smiling, beckoning them over, at the same time marshalling drinks for the new arrivals. The barman nodded routinely.

"Excuse the mess. Just getting my notes in order." Sidney cleared part of the table for them as they sat down. He was dressed in regular country gent splendour, gold cufflinks twinkling in the light as he shuffled papers around. He was around five feet seven in height, his salt and pepper hair with a smart parting sweeping just above the eyebrows over a face with a ruddy complexion.

"Please sit."

Drinks arrived at the table swiftly, a G&T for Helen and sparkling water for Marius, the 'designated' driver. Sidney had a top-up, which informed him that he would also be dropping his friend off later.

"Right. What's so important that it just can't wait?" Marius projected with his usual rich, deep, soft tone, a voice which matched his large six-two frame. Unlike Sidney, Marius was a more casual dresser, not scruffy by any standard, but he rarely wore a tie. Smart shirts and chinos were his mainstay.

"Had a client in recently; very strange session it was too. I have a recording that we can listen to back at my place. In the meantime, this is the transcript in front of you along with some rather interesting notes and drawings that he could recall after the hypnosis."

Sidney spread the papers out for them.

What struck Helen immediately was the subject matter. Pictures of a flying craft, chubby and round with lights in the middle, the dimensions written neatly together with description of colour, speed and movement, the detail remarkable. This theme continued with the interior of the craft, including its occupants.

Marius could guess what she was thinking; the similarity of some of the transcript from their own client. But Clarke's whole experience was on another level, far more involved.

Maybe, if he saw Caroline for another consultation, she could possibly reveal more regressive memories that would chime with that of Sidney's patient. It could be worth a shot; after all, Caroline had asked for his help on the matter.

Wait a minute ... What the hell was he thinking here? Two therapists with patients who both wanted to quit smoking, but then began to regress about the same experience. The analytical mind of Marius came to the logical conclusion that this was one to walk away from, yet simultaneously, his enquiring mind could not let it go.

He was suddenly made aware of the others at the table.

"Marius, old chap, you were miles away there ..." Sidney was staring at him.

"Look, I don't like this, Sidney. Bit hard to take it seriously, don't you think?"

"I didn't say that I believed any of it, but it still happened."

Sidney sighed. "I'm the same as you, a sceptic looking for answers."

They finished up at the country club and moved the meeting back to Sidney's place. It was a Georgian pile nestling in the centre of Melworth, a very salubrious little Hertfordshire village a mile from the A10.

The three of them settled in to the Garden Room at the back of the house overlooking the pristine grounds. Sidney linked up his digital dictaphone to the computer speakers.

"Perhaps this will convince you a little more," he got in before the recording started.

Not a word was spoken as they heard Clarke describe his experience.

In simplistic terms, he was taken against his will in a strange craft to a facility where he was experimented on. Then they took him back.

The recording stopped.

"Rather disturbing, wouldn't you say?" Sidney was up and pouring himself a scotch from a Georgian decanter. He offered one to a shaken Helen who accepted gratefully.

Sidney was right; it was disturbing, and as Marius contemplated some solution to it all Helen told Sidney about their own client, Caroline.

He gave them both a humourless smile. "I can see why you suspect skulduggery. It is a bit of a coincidence."

Both clients with similar regression but with very different backgrounds. Were they collaborating? The thought had struck Marius, but Helen's background checks had yielded no connection to Clarke. It would still be wise to proceed with caution, though.

"Are you seeing Clarke again, Sidney?"

"No. The funny thing was, the man claimed that he would

no longer be accosted. He seemed rather pleased, thanking me profusely as he left the office. He even paid me double for the treatment."

"Well, my client has asked me to help her further," Marius exclaimed.

"Are you going ahead?" Sidney asked hopefully.

"I know you would like me to. I can tell that." He smiled. 'But you know this is out of my field of expertise, and yours too."

Sidney had to agree there. "Surely there's no harm putting your client under one more time, though. It might help me to understand as well."

Marius considered this. He looked at Helen occupying a wingback chair in the corner of the room, finishing her scotch, the ally of impartiality, a woman that he had only known for three months and who had a growing reputation for sensible directives.

"This kind of regressive incident is more common than you might imagine," she exclaimed, delving into her case and producing some notes. "In quite a few circumstances, hypnosis clients have been known to retrieve memories on quite a variety of different subjects.

"They can vary from a childhood trauma, or a past life, even taking on and speaking in a foreign language, but an alarming number will recollect instances of abduction." Helen referred to her notes and continued. "There have been some very famous cases, some where the subjects were taken as they were sitting in their homes or driving along a highway. They knew something had happened to them, but it was only when some of the victims were put under hypnosis that a far more detailed and alarming account of events was revealed."

As she recited a few of the many documented abductions,

one thing that stood out above all the accounts was the consistency of the details. There was the strange craft; the lights, strange beings, the sheer feeling of terror, the fact that victims were repeatedly abducted, and the varied backgrounds of the people involved who had no reason to make up stories.

"Then there are the even more alarming abductions, the victims sometimes returning years later, others sometimes never returning. Over 300,000 people disappeared last year in the United States alone."

'It's only when you witness this at first hand. I mean, this guy Clarke, you should have seen the state of him ..." Sidney's voice had an audible wobble.

"That's not all." Helen opened a book to a page with several sketches on it. "These were made by some abduction witnesses."

The drawings, all of a flying craft of some kind, carried a remarkable likeness. Even more to the point, they were similar to the ones made by Mr Clarke.

Marius felt himself being sucked into a world that he wanted nothing to do with, and all he could sense was a world of trouble ahead. But the facts were there. Not all these people could be hallucinating or lying.

"So you think I should see this woman again?" he sighed.

"I would go ahead. She seems to trust you."

"I'll think about it."

Chapter 6

Cambridgeshire

Valerian glanced at his watch. The buzzer had sounded at precisely two o'clock, a simple organised punctuality informing him who was at the door.

He strode down the wide splendour of the corridor, reassured that some standards were always maintained. He opened the door to his colleague, who was wearing her usual optimistic bright smile.

"Caroline, do come in." He beamed, standing aside for her.

She ambled down the spacious reception hallway and into the much-loved Queen Anne period house. It had only known one family, being built by astronomer and inventor Benjamin Valerian in 1608 to exacting standards. The current owner, Hector, or 'H' to his friends, had occupied the residence for some thirty years, always insisting on being a custodian rather than the owner of the splendid manor house.

To a degree, Caroline knew what he meant. With his wife Eve and their son in current residence, it was the role of Valerian to carry on the family traditions. Fortunate to be blessed with a brilliant business background, his prosperity would keep the coffers full for a long time. Plus, there was always the safety of the DHvSS.

She was shown into the Garden Room at the rear of the

house, overlooking splendid lawns and architectural features. Afternoon tea was waiting, Valerian encouraging his guest to sample the large selection of cakes and pastries.

"Hector, I am going to have to be careful here."

"Oh, nonsense, there's nothing of you." He chuckled, sliding a millefeuille onto a plate. "So, how did your little appointment go?"

"Very well, I think. He has good strength of character." Caroline attacked a fully loaded doughnut. "Mmmm, wow, that's good."

He nodded, raising his eyebrows. "How did he respond to the test?"

"I think he was suspicious; tried to fob me off when the session finished." She licked sugar from her fingers. "I tried probing his mental barrier. It is the strongest that I have ever tested."

'H' poured out the tea. "You think he would come on board, join the team, so to speak?"

"Hmmm, not sure; he seemed very stuck in his ways. I liked him, though."

He thought for a moment. There was not an abundance of time. Opposing forces were always trying to infiltrate their ranks.

"Did he like you?"

"I could not say for sure but, maybe, yes. Wait, you're not saying I should … "

He waved a hand of dismissal. "No, of course not! What do you think we are, Special Ops?"

Caroline laughed. No, they were far more than that. She knew of units where they expected you to do anything to get the job done, no exceptions. Although, this was no military unit. True, they had connections within the armed forces, but the inner workings ran independently and answered to no one.

"How about another session with this Marius guy?" 'H' enquired.

"Not sure if he'll see me."

"My suggestion would be to see what he says and, if he refuses, level with him."

"What, tell him the real reason for my visit?"

"Some of it yes, if it helps." He leaned forward. "We need to sort this problem out, Caroline, and fast."

"Okay, when's the next meeting?"

"Next month."

"Alright, I will try to fix something up."

Chapter 7

Hertfordshire

Marius cruised around the kitchen, a childish spring in his step. He had prepared a full complement for breakfast, and felt better than he had done for years.

He was pleased to have his female guest to look after. It had given him a new sense of purpose to an otherwise very mundane existence. The fact was, he had no idea just how dull his life was before Helen Collins had breezed in. She had to leave her rented flat at short notice. Marius had plenty of space. It seemed like the ideal solution.

He could hear Helen getting dressed upstairs, the Georgian floorboards creaking merrily up above. He liked having someone around and was glad of the company. Helen had occupied the end wing of the house for convenience purposes. It had meant a few changes to his daily routine, but one which he now welcomed with a relish.

The creaking stopped, replaced by the wail of a hairdryer with a subtle overtone of tuneless singing. The humorous cue to this event was to get a move on as Helen's appearance was now imminent.

Marius had thinned out his appointment book to a five-day schedule and, to his surprise, he did not care at all. Deep inside was a yearning for something missing in his life. Up until now, he had been fooling himself that it did not exist. But here it was real, alive, and there to be discovered. Helen had been the key to opening the door to something worthwhile, something that was so important that he knew it must be worth pursuing.

She appeared at the kitchen door, the usual look of an excited child as she saw the plates of eggs and bacon with all the trimmings. Marius, with a cursory nod, produced two mugs of tea, and they settled down to watch the morning news.

Three weeks had passed since the disturbing consultation at his office, enough time for him to mull things over. He was in a good place at the moment, and was very reluctant to invite controversy in his direction. So it was against his better judgement, and the persuasive abilities of his two compatriots, that he had set up another meeting with Caroline.

Helen munched her way through a rack of toasted bread as she scanned her inbox on her laptop computer. There it was, the confirmation for the seminar at 2 p.m.

She had managed to seek out Derick Mills, a leading expert in the field of the unusual. It was almost a relief that Mills had been particularly apprehensive and cautious. He was no stranger to controversy, having attracted media attention for his views on evolution and conspiracy theories. He had carved out quite a successful career for himself as an author of several bestselling novels. But it was his non-fictional works that had attracted Helen's attention.

There were remarkable similarities in his writing to their own recent experiences, and when Helen gave him a brief overview of the cases, it seemed to go a long way towards securing a reluctant meeting.

Mills had suggested the two of them come along to one of the venues where he was giving a talk on related matters. There was absolutely no chance of a ticket; such was the popularity of the man. Instead, he had got them permission to watch from the wings backstage.

Helen wore an expression of optimism. She swigged down the last of her tea, and fiddled with her hair in the mirror on the table, an essential item that had to remain there at all costs as Marius had discovered when he tried to remove it one day.

Marius had eventually been won over by his guest. Although he could not be described as elevated to the realms of perfect contentment, he had brightened with optimism, plus he was intrigued by what this Mills character had to say. Maybe it would help him to understand the complexities of his concerns.

Helen had used her research skills to great effect, to extensively investigate many abduction cases in more detail, cross-referencing similarities of which there were many. She had also gleaned as much information on what was known about secret bases and laboratories. Much of this was speculation, but she was hoping to question Mills who she hoped could authenticate some of the subject matter.

Chapter 8

Washington DC

The deep cleaning team had done a wonderful job, arriving at East Point in no time at all. The rug had just arrived totally unblemished, and was now back in position. He took the liberty of having the floor waxed just to rejuvenate the lustre of the eighteenth-century floorboards. The leather chair was not to his taste and had since been replaced by a designer model by Guy Lefevre. The dimensions made it far more comfortable, being an essential item when meetings regularly dragged on into the early hours.

Although he was not offended by the Bouvard artworks, he thought of them as much more suited to the hallway. They were swiftly replaced by large-scale maritime scenes by Edward Seago, the gilt frames and angry seascape colours blending particularly well with the flame-mahogany wall panelling.

He straightened the picture nearest the window then admired the surroundings from the boardroom balcony. It was a beautiful day, a pleasant breeze rocking the avenue of trees below with a gentle sway, fish topping all along the lengthy rectangular lake. His eyes dreamily followed the swirls along the waterline and on to the boundary way off in the distance. Beyond this, he could make out the busy ant-size traffic.

He had admired the house for a very long time, with its

prime location and views, the architecture of a tasteful classical design, with high ceilings and generous dimensions, all the original fittings still in place.

In many ways, it had a lot in common with his own large estate located in Vermont on the edge of Lake Champlain. Many of the New England properties had a bit of age to them compared to the rest of the continent, due to the settlement in the area of the first Pilgrim Fathers. He had a fond affinity with the area and regularly visited friends both in Cambridge and Boston.

Buchanan's body had been disposed of in haste, the post mortem and cause of death taken care of in-house. His wife and two sons had been informed of the terrible accident that befell such a cherished and valued colleague. Honestly, the audacity of some criminals, ambushing him at a filling station downtown. It was simply outrageous. He told the family that he would do all he could to bring the culprits to justice. He had already given the police details of a car that was seen in the area. A few other convenient witness statements and the unfortunate chosen ones would be fitted up sufficiently to take the fall. This was essential as it would stop unwanted attention pointing towards their own direction.

And now down to business. His own wife and two daughters would soon be joining him. As the new President, he would be able to implement total control protocol over the organisation.

Korzak knew his place and had not challenged for the top spot. This would be unusual in the realms of the Uber Government; but here, where the real power lay, they did what they damn well liked. He was the natural successor, Korzak playing his charade well. True, Buchanan had been useful for a time but, in truth, he was the stopgap for the inevitable. There was no room in their organisation for doubters.

The circle was now complete.

It had all started with the convenient accident of Bailey Scott and his entourage. Why, a cynic might imply that the accident was deliberate. Who would dare make such an accusation? Certainly not the new President. Why, some would dare to argue he manufactured his own ascendancy to the top job. Simply outrageous.

The new President allowed himself a wry smile. This truly was a monumental moment. Dare they even contemplate what lay ahead: after all these years, the incredible set of circumstances that now saw him in the most important position in the world? One thing was certain, and that was he would not squander the opportunity, and would use this position to the best of his advantage.

He'd better get the other members in and explain his plans in more detail, but this time he could ensure that there would be no distractions.

Good timing, that was the key to it all. And patience.

Buchanan's big mistake was testing his authority too much. It was far too simple to subliminally steer the rest of the board in the opposing direction, the main weapons at his disposal being the promise of power and wealth and, above all else, the knowledge that they would all gain.

The board were far from naïve though, collectively boasting some of the most brilliant business and scientific minds in the country.

Complacency was for the weak. Seize the moment, thinking on your feet, negotiating, but always having the best hand if the need arose to play the cards.

That hand had been played to perfection.

Chapter 9

Cambridge

Marius guided the Range Rover into the parking bay and killed the engine. The two occupants emerged from the climate controlled cabin into the sticky humidity of the August afternoon. It was a short walk from the car park onto narrow streets, with a seemingly appropriate apocalyptic dark grey sky looming above them, the tall Gothic architecture engulfing the light, a rumble of thunder serving to quicken the pace to the awaiting stone steps of the Cambridge Corn Exchange.

Sure enough, Mills had left instructions for them to be guided to the backstage area.

A very polite and helpful assistant led them out of an emergency door and down the outside of the building. They re-entered through another door and were led to a vantage point next to the stage.

It was only when Marius peered out into the large hall that he could see the point of their mini detour. The place was absolutely packed with the murmur of an 1800-strong audience. Marius had to admit that until recently, he had never heard of Derick Mills.

It was abundantly clear that a lot of people had, though.

He could feel Helen's breath on the back of his neck, her hand gripping his shoulder in anticipation. He caught her feminine body fragrance; it was pleasant.

The lights went down to reveal a star-filled ceiling, green and blue lasers washed the stage, the sound of *Rush 2112* filled the air. He was familiar with the iconic first track entitled 'Overture', the lasers now dancing around the large hall. This guy knew how to make an entrance. Even more impressive was the almost rock concert-like reception Derick Mills received as he took to the stage, arms aloft applauding in response, showing his obvious appreciation for his audience.

The music faded and the applause died down to an almost deathly silence as Mills took to the rostrum. He let that silence hang in the air for a while as the haze machine did its work creating an eerie smoke that hung in the lighting and spewed out into the masses. Marius could not help but smile at the theatrics. The man had not uttered a word, but he liked him already.

Mills was a diminutive figure, about five feet six, well-tanned and completely bald. He wore neat round spectacles and was dressed in a smart powder blue jacket with crisp white shirt, blue jeans resting on brown leather brogues.

The clever lighting had already illuminated him into something ethereal. Marius looked around at Helen who was beaming in anticipation.

The silence was suddenly broken by a surprisingly aggressive volley of words that echoed around the vaulted building.

"Let me ask you ... to go out and kill five women, then go to confession and to be told you are forgiven. Is it reasonable to expect this?

"A military regime that controls a country by fear, starving and murdering their own people, will be seen embracing their religion in prayer. Is it reasonable to tolerate this behaviour?

"Protestants and Catholics in Ireland have to build walls and fences to segregate each other in the name of religion. A man in India is displeased with his wife's behaviour so he sets fire to her; permitted within his religion, apparently. Jewish people are persecuted for being Jewish, in the name of religion.

"Would the world not be a better place without all of this? I put this to you all."

The noise was deafening, the applause bordering on fanatical. Marius had found nothing to dispute so far, although he would argue that not all religious bodies were bad.

Mills continued.

"The various religious leaders around the world would like you all to believe what they preach because it makes them very wealthy, and gives them control over their people. Socrates and Galileo dared to speak out, citing factual evidence that the world we live in is more down to natural and scientific events rather than the religious miracles that made us all."

More applause echoed around the hall. Mills paused for effect and then continued. He had them in the palm of his hand already.

"Now, let us not dismiss the existence of God. That's not what I am saying at all. Indeed, we now know that the universe is thirteen billion years old. Is the Church going to also dispute this? I ask you, what came before this? Possibly only part of the universe is thirteen billion years of age, some parts are likely to be older.

"I believe that God is real, and that he does indeed exist within a spiritual realm in all of these universes. There's so much evidence to support this, but in a form and purpose that has been distorted by religion throughout the centuries." Mills paused to view his audience who were in complete silence, hanging on his every word.

"What if God created the souls of men to journey through many bodies until the time came to reach a higher level? After this long journey of learning, the soul eventually returns to its creator to rest by his side in the real kingdom of heaven.

"I believe that God is the caretaker of the universe. He sows the seeds of life and then harvests them in a complex cycle of evolution."

Marius eyed the audience who seemed mesmerised by Mills' rhetoric. This was a powerful man who, on the surface, was very convincing indeed. Mills continued.

"Ladies and gentlemen, if you use the Bible for an answer, God does indeed travel in a very fast, very big and powerful, spinning, glowing, metallic flying machine.

"When you observe how the Church handles these theories, the only response they have is, as always, to the satanic and delusional. We are the blasphemous ones who have no voice. Well, I am your voice, I am your portal. I can try to explain what others refuse to believe."

Hysterical cheers at a deafening level. Marius looked at Helen and they cheered too.

"Try to imagine what is beyond our universe. The answer is many more universes of different kinds, with no beginning and no end; they simply *are*. These places are beyond human thought capacity. Time and distance are human inventions; these laws only apply on Earth. Try to think of universes in dimensions rather than in straight lines. They come into being, and develop not only in the present but, at the same time, in the past and the future. In some circumstances, this would give the impression of some objects appearing and then vanishing, and appearing again somewhere else. This explains the ability to travel great distances in a short space of time. Many authorities will try to dismiss this because it does not serve their purpose, but the objects that so many have witnessed in our own skies travelling at great speeds, the huge size of them, the unusual shapes and lights; are they all to be dismissed as a fabrication of the mind?"

Cheers of support from the audience mixed with negative sentiment towards those who would dispute Derick Mills' way of thinking.

He went on to accuse governments of starving the public of information, playing God themselves, deciding on what we should be allowed to know and what they should keep secret, the numerous UFO sightings and abductions that were of particular interest to Marius and Helen. He then moved on to the subject of secret underground bases.

"Friends, these bases do exist. Too much consistency in eyewitness testimony tells us as much. They are known as D.U.M.B.s, Deep Underground Military Bases, with many levels that descend vast distances, connected to each other via a network of tunnels made by massive boring machines. Now, we suspect that secret tests on state-of-the-art technology are carried out on these bases: weapons, aircraft, of a very advanced kind. But here it gets much more interesting." He leaned forward on his pulpit. "Brave individuals, ex-employees, have given detailed accounts about what really goes on in these bases. Forget the weapons and craft. In the lower levels of these bases are vast laboratories where experiments are carried out in mind control, genetics, animal crossbreeding, cryogenics, with an agenda that no one knows about."

The audience were silent again.

Mills eyed them all with a look of steel. "They were there all the time: deep, natural, underground caverns that just needed to be connected. The most well-known of these bases resides under the Archuleta mountain range, just inside the border of

New Mexico not too far from a town called Dulce, a name I'm sure a lot of you will be familiar with."

Marius had heard of the base; it was mentioned a few times in the books used in his research. Mills continued.

"The underground bases are heavily guarded with state-of-the-art security on each level. The lower down into the bases, the more clearance is required. It is in these lower levels that the worst experiments are supposed to take place."

Another pause from Mills, working the room for all it was worth.

"Ever wondered how they test cosmetics these days, or how many of the amazing breakthroughs in medicine are discovered? Well, a lot of the medical world would like to know too, because these new treatments and beauty products keep hitting the market and, in many cases, no one can trace their source."

Mills sighed heavily.

"Cattle mutilations are rife around Dulce. Parts are removed with surgical precision. Maybe this is connected, maybe not. A little strange nonetheless.

"And then there is the alarming number of missing persons and not just in the Dulce area. I mean nationally. Every year, over three hundred thousand human beings are reported missing in the USA alone."

Mills pointed at the audience, his arm moving in an arc from left to right.

"People like you, my friends, just vanishing into thin air and, in most cases, never to be seen again.

"There is strong evidence that all the procedure and practice laws are ignored in order to get to the end objective. And what test subjects could be better than the species these products are made for?"

Audible gasps from some of the audience, followed by muttering. Mills put up an outward palm and soon had the silence back.

"According to eyewitness testimony, the lower level of these bases are crammed with humans, kept as slaves, experimented on until they are no longer of use. And it gets worse."

Marius cast a glance at Helen thinking what could be worse than that?

"Friends." Mills' voice had risen in volume somewhat. "There is strong evidence that these poor human souls are being used to grow body parts. The scientists at the base are conducting experiments on animal-human cross-breeding, with huge vats preserving horrific mutations of all kinds, all not only completely illegal, but ignored by many people in high government who know exactly what is going on at these bases."

Mills voice dropped down to normality; he nodded to all in front of him.

"It is now time to expose these practices and demand them outlawed, and the ringleaders brought to justice. We demand to know the truth and we demand to know it right now. Thank you all for listening."

The applause was deafening, people cheering, trying to get to the stage, shouting for Mills to reappear, but Mills had gone back to his changing room, security firmly in place outside his door.

Marius and Helen made their way down the corridor to the room with Mills inside. As they eyed the huge pair of suits that flanked the doorway, he feared the worst. He was just about to try his luck when one of the men spoke.

"Dr Marius, Helen Collins? Dr Mills is expecting you," the guard said with a cheery lilt. He opened the door for them.

Marius was a little puzzled by the welcoming nature, given the hasty retreat and the controversy surrounding Derick Mills. He was even more surprised that they had secured a private meeting.

"Hello, you two, do come in." Mills beamed.

The two squeezed into the small dressing room and made their introductions.

"Delighted to meet you both. I think the talk went well tonight," he enthused.

"They wanted to hear more," Helen stated.

"And always leave the audience wanting more, my dear," Mills said playfully.

Marius guessed Mills was over sixty and appeared to be in good shape. He had an expression that gave the impression of a man who was continuously studying everyone and everything with great interest. Mills took off his spectacles and cleaned them on an initialled handkerchief.

"So, where shall we start?" he prompted.

"Dr Mills, I will come straight to the point. We need answers." Marius tried not to come over too emotional. "Myself and my colleague, for that matter, are in way over our heads with this. We deal with addictions for the most part and are really not qualified to handle such delicate subject matter."

Mills flicked a glance at a notebook nestling in his left hand.

"Ah, yes, the regression cases." He nodded thoughtfully. "The ones with strange craft, abduction, strange beings ... hard to believe, don't you think?"

"Very," Helen exclaimed.

Mills looked at them both with a look of sincerity.

'So what do you want me to do? Convince you that it's not all a load of rubbish, a fabrication, some conspiracy?"

"It is very difficult for a sceptic like me to understand recent events," Marius said.

"Tell me how you feel first; how the hypnotic regression experience has affected you?"

"Well, I'm not the client here, Dr Mills. I just want answers."

Mills nodded, smiling, holding up a hand. "Of course, I'm just interested in your own opinion. By the way, I'm not a doctor. People just assume that I am."

Marius broke into a grin. "Me neither, same reason." What the hell, he thought, what harm could it do?

Marius recalled the hypnotherapy session in as much detail as he could; the routine addiction treatment, the sudden deviation and alarming change in his client, the craft with its weird crew, and the terror she was clearly experiencing with them and what they were doing to her. Then there was the new set of questions that the whole situation threw up.

When Marius had finished his account, Mills leaned back in his chair puffing out his cheeks wearing a knowing look.

"Sounds like a textbook abduction to me. Are you seeing the client again?"

"That's why I'm here. I'm not sure how to proceed."

Mills eyed them both with a serious frown.

"Look, this is a very emotive subject, not to be taken lightly. It demands that you both go into this with an open mind."

"I'm curious, Mr Mills," Helen cut in displaying a look of concern. "Why did you agree to meet us? I am told you are a very difficult man to see."

Mills eyed them both, hands on his knees, glasses back in position.

"I believed you, simple as that. You wanted answers, as we all do, to these incidents." He sighed and tapped his knees. "Okay … you mentioned a box, a rectangular black box."

"Yes, she showed us the box at the end of the session. Said

she had no idea what it was or where it had come from," Helen stated.

Marius eyed Mills curiously. "So, you've come across instances like this before?"

"A few times, yes, but that said, the boxes do not get mentioned very often, and when your notes mentioned Clarke's mysterious black box also, curiosity did get the better of me."

"And so you would recommend that I see my client again?"

"Well, it might give you those answers that you seek, for sure." Mills paused for a second clearing of his throat. "Look, if it would make it easier, I could sit in with you."

Marius could see the benefit in this request. To have one of the country's leading authorities as a first-hand witness was too good an offer to pass up. Besides, he had a lot more questions that needed answering.

"Okay, Mr Mills, it's a deal. I will arrange a meeting with my client."

Chapter 10

Kecksburg, Pennsylvania, July 19th 1985

Don Hubbard was enjoying some downtime with his son Cory. It was a pleasantly warm evening as the two made their way across a field to the edge of some woodland. This area would be their campsite for the night. Don started to undo his backpack, deciding on a flat area of grass to erect the tent while Cory made off to the trees to collect firewood.

The star-filled sky suddenly lit up. There was a whoosh which made the two of them look up. They saw a comet-like object streak across the skyline heading in a downward trajectory. The noise became deafening as the object bore down upon their position, hitting the trees, smashing trunks clean off, sending branches scattering in all directions. The object ploughed past the father and son only a hundred yards away, gouging out the ground, sending earth clods flying all around them, small fires igniting in a straight line, the earth eventually engulfing the object, grinding it to a halt.

Don dropped the tent poles, staring at the fiery mass, mouth wide open.

Cory ran back, wide-eyed, to his father's side, demanding, "Get the camera, we gotta get down there."

Don felt himself shaking, just staring where the object now lay glowing red in the night. "C'mon, Dad, let's go," Cory pleaded excitedly.

Don broke from his gaze. He turned to the backpack, fishing the camera out of a side pocket.

Stumbling forward and full of shock, the two of them made their way down a gentle meadow to the next set of trees where the glowing object lay. They came upon the deep groove in the ground, following it the short distance, Don snapping off a few shots, trying to keep his footing in the uneven woodland.

He staggered to where Cory was now standing, excitedly pointing to a dark metallic object shaped like a bell, half buried in the earth. Don could just make out something around part of the base, weird, indiscernible lines and curves. He could see no additional markings anywhere else. One thing was for sure, this was no comet.

"It's a spaceship, Dad, it's the real thing."

Don took stock of the situation, his son's comment resonating in his head. He had twenty-five years service as a fire officer and had seen some sights in his time. Now his training kicked back in, telling him to assess the situation. He looked for danger. Thankfully, the fires that had broken out were now nothing more than smouldering embers.

"Careful, Cory, we don't know what we're dealing with here."

"Maybe we should get help," his son replied. "There could be something alive inside."

Don stared at the object, the redness fading now into black, but the heat on his face, still intense.

They decided Cory should go. He was the faster of the two. They remembered passing a farm half a mile back. A careful jog and Cory could be there in five minutes.

Without further encouragement, Cory ran off in the direction of the farmhouse.

Don eased himself down into the trough made by the crash. Even through his boots, he could feel the warm earth on his feet. He could see a row of cast-iron rivets just above where the strange inscription started. He took a couple more photographs, advancing the film wheel on; about to take a third snap when there was a noise from inside … a banging sound … three dull thumps.

Don picked up a lump of wood and, holding it like a baseball bat, struck the side of the craft. Another thump from inside. Something was alive in there.

Don searched for anything that could be an opening, tracing the side of the craft with his eyes.

He suddenly stopped, rising up, his hearing detecting something else, a low hum, or was it droning? It sounded like a vehicle. No, wait … he could hear more clearly now, the noise getting closer. Yes, they were vehicles; guttural engine sounds unmistakably that of trucks.

Surely his son had not raised the alarm so quickly? No, he would be way off the farm yet.

Don could now make out a convoy coming down a dirt track in his direction.

This was not down to Cory.

During Don's career, he had worked alongside all manner of services and authorities and in that time, he had become familiar with most of them, even helping with training the army in firefighting techniques. Something about their timely appearance made him uneasy, though, and rather than breaking from cover, he instinctively retreated back into the trees and crouched down.

From his vantage point, he watched as a number of trucks and jeeps pulled up at the crash site, groups of personnel spilling out in all directions.

Don squinted through the night-time gloom to catch a glance of what division of the army this could be. Maybe he had worked with them in the past; that would be reassuring. One of the troops climbed down to the spot where Don had been standing. He was examining the craft and the faint diminishing glow was enough to illuminate the soldier's uniform. It was black. The only insignia he could make out was a triangular patch on the top of his arm; inside the triangle was an upside-down letter T. The vehicles themselves carried no discernible markings that he could make out. This was a unit that he had never seen; reason enough to stay hidden.

Don watched as more troops appeared next to the craft. The banging from inside started up again, making the men shout up for help. An officer appeared with a notebook, looking towards the top of the craft. Apparently, the opening mechanism had been damaged in the crash. The officer was tall with a hard, rugged face. He sidled his way down to the craft, referring to his notes. He ran his hand over the metal until he was almost at the part that was buried at ground level. He pulled earth away with his hands and then suddenly called for cutting gear. As Don continued to watch, he saw a flurry of activity. He could not make out the majority of the dialogue, but it was clear that the officer wanted to open up the side of the craft. The banging emanating from inside had increased, the occupants showing more urgency to get out. A huge drill appeared on a tripod along with a torch and line. The troops worked on the area as instructed, the officer nodding tight-lipped. The drill was operational for thirty seconds until there was a loud click, and then the torch was administered.

When the group stood back, the officer pushed on the craft and a door suddenly slid open. Don watched wide eyed as the troops murmured, looking uncertainly at each other, probably thinking the same as Don. Who or what was inside?

The officer reached inside, his entire arm disappeared into a white swirling mass of steam. He pulled himself up, retrieving his arm which was now connected to something. Don could make out a gloved hand grasping that of the American officers, followed by another arm ... a black uniform, then he saw the head ... the face of a human, donning a peaked cap. The man climbed out, followed by another dressed in identical fashion. Don gasped, realising at once that they were in Nazi uniforms.

What the hell was going on here? A third man climbed out, again a Nazi although dressed in khaki, followed by two men in civilian clothes. Troops moved in, taking the occupants away. Suddenly there were bodies everywhere digging debris away from the craft. A crane swung out from a flatbed truck, chains were swiftly connected up to the craft and with a groan, the metal object broke free from its earthen burrow.

Don could see that the craft was about fifteen feet high and about ten feet wide. The top of the object was damaged but still in one piece. The occupants seemed shaken but otherwise unhurt. They were all shown to an SUV and whisked away, shortly followed by the craft safely strapped onto the flatbed. The rest of the troops did a quick ground search collecting up a few pieces of debris. After bagging them, they made their way to the remaining vehicles. Don guessed that the whole operation had taken no more than ten minutes.

There were voices to the left, and torchlights cutting through the dark, the beams waving from side to side. The voices were audible now, shouting to each other excitedly. Don could see some of the detachment break away from the crash site, possibly three soldiers, arming weapons as they went. Along the top of a ridge of trees he saw a man appear, shouting,

"Hey, fellas, what have you got there?"

To Don's surprise one of the soldiers beckoned the civilian down towards the crash site. Three other men appeared behind him, scurrying down the ridge following the torchlights. Soon they were face to face with the troops.

"Is this all of you? Wouldn't want anyone to have an accident," one said matter of fact.

"It's just the four of us. We heard the noise and came to see what was going on. Is it a spaceship?"

No answer came from the troops. Instead there was a hiss followed by bright beams of light emanating from their weapons. It happened so fast, the civilians had no time to react. Their forms became engulfed in the beams, followed by brief screaming ... and then nothing.

The troops shone torches where the men had been standing.

Whatever the troops had fired, Don had never seen anything like it. Their targets were completely vaporised; not the slightest trace of them remained. Still in hiding, he watched as the troops returned to their colleagues, climbing briskly into the back of a vehicle.

There was a roar of engines and crunching of wood as the huge tyres began to turn over debris back in the direction of the track nearby, but this time the drivers wore night vision helmets and the headlights remained off, Don guessed, to stay undetected until they were well away from the scene.

As the noise faded, he heard the engine of another truck, this time approaching from the opposite direction. He could make out headlights coming across the grassland.

The truck came into view and he could see Cory waving from the passenger seat.

The farmer pulled up. Jumping out, he briefly introduced himself. Don thought he caught a name, Clanton or something. He made his way past Don to the crash site to see for what the fuss was all about. Cory wanted to go too, but his father ushered him over to one side.

"Cory, we have to get out of here right now," he whispered.

"But, Dad, I want to see …"

Don cut him off. "It's gone, everything. The army came and took it away." Don pointed to the backpacks. "Just put that on and let's get going now!"

The look on Don's face was enough to halt a protest. Cory did as he was told. They hurriedly packed up and made off, with Don setting the pace.

The farmer stood at the crash site, surveying the impact, trying to guess what might have caused the commotion. He picked around through charred foliage and mounds of warm earth. The kid had mentioned something about a spacecraft, but there was nothing here, nothing at all. He decided to see what Don and his son had to say about it.

But the father and son were now pacing across the grassland to the nearest town where Don had parked the car. If they carried on without stopping, it would be possible to make it in a couple of hours.

On the way, through laboured breaths, Don said little that made sense to Cory. But he could tell that his father was rattled; terrified, even.

The six-vehicle convoy made its way back to the highway, and only then was the decision made to turn the headlights on. The convoy was made up of an M939 flatbed that housed the craft safely out of sight under a green tarp, followed by two more 939s full of troops. Then came two black Lincoln SUVs. Up front was an LAV25 eight-wheeler recon vehicle, the gun turret housing a 25mm M242 Bushmaster chain gun. Any of the six personnel inside could take up position if necessary.

The convoy pushed on, driving through the night, over the border into Ohio, destination ... Wright-Patterson Air Force Base.

Chapter 11

Antarctica

Hans Schumann looked around his own current view of the world, a complement of untamed wilderness and unparalleled beauty.

He trudged through the snow, viewing the contrasting blackness of the rock blending with thawing ice shelves, the pink sky delivering an array of dancing reflections from the sun that could be witnessed in all their glory at this time of day. The sights here were always to be admired.

Suitably protected from the sub-zero temperatures with state-of-the-art clothing, Schumann had endured the outside world for two hours, much of the time stationary, running tests, and he was pleased to report back that the latest gear held up remarkably well. His bib and brace with matching anorak were all lined with alpaca and experimental man-made weave that had the capability of operating in any recorded low temperature. The outer layer was a breathable waterproof anti-tear compound that trapped the heat inside. Also on test was the latest polarised balaclava with reactive sunlight filtration. This meant that the mouth could be shielded without fogging up. What amazed the officer the most was how little the whole kit weighed. It enabled the same mobility as if just wearing a T-shirt.

He checked his bearings, running a sweep of the area. There should be no one else in this sector, but it was best to be on the safe side. The Norwegians were an inquisitive lot and could stray uncomfortably close to the sensors that were discreetly situated in the surrounding mountain range. That was the cue to drop out of sight until they passed, oblivious of what lay way down beneath their feet.

New Swabia was a place of isolation and tranquillity; it was his home.

He was born here, part of the colonisation after the war, his great-grandfather being a serving officer in the German navy, the discovery of the thermal layers far beneath the ice the key to sustaining a colony. And what a colony it had now become!

Schumann was himself a serving officer, part of the healthy Aryan population the Führer had always striven to create, strong and powerful with plenty of good female stock, the infrastructure a vast network of underground tunnels connecting to naturally heated caverns so vast that you could fit the whole of Manhattan into one sector. And there were seven sectors in all.

The population now stood at two hundred and eighty thousand, carefully regulated and nurtured, everyone with a role and a purpose, the technology way beyond surface comprehension.

A perfect civilisation? Possibly.

Schumann made his way to the water's edge, signalling that he was ready, making sure his departure was as swift as possible.

He stood at the precipice, the icy cliff face curving away in both directions, his position the lowest and nearest to the water's surface for miles, and still he must have been thirty feet up.

The inlet subtly carved from the land allowed for safe and discreet passage as the specially converted submarine emerged from the freezing black depths, gently parting the flotsam of floating ice, the foul weather bridge opening the hatch to receive their sole cargo. Schumann stepped aboard in a well-rehearsed manoeuvre, slid inside, the door closing tightly above his head as the vessel slipped below the surface, gone in an instant, heading back the short distance through the Southern Ocean to New Swabia.

Schumann got out of the dry mesh suit and changed into his uniform as the sub made the fifteen thousand feet descent to where the crew would follow the seabed to the entrance to the underwater cavern where the dock was situated.

He took a look in the mirror, making sure he looked acceptable. He donned his peaked cap, straightened his shirt cuffs and saluted himself, a tradition encouraged by society. He joined the other officers in the observation deck, helping himself to the refreshments on hand. He looked out through the thick glass, the powerful lights illuminating the way being met by other lights in the distance closing fast. Schumann soon recognised them as the usual pair of scout craft on hand to escort the sub through the entrance and to ensure that nothing else followed.

From a distance, the huge overhang of rock made the entrance invisible, but ducking underneath revealed the undersea cave that led to the dock. The sub, now on automatic settings, was guided the length of the mile-long journey, eventually surfacing into an underground cavern, some of the crew taking the advantage to go up on deck. The river split into five sections, all with docks for different divisions and destinations. Schumann liked dock one the best as the geological layout allowed for the mag air rail system to have a platform right by the dockside. As he lived in New Berlin, this meant that he could be home in fifteen minutes, stepping across the road at the other end and into his apartment. First of all, though, he must report in and be debriefed about his findings. The scientists working with him on the new version of the dry mesh suit would be very pleased; this technology could be filtered into many scenarios. He was glad to be part of the progress. The sensors that he checked were all serviced, samples of the ice taken as usual, and if it all went to routine, he would not have to venture out again for quite some time.

The sub glided to a halt dockside and the crew disembarked.

Schumann swept his blonde hair back into place with his hand and replaced his cap. He tapped in the report on the keypad, the runes neatly documented on the daily schedule. He chatted to a few of the scientists for a while about his findings, sharing some good-humoured banter.

Satisfied that all was in order, he stepped onto the shuttle, nestling into one of the memory foam seats that tilted back into position. A few colleagues joined him, exchanging pleasantries. He recognised one as Steiner, a young officer who lived in the next building to his. He had seen him a few times in the tavern close to where they both lived. They both politely acknowledged each other as the shuttle pulled away from the station.

The shorter distances were covered by the shuttles, but these were still capable of four hundred miles per hour. It was difficult to quantify just how vast the cavern system was. Even more so since the interconnecting tunnels were created, making travelling around simplicity itself. It was just over fifty miles to Schumann's stop in the centre of the capital, a much-admired area. Schumann had his grandfather to thank for this. Although he had been killed during the Second World War, his superiors had seen to it that the family were well looked after. His family was allocated one of the prime sites usually reserved for VIPs. Schumann knew that Steiner's father was a high-ranking army officer attached to the nation's border security. It was their job to make sure no one entered the boundaries unless they were a citizen of the country.

Schumann was pretty sure that no one had ever been to New Swabia from Terra since the first settlers found the caverns at the end of World War Two. And what strides they had made since that time. The seven provinces developed into a strong society, with technology way beyond that of the surface dwellers, down here, thousands of feet below the surface, the thermal underworld with its pleasant ambient temperature having been discovered in the late '30s by Rudolph Schmitt.

Schumann was well versed on the history of New Swabia; it was part of the curriculum that all citizens studied at the academies. He reminisced on his time there at the Kammler Academy, the nation's first and finest college; about how he captained the football team to victory, earned a distinction in his field of science and was awarded a very lucrative position in the research wing of the military. All citizens were expected to do at least five years' active service before being given the option of going into more specialised roles.

The Kammler Academy was named after Jan Kammler who was in charge of many scientific branches of the Third Reich. Towards the end of the war on April 17th 1945, when all was lost, Kammler assembled the fleet and headed south for Antarctica. With personnel of over two thousand, the U-boats and warships stacked with research equipment and supplies left Germany on the dangerous journey through Allied waters.

By some miracle they managed to avoid detection and reached their destination unchallenged where they liaised with the small colony, secretly established there for seven years. From this modest foothold, a new nation was born, a nation the Führer himself would have been proud of. In many ways, New Swabia was created to immortalise their great leader taking many of his own visionary ideas and implementing them into the architecture. This was the ultimate compliment that could be paid to the man who had started the movement, who had instilled the drive and desire, who taught the nation to rise up and to fight for what they believed in. Even now, the country was of pure Aryan population with no exceptions.

Kammler wasted no time in putting his people to work. There was no shortage of motivation with all striving for the same cause to create their own society with their own rules, with no one else to tell them what to do and how to do it. With a blank canvas to work with, it was easy to set out the structure for the capital. The willing and skilled workforce using the abundance of natural materials, along with the classified scientific technology at Kammler's disposal, soon had the makings of a nation. A lot of the geographical landscape was incorporated into the design of the stone structures that were hollowed out and made into buildings. Kammler had done his homework. The evacuation had been months in the making, and nobody got a free ride unless they had the right abilities. The females had to be brilliant and of good breeding stock, the males had to possess the requirements for the new society about to be created. If you were a stonemason or a sculptor, you were top of the list; and as Kammler was in such a prominent government position, it was easy for him to access the military records, discovering the skill sets relevant to his needs.

Also cherry-picked were all the top scientists he could amass, along with the finest military minds, engineers and academics. There was no shortage of takers; farmers, chefs and doctors were also keen to escape. With the alternative, imminent failure and occupation of their country by Allied forces, the decision was an easy one.

Kammler was confident that if he set out with a high level of intellect within his small community, this would ensure a good basis for super genes to be inherited through the population expansion programme. He was proven right with the IQ average at a consistently impressive level, nurtured by the rigid education that all citizens received.

Kammler instilled discipline way beyond the school gates, citing it as an essential attribute to a successful society. The population were constantly monitored, expected to abide by the strict laws and protocol. This was reinforced by the assurance that this would protect and safeguard the survival of New Swabia.

Rudolph Schmitt, the founding father who had discovered the underground caverns, was only too pleased to be able to hand over leadership. He was a much older man; a scientist, not a soldier. He was far more comfortable with his research programmes, overseeing the staff in the laboratories.

Kammler had been the obvious choice. The new Führer carried on the good work, a model leader overseeing zero unemployment, zero poverty, zero crime, and extended lifespan. Still he was not satisfied, the laboratories working long hours researching advanced weaponry and craft, healthcare and his main obsession, the secret of the brain.

Schumann knew where he was with Jan Kammler, the ruler he had grown up with, in power right up until his death, exact age unknown, but very old indeed.

He remembered as a ten-year-old boy disturbing Kammler who was trying to mend one of the harvesting machines. Kammler got him to pass up the tools as he worked. He chatted to Schumann cheerfully about all manner of subjects. He seemed to have a genuine interest in the youngster's aspirations.

They met eight years later when Schumann joined the armed forces. Kammler recognised him, they joked about the farm machine and a mutual respect developed between them. The young cadet was selected for the advanced runic and scientific training alongside the usual military curriculum. He was eventually transferred into Kammler's Spezialeinheiten.

Schumann was suddenly disturbed from his reverie by the announcement that he had reached his destination. The shuttle stopped seamlessly and he disembarked into the bright phosphorescent skylight. The weather never changed in New Berlin, the temperature constant, the unique geological climate and thermal lakes a source of free energy. The natural mineral content throughout the caverns had dictated where the country began and ended. There was more vastness beyond, but away from the geothermal lakes the temperature fell away somewhat, and without the phosphorus the light was poor. With the population now at a wholesome level, and the regulatory one child per family introduced, the need to expand to these extremities would be centuries away.

Schumann waved a farewell to Steiner, thinking of his father out there in the vastness on the edge of the light.

He entered the apartment complex through a series of security procedures before stepping into one of the mag lifts. Magnets and air pressure were in abundance in New Swabia; their uses could be seen everywhere. Schumann had been instrumental in advanced magnetic developments with new compounds. This was one of the reasons why he had spent time on the surface of Antarctica, testing metals and lodestone magnetism in extreme temperatures.

The mag lift rose effortlessly to the top floor of the complex. He stepped out and took the mag conveyor to the far end of the building, where he lived. The front door recognised him and opened as commanded. Once inside, Schumann opened up the mag screens and let the light into the open plan apartment. He took in the sights: a splendid disc pilot's view of the Grand Central Dome, only a kilometre into the distance, and the same height as his own building. The dome was flanked by a series of interconnected buildings all with matching Roman column frontage and large carved stone steps encompassing the capital's square. It was here that most of the official parades took place; the square itself, two kilometres long, was always well attended on those occasions. Soon they would put on the uplighters turning the dome a magnificent deep blue that could be seen from a great distance. The Grand Avenue ran from the centre of the dome for twenty kilometres either side, which was the entire length of New Berlin. The shuttle that Schumann had recently occupied ran underneath this road.

A great deal of thought had been put into the layout of the six cities to make them efficient with synergy to give a very smart and orderly appearance. The seventh massive cavern had been put over to farmland to provide for the nation.

Schumann could count himself lucky as one of the offspring of the chosen few. When he considered the alternative, a life of conflict, chaos, extreme weather, starvation, crime and a very primitive existence, the thought of a life on Terra horrified him. The fear of living permanently in that world certainly helped as an excellent way of keeping order down here in New Swabia.

His thoughts drifted to the next day. He had an appointment at the Chancellery, a very rare occasion to meet with the governing body in person. They had requested his presence to discuss work-related matters. That was all the information conveyed to him. He was to be at the NewBav base headquarters first thing to be instructed on this very important issue. The message had come through to his personal mailbox, and not at the military base, to ensure discretion. He was to tell no one of the meeting; *strict confidentiality* were the exact words. He wondered what the meeting could be about. He knew of no one who had been summoned in this way.

Schumann knew his duty, though. He was well versed in protocol, but even so, he still felt out of his comfort zone. This, and a sense of unease, crept into his thoughts. Should he be concerned? He would find out soon enough.

Chapter 12

Wright-Patterson Airbase, July 19th 1985

The vehicles were waved swiftly through the checkpoints, the convoy making its way to a hangar at the far end of the base. On approach, the two Lincoln SUVs left the rest of the convoy behind, passing under a large shutter. The rollers lowered the shutter door behind them.

The occupants were escorted from the Lincolns across the hangar and into a large office. The five men were placed in separate rooms and made as comfortable as possible. Outside, Captain Hul Prowse scanned through the notes. Three men in uniform, two in civilian clothes. He looked at the men through observation windows as they were being photographed and checked over by medical staff.

He studied the very old photograph in his hand, that of a German officer going by the name of Kessler. He looked long and hard at person number one, at his uniform, distinguishing features and facial structure. The man appeared fairly calm, slightly apprehensive, but that was to be expected.

Prowse shook his head in disbelief, staring through the glass, trying to come to terms with the situation. *Christ, they really did it, they actually did it!* he thought inwardly.

He took a deep breath, checked himself and entered the room.

"Good evening." The man seated opposite nodded. "For the record, could you please state your name and status?"

"My name is Oppengruppenführer Heinz Kessler."

Prowse nodded slowly, getting a measure of the man, observing the numerous military decorations adorning his black uniform.

"Your English is good, very good."

"And yours also," Kessler replied.

A German with a sense of humour. Maybe this would be easier after all.

"Okay, Herr Kessler, let's start at the beginning from when you entered the craft."

Kessler eyed the captain with interest, weighing up his own situation. He had to take a chance. Co-operation seemed a sensible option.

"I entered the craft and dialled the numeric code."

"Which was … ?" Prowse coaxed.

"Five, five, two, six, one."

"That matches what I have here. Welcome to America, Mr Kessler."

Chapter 13

New Swabia

The surface world was not without its uses. Many of the citizens of New Swabia would venture out on specific missions, be it for educational purposes, fact-finding missions or to obtain useful resources and luxuries not available subsurface. The main reason, though, was to spy on Terra, to see if any of their actions would pose a threat to their nation.

The favourite method of doing this was to travel at high speed in one of the Haunebu, the ultimate dispatch and extraction craft, which could evade radar detection, ensuring all missions were conducted covertly.

The main military base of New Swabia was located in the sector known as New Bavaria. Here the terrain differed somewhat with the ceiling height of the cavern at a consistent nine hundred feet, also the Wohltat River at this point was very wide, enabling easy passage through to an exit onto the ocean floor.

All the Haunebu craft were amphibious and had been for many years, providing versatility and extra flexibility. Sometimes it was necessary to mix air flight with underwater propulsion, depending on the destination. None of the Terran craft could match the speed, but it was important not to be complacent. If any of the craft were shot down, the crew were drilled in protocol, an option no one in New Swabia wished to consider. To date, no Haunebu craft had been lost.

Schumann banked his mag car around and descended to hover at the main entrance. As his pass was checked by the military police, he admired the Junkers 390, taking pride of place just inside the gates, a reminder of times gone by. He noticed the cramped cockpit and tiny gunnery ports, the immensity of the actual fuselage. One of the last warplanes built, capable of flying great distances, this particular model was fitted with seaplane skis enabling it to land in the Antarctic waters. It was the only aircraft under the command of Jan Kammler. There had been two others rumoured to have landed somewhere in Argentina, but this had never been substantiated.

His pass checked and approved, Schumann followed the guide line illuminated on the ground taking him past an impressive array of the latest amorphous Haunebu squadron, technicians busy running checks in the hangars, pilots making ready one particular craft hovering nearby, the unmarked matt black body like a perfect ellipse being taxied remotely into position.

A group of buildings came into view, then large avenues of trees, original descendants of the old homeland, planted in regimented fashion, a regular feature in New Bavaria. Schumann parked the mag car and made his way up the impressive stone block steps to the main entrance. He was greeted by a smiling receptionist flanked by two MPs and offered a seat while she called through, announcing his arrival.

In no time at all he was being escorted down a long corridor, every doorway, he noted, with its own guard, all immaculately turned out as was only to be expected. The escort waved a hand over a pad to the side of two large wooden doors. The doors opened into a vast room of opulence, with floors of marble and pedestals with classical busts. Three men were seated behind a huge, profusely decorated bureau plat. Schumann was offered a Louis XV gilt wood frame armchair. He glanced around as he sat in wonder before addressing the men opposite.

The man in the centre gave the informal customary Swabian salute. He wasted no time in getting to the point.

"Herr Schumann, are you familiar with sonic weapon technology?"

"I have basic knowledge, yes, but it is certainly not my area of expertise."

The third New Swabian Chancellor was about sixty years of age, selected carefully from a strong field of candidates. He was tall and in good shape, still blond, with sharp features and a chiselled jawline. He looked every inch a born leader. In his considered, measured tone, he continued, "There are not many people who do understand this science completely, and that is why in the wrong hands it is so dangerous."

Chancellor von Gellen prompted a high ranking official Schumann vaguely recognised, who produced a remote device and gestured for all in the room to look at the screen that now appeared on a wall. He clicked the screen into life, which appeared to show a nuclear submarine cutting across the surface of the sea.

Von Gellen continued.

"This is an American submarine of unknown origin on exercise earlier this month in the South Atlantic, and this is what happened when they tested their latest device."

The film moved on to show personnel transmitting sonic waves at specific frequencies inaudible to the human ear. About a mile away on the horizon, a large container ship drifted motionlessly. Suddenly the ship pitched; a large hole appeared in the stern, and the ship was sunk within a minute.

"As you can see, the American target was destroyed very

effectively."

Von Gellen paused before showing more still images on a slideshow. A beached school of whales, dead seabirds, seals, many species of fish and then the crew of a Brazilian container ship, all apparently dead, the crew of another vessel holding their heads, some being stretchered off at the mainland and away by ambulance.

The Chancellor spoke with despair in his voice.

"And this is what also happened on the same testing; one crew member dead, another with serious injuries and huge amounts of wildlife killed."

The other man, whom Schumann recognised as Vessels, interjected.

"Herr Schumann, you are now promoted to the thirty-fifth degree. This also comes with privilege of knowledge disclosure, which will make the situation even more obvious, but in a nutshell, we need to stop these tests at once."

Schumann could hardly contain himself. No ceremony, no public declaration; he had not been prepared for this. This was a great honour.

As far as he knew, there were very few citizens attaining Level 35 clearance. This gave him access to super-secret protocol and was regarded as a highly important level. "Thank you, sir. I am honoured," he said.

"You deserve it. You have served the nation well," the Chancellor said warmly. "But with reward comes responsibility. The information within this file will explain your new role. I hope you will find it fulfilling. Oh, and by the way … you work for me now."

Schumann remained calm and measured. This was too much to take in. He managed a reply.

"Mein Führer, I will not fail you."

Chapter 14

Hertfordshire

Marius coaxed himself out of bed – more of a tumble than a smart ascent – into the late autumnal coldness. His head ached from too much Canadian Club the night before. Sidney was an awful influence, and he convinced himself that this was the probable reason for his over indulgence.

He looked at himself in the mirror, a Georgian gilt wood example far too good for his reflection. He smiled at the thought; quite witty really, all things considered.

He looked every day of his forty-two years. Stress and worry could do that to a man, especially when that man knew he was out of his depth. He trudged downstairs, the idea of a walk to shake off his current state emerging through the foggy haze. With Helen out shopping, though, and the house so quiet, he needed to leave it for a while.

Later, as he walked along the footpath which led to the local heath, a neighbour crossed his path with a cursory nod of recognition. Marius nodded back, and a sudden sense of shame coupled with embarrassment made him instinctively turn his gaze away.

How he resented his exposure into the world of hypnotic regression.

Looking ahead through the trees, the mist swirling around

his feet, the sound of a dog barking playfully in the distance, and the heat of the sun trying to break through the haze, he felt sorrow for a life infiltrated by things he thought could only exist in the imagination of some sad sci-fi geek. The innocence of the waking day around him, the normality seemed to touch his very soul as if to awaken unknown resolve, commanding him to believe, to let go of what was such a safe life of normality, and to take a step, even a leap of faith, and to try to understand what all of this meant, and more importantly, what he was going to do about it.

It was true what Derek Mills had said to him: once you knew, everything changed forever.

Despite his resentment, Marius was grateful for the waning ache that was gradually fading from his head, the glorious morning almost forcing a smile as he enjoyed the circuit leading back to his house.

The mobile in his pocket sounded. Sidney's number appeared on the screen. The smile broadened as he answered, but was halted in equal measure in a second.

"It's Clarke … he's dead."

Chapter 15

Washington DC

The new president of MJ-12 looked around the table at the eager faces enthusiastically expecting their new directive. He eyed them all one by one, wearing his best face of reassurance; and delivering a volley of reports, all with positive results reassuring the board members, simultaneously lining their pockets with handsome dividends, skilfully skimmed off from the hapless American government.

President Kessler took a brief discreet moment to congratulate himself on a stellar performance. The journey had been an eventful one to add to his colourful past, but here he was with yet more quirks of fate handing him the most powerful position in the world.

Always best to start off in a new job with good news, which he had been able to deliver with relish. With funds at an all-time high and business and research results returning positive figures, it had been a dream start for the man who had played the perfect hand. There was just the small matter of updating the board on current affairs.

"Gentlemen, I am highly delighted to declare that our new underground wing is now operational. I am expecting you all to accept the invitation to inspect the facility for yourselves."

There was a brief pause followed by murmured approval

by all. Kessler had expected no less. It was important for all the board to observe first hand the advances being made at the Dulce base.

The eager faces all appreciated the disclosure of knowledge that only they were privy to. Soon they would be among the few to ever visit the base in person.

Chapter 16

Somewhere over the Atlantic Ocean

The craft emerged seamlessly from the sea and into the sky. The veteran pilot, going by the name of Weisse, chatted casually to his colleague, the equally experienced Kauffman, who was seated next to him.

At the rear of the craft Hans Schumann flipped over a large envelope and tore the back open as instructed. He fished out the documents and began to read. After a brief introduction to his new rank and expected duties, he arrived at his mission profile. Wide-eyed and in astonishment, he digested the details.

They were to fly to an American airbase located near Dulce in New Mexico where Schumann would be cleared to access the scientific research facilities and meet the staff there. His cover had been elaborately implemented to coincide with a Terran scientist.

Choosing Schumann for this mission was obvious from an academic point of view, but this would be his first liaison with surface dwellers. True, he was well versed in protocol, but that did not prevent him being as nervous as hell at the prospect of social dialogue. The last thing he wanted to do was to arouse suspicion. Although there was one small modicum of assurance.

As if on cue, a tall reedy spectacles-wearing Klaus von

Getz appeared with a plate of bratwurst, and a bundle of papers under his arm. Schumann took a bratwurst and munched away with a gesture of appreciation.

"No telling what the Americans will offer us, so best make the most of it," von Getz said in a surprisingly deep, authoritarian voice.

Without warning, he produced a portable scanner and swept the device in front of Schumann's body. There was a brief pause while von Getz studied the results. After a while, he looked up. "Hmm, yes, I see why you were selected. There are the obvious signs of apprehension, a slight rise in heart rate, but you display excellent levels of composure … taking into consideration that this is your first time … er, sir."

Schumann shrugged and smiled, partly because it had dawned on him that he was in charge of the mission. Maybe it was like this for all who had gone before him. Indeed, that in itself was a great mystery. Just how many had made contact with the outside world was still above his pay grade. Up until a few weeks ago, he would have guessed at zero.

The craft banked towards a mass of land he guessed must be America. He could see Weisse operating a series of controls. They sat there in silence as the mag shaper realigned the craft from a Haunebu into a private jet. Weisse activated the cloaking device just to be safe. He would wait until they were just shy of Dulce radar airspace and then de-cloak. It would then be a case of radioing in for clearance to proceed and land at the base. The advanced avionic technology would prevent the Americans from tracking them on departure and ultimately stop them from discovering New Swabia.

Von Getz used the time before their arrival to go through mission specifics one last time, his booming voice constantly reminding Schumann that he would be right there every step of the way with him. All he had to do was the job as instructed.

In no time at all, Weisse slowed the aircraft to a regular speed as they approached contact. As if on cue, the coms sprang to life. For the first time, Schumann witnessed the dialogue with the Terrans.

"Aircraft, you are about to enter restricted airspace. Please change your route."

Again ...

"Aircraft, if you continue into restricted airspace, you will be shot down. Acknowledge!"

Weisse made contact. "This is aircraft Vector Ten, Delta November Mike requesting permission to proceed to base. Check."

There was a pause, Schumann assumed while control checked the passwords.

The coms sprang to life again.

"Vector Ten, what is your current status? Check."

Weisse changed the channel and sent though a code via a keypad. Another pause before the reply.

"Aircraft, permission denied, I repeat, denied. Please re-route immediately."

Schumann was shocked. Surely the Americans knew who they were. Weisse, though, seemed unfazed and continued on the planned heading.

The aircraft continued over sun-parched desert floor, a mountain range appearing in the distance. The Swabian crew could make out camouflaged military vehicles with surface-to-air missiles positioned on an invisible boundary. They passed over without incident. Schumann now understood that the base had cleared their craft in coded format sent to them in text.

The aircraft passed over the summit of Mount Archuleta and banked left into a canyon. The base came into view for the first time. Schumann looked down at the arrangement of buildings, completely underwhelmed. He could make out five hangars at the end of a single runway and a modest group of smaller structures beyond that. There were a few jet fighters parked in a neat row and various vehicles parked randomly around the complex. Weisse banked the Haunebu and levelled out, descending smartly onto the tarmac of the runway with barely a jolt, and applied the airbrakes. The aircraft taxied to the end of the runway and parked up as instructed.

Schumann waited for Weisse to give the okay to release the door seal and, as instructed, he was led down the steps by von Getz and onto American soil for the first time. A welcome committee had assembled as they taxied in, and was now standing rigidly to attention. Base commander George Holt marched forward brusquely with a confident swagger, extending his arm and wearing a tight-lipped grin. He tilted his head up.

"You must be the German scientist Hans Schumann."

Schumann was prepared for the strange American manner and responded accordingly.

"Yes, Commander, and this is my colleague, Klaus von Getz."

Holt gave the man a cursory nod and moved off, gesturing for the two men to follow. The three of them headed for a building incorporating itself into the rock face at the end of the runway. The entrance had a bowl-like roof of concrete overhanging two enormous double doors.

Inside, the road continued in a straight line down a large tunnel as far as the eye could see, the illuminated ceiling exposing neatly excavated walls. Where they stood, a series of steel cross members and concrete had been united by industrial grey paint. The only other colour in peripheral view was the odd splash of black and yellow indicating hydraulic locations.

Marching smartly across, the three men were introduced by Holt to Clare Logan, Head of Department for sonic research.

She was about five-seven, attractive and slim. She had a pair of reading glasses nesting in her dark brown hair which met the top of her shoulders and was cut into a neat bob. She wore a look of officialdom and authority which told admiring eyes not to mess with her. She greeted the men straight-laced with a firm handshake, her face giving away nothing at all.

"I will leave you in the capable hands of the professor here." Holt gave her a knowing glance and made his excuses.

"Gentlemen, if you would like to follow me," she said.

They made their way through a doorway and into an office. It was much the same grey affair in décor, with functional computer layout with the usual peripherals in place. Schumann observed the similarities with some of their own tech back home, although it appeared far more primitive. The staff in the office were very civil and professional, guiding both himself and von Getz onto a platform built into the floor where their body weight was recorded. Von Getz had his briefcase put into a locker, it would not be allowed beyond this point.

Clare, or Professor Logan as she was known officially, explained. "You will not be permitted to take anything other than what you are wearing beyond this point, not even a pen. Your weight will be recorded here each day and you will be expected to use the scales within the facility levels to gain access. In addition to this, you will be issued with a swipe card and a numerical code which will change each day and will be issued here in this office. All these will be programmed to get you to the required working areas. Any questions?"

The two men said no, and were duly processed. The credentials checked out with the information given, a great attribute to their elite training, enabling the men to show no concern at this point. They had to trust the identities and covert placement that had got them this far. Now it would be up to Schumann to play his part and gather the intelligence requested by his new commander.

Professor Logan seemed satisfied, her mood seeming to lighten somewhat. She gestured towards a vehicle that had arrived for them. It was a white electric open-plan car that could accommodate eight people. As the car headed off into the gloom of the tunnel, Schumann actually relaxed a little. It was his first time in such a vehicle and he enjoyed the gentle breeze on his face that the swift ride generated. Although the vehicle propulsion was primitive in comparison to their own, he could see the practicalities of electricity as they sped along the centre of the tunnel. What caught his attention most of all were the walls of the tunnel. The way the rock had fused itself looked very familiar. He would try and discover what technique had created this.

They arrived at a platform with the same grey décor and disembarked, the driver waving a hand as he went on his very relaxed way. The professor took the lead with the floor scale, swipe and code. The men did as instructed, the three permitted entry into a room with a lift. For the first time, they were met by armed guards, but rather than the official smart uniforms of New Swabia, these were quite plain jumpsuit affairs, bulked out with built-in body armour and utility belts. The guns were slung over the shoulder behind their backs, one hand ready to react to an incident. They carried out a second manual check before parting the way for the lift.

Inside, Logan punched the control panel and the lift descended smoothly to Level Three. The doors opened to a repeat scenario with security and two more armed guards before entering a stark corridor, each doorway they passed also having armed guards. Schumann could guess from the look on the face of von Getz that he too was surprised at the level of security.

After a short time, they arrived at the lab. Logan opened the door labelled 'Sonics'.

The room inside was much bigger than Schumann had expected, with a large number of people busily working away on scientific duties. He could also see isolation booths and soundproof rooms with observation windows. Some of the scientists looked up from their work, acknowledging the three.

"For today, you will be permitted to work in your own uniforms. That way the staff here will know you are new consultants. From then on it will be the standard issue jumpsuit. Some of the lab areas are cross contamination sensitive."

The two men nodded their understanding. Schumann carefully let von Getz take the lead. He had a scientific background of his own and would know what to say. They would have to be careful with dialogue; it was likely that they were being monitored and recorded. He wasted no time;

"So, first a guided tour, perhaps?" delivered with a confident crisp clip.

Logan did not bat an eyelid "Of course. I will introduce you to the heads of department and show you what we are currently working on." She sauntered around the lab, pointing out various experiments, most of which were of no interest to Schumann. He nodded with a studious frown, asking the odd innocuous question. The professor was very thorough, giving a very detailed account of how far they had progressed with the experiments. He liked the way she spoke; the unusual mannerisms he found quite fascinating but, at the same time, quite unnerving. Her appearance was like something he was not at all used to. They spoke the same language, but they were so very different in so many ways. Yet, he liked her.

"Gentlemen, I need to take care of a few matters. Feel free to observe and ask the staff questions." She handed Schumann a tablet. "You can take notes on this if you like, Doctor." She gave him a tight smile, turned on her regulation shoes, and marched off.

Schumann looked at the device. It was some sort of old-fashioned recording touchscreen. It might come in useful, so he tucked it under his arm. He and von Getz started their observations.

They were careful in conversation with each other. A lot of what they saw would have to be committed to memory and documented when they got back to Weisse. Von Getz did an excellent conversing job. Some of the phrases he delivered to the scientists sounded like utter nonsense to Schumann, but seemed to assuage them in the necessary way. The real value of having himself in Dulce came after an hour into the lab visit.

It was immediately obvious that the Americans had part of the weapon perfected, but at the expense of having no restrictions on its limits. When employed, the weapon would destroy the target but could not be stopped from expanding out of the kill zone. He needed to find out how many of them had the knowledge to build one of these weapons. First job would be to get to a test site. There he could manipulate the results. The main tactic would be to install a much safer device. The last thing they wanted was another Hiroshima or Nagasaki. Schumann knew that, given the right modifications, the capability of these sonic weapons could easily surpass that devastation. The two Swabians continued with their observations until the shift ended.

As if on cue, Professor Logan appeared.

"Make any interesting observations?"

Von Getz took the lead. "You have a very impressive lab, Professor. There is a lot to take in," he exclaimed in a flattering tone.

"Yes, the work here is extensive," she responded, clearly pleased that the two visitors were impressed. "Time to sign out now. Work's over for today."

She led the way out past the vast array of security measures until they reached the lift. Once again she took charge of the controls and hit one of the large buttons.

"Time to show you where you will be staying."

The lift gracefully ascended to Level Two where they got out. By all accounts, it looked similar to Level Three. Only the directional signs were different. They headed a short distance up a corridor where Professor Logan led the way into a recreation area, the relative silence of their day replaced for the first time by large groups of personnel dining and chatting. Schumann recognised some of the scientists from earlier. Even the off-duty guards seemed to grow a personality. Von Getz's eyebrows arched up as he spotted the menu on the wall. In neat chalk marks was a selection of bewildering names, most of which he had never heard of. He took the lead and played safe.

"So, what do you recommend, Professor?"

"Italian for me; pasta is always good here."

"You mean there are more places like this?" von Getz's surprised look grew even bigger.

"Each sector has its own facilities. It makes it easier to cope with the numbers."

"Do you mind me asking how many personnel work here?" Schumann asked.

"I'm not sure of exact numbers, but certainly, more than fifty thousand."

Schumann nodded matter-of-factly, disguising his shock. Due to the fact that he came from an underground country, he knew that this place must be colossal.

The very modest layout on the surface, should anyone be fortunate to capture it on film, would show up as nothing but a small airbase of no consequence. As the Swabians knew only too well, the only way to spy on someone or something underground was to obtain direct access. No one could observe what was happening from the sky.

Although hardly luxurious, the dining area was much more inviting than what the two had visually experienced so far. Across the food hall, Schumann could see Weisse and Kaufmann chatting away to some of the military guys without a care in the world, munching on lumps of meat and vegetable matter locked together with some sort of bread. They looked like they were enjoying them immensely. A staff member came by with the same meal. Schumann smiled to himself at the main component, resembling the shape of their craft.

Accompanying the bread 'Haunebu' were a series of rectangular golden objects and what looked like a pot of shredded cabbage in a white sauce. As the man walked past the table, he caught the aroma coming off the plate and his mind was made up.

Above the droning of voices and kitchen noise, he heard the staff at the serving area announcing two burgers medium rare and two more 'Haunebus' made their way to a waiting table.

"Okay, guys, what are we having?"

"Have we all got to have the same?" Schumann exclaimed quite indignantly. Professor Logan looked startled.

Von Getz gave him a discreet glare and he realised his mistake. American turn of phrase sometimes made no sense to him at all and he had fallen foul of the generalisation.

"My German humour. Please excuse me."

Clare Logan looked at the man opposite and burst out laughing. Von Getz hurriedly joined in.

"You got me there, Dr Schumann. And I thought you Germans had no sense of humour."

"We Germans are full of surprises." He smiled playfully.

"So, what are we having then?" she asked expectantly.

"I will have a burger, medium rare, I think."

Von Getz, again surprised, gave him a look not to push it and he understood. Logan, though, nodded, seemingly impressed.

"Good call, Doctor. You want that with fries?"

"Of course." It was an educated guess.

Dinner arrived promptly; two pasta ragus, and a burger for Schumann. It was a strange creation, seemingly; on observing other people, you had to almost dislocate your jaw to get the right bite ratio as you ate with your hands. He picked up the 'Haunebu', surveying the best approach. By squashing the toasted bun down in his grasp, he was able to get the thing in his mouth. The whole thing together was a taste sensation, but at the same time familiar. It definitely tasted of beef; but then why call it a *ham*burger? Most strange. He decided it would be better not to ask.

The fries turned out to be potato sticks fried in vegetable oil.

As he discreetly studied others in the canteen, he surmised that most of the food items in their basic format existed in New Swabia; they were just assembled in a different way from what he was used to. This would help in his understanding of Terran cuisine.

Von Getz seemed to be enjoying his Italian meal, a construction of flour, eggs, water, a few herbs and tomatoes, used to create something delicious yet quite simple in format.

He studied Clare Logan as she chatted quite freely, a different person from the officious version that greeted them earlier in the day. She was very at ease with von Getz, a fine scientist himself, discussing matters of sonic theory.

In truth, soon after their arrival, the two Swabians had identified basic errors in the delivery system. Schumann would stretch it out a bit to make the knowledge they possessed seem less suspicious.

"Tomorrow we will go to the test site. You can witness a demonstration for yourselves," Logan announced. "We will meet in here for breakfast tomorrow at 0800 hours. Gentlemen, when you are ready, I will show you to your quarters."

The rooms were on the small side, reminding Schumann of old-fashioned naval quarters: metal-framed beds and lockers, everything functional but well-made. The only technical item visible was an aircon control on the wall. Schumann detected the gentle hum. It was an ancient version of their own system.

"Showers are down the hall. You can use the dining hall and recreation room till 2300 hours, then its lockdown. All levels become out of bounds."

The professor said goodnight to them and marched off towards the lift. Schumann nodded to von Getz and they retired for the evening, choosing not to discuss anything in case someone was listening in. There would be plenty of time for that.

Schumann retired to his room and stretched out on the bed. The time alone would serve him well as to how to proceed from hereon. He was pleased with his performance as a German citizen. Apart from a few minor hiccups in dialogue, it was a lot easier than he had anticipated to meld into the surface world.

If only the Terrans knew how close they were.

The next day saw Schumann and von Getz meet up as agreed in the food hall where, after a very brief meeting, they were escorted to the elevators by Professor Logan.

This time the three of them journeyed a lot deeper into the base. Schumann managed to get a quick view of Level Seven on the control pad.

"Nice and quiet," Schumann remarked at the sound of the propulsion.

"I remember when I first came to work here. They were much louder. I suppose that's progress for you," Clare Logan replied.

As the lift came to a slow, controlled halt, the doors opened smartly, giving Schumann just the briefest of glimpses at the shutter mechanism. Curious, he thought to himself, the technology here was quite advanced; familiar, even.

No time for that now, though, as they were whisked along by security, again through a warren of identical corridors. He noticed some of the signs were in a strange language he was not familiar with.

"We are on the lowest level of the base," Clare Logan announced. "This will take us to the test site."

The two security guards seemed rather nervous to Schumann. He thought they would be used to working here. Clare was slightly ahead, talking to them about the day's arrangements. Occasionally one of the guards would look behind the party.

He glanced at von Getz, who gave him a look that told him the other man was also puzzled. They could be miles underground; there was no real way of telling. The fact that the layout or décor rarely changed gave very little away. There was also a strange feeling that he knew all of them were experiencing. The conversation in front had stopped and there was silence. Only the footsteps striking the screeded polished floor could be heard.

They arrived at a tunnel. A driver wearing a solemn expression ushered them into an electric car. He made his way off into the dimly lit roadway, the two guards left behind to return to their posts.

"Not far now." Clare's voice echoed around the vast cavern.

It was much colder; Schumann was now grateful for the coat with which he had been issued earlier. A dampness of hostility crept into his bones, combined with a feeling of apprehension. Was it just the mission, the pressure getting to him, or was there something more?

The car came to a halt at a platform where they were instructed to disembark.

Clare guided them through an alcove where they suddenly looked out onto a huge expanse of water, illuminated by powerful lighting. It was a spectacular sight with large numbers of personnel working on a mix of submarines.

"This, gentlemen, is our underground dock." She gestured with her hand. Schumann now realised why he had felt the cold damp conditions as they had approached. "We can keep this fleet here until needed. The river connects further down under the sea and into the Gulf of Mexico."

He and von Getz nodded studiously, but inside they were both secretly impressed. The cavern was magnificent. Schumann imagined what an asset a place like this would be back home. They climbed aboard one of the subs, where the two Swabians were drilled in procedure. They knew most of it already, but went along with the charade.

The submarine glided smoothly into the depths, and into an underwater tunnel. It would be a short journey to the test site, their destination, connected underground by the tunnels. Here they would witness the sonic test.

Although Schumann could understand the principles behind the sub's construction and layout, there were a few subtle features that seemed a little out of place. He had also observed this back at the dock.

"How fast are we travelling?" von Getz enquired.

"They tell me these submarines can reach speeds of eighty knots," Clare replied.

That was certainly a lot faster than the intelligence reports, thought Schumann, but was thankfully still way off their own submersibles' top speeds. This insight into Terran weaponry was certainly an eye-opener. They appeared to be on the brink of some huge leaps in technological advances.

The sub made its way swiftly through the underground river, eventually arriving at another wide, half-submerged cavern.

The dock lit up. Von Getz removed his spectacles, cleaning them thoroughly as the sub glided into place, dock personnel tending to the vessel. A large number of buildings came into view. They were helped onto the dockside and escorted along the gangway to join a group of dignitaries who, Schumann guessed, had also been asked along to witness the test.

They were introduced to the various Terran representatives, Professor Logan ushering them over to the monitoring equipment where several scientists were stationed. Schumann did a visual sweep of the layout, taking in the other figures nearby.

Clare Logan could see he was impressed. "Magnificent, isn't it? The network was discovered in 1965; a real geological wonder."

Schumann nodded, hands on hips. Clare continued, "We are in very esteemed company today. The man over there on the end is head of the whole underground base network."

Schumann observed him; around seventy years old, average height, wearing civilian clothes but retaining a military air about him. His hair was cut short, his stern expression accentuated by a neat pencil moustache.

"What's his name?" Could be useful to know, he surmised.

"Albert Hebb." Her words carried bitterness. "He has been in charge for the last eight years, though I have only seen him down here once before."

Schumann decided not to question the displeasure in her voice. Besides, the delegation with Hebb was fast approaching. Von Getz tapped his side as if to hint that he would handle the dialogue. Schumann had no problem with that.

"You must be the two consultants from Germany." Hebb extended his hand. Von Getz took it and gestured to his colleague. Schumann shook hands, giving a curt nod, meeting the other man's stern gaze.

"Good to have your expertise, Mr …?"

"Hans Schumann, sir."

Hebb nodded, a faint smile appearing for a split second. "The test starts in a few minutes. We should take up our positions."

Schumann could not be certain at first, but the more the high ranking official spoke, the more convinced he was. Although very Americanised, there was no doubt that Hebb had a Germanic accent.

As he consulted with the base scientists, Schumann could see some more subtle military mannerisms. He felt a dislike for the man which was unusually pre-judgmental of him. He was not sure why.

He took up his position at a monitoring station with von Getz and four other scientists. Here they explained there would be a series of tests, getting stronger as they went on. This made sense as there would be ample opportunity to adjust the settings on the weapons. That was where the two Swabians would be expected to deliver.

In truth, the two of them had solved major flaws in the sonics almost straightaway. Luckily, they did not have to introduce any suspect machine parts. It was just a case of reprogramming the settings.

Schumann could see Hebb conversing with other dignitaries, their expectation clearly optimistic for all to see.

Despite the cavern's enormous size, it puzzled the Swabian what the target could be. He could see no obvious destination for the sonic weapon.

Von Getz joined him studying the first test settings. It was in a basic programming language that they were both familiar with. Schumann could make out some other figures who had gathered behind the smoke glass of the buildings nearby, their features impossible to make out. It would seem that there was a lot riding on this test; the scientists looked very nervous at this sudden extra presence. Schumann took a discreet long breath to compose himself. The test, he could feel, was now imminent.

An announcement came over the tannoy system to not be alarmed at the noise, and suddenly a light appeared way above them; at first just a glint, then soon like an enormous strip light, thousands of feet above their heads.

The light was now an ever-growing rectangle illuminating the cavern. Schumann realised that the light was emanating from the Terran surface, opening up like a zipper to reveal the sky above. An image appeared on the screens in front of them showing bleak terrain with a rocky outcrop beyond. On the rocks were a series of military vehicles numbering around twenty, all parked side by side.

The first concentrated beam was dispatched, taking the power out of three of the vehicles to the right of the pack. Schumann also observed numerous wildlife casualties.

Enough of this. There was no need to draw it out any more. He held a hand up before the second sonic wave could be released, busying himself on the keyboard, checking readouts and calculations until he was satisfied with the outcome. He nodded for the next sonic test to be dispatched. A bewildered scientist looked toward Clare Logan who shrugged and gave her authorisation.

There was a deep guttural hum as the next sonic wave left the cavern. They all crowded around the monitors, watching the electrical readings. The sonic beam found the target, disabling all the remaining vehicles.

A sweep of the area displayed no other organic casualties. Even a rather gruesome looking vulture that had taken up position on the roof of a personnel truck remained unharmed.

There was a very long pause. Clare Logan looked at him; a look of complete shock. A ripple of applause grew, echoing around the cavern, Albert Hebb joining in, nodding his approval, a pat on the back from one of the scientists.

In truth, it had been an educated guess, but there was no disguising the glee on the face of von Getz.

Schumann caught his glance and stifled his emotions.

The subtle adjustments were clever, enabling the sonics to be dispatched at a far more efficient level; but, at the same time, he had restricted the distance to a mile, explaining to the Terran scientists that it was a vital compromise to improve the accuracy of the weapon. It was a very plausible explanation that seemed to satisfy them all.

Schumann could waffle his way past any awkward questions avoiding any quantum leaps in the machine's efficiency. He knew it would take them a very long time to work out how he had managed it.

"Well done, Mr Schumann, very well done indeed." Clare Logan applauded him as she joined his side.

Schumann gave her a curt nod and checked over his settings for the last time. He busied himself consulting with the scientists for a while, making small talk, bluffing his way through the barrage of questions, modestly putting a lot of his problem-solving down to guesswork.

They had accomplished the mission. Now it would be a case of gathering as much intelligence and information as possible before leaving for New Swabia. The more they knew about the Terrans, the better they could deal with them in the future.

Chapter 17

Hertfordshire

"Police were here a while ago following up on a few leads." Sidney took the coats of his two friends and hung them in the cloakroom. "Such a nice chap. Still can't believe it."

Helen and Marius stepped out of the stubborn misty chill of the morning and into the inviting Georgian haven.

"Where did it happen?" Helen asked.

"Village where he lived. Do you know Westhill?"

"Yes, I do," she exclaimed. "Just the other side of Royston."

"That's the one. Nice quiet village."

Marius knew the place. It was linear with several other villages. He had used the road as a detour on occasions if there had been problems with traffic on the A10.

Sidney handed out the tea.

"He was walking along the High Street. Just left the pub around 10.30 p.m. Couple of witnesses say a black MPV mounted the pavement, taking him out at high speed."

"Have they arrested anyone?" Helen asked hopefully.

Sidney shook his head vigorously. "No one. Police are not even sure whether it was intentional or not, but I have my suspicions."

"Why so?" A surprised Marius.

"Well, after I helped him awaken those suppressed

memories, he thought it would be a good idea to speak to the press. His story was in the local *Gazette* last week."

"Surely you don't think he was deliberately targeted?" Helen, incredulous.

"I do. With all that's gone before, it's too much of a coincidence."

Marius frowned, listening intently. The more he tried to dismiss the whole thing as a tragic accident, the more he had to agree with Sidney. The High Street of Westhill village was well-lit and straight as a die, plus there were traffic-calming speed bumps all along the road.

"I went to see his wife this morning. She was incredibly complimentary considering the dreadful news. She said how his manner had brightened since the hypnosis session." Sidney handed over a large jiffy envelope. "She said he had put some notes together on the subject: thought I should have them."

Marius emptied the contents onto the coffee table in front of him. Out tumbled a leather-bound notebook and a rectangular black box.

Sidney's head snapped back, eyebrows raised. "Well, will you look at that."

Marius ignored the notebook, picking up the box, identical to that of his own client. He examined it for a while, not really knowing what he was doing, before handing it to Sidney. The same dread seemed to pass from one man to the next, as if the box was almost alive. It was a very strange feeling, as if they were handling something forbidden.

"This box … I think Clarke meant for me to have it. Don't ask me why. Maybe he wanted me to try and find out its purpose. All I know is he was quite satisfied that he no longer required any more treatment."

Helen picked up the notebook. Flicking through the pages,

she could see nothing out of the ordinary that would help. There were more drawings of the craft that Clarke claimed had abducted him. They were a little more accomplished and less childish than before, but the notes were more of the same, repeating what he had documented in Sidney's office.

"So what do we do now?" she said.

"I think it's time for us to introduce Sidney to Derek Mills."

Chapter 18

Dulce, New Mexico

Schumann met von Getz in the corridor outside his cabin where they made their way to the conference rooms. Through the mass of staff, Clare Logan spotted them as they entered, holding up her arm so they could see her. The two Swabians wove their way through the throng, a few compliments aimed at them referencing the success of the tests the day before.

"Gentlemen! Sleep well, I hope?" She beamed as they were handed coffee.

They'd slept very well and acknowledged the fact. Logan wasted no time sliding into her official mode by explaining the day's schedule. There would be a spell in the lab going through settings and checks before a final review of the sonic weaponry for the people who would be using it. It all seemed fairly straightforward to von Getz until she announced that she would be taking Schumann to the surface.

He gave little away as she made her matter-of-fact announcement.

"I thought I would give Mr Schumann a tour of the grounds. We have a few testing areas on the other side of the base and I could do with his advice on the best one to use."

Von Getz relaxed a little, but shot his colleague a subtle glance. Schumann could read him by now and knew what he was getting at. But he was getting the hang of his alter ego now and had assimilated himself into a far more relaxed mode that was far less likely to make a mistake.

Von Getz took the opportunity to check in with the other crewmen on their craft. Schumann could meet up with them later in the labs.

Logan led the way out of the noisy conference room and down the corridor to the lift that would take them to the surface.

"I must say, a lot of people have trouble getting used to being underground for a long time. You both seemed to cope very well."

Schumann smiled inside. "It must be the company," he replied.

She gave out a short laugh, caught off guard by the unexpected compliment. "We Americans have a reputation for being good hosts, Mr Schumann." She gave the guard a familiar nod and ushered Schumann into the lift. The doors closed in front of them, exposing the inner workings for just a split second.

Logan caught his gaze, breaking the silence. "They are all very impressed with your work and I would like to take this opportunity to thank you personally." She extended her right hand. Schumann took it in his own, delivering a firm handshake.

"I'm glad I could be of service, Professor."

"Hope you don't mind me stealing you away from the others. We won't be too long."

The lift reached the surface and they emerged onto the level. A car was waiting and took them the short distance to the hangar doors. Schumann recognised the processing office across the way as the doors opened to bright sunlight, illuminating the building with a pleasing natural glow. They stepped out of the car and made their way on foot outside, across the road towards some outbuildings. Schumann could see Kaufmann in the distance talking to Weisse, pointing to the undercarriage of their aircraft.

Logan led the way around the buildings. She turned from the solid ground into the scrubland, through the trees, negotiating the steep incline with ease. Schumann following behind admiring her fitness and her attractive form. She had dispensed with the jumpsuit and white coat and was sporting a military issue top with backpack, dark combat pants and hiking boots. Schumann had also been kitted out: the boots, he now realised, were an essential requirement to grip the loose dirt track that wound its way up the hillside.

They reached the summit in around ten minutes and dropped down out of sight from the base. The terrain became a lot more level; the trees also became denser as the track vanished. Logan seemed to know where she was going, though. Schumann maintained close proximity, parrying branches from his face, ducking occasionally to avoid them hitting his head. The air filled his nostrils with wonderful aromas, some of which were a first-time experience. A rabbit broke cover and scurried away through the undergrowth. Schumann looked astounded as the white tail bobbed and disappeared from view.

"What's the matter, never seen a rabbit before?" she teased.

He waved a dismissive hand. Actually, he had never seen one. He suddenly started wondering what else might be waiting for him in the woods.

To his relief, the trees started to thin and they soon emerged into a clearing, the sunlight heating his face. Logan looked at him.

"Are you one of those guys who finds everything interesting, Mr Schumann?"

He realised that he was smiling broadly, but came back smartly.

"Forgive me, Professor. The weather has been quite terrible back home. It's good to see some sunshine."

She shrugged and headed off, making her way towards a rocky outcrop.

"Keep up, Mr Schumann."

He did as he was told, following her until they rounded a corner exposing a narrow opening in the side of a cliff face. By sliding in sideways, it was just possible to squeeze through the opening. Once inside, they were met by blackness. Logan fished out a torch from her backpack and switched it on.

It was a small cavern, about the size of two cars stacked on top of each other, narrowing at the other end into a door-sized corridor. Schumann did a three-sixty of the cave, suitably underwhelmed.

Logan could see the puzzlement on his face.

"S'pose you're wondering why I brought you up here," she said, her voice bouncing around the walls.

"This does not look like a test site," Schumann replied, trying not to sound too concerned.

She faced him, her body at a distance that he could tell was no longer official. Logan eyed him with a wry smile in the corner of her mouth. He knew that he was at a distinct disadvantage and she seemed to detect that.

Knowing very little about the surface world gave him few clues as to what to expect from the Terran. There had been very little warning before they had left the safety of New Swabia into this world that he had always been warned was mad. He had no time to research properly, so much was left down to instinct. When he thought about it too much, it was a miracle that they had got this far without being found out.

He realised Clare Logan was sizing him up. The look on her face had now changed into a more serious format. He realised that she was still waiting for a reply to her question.

"Alright, what are we doing in this cave?"

"I like to come up here every now and again to be on my own, have some time to myself and get some privacy." Schumann eyed her with confusion. She continued looking around the walls. "I found this place by accident while out walking one day. I checked it out very carefully and I am confident that no one on the base knows it's here." She turned to face him again. "The whole base is fitted with cameras and listening devices; you can't do or say anything without being monitored. I brought you up here so no one could hear us."

So the cave was a blind spot. It now made sense to Schumann why they had left the track a while back. She was obviously being very careful so the least he could do was to find out what was so important.

"So, what do you want to tell me?"

Clare Logan looked pretty uneasy, not the usual in-control persona that he was used to. It actually bothered him more than he knew it should. She took a deep breath and told him.

"Straight off, I am trusting you with highly classified information." She could see Schumann looking unsure, but kept going. "I mean it. This base does not only experiment with new weapons systems. That is just a very small part of what goes on here."

"But why would you risk your career telling me this?"

"Look, there's something that you should know about this place. If you step out of line you lose more than your job … you go missing, and no one will ever find you." She took another breath; she was struggling to express the gravity of her situation. "Mr Schumann …"

"Please call me Hans," he said soothingly.

"Okay, Hans, and you call me Clare, then. Okay?"

"Sure."

She continued as best she could. "This place is full of dark secrets. A lot of the staff do not know what goes on down in the lower levels. There are rumours, of course, but few have access to Base Level. That man you saw yesterday, Hebb ... his speciality is cryogenics and worse."

Schumann's eyes widened. Human experiments. He had heard about similar atrocities carried out in the homeland during the Second World War, the leaders trying to create a super army, soldiers with great strength, advanced mental powers and with amazing resilience. And in the quest to discover the answers, they experimented on the prisoners in the concentration camps ... thousands of them.

"Go on," Schumann coaxed.

"It's called 'nightmare hall'. I have to go down there on occasions as my field crosses over from sonics to mind control."

"Mind control?" Schumann gasped.

Logan hung her head in shame.

"I was recruited originally for my work with effects on the brain induced by soundwaves."

Hence the reason for heading the sonics department, Schumann thought.

"I thought it would further my research. I had no idea what they were doing on Base Level, taking my findings and administering them to live human subjects."

"Where do they get the subjects from?" Schumann asked.

"They grab them off the streets and in their own homes. Some of them are the ones I told you who dare to speak out, go missing and end up on Base Level."

Schumann was shocked. He never thought that the Terrans

could carry out such barbaric acts. It sickened him to think that this was going on in the very facility under their feet.

"But what can I do? I have no authority here."

Logan walked the short distance over to a boulder next to the wall. She bent down, sliding a notebook from its hiding place. She stood back up, handing it to Schumann.

"Here, take it. It's all in there. It will be easier to read my findings rather than me try to explain it all. Anyway, we don't have much time."

It had a tatty red leather binding, being around only four inches high and about three wide. Schumann flicked through the contents briefly and tucked the notebook snugly into his trouser pocket.

"When we get back to the base, you can make an excuse and stow it away in your aircraft."

"Of course, but what do you want me to do with the information?" Schumann was trying to be helpful. She was traumatised even trying to explain the gravity of the situation, and he did not want to create further anguish.

"Take it back to Germany with you and keep it safe," she said. "It is important that the world gets to know the truth, then maybe we can bring an end to all of this."

Schumann's heart sank. He had no Terran allies to call upon. The situation was hopeless; there was nothing he could do. Telling others back in New Swabia would only provoke mild interest. Unless the appalling activities posed a direct threat to the homeland, his superiors would not act.

"I will keep it safe for you, I promise."

Thankfully, Logan did not press him any further. She seemed satisfied with his co-operation.

"I know I can trust you, Hans. When I get some leave I will contact you in Germany. Don't worry, I will be careful."

This was getting worse, although, thankfully, the Swabian facility that dealt with their cover in Bavaria could deal with any unwanted enquiries. On this occasion, he actually felt a desire to be Terran for a while.

"You can get a message to me at our facility, the usual address."

"Is there a home address, perhaps an email?" Logan enquired.

Schumann tensed up. "Might be unsafe to do that. Better not risk it."

"Oh, yes … You're right, of course, that makes perfect sense."

Schumann breathed an inward sigh of relief. It did make perfect sense … got away with it again.

Why did he feel the need to help this Terran woman? He could see no realistic solution to her plight anyway. There was no guarantee that the team would be required to return to Dulce. This could well be the last day that he saw Clare Logan.

He would have to see what happened when he returned with the others in New Swabia.

In the short spell of silence between them, Schumann became aware of a faint hum emanating from the back of the cave.

"Do you hear that?"

Logan nodded. She led him over to the natural corridor, about five by four, that ran for only a maximum of ten feet. Schumann borrowed the torch from her, sweeping the beam from left to right as he entered. There wasn't much to see; evidence of a rock fall from the roof of the cave, a few rocks scattered on the floor.

Logan pointed to the left-hand corner.

"Over there … that opening."

Schumann had not seen the opening, obscured by a boulder,

the shape of a table top, that had fallen against the back wall.

"It's an air conditioning vent from the base," she explained, showing him the gap in the floor. "The rock fall must have created a breach."

Schumann observed the dimly-lit hole. Some of the rocks had stoved the top of the air con duct open; beyond that, there appeared to be little damage. Peering further inside, the hum grew much louder where he could also make out the dusty tunnel that housed the air con vent. It was visible for about ten yards in either direction before the light faded away. Satisfied that they could not be overheard, he backed out of the hole.

He was suddenly reminded of the immensity of the base. They must have walked nearly a mile to reach the cave.

"We'd better get going." Logan signalled with her head in the direction of the way out.

Back in the bright sunlight, she pulled a large bundle of brush scrub over to conceal the small entrance. "Just to be on the safe side," she exclaimed.

They made their way back to the trail, down the sloping hillside, and back to the base. Schumann casually sauntered over to his aircraft where Kaufmann was still checking over the undercarriage. Schumann climbed the steps and opened the side door. Inside he was greeted by Weisse and von Getz.

"Everything in order for departure?" Schumann enquired, taking his seat.

Weisse nodded. "Yes, sir, we are scheduled to leave tomorrow."

"Good, that just leaves us time to do some final checks." Schumann slipped the notebook from his pocket and jammed it safely down the side of the leather upholstery. He waited a while, making idle chat before announcing his plans to go below surface. Von Getz complied by shedding himself of any foreign objects before following his superior out of the aircraft and over to the hangar doors of Dulce base.

The two of them were checked through by security measures and taken by the driver to the lifts, all in the same routine manner. The staff were used to seeing them come and go by now and acknowledged them from time to time, although the same level of security was maintained during their descent to Level Three.

Logan was there as expected, back in her lab coat, supervising the test reports. These would be passed on to Hebb to sign off, giving authorisation for weapon deployment. She broke from her duties and came over to where the two men were standing.

"Gentlemen, time to sign off your work and make sure you approve of the details. Here is the total payment for the work carried out."

She showed them the amount. Schumann looked at the sum: six hundred thousand dollars. He was vaguely familiar with Terran valuations, and this, he knew, was a very large payment for what was a very small amount of work. They must have been very happy with the results or very desperate to achieve them. Maybe both.

The fee would be transferred to Germany where Schumann assumed the money would be used to buy Terran goods for New Swabia. He showed no emotion as he checked through the document. It all seemed to be in order. He nodded, and von Getz concurred.

Schumann signed the document. Logan took it and passed it over to her assistant.

"Right, gentlemen. If you would both follow me, please."

The men followed Logan without question, back out of the lab, down the corridor to the lift. The three of them stepped inside, Schumann doing his habitual observation as the lift doors closed. Logan hit the control panel and the lift descended into the depths, down to Level Three, a wait, past Level Four, then past Five. Schumann stiffened as the lift approached Level Six, Logan cast him a fleeting glance and then turned her head away. The lift continued downwards. Schumann breathed an inward sigh of relief. The lift came to a halt on Level Seven and the doors opened.

Logan led the way, the same direction as before, the two guards escorting them wearing the same concerned expressions.

As the corridor split in two ahead of them, the party was guided towards the left-hand tunnel. Schumann observed three figures in the tunnel on the right. They seemed to be arguing, the figure nearest to them pointing to a motif carved into the tunnel floor. The other two interested him the most. One of the figures appeared to be only four feet tall, with very pale skin and a large head. Next to this one was someone or something much taller. It was difficult to see through the gloom, but this figure appeared to be the most aggressive of the three although he could only hear one voice.

Logan ushered them into the left tunnel. "Nothing to do with us, gentlemen. This way." She directed with her hand.

The guards looked unsure what to do, which struck Schumann as quite strange in itself. Added to this was the nervousness of Logan. Surely, in a facility like this there would be a very strict code of conduct. Certainly, back in New Swabia this kind of behaviour would not be tolerated. He could tell that von Getz was alarmed at the absence of discipline shown. Also, there seemed to be a complete lack of decisiveness from the people who were supposed to be looking after them.

Logan seemed to relax a little as they put some distance between themselves and the minor skirmish. She guided them over to a ten-man Zodiac tied up at the water's edge. It was far more practical and faster than the sub.

The loud engine noise made conversation difficult. Clare Logan was sitting by his side. She touched his hand discreetly, a signal he took as not to forget her plight. He had not forgotten at all.

The rest of the journey passed by without incident which gave Schumann time to ponder the ever-mounting collection of anomalies that seemed out of step with his rationale. It could be just the Terran way. He had no way of knowing for sure.

They arrived at the now familiar dock cavern where the test had taken place. Hebb and the scientists were waiting for them, and came over to the dockside. The same warm congratulations were echoed from the day before on the two men.

Hebb drew Schumann over to one side, away from the group. "Let's take a walk, Mr Schumann." He complied without hesitation.

The two men walked side by side along the dock, Hebb arched his left arm above his head.

"When I saw this place for the first time, I could not believe my eyes. I still marvel every time I see it, even now."

"It is a wonderful place, sir."

Hebb nodded appreciatively at the respect given by the other man. He continued his spiel.

"While the world burns above our heads and society falls apart, we have the power and the resources down here to survive it all. Just imagine a place with no crime, no conflict, no unemployment and no famine."

As a matter of fact, Schumann could easily imagine such a place, and he was keen to get back there as soon as possible.

Hebb went on. "We are all very grateful for the work you have done, none more so than myself. You should be proud to be a part of all this." He carried an air of arrogance that Schumann found unsettling.

"I'm glad we could be of service to you." He hoped that he would not regret those words.

"You could play a very important role in our future plans. I have many ambitious projects that would benefit from your input. I could offer you a lucrative consultancy job, full expenses."

Schumann nodded at the ground in a studious manner. Hebb continued, the German accent surfacing as he struggled to contain his excitement.

"I will be sure to let your superiors know how pleased I am with your help on the sonics."

Schumann made sure his face gave nothing away. He knew Hebb was on a fishing expedition, obviously curious as to how they had solved the weapon fault in so little time. In hindsight, they should have held out a lot longer. The trouble was that they had very little instruction from their real superiors.

"I must admit that I was unaware of your knowledge in this field, Mr Schumann ... or is it doctor or professor?"

"No, I prefer to be informal, sir. No titles, please."

"Oh, come now," Hebb scoffed. "You are far too modest."

Schumann needed to stop this before personal questions started being fired at him. He stole a glance in the direction of von Getz who was standing, going over final details with the scientists. Thankfully, he was watching, could see the discreet hand signal and reacted accordingly. He held a hand up as if to attract Schumann's attention.

"Looks like I am needed," said Schumann. "Please excuse me, sir."

"Of course ... yes, go ahead, Mr Schumann." Hebb delivered this with a slight hiss.

The Swabian officer walked smartly over to von Getz who

bluffed his way through a conversation that no one would admit to not understanding. Schumann was eternally grateful for the backup.

Hebb eyed him for a while before wheeling on his heels and marching off. Several men scrambled to join him before they all vanished into a building on the far side of the dock.

Logan sidled up to Schumann, smiling. "Everything alright?" Her eyes carried a disguised look of concern.

"Fine, Professor." Schumann smiled back as broadly as he could.

After the formalities were all completed, the group made their way out of the cavern, the Zodiac rising effortlessly through the jet black waters of the cave system to rendezvous with the dockside driver, and back to the edge of Level Seven where the guards were waiting patiently.

Chapter 19

Cambridgeshire

Marius followed the instructions conveyed by his satnav, the soft female voice guiding him over the border into Cambridgeshire. They left the busy A14, skirting the market town of St Ives and headed for the village of Wyton. Just before the village, along a country lane bordered by dense greenery, lay their journey's end.

"You have reached your destination," the soft female voice announced.

A green-and-white chequered flag appeared on the screen just as two huge brick pillars with stone ball finials came into view. They flanked a pair of black cast-iron gates that opened remotely on arrival. Marius eased the Range Rover onto the pea shingle driveway and drove the short distance to the gatehouse.

The red-brick house had a substantial wing either side of the driveway, united by a first floor enclosed archway. The void below this part of the building was filled by another pair of iron gates. Marius slowed the car as these gates also parted to allow him entry. He saw Mills at the front door signalling him where to park up.

Marius manoeuvred the Range Rover into the drive of the gatehouse. The lecturer walked down the steps as Marius killed the engine and got out. He introduced Mills to his great friend, Sidney Cross. The two of them were dressed in almost identical fashion and seemed to be mutually impressed with the other man's choice of garb.

"Delighted to meet you, Mr Cross. Please come in, all of you." Mills ushered them into his home. "Helen, Marius, glad you could make it. We can go through here." Mills led them to the drawing room where they were met by the housekeeper. "Martha, could you make tea for our guests, please."

Martha was tall and slim and of retirement age. She fitted her smart black uniform with a neat appearance. She was very well spoken. Marius thought he could detect a slight Scottish undertone.

"Sorry to hear about your client, Clarke. Terrible news." Mills beckoned them all to sit.

Marius took up residence in a comfy overstuffed Bergere chair. The room was an antiques collector's dream. He could see his friend salivating at the collection of agate boxes that were arranged on the bay window sills, the afternoon sunlight casting a pleasant glow into the room through the stained-glass window panels.

Sidney cleared his throat. "Yes, it was a real shock."

"Think it was just an accident?" said Mills, eyebrows raised.

"Well ... "

"It was no accident. Sorry to cut in, Sidney." Marius could see no point in dancing around what they all suspected. "It's too much of a coincidence. Clarke tells the press about his experience, and then he gets mown down in a sleepy little village."

Mills pondered the theory for a few moments.

"So he is killed before he can talk any further. So what did he know that was so important?"

Helen handed Mills the newspaper article. He scanned down the lines looking for anything other than the usual abduction recollections.

"I can't see anything that is not like many other claims of abduction … mmm, wait a minute. Yes, it could be this paragraph here." Mills pointed to the page. "It says here that Clarke claimed to have been taken to a secret base where he was experimented on. He goes on to describe in detail the layout of the base he claimed was in northern New Mexico, where he talked extensively to human scientists and strange beings alike. They told him many things about the base and why they were abducting all the people against their will." The lecturer sighed in understanding.

"This part, announcing a series of articles to be run in the near future. I imagine Clarke must have struck quite a substantial financial deal with the press."

"One that cost him his life," Helen interjected.

"So before he could reveal the great masterplan, somebody silenced him," Sidney hissed.

"That would be my guess, Mr Cross."

Sidney pressed the point. "But why would the people at the base tell him anything relevant? It doesn't make sense."

"Could be that there are some workers who do not approve of what is going on."

"That's some theory, Mr Mills," Helen mused.

"Okay, then." Mills leaned into his wingback chair and puffed out his cheeks. He tapped the arms a few times and then stood up. "If you would be so kind as to follow me."

They followed Mills through the house, admiring all his treasures collected over many years. He led them into what turned out to be a library, the walls with shelves of books from floor to ceiling. A large table in the centre of the room housed a computer, several books, and some notes were scattered next to it. There was a large-scale world globe in the corner next to a set of steps on wheels.

"This is my study, where I prepare my speeches and do some of my research." Mills waved his arm around the room. 'If you care to examine the books on the left, they are all on the same subject."

They took a look at the spines: books on abduction, extra-terrestrial life, secret bases, cattle mutilation, strange craft. There were literally hundreds of volumes.

"I want you to take a long, hard look at them. They are, for the most part, theory-based with a few of them being factual in places. Most of them, though, are complete fiction."

Marius looked puzzled. It seemed strange to him to behave in this way. "Why keep all these if you don't believe in them?"

Mills nodded, with a half-smile. "It's good to be reminded of what's out there, what people are permitted to know, what confusion and disinformation exists in the public domain. I thought it was important for you to see this."

He could see the confusion on all the faces in front of him, and without further delay walked over to another bookcase. Mills reached in and pulled a hidden lever. A whole section sprang away revealing a solid wall. He twisted another lever and the wall slid to one side revealing a stone stairwell.

"Please, if you would …" gesturing to all to follow him once more.

Marius descended the stone steps, the others following closely behind, sensor-activated lighting illuminating the way. The walls were bare rock, slightly clammy to the touch, the stairs curving down for some one hundred feet, eventually coming to a dead end. Mills leaned over to the left. Marius could see him fumbling around in the gloom until he found another switch. The dead end turned out to be another stone door that slid away in the same manner as before to reveal a large room. Mills flicked on the lights and the place illuminated, wall panels decked out in oak, books galore again, a table in the centre with another computer.

They all filed into the space, Mills with his hands on his hips surveying the room with great satisfaction.

"Now these books, these really do mean something."

Mills marched over to the far right-hand corner of the room. He carefully prised one of the ceramic floor tiles up and lifted it away. There was a circular plate built into the floor. He removed this and fished out a cardboard document folder. He got up and came back over to where the others stood. He opened the cardboard folder and carefully removed the contents onto the table for all to see.

"The reason for all of this cloak-and-dagger stuff, my friends, is because these are probably the most important documents in the world."

Encased in their own individual clear plastic pockets were around fifty sheets of paper with handwritten drawings, maps and notes on a similar theme to those of Mr Clarke.

"Feel free to read through them all, but to spare you time, I will give you the shorthand version."

Mills nodded at the floor which Marius deduced as being a customary trait before launching himself into lecturer mode.

"The first thing I must say is that what I am about to tell you will change everything. Once you know, nothing will be the same." He noted the scepticism with measured tolerance; the academic was never far away from controversy, and he was used to the uncertainty. "If you wish to leave now, that's absolutely fine by me."

There were no takers. Curiosity had got the better of them; plus, the death of Clarke had definitely convinced them that closure was needed.

"Right, the first thing to point out is that Clarke was totally factual in his recollection. I have gone over his notes and they only add weight to what I already know. I touched upon some of this in my lecture you attended recently."

He eyed Marius and Helen in turn. "The papers on the table were smuggled out of the very facility that Clarke describes. It is indeed an underground base of immense size located near the town of Dulce, New Mexico. The base resembles the Pentagon in shape and has at least seven levels. At the lowest level is a shuttle system connecting other bases via a high-speed rail network. There is also an underground river system that connects to the sea. Its remote location allows experimental aircraft to be tested away from public view. They also test advanced weaponry here. But it is on the lower levels where the real atrocities take place."

The others listened intently without interruption.

"Victims are taken to the facility against their will, where they are experimented on in various ways, some multiple times. The lucky ones are returned. Many of the women are impregnated and then have their embryos removed."

"What about the scientists?" Helen asked. "You mentioned some of them were sympathetic to the victims. They seemed to like Clarke, for instance."

"That's right, and I know this for a fact as those notes on the table over there were written by one of the scientists who worked at the base. He secretly documented what was going on down in the lower levels. There are accounts of experiments in mind control, cross-breeding of species and human cloning."

Mills paused to let them digest the rather appalling revelations. He suspected that his guests were hovering in a place between disbelief and denial. It was hard for anyone to hear accounts that many would dismiss as science fiction. Mills would not blame them. He had some individuals attend his seminars leaving at the end convincing themselves that it was far easier to ignore an unpleasant truth than to face it head-on.

Sidney was incensed. "Surely this is totally illegal. Can we not report these findings to the authorities?"

"Who would believe you? Just supposing the powers that be did make some enquiries, they would get nowhere; and in the process you would become a target just like Clarke."

"Do you know who killed him?" Marius asked slowly.

"I could make an educated guess," Mills replied knowingly.

They all waited expectantly, Mills eyeing them all with a look of uncertainty. He sighed heavily, knowing that a point of no return had been reached.

"He was killed more than likely by a secret organisation based in the USA. They are the ones who fund the research at the Dulce facility."

"But surely the American government would not allow this?" Sidney blustered.

Mills gave a look as if to say 'Where do I start?' There was so much to explain.

"This world of ours, Mr Cross ... it can be a very frightening place, and a dangerous one, too. The organisation behind all this operates separately above the US government. They are called MJ-12 and are completely off-grid. They are extremely powerful and have unlimited resources."

'Is that the Majestic 12?" Marius probed. "I thought they were disbanded in the sixties?"

"That's the one, although originally the Majestic 12 was formed to investigate UFOs and strange phenomena. When the government funding was cancelled, the organisation was shut down, or so we thought. We then started to get reports of its existence with new funding and new members. MJ-12 now control some serious business interests and are considered by those in the know to be the real American government. They have military capabilities and advanced technology all skimmed off taxpayers' money."

"And the US government don't even suspect anything?" Helen asked, baffled.

"Some of the senate, possibly. I'm sure one or two may even work for them. We are quite sure that presidents have been excluded since JFK was in power."

"So how do they get away without being discovered?" said Marius.

"Threats, swearing workers to secrecy, sectioning departments so no one knows what is happening, and strict discipline."

"You mentioned President Kennedy. Is that how far back this all goes?"

"Oh no, it goes back much further than that."

Mills gave them a detailed insight into the Majestic 12, starting with its origins.

"It all started at the end of the Second World War. The Germans had lost a large number of officers and scientists, who had fled the homeland to various destinations. Part of the exodus was processed legally by the Americans and the Russians, under the name of Operation Paperclip. It was agreed that a certain number of scientists and officers were to be divided between the two countries. They were granted complete amnesty and continued with a lot of the programmes that they were working on in Germany, almost seamlessly and with generous funding.

"World War Two had changed the way in which technology was developed. It became ultra-secret, off the record, after the Nazis managed to produce a new kind of physics which they factored into the propulsion systems of their latest aircraft.

"But the most puzzling thing about these breakthrough covert technologies that found their way into aerospace industries suggests that they were never intended to rescue the German war effort, and were for some other cause, as if the people involved were working for some future unstated goal of a greater magnitude than even rescuing the war effort."

"But why would the Americans want to help the very nation that they were trying to defeat?" Sidney asked.

Mills was morphing into his habitual lecturing mode, clearly enjoying the questions aimed at him by his mini audience.

"The Military Industrial Complex were holding secret talks with some of the German scientists many months before the war ended. As it became more likely that a German victory was unlikely, the plan was to try and get them to defect, selecting the very best subjects, promising them work and their families a new life. It is highly likely that many scientists agreed to the terms and kept their work a secret from Hitler. That would account for a large number of them being executed just before the German surrender to stop them from talking. There were thousands of Germans granted safe passages into the USA after the war. Many of the scientists carried on where they left off; a large number of them went on to work for NASA on the space programme; and a large number joined the American Psychiatric Association to study peoples' minds."

Mills paused to clear his throat and continued. "You have all heard of the 1947 Roswell incident, I assume?"

"Yes, an alien craft was supposed to have crashed near the town," Sidney answered.

"Maybe up to three craft, so some reports claim," Mills suggested. "A communication glitch allowed the *Roswell Daily Record* to print their now famous headline. As soon as President Truman, General Nathan Twining, and Dwight D Eisenhower, who was chief of staff at the time, were all informed, the story was suddenly changed to a downed weather balloon. Let's just assume the original version is true for the time being.

"Almost immediately after the incident, President Truman formed the Majestic 12 to investigate similar occurrences. Now why form a well-funded organisation like MJ-12 to respond to a crashed weather balloon in the desert?"

No one could argue that point, so Mills carried on.

"There is no doubt that MJ-12 existed. Not only that; almost simultaneously, Truman formed the CIA and the National Security Council. The first leader of MJ-12 was the Secretary of Defence, James V Forrestal. Other members included Head of the CIA Admiral Roscoe H. Hillenkoetter and General Nathan F. Twining."

"Did Forrestal not die in suspicious circumstances?" Helen seemed to recollect.

"Good, yes, that's right." Mills pounced as if his star pupil had beaten him to the answer. "In 1949, Forrestal decided to go public with proof of extraterrestrial existence. Suddenly he is sectioned in a hospital suffering from depression and manages to jump out of the sixteenth floor window to his death."

"Sounds a bit suspicious," Sidney mused.

"The people who knew him well certainly thought the same," Mills confirmed. He continued. "Truman and his government went to great lengths to keep their activities a secret. Then some years later a document was uncovered." Mills rifled through his papers until he came to a portfolio. He fished out a twenty-six page manual.

"This is a copy of SOM1-01, the Majestic Group special operations manual." He handed it over for the others to see. "Inside you will see chapters on craft recovery operations, handling material, UFO identification, and much more besides." Marius and Co. seemed suitably impressed. "Pretty wacky stuff for the president to endorse, I think you will agree."

"Is this real?" Marius asked, looking through the pages.

"It is."

"And all the presidential governments have been complicit in this?" Helen asked.

"Well, then it gets even more interesting," Mills replied. "Allow me to explain. The Cold War started soon after. To enable the work to continue away from prying eyes, the Americans created a number of underground bases. The scientists could continue their work in isolation with the complete authorisation of the government, although most of the information was classified to the public.

"During the term of John F Kennedy something happened. It was probably due to the president not approving of what was going on in the bases. The reasons are not certain, but soon after he threatened to cut the funding, he was assassinated. Coincidence? Maybe.

"But there is another document that backs this theory, signed by ex-Director of the CIA and MJ-12 member Allen Dulles. The document highlights – and I quote this section – that 'Lancer has made some enquiries regarding MJ-12 activities which we cannot allow. Please submit your views no later than October 1963."

Mills could see the confused looks on the faces of his mini-audience. He explained. "Lancer was the code name given to President Kennedy by the Secret Service. He was clearly ruffling a few feathers and making too many enemies. This document has Dulles going directly against the wishes of the President of the United States. He must have had a great deal of influence because less than a month later JFK was dead.

"From that point, the presidential governments were excluded. An alternative shadow government was formed, funded by rich businessmen, later added to by sophisticated money embezzlement. The lower levels of the bases were kept secret from official visits. Over the years, the real government became more and more oblivious as to what was going on under their noses. The alternative government became far more powerful and expanded the bases. They have people everywhere; their goal is to take control of the US. They are without conscience. Most of the research and practice is totally illegal. Anyone gets in their way, and they will eliminate them.

"Intelligence is continually being collated to find out what are in the bases, what their capabilities are, and who runs these facilities. Very little is known about the current MJ-12 members, who they are or where they meet. One thing is certain: they do exist, and they are very dangerous."

Marius studied more of the papers on the desk, handwritten, accompanied by a series of crude drawings of the Dulce base including some of the craft being tested there. They certainly looked futuristic. The author went on to describe the sophisticated security around and within the base, listing microwaves, motion detectors and heat sensors. Inside the base there were seven levels, each forty-five feet apart in depth. The width of the base was a mile in places. It was hard for Marius to quantify just how massive the base must be. Mills could see him poring over the information.

"They are truly fascinating, are they not?" He turned to the others. "There have been several people with credible backgrounds that have made similar claims to that of our own man. They have all died mysteriously."

"What about your man? Is he still alive?" Sidney enquired.

"To be honest, I don't know. He is a wanted man, and while he remains alive, he is a threat to MJ-12."

Chapter 20

Dulce, New Mexico

Schumann and the rest of his crew had assembled on the runway. Base Commander Holt shook hands with the men. Professor Logan did the same. The others peeled away as Schumann said his goodbyes.

"Keep in touch, Dr Schumann. I'm sure we will have need of your experience again."

"Yes, possibly. I have enjoyed my time working here. Thank you for your hospitality."

"A pleasure. Have a safe journey home."

Schumann walked over to the craft. Climbing the steps and into the fuselage, he chose not to look back as he shut the door behind him.

Weisse and Kaufmann took their places in the cockpit and fired up the Haunebu. The craft creaked and groaned a little, the shape-changing device in operation for longer than they would have liked. The craft taxied down the runway effortlessly and rose off the tarmac into the air.

All four men turned to look at each other, the relief apparent on all of their faces as the craft rose into the heavens.

Weisse liaised with Base Control, following protocol before they slipped out of airspace. He allowed a reasonable distance, as the nearby town of Dulce with its population of 2800 became little more than a speck, before engaging shape-shift back into the more malleable disc craft. Kaufmann activated the cloak, making them invisible until they reached the coast and were able to plunge into the ocean.

Von Getz reached over, patting Schumann on the back. "Well done, sir. Mission accomplished."

He felt good; all of the training coming to the fore, leading his team for the first time on Terran soil. He was, however, relieved to be going home to his own, familiar land. The camaraderie had grown between the four men. Schumann had gained their trust and knew that he could rely on them in return.

Von Getz ran a scanner over the ship, just to make sure. It was all clear.

"Did you see the weapons on the guards? They were flash guns," Kaufmann exclaimed.

Schumann had seen them; not the first time that he had been surprised by the Terran advances.

"Something very strange with their technology. I see antiquated practices and machinery all over the base, but then I see electromagnetic drive systems in the lift shafts."

"Maybe they just got lucky, like they did with their basic sonics," Weisse stated.

Schumann gave out a short laugh. "No, it was more than that. It's just too much of a coincidence."

"What do you mean?" von Getz said quizzically.

"Well, the components were just too similar. There cannot be any other explanation." They all looked at their commander curiously. "The magnetic drive system ... it's the same as ours in New Swabia."

"What?" von Getz burst out. "How could that be?"

"I don't know how it got there, but there is no way someone could have designed exactly the same components," Schumann stated.

"Are you sure, sir?" Weisse pressed.

"I checked the mechanism three times while using the lifts. There can be no mistake. It's mine. I invented it."

Chapter 21

Essex

The Black Mercedes Vito came to a halt in the yard. The two men jumped out. They were sporting navigator sunglasses and dressed identically in black combats with baseball caps, the peaks pulled down tight over the eyes. One of them walked over to the yard owner, gloved hands meeting in the air, slapping together. The other man did a three-sixty of the vehicle, satisfied that the minor damage on the front passenger side would soon be eradicated forever. He did a final check of the interior and tossed the keys inside.

His colleague fished a brown envelope from his inside pocket, handing it to the other man just as a Manitou teleporter trundled across the yard, the top armed with a magnetic disc on a chain.

The teleporter moved into position, lowering the chain until the magnet dropped on the roof of the Vito with a loud clang. The teleporter moved off, with its metallic captive swaying gently through the scrapyard passing vast mountains of redundant transport until it came to a halt in front of a large blue container. The Vito was lowered into the crusher where it was released. The teleporter then retreated out of the way.

The two men in black hung around just long enough to hear the groans and squeals of the powerful machine compressing against metal and glass, squashing the Mercedes into a compact square cube.

The two men ran through the gates to a silver BMW M5 idling in a layby on the far side of the road, driver at the ready. They jumped in the back of the car and sped off at high speed in the direction of London.

Chapter 22

Cambridgeshire

Marius graciously accepted tea from Martha, who was clearly entrusted with the knowledge of the secret room. She served the others before retreating, almost floating angelically out of sight.

Sidney was studying the books on the far side of the room. A lot of them were in a foreign language with transcriptions next to them. There were also volumes in Latin, some of which looked very old indeed. There were hundreds of books ranging from ancient weapons and science to alchemy, the dark arts, even Nazi involvement in the occult.

"Some very rare examples there, Mr Cross," Mills proudly exclaimed.

Sidney pulled out a book on Vimana, the ancient drawings inside showing pyramid-shaped flying machines.

"It says here that man created these machines thousands of years ago."

"Yes, there are many examples of Vimana's. They are documented extensively throughout history along with stone carvings and drawings, but are largely dismissed as folklore and fantasy. But there are those who believe that we did have the knowledge to build flying machines and other advanced machines too, as well as being equipped with powerful brain powers. At some point in history, this knowledge was lost. Many have tried to rediscover the forgotten secrets; this was one of the quests of the Nazis in World War Two."

Marius listened intently. No wonder Mills could pack out the venues he hosted. He had a great ability to explain things without all the complicated jargon. What Marius found so fascinating, though, was the possibility that all of what he had heard could actually have a ring of truth to it. Mills revealed more.

"The Nazis invested a great deal of time and money into exploration to find links to the true Aryan race that they believed they were descended from. They tried to discover occult powers that they could administer to their troops to create a super army. The high order in Germany took this very seriously. Why else would they be so distracted when they had a war to win. Due to the enormous devastation from the allied assault, and coupled with what the Nazis destroyed themselves, a lot of what they discovered was once again lost. So you see how easy it is to eradicate advances in technology if war or natural disasters occur on a large enough scale."

"And maybe how easy it would be for a few people to keep that lost technology a secret," Marius said.

"That's right," said Mills, delighted with the comment. "But to make matters more confusing, certain factions who do have advanced technology continually release hoax information in the public domain to discredit anything that could be believed."

Mills walked over to his huge collection of books, removing a volume with some loose photographs inside. He pulled two out and set them on the table.

"On the left here we have a high-resolution snap of a UFO taken on a bright sunny day in July."

The others gathered around to look at the photo.

"And here is a second photo of much poorer quality taken at dusk. Now which one is the hoax?"

Marius chuckled inside to himself. It was obvious. The one on the left was almost cartoon-like with far too much detail showing on the craft and the light just seemed too artificial. The picture on the right was a lot grainier, seemingly taken in haste during a poor overcast skyline.

"The one on the left." The others nodded in agreement.

A wry smile appeared on the face of Mills as he shook his head.

"Wrong, I'm afraid, it's the one on the right."

There was a look of surprise from the mini-audience as Mills explained. "The two pictures have been examined by some of the country's top photographic experts, and they all came back with the same verdict as yourselves. But the picture on the left is definitely a hoax."

"So what makes you go against these so-called expert findings?" Helen pressed him.

Mills stroked his chin, nodding slightly in expectant mood.

"I am the first to admit that the photo on the left does look as if it has been tampered with, but it is a typical example of how the light and too much detail can present a subject in an unrealistic manner, as if appearing to be computer-generated. The one on the right, at a much greater distance, a little distorted, would appear to be the more genuine of the two. But I can guarantee that the one on the left is the real picture."

"How can you be so sure?" Sidney quizzed.

"Because I took the picture of the object on the left myself, one sunny afternoon, just by chance. It is completely genuine and the reason that I became obsessed with the subject."

"And the one on the right?" Marius enquired.

"That, my friends, contrary to all the so-called leading

experts claiming that this is a totally genuine untampered photograph, is a complete and utter forgery created by yours truly."

They looked confused to say the least.

"The point of my exercise in deception was to prove that even the top names surrounding these particular subjects have no idea what they are doing. All I did was take a small homemade model which I threw into the air, repeatedly taking photographs as the sun went down. I then chose the one that looked the most authentic. Simple as that."

Mills eyed them all in turn with a stern expression.

"As we proceed, you will see and hear things that you may doubt. It is imperative that you all continue in this manner, because I, for one, have no time to constantly keep persuading you all that I am telling the truth. If I am not sure about certain facts then I will tell you; otherwise, all that I reveal to you will be absolutely genuine."

Marius listened intently as Mills gave out a few historic examples to back up his own claims of belief. He was not entirely sure what to make of it all, but it was clear that something was going on. The more the academic explained to them, the more layers of complexity revealed themselves, which only made it a growing obsession on an addictive level.

"Getting back to Clarke, should the press start snooping around asking questions, it goes without saying that you should deny everything."

Marius had not thought about any danger to themselves before. They would all have to be careful. He fished out the notebook from his pocket along with his recording on a memory stick and handed them over to Mills.

"I think you should keep these."

Mills nodded. "Ah, you beat me to it, my good man," He

took the items.

Sidney produced his own documents and handed them over.

"Oh, I almost forgot this." He produced the box from the inside of his jacket. Mills' eyes lit up as he took the object, handling it reverently.

"That is most fascinating." He examined the box for some time, clearly quite moved by its existence.

"Ever seen anything like this before?" Sidney asked.

"Only once." Mills put the box with the other documents and placed them inside a folder. "Remind me. How did Clarke say he acquired one of the boxes?"

"He said they gave him it at the Dulce base." Sidney reaffirmed.

"Very strange that, very strange indeed." Mills seemed to retreat into a world of his own for a few moments before remembering where he was. He sighed heavily, leading them over to the other side of the room to where he once again triggered another secret door open. The mechanism was of the same ancient design, the door rumbling to one side allowing the four of them to step into a long corridor.

"A lot of these old estates had a network of underground passages and secret rooms built in case the occupants needed to escape conflict." His voice echoed around them as they followed in single file.

The tunnel was about four feet wide with a rounded ceiling, the walls of rough stone, built to last. Mills was shining a torch ahead of them, lighting the way. The tunnel seemed to go on forever.

"How long is this thing?" Marius enquired.

"Oh, it's a few hundred yards. Had to be to ensure safe escape. Some are a lot longer than this one."

They trekked along in silence, the torch beam offering only

an identical view up ahead until they finally came to another dead end. This time Mills reached up above his head, pushing on the ceiling, and then stepped back. A stone doorway slid downwards into the floor, revealing a room similar to the one they had recently left, books adorning the outer walls, the only clear difference being a very large table in the centre surrounded by chairs. They followed Mills, bypassing the furniture through another stone door, up another stone staircase, to a far larger concealed door which resembled more of a wall panel, sliding to open into a long corridor. There were marble busts on columns facing each other in twos, spaced regimentally, that ran from one end to the other, huge classical paintings over rich wall coverings of gold and red, the wooden floor with a single carpet runner down the centre.

They followed Mills, stepping into the hallway, the wall section sliding back into place, engulfing its hideaway behind them.

Marius could hear Sidney picking out objects and explaining what they were to Helen as they walked the vastness of the ground floor. It matched any stately home that Marius had ever visited, and he had been to a few. He had Sidney to thank for that.

"Here we are," Mills suddenly announced, stopping in front of two huge oak doors with highly polished brass handles the size of grapefruits. The doors clicked open with a weighty glide into a drawing room extending into an orangery at the far end.

"Oh, it's magnificent," Helen exclaimed.

"It's my favourite room in the house," an authoritarian voice boomed, as a large frame rose out of one of a pair of serpentine backed sofas. Marius caught Sidney mumbling the name John Adam, and "bloody fortune" as the owner of the house came over and introduced himself.

"Everyone calls me 'H'. Come in and make yourself at home. Derek has told me all about you."

Mills could see Marius and the others looking rather wary, which was to be expected.

"Sorry, I should have said, but one thing led to another," he said. "Anyway, this is Hector Valerian; he is the owner of the estate, and an extremely good friend." He could see them relax a little. 'Trust me, this man knows as much as I do.'

"Alright, Derek. Please excuse the rather covert entrance, but we have to be careful." H exuded a stern but cheerful authority, positioning his great frame to shake hands. Marius was not a small man himself, but Valerian towered over him, his huge jawline wearing a tight-lipped smile as he welcomed his guests. Marius guessed his age around the same as Mills, his brown, shaggy hair slightly untidy, and his face with a ruddy complexion.

"Can you elaborate on *careful*?" Marius was keen to get to the point.

Valerian eyed them all in a downward motion while Mills fixed some drinks.

"Just to reinforce what Derek has already explained, the people probably responsible for Clarke's death work for Majestic 12. They are heavily connected to the Illuminati, which is where most of their power comes from. This is an international organisation with a lot of resources. They would like nothing more than to eliminate us."

Satisfied that he had their full attention, he continued.

"We have existed alongside each other for centuries in many differing formats, but always with the same purpose. Majestic 12 is a more recent and far more radical branch of the Illuminati. They are, as many rightly believe, the shadow government that controls the underground bases including the one Clarke described. We have no idea, to date, who the leaders are. The only consolation is that they do not know who we are either. That is the reason for being careful and why we maintain our secret status."

"So why reveal yourself to us?" Helen asked.

H appeared to expect this question. "Derek told me about the hypnosis patients and their regressions. I, too, was intrigued with the detailing recollected. We are sure that most of the abductees are being taken to the same destination. There was a reason that Clarke could recall so much information about his own abduction. It is such a pity that we did not find out sooner, then we could have stopped him going to the press."

"But he did reveal that the scientists told him that he was in Dulce," Mills interjected.

"Right," said H, accepting a crystal tumbler of Johnny Walker Blue Label. "We are fortunate enough to have people on the inside, within the base itself, but getting the information out has been very difficult. Our scientists have been using trials subliminally messaging abductees in the hope that a few of them will recollect what happened to them, helping us in turn to expose what is going on down there. The conditioning, though, is very intense, making memories very hard to extract.

"Suddenly we get the Clarke incident whereby he can recall an amazing amount of information, along with extra knowledge that was highly classified. This information came under hypnosis. We want to know how this was possible."

"And that was enough to gain your trust?" Marius asked.

"Well, it went a long way, yes," Mills cut in.

"Also, there is something that you can help us with." H looked at the three guests in turn. "We have an abduction victim of our own and would like you to put them under hypnosis."

"Look, I'm really not sure that we ..." Marius was cut short.

"We are willing to pay you both twenty thousand pounds."

Sidney and Marius exchanged glances, both men's faces failing hopelessly to disguise their obvious surprise.

H went on. "It is a matter of great importance. The information you extract could help us immensely."

Sidney sighed heavily. "Look, speaking for myself, there are no guarantees, and to be honest, I am not experienced at all in regression."

"That goes for me too," Marius added.

The enormous face of H broke into a broad smile. "I know we may end up with nothing, but that's a risk we are willing to take. Don't sell yourselves short, though. You must have done something to unlock those memories. I suspect that it was the way that you both put your clients under."

Marius thought about this for a moment. It was true that they both used the same techniques to hypnotise. He could see Sidney's mind ticking over, probably digesting the massive financial offer. It was clear that their organisation was desperate for results.

"All we ask is that you try, nothing more," said Mills, enthused.

Chapter 23

Atlantic Ocean

Von Getz was transferring data from the visit to the Dulce base, while Schumann took the opportunity to flick through Clare Logan's notebook. Kaufmann checked that they were not being followed before banking the Haunebu into the ocean, the craft gliding steadily into the depths to the safe haven of the ocean floor; a sensible decision to err on the side of caution just in case someone was trying to track them. The craft bottomed out following their underwater flight path. It would take a lot longer to get back to New Swabia this way, but this would also enable the crew to go over their mission intel. There had been an uneasy silence for a while between the men, while protocol was followed. Now the weight of tension had lifted, it was Weisse who offered up a theory that was far too alarming for comfort.

"Sir, if your invention has been used in the magnetics at the Dulce base, then we have to face the strong possibility that someone in New Swabia has betrayed your work."

"But why would they risk our nation to help another?" von Getz exclaimed.

That was a very good question indeed, but Schumann knew his work, and it was absolutely impossible for another person to replicate his design.

"So, we have a traitor in our midst."

He could see the worried looks on the other faces. This was something new for all of them. Right now, the job of how to proceed fell squarely onto his own shoulders.

"Okay, let's dispense with rank for the time being. There is something else." He held up Clare's leather-bound book. 'Professor Logan gave me this in total confidence. She has been secretly documenting what goes on in the lower levels of the base." They all looked at him intently. "It would seem that Albert Hebb is heading illegal genetic experiments of a kind not seen since the last great war, totally off grid, using human subjects."

They all looked shocked. He continued.

"According to her, this has been going on for some time, and is on an unprecedented scale."

"Why did she tell you?" Weisse asked.

"Well, she thinks we are from Germany, and I could hand over the evidence to the authorities there in the hope that they would expose what the Dulce facility is up to."

"What are you going to do?" von Getz added.

"I don't know. I could not reveal our real identity; that would have been too dangerous."

Schumann thought for a minute. The situation was becoming complex. They needed an overall picture of everything they had.

"Let's see what information was gathered from our time at the base." Schumann looked at von Getz who was putting his spectacles back in place.

"The micro camera from my glasses has worked well. See here."

Kaufmann put the craft on autopilot and joined the others around the monitor screen. They could see a series of images that von Getz had managed to take when the opportunity arose. They had a very good overview of the base layout including some spectacular shots of the submarine cavern and the laboratories. He had also taken pictures of some of the personnel that could be profiled from their database. New Swabia carried extensive information on Terran procedures, and regularly accessed their computer servers. It was called 'ghosting in', and could be done without detection. Von Getz flicked through the images just to see what he had. There were shots of Holt, the base commander, some of the scientists, security, a few of Clare Logan, and the people assembled for the sonic testing, including Albert Hebb.

As they pored over the images, Schumann made notes, referencing his own observations, comparing them with notes made by the others. What became apparent straightaway were the impressive pockets of technological advancements that seemed to almost contradict the naivety in other departments.

One example of this was shown up in a shot of a security guard carrying a flash gun.

Schumann was very familiar with the system. They possessed similar weaponry called Armorlux. The guns fired an intense beam that could vary from stun all the way up to complete vaporisation. Along with the revelation of the Terran submarine top speeds and some of the building techniques employed at the base, it was quite a mystery how they excelled in certain departments and lagged behind in other areas.

"Look at this," von Getz announced abruptly.

They all crowded around the monitor to view a picture of Albert Hebb, the chief of the underground network.

"I've been running checks to see what I could find out. So far nothing very interesting until I put Hebb through the database."

They looked at a split screen; on the left, the recent picture of Hebb at the cavern, and on the right, a much older picture of three German officers, Schumann guessed, from the Second World War. Standing together were Heinrich Himmler; next to him Karl Wolf, his chief of staff; and a third officer who looked the spitting image of Hebb.

"According to the archives, the man we know as Albert Hebb is an exact match with this man."

There was no doubt; it looked like the same man. But that could not be as the man they had been introduced to had hardly changed in appearance.

Schumann took a long hard look at the images. Sure, he looked older, but to still be alive was impossible.

"There can be no doubt. There is a fifty-point facial structural match. The small scar on his chin matches exactly. This is the man listed as missing at the end of World War Two: Obersturmführer Karl Beiger."

"So how do you explain his youthful appearance?"

"I don't know, but the profiling cannot be wrong ... Wait, look, here is some more information." Von Getz read out the file on Karl Beiger.

"He was a high-ranking officer in the SS, heavily involved in experiments on humans in the concentration camps, that certainly tied in with what he was doing at the Dulce base. He had a great deal of power, also being involved in experimental aviation projects, and was a regular attendee of occult SS meetings at Wewelsburg castle in Buren, Germany."

Von Getz had further information to reveal.

"How about this? In 1985 there was a mysterious crash in Kecksburg, Pennsylvania involving what was described as a bell-shaped craft. A witness claimed that the occupants emerged dressed in Nazi uniforms and were taken away, craft and all, by the military to some undisclosed destination."

Schumann looked at von Getz with a look of vague familiarity, for there was an account that he remembered from his college days of a highly classified craft nicknamed Das Glocke, or The Bell, that the Germans had developed with the intention of travelling through time. While under interrogation, former SS man Jakob Sporrenburg mentioned The Bell himself, a powerful craft that ran on red mercury or Xerum 525 to give it its proper name.

There was a plan to unite the remnants of the Third Reich after the war, in Argentina. Somehow, it appeared that the occupants miscalculated their journey and did not make their planned destination. It was well documented that this was the plan and that such a machine did exist, but to think that someone travelled through time in 1945 seemed completely ridiculous.

But Schumann knew his history well, particularly science-based accounts. It was well known that the Nazis were experimenting with reverse engineering towards the end of the war, phasing electromagnetic fields in a strange way to make objects vanish and reappear. The theory behind this was to slow time down when incredible speeds were reached.

Maybe they had discovered the basic principles of time travel. Schumann, like many before him, had researched the subject without much success. But could a small band of scientists have solved the incredibly complicated procedures and sent a group of their men forward in time?

Schumann took another look at the two images. There could be no doubt; it was Hebb alright.

This put yet another layer of complexity on top of it all. The man in question was overseeing operations at the Dulce base. How on Terra had he managed that? And what had become of the other Bell occupants?

Schumann was certain that the Americans must have known about The Bell. It could be that, among the thousands of seized documents at the end of the war, the Allies knew what had been achieved. What looked even more certain was that a deal must have been brokered in exchange for intelligence: a prominent position, generous salary, and obviously complete exoneration of all war crimes for all inside The Bell.

But who to tell? Back in New Swabia, Schumann was sure that somebody was responsible for handing over some of their own technological state secrets to the Americans. But in return for what? The thought horrified him.

He needed to think. He was the commander, Level 35. Any decision had to be taken with the security of the nation as the number one priority.

"Okay, this is what we are going to do. Until I have time to investigate our findings in more detail, we will submit our own report version. We can keep the photos of Beiger to ourselves for now."

"What about Professor Logan?" von Getz suggested. "Shall I leave her out of the report too? I mean, after all, you seemed to get on very well; she could be a useful ally, perhaps."

Schumann knew what his colleague was getting at, but was grateful for the respectful approach.

"Okay, no point in endangering her unnecessarily." He felt a more personal connection to the decision than he should have done. "I know that this is a very unusual request, and I will take full responsibility if we are discovered." He eyed them all sternly.

"Hans, we are all in this together," Kaufmann replied. "The most important thing is to discover who is leaking our secrets to the enemy." Murmurs of agreement.

Schumann nodded appreciatively. He had quite forgotten that the Terrans were regarded as the enemy. They had always been reminded never to trust them.

Surely, not all of them could be bad, though, he hoped.

The amphibious craft swept around in a graceful arc, barely disturbing the sandy seabed as it straightened, navigating through a narrow ravine, then plunged into darkness. The automatic lights remained off as Schumann saw no need to observe a view they had all seen many times before. The interior lights of the craft gave out a soft pinkish hue; it had a therapeutic calming effect that they all appreciated.

"Not long now, sir," von Getz announced as he appeared with a new plate of bratwurst.

Schumann smiled. He took one eagerly and took a large bite. "The best yet," he mumbled, grinning like a New Cologne cat.

The gesture was much appreciated; he could hear the others up front laughing at the humorous respite. Now all he had to do was to think of what to do next.

Von Getz returned, taking up a seat next to his. "Might I suggest that we meet up in a few days at the Great Falls in New Berlin?"

Schumann was puzzled at first, but then realised the logic behind the unusual rendezvous point. The thunderous noise of the water would mask out their private conversations. He nodded to concur, then slid back into the leather chair, polishing off the remainder of his bratwurst, his arms falling down by his sides. He was exhausted.

Chapter 24

Cambridgeshire

They did not have to wait too long for their client to arrive, who was only too eager to take advantage of their close proximity. Marius could hear a female voice being guided to the drawing room where they were all assembled. A cheery fire crackled away creating a warm glow, the curtains drawn, soft lighting activated, creating a relaxing atmosphere.

H and Mills intercepted their guest, exchanging greetings before they all appeared at the doorway. Marius and Helen traded bemused glances. Sidney looked bewildered by their reactions as she walked in.

"Sidney, allow me to introduce my client, Caroline," Marius said, glaring at Mills and H.

Helen parted her arms, miming her objections.

"What's going on here?" Sidney demanded.

Caroline extended a hand to them all. "Sorry for not telling you my reasons, but I had to know I could trust you."

Now the carefully paved introduction by Mills made a lot more sense to him.

"So when you came to me to give up cigarettes, that was just an excuse?" Marius delivered this with a tone of displeasure.

"Oh no. I heard that you were very good, and I did want to quit. Still haven't had one." Caroline held up crossed fingers sheepishly. "It was only on awakening that I realised what had happened. I suspected something was wrong, but I did not know for sure."

H took up his usual position on the Adam sofa.

"I should point out that many have tried, on numerous occasions, and have failed to regress these memories, but both of you have been successful for whatever reason. The point is, you did succeed."

That much was true, Marius thought.

"Caroline may be carrying vital information that could help us," H added.

"Well, we're here anyway." Sidney resigned. He looked at Marius who shrugged.

The two men had never worked together before, so it was decided that Marius would take the lead with Sidney giving advice via pen and paper. Caroline made herself comfortable on the chaise. Marius began using his procedural calming voice, sending her into a trance-like state. She was able to respond to a series of test questions that told Marius that she was in a place that he was satisfied with. The questions and answers continued, Caroline responding with a slurred quiet lilt.

Marius looked at Sidney who nodded in approval. He decided to start by replicating his treatment for smoking, sticking to the same script.

"Where am I …? What do you want …? Who are you …? How dare you touch me …"

Marius jolted, taken aback and caught out by the sudden outburst. There could be no doubt. She was under and could not be faking it. The breakthrough was almost immediate. He had to check if it was directed at them. He let go of her arm.

"Who's there with you? Can you describe them?"

Caroline moaned, struggling on the chaise, mumbling

incoherently for some time. She became tearful. Fear cut through her demeanour, her body now shaking.

"They want to hurt me again. I don't like it. They say it does not hurt, but I can feel it. I can't move … the lights are bright … can only see outlines … I'm scared … I want to go home."

"Tell them, Caroline. Tell them you want to go home."

Sidney nodded his approval at the tactic. The others looked on wide-eyed. Helen stood nearby, barely able to breathe. This was far more intense than the last time.

Caroline did as instructed. "I want to go home, let me go home …" Her body became still; she went silent. Marius checked her status; she looked alright. She seemed to relax a lot more and it dawned on him that she could have been released from her abduction. He may have employed the wrong tactics.

Mills and H stared anxiously; Sidney stared too. Helen was biting her hand.

"There are pink walls, I like them … I like the walls … the walls move sometimes."

Another sudden outburst; this time she seemed to be more relaxed in her surroundings, although her response seemed to be altered. Her mannerism had also changed.

"Oh … there are three … yes, three. One is tall, and the other two are a lot smaller, like children."

"Can you talk to them, Caroline? Will they let you do that?" Marius tried asking.

"I … I … is that okay? Do you talk …? No … I don't know." She nodded her head, eyes shut, still well under. "They don't talk, they can't talk very easily … they don't have to … I can hear them in my head." Caroline nodded again as if they were talking to her, acknowledging the dialogue. Sidney could see Mills and H stunned by the sudden breakthrough.

"They are not going to hurt me … they do this all the time

... I feel okay now. The tall one told me his name, but I can't say it ... I like him, he's okay ..."

"The tall one is a male?"

"Yes, he has a male voice ... in my head ... It's the little ones ... They can be mean, they don't talk much ... They sound funny ... Wait ... Over there is a green machine ... It's really weird, but I'm not scared now ... They told me not to be scared."

"Is there anyone else that you can see?"

"Oh ... It's misty over there ... I ... Yes, I can see a ... It's a ... a man."

Marius felt a nudge as Sidney passed him a note. He tried the suggestion.

"Caroline, will the man speak to you? Can he do that?"

She looked puzzled, a frown developing on her face, nodding to some invisible presence.

"He says that he works with them ... he tells me not to worry, they are not going to hurt me ... he says that I can go home soon and I will wake up and nothing will have happened ... That's good, isn't it?"

"Yes, Caroline, that's very good." Marius kept his voice measured. "What do they want?"

She nodded again to herself. "They want ... they want to monitor me ... they do this a lot ... the man is called Aral ... Aral is nice ... Aral says not long now."

"Where are you, Caroline? Can you tell me that?"

"I am ... here ... I am here ... Wait ... Okay, Aral ... Aral is telling me now."

Marius held his breath. He felt like he was going to burst. Caroline continued.

"I'm at the base ... I'm at the base and it's nice ... they are being nice ... I can see the small ones now ... the mean ones.

There are a lot, but they are far away, they are on the other side of the glass."

"Are you in a laboratory?"

"Oh … yes … Aral says yes I am … they will look after me."

"Can you describe the room you are in?"

"It's got pink walls … The lights are soft … I am on a gurney … I can't move … don't know why … I don't mind, though … I don't mind."

"Do you know the name of the base?" Marius tried.

"The base … is … it's called … Dulce … It's in America … I'm in America." She smiled broadly as if she was on vacation.

H rolled his hand in the air silently as if to signal a continuation of the line of questioning. Marius nodded to him.

"Does Aral like working at the base?"

"Yes, he has been there for a long time … he likes his work … he likes the others."

"Are the others from this planet?" Marius could sense that the answers were becoming less restrained, as if a censorship was being lifted.

"Oh, yes … they are all from this planet … They live at the base."

He could see Mills looking confused. "Do they fly the ships?"

"Yes, they fly the ships … What's that, Aral?" She had another conversation with herself. "Aral said that some like him fly the ships too … Aral says my son wants to fly a ship when he grows older."

Marius took a sharp breath. This was becoming confusing. He still pressed on nevertheless. Another note was handed to him with the writing 'She has no son'.

He took a chance. "I did not know that you had a son,

Caroline. How old is he?"

"Oh ... he is seven now ... he is very clever." He could see the others shaking their heads.

"What is his father's name?" Brilliant, acknowledged Sidney tapping his arm.

"I can't ... I can't ... It's too hard to say ... It's a nice name, though ... He is kind."

"Does he work at the base too?"

"Yes ... he works at the base; he has always worked at the base."

"Is he your husband?'

'No ... of course not." She laughed, eyes still tightly closed. "He is the father."

"Okay, Caroline, what is your son's name?"

"His name is Bek ... I can call him Bek."

"Did you name him?"

"No." She chuckled. "They name all the children."

Marius could see Mills' shocked expression. It was clear he had guessed what she was talking about. The notes came thick and fast now with H joining in too.

Marius tried another question.

"Caroline, did they take the baby away from you?"

"Oh, yes," she replied matter-of-factly. "But it's alright, they do it all the time ... I can visit any time I like ... they said I could ... I can see Bek any time."

Christ, what was this? Marius thought to himself. It was very alarming. He could see Helen was shaking her head in disbelief.

"What does Aral think? Has he any children there at the base?"

"Oh, no, Aral cannot father children. That is not his job."

"What is Aral's job?"

"Aral is here to help ... that is Aral's job ... he is here to work ... like the others."

"Are there many like Aral."

"Oh yes ... there are ... they are all Aral."

"Is Aral human?" Marius could not believe his own question.

"Aral is not human. Aral is Aral."

Marius was shaking now. He was filling up with dread.

"Can you elaborate?"

"Aral was human; now Aral is Aral."

"How did Aral change from being a human?"

"Aral was changed by the little ones ... Aral says they are called Caste."

Mills nearly fell on the floor. It meant nothing to Marius although it was clearly important.

"Can you ...?" He was interrupted.

"Someone here, someone new is here ... They want to talk to me."

"Who is it?"

"No time. Listen." Caroline was suddenly more serious and businesslike. "Enoch."

"My God," he heard Mills hiss, followed by rapid scribbling.

"Enoch, go ahead." Marius repeated the instruction handed to him.

"Seven levels at least, need Umbra clearance, base a mile wide, high security, weight, retina, swipe card, body frequency alignment, surveillance cameras, microphones. Outside heat sensors, microwaves, satellites, patrol vehicles, gun installations, GPS tracking. Levels Six and Seven and lower caverns controlled by Greys and Draco. Seven connects to river and sub base testing area. Base connects via sub global shuttle system to other bases ... Recent visit here by Germans working on sonics ... Have to go ... Out."

Caroline fell silent as if asleep. Marius checked her over. She seemed okay.

"Caroline, can you hear me?" Nothing. He waited for a full minute then tried again. "Caroline, can you hear me?"

Again, she was unresponsive. He waited a while longer.

"Caroline, are you alone?"

"No."

Marius breathed a sigh of relief. "Where are you?"

"I'm in the craft now." Her voice, unemotional.

"Do you recognise anyone?"

"No, they told me I am going home now."

"So Aral is not there?"

"I don't know Aral ... I don't ... Wait, it's time ... it's time to go now, time to ... go ...'

Marius saw her eyes flicker. Sidney held her hand. They allowed her to stir a little more before Marius employed the recovery procedure, taking his time to alleviate any chances of trauma.

Caroline opened her eyes, looking up at Marius, her face giving nothing away. She sat up and stretched.

"How did I do?"

"Very well, my dear," Sidney answered. "Feeling okay?"

"Yes, I feel pretty good. Not remembering that much, though."

"Better not to rush it." Marius turned away, wide-eyed, as he switched off the recorder.

Chapter 25

New Swabia

Schumann stepped into the street from his apartment building to the nearby terminal. There were two main rail/vehicle routes that cut across the cavern systems. Schumann's favourite method was to use the rail and book a mag car where needed. The short one-stop hop to the military HQ was very straightforward, New Bavaria being the next cavern to New Berlin. The base was located at one end where the river met the exit that linked to the outside ocean.

The shuttle was almost empty as he stared down the corridors steeling himself for the meeting with his superiors. His thoughts were full of his first Terran mission, his guilt about not being able to help Clare Logan. And then there was Albert Hebb. Just what was he going to do about him?

The Chancellor was sure to be pleased with his work on the sonics. There were bound to be many questions at his debrief regarding this, along with intelligence gathered.

Soon he was skimming across the countryside, his eyes greeted by the brightest of all the caverns, a masterpiece of creation. It was a glorious place that did not really suit the aggressive-looking base that now came into view, but its location covered a very strategic position.

The whole journey had only taken ten minutes and he was

soon cruising by the Haunebu fleet, his own craft now in place, a crew busy checking it over. Kaufmann and Weisse would be among them for sure, he thought.

He parked up in the same place before and entered the main building. Inside, he was met by the same female officer as before, the only procedural change being that she escorted him immediately along the lengthy corridor, guards in place as always, immaculate as usual, and onto the great double doors where the Chancellor would be waiting on the other side.

His arrival was announced as the doors opened promptly before him. Schumann marched smartly inside. He could see the men behind the great desk; only two of them this time, though.

"Please, Herr Schumann, take a seat," Vessels requested. "The Chancellor could not be with us today; he has other matters to attend to." He turned to the man next to him. "You met Great General Brunner at our last meeting."

Schumann acknowledged the other man with a smart nod, and sat down.

"I have read your report," Vessels continued. "Very impressive. You handled the mission very well."

"I think their sonics will be a lot safer for quite a while, sir."

"Excellent. And I see you managed to capture footage of the base layout, too."

"Yes, sir, as well as a good overview of their technology."

"See anything interesting?" Vessels enquired matter-of-factly.

"Nothing very remarkable, sir, although the underground base is very impressive."

"So it would seem," the Vice Chancellor purred. "Right. Follow me if you would."

The two men opposite stood up smartly, beckoning him to

follow them through a nearby door.

Vessels flicked the lights on to reveal a very large map table in the centre of the room, communication hub on one side, banks of workstations and monitor screens on the other. A war room, no less.

"Recognise the map?" Brunner asked him.

"Yes. I believe that is South America, sir." Schumann could see a lot of miniature objects that represented military campaign positions and weaponry. Rather worryingly, it looked like the map was set up for an invasion.

"Correct; one thousand kilometres north of our current position."

"Obviously, your new promotion gives you access to our war room," Vessels reminded him. "Impressive, is it not?" He beamed.

"Yes, sir, very impressive indeed." *What the hell is all this?* he thought inwardly.

"So, I suppose you are wondering why we have set out our room in this way," Vessels prattled on. "Well, South America is of great interest to us. Not only is it reasonably close to our own continent, but it has some very advantageous geographical features."

"I know a lot of our ancestors settled there after the last great war," Schumann offered.

"Indeed they did, yes, indeed; the Odessa Project as I recall." Vessels was pacing slowly up and down. "And those surface dwellers could prove to be useful." He nodded, stroking his chin. "But we are more concerned with what is underground."

Schumann studied the large map in more detail. He could see the continent divided into countries, all in German as expected.

"This is the area we are most interested in." Vessels

indicated with a campaign baton.

Schumann could see a mountainous region in Southern Brazil known as the Matto Grosso.

Brunner poked a few pieces around the map, rather like a child playing with a toy.

"The region in question has a network of caves. They go down a long way, some of them opening out into caverns. Some of these caverns are supposed to be massive."

"Is the intel reliable?" Schumann asked.

"Oh, yes, we think so. We have studied the maps made by the Terrans. The biggest interest for us, though, is that most of the cave network is unexplored. There are stories of some of the caves going down for miles."

"That would be perfect for our expansion," Vessels barked.'

Expansion? Schumann thought. *What did they think this was; some sort of game that would risk their revealing the New Swabian nation's existence? And for what? They had plenty of room to expand right here if it was deemed to be necessary.*

"We will expand into South America, creating tunnels to link with the Brazilian caverns. We can be great again, Herr Schumann; we can come out of hiding, join forces with Germany, share our knowledge with the old fatherland," said Brunner excitedly.

"Let's face it, we are far more advanced than anyone else. They will be queuing up to get hold of our technology," Vessels ranted.

Schumann was reeling. He had to derail this idea, or at least sow some seeds of doubt into the two men.

"Sir, we have always been very careful not to trust the Terrans. What makes you so sure that they will keep their word?"

Vessels looked pleased with himself. "We have been

liaising with them for some time now at the Dulce base."

Schumann felt his heart sink. "I still would not trust them, sir."

"Who said we need to trust them? As long as we get what we want."

"And we know how to get it," Brunner added.

"How so?"

"We had a message, sent through from Albert Hebb via our German facility."

Schumann baulked at the name. "What did he want?"

"He wants to offer you a job, a temporary contract troubleshooting some of their technical issues."

"But I have my place here in New Swabia."

"Come now, Herr Schumann; with promotion comes responsibility. Your new rank gives you the opportunity to help shape our destiny. This is a big moment for you."

Schumann felt utterly devastated. He was being used as a bargaining chip in a very dangerous game. He felt like beating them both senseless. How could they both be so irresponsible?

"Of course, sir. How long will the secondment last?"

"Well, there is no time limit. For as long as you are needed."

"Very well, Vice Chancellor, anything to help."

"One more thing," Vessels sneered. "Better choose an assistant. No telling where they will take you on the base, and I want all the information you can get for me."

"Okay, sir, I will give it some thought and get back to you"

"Don't think about it for too long. You leave in two days."

The next day saw Schumann immersing himself up to his neck in the warm natural lagoon at the far end of his hometown of New Berlin. He casually swam across the expanse of water, ducking under the large man-made waterfall tumbling over giant rouge-coloured boulders, emanating from the source two hundred feet above his head.

Inside, the rushing water echoed around the cave. Shouting was the only way to make oneself heard. Perfect.

Von Getz and the others appeared through the mass of bathers. The lagoon was a popular recreation destination and was always busy.

The first thing Schumann did was to bring them up to speed with his meeting at NewBav HQ. They were suitably alarmed, and agreed that something had to be done. That problem would have to wait for the time being, though, until they could come up with a plan of some description.

The South American situation worried him. It reminded him of the Nazi era, with its obsession with domination. The end of the Second World War had brought a unique opportunity for them to start over again from scratch, taking all the good parts and leaving the bad things behind. It was true at first that the remnants of ambition still burned brightly among the new settlers of New Swabia, but those thoughts soon eroded as the colony flourished and news reached them of the atrocities and disasters on the surface. While New Swabia advanced, they watched from afar as Terra became more and more unstable. Now it would seem that the idea of an opposing underworld order was a very real threat indeed. He needed to find out how many of the population actually knew what was going on. He was sure that if they were allowed to voice an opinion, they would strongly object.

Vessels was of the same mould as Albert Hebb, arrogant, full of self-importance and dangerously ambitious. People like him could ruin it for all of them.

Chapter 26

Vermont

President Dalheim of the Shadow Government was studying the document in his hand. Very interesting. Apparently, while at the Dulce base, a scientist had succeeded in correcting the erratic performance of their sonic weapons. Hebb, or Beiger as he knew him, had offered the scientist a position at the base. That was a good idea: keep the best minds for themselves.

But just who was this Hans Schumann? Surely they would have heard of him. If that wasn't strange enough, another scientist going by the name of von Getz was helping him. Not heard of him either.

The two men were due to arrive at the base in a short while to assist with another matter. It might pay him to fly down there and meet them himself; get the measure of them.

Heinz Dalheim, formerly known as Heinz Kessler, was intrigued. To think that these scientists were German citizens made it all the more perplexing. He was very pleased. The sonics would play a vital part in their future plans, plans that had been steadily set in motion since he stepped out of The Bell in 1985.

He remembered that night vividly, leaving the wasteland of war-torn Germany to emerge in a matter of seconds in Kecksburg, Pennsylvania. Driving to the air base, he knew at once that something had gone wrong with the coordinates. The most puzzling aspect, though, was how the military seemed to appear almost at once to take them away.

At the Edwards Air Force base the interrogation had been cut short by an MJ-12 operative, a high-ranking CIA official who had swept in, taking the five men away, and The Bell craft to Dulce, New Mexico, out of sight and out of mind.

They were there quite a while undergoing tests to see how they stood up to the rigors of their incredible feat. It was at that point, the high command told them the date.

It was clear to them that unknown perpetrators had adjusted the coordinates to catapult The Bell onto an alternative course. But the end result gifted the five occupants an unexpected lifeline. Arriving forty years later, they distanced themselves from the controversy of the war and, after overcoming the shock of it all, gave them a chance to start over.

It was unfortunate that none of them knew how the craft actually worked. The coordinates had been set in advance covertly. The two scientists on board only had operational knowledge, which was typical of the time. With all the paranoia that existed among various factions within the German hierarchy, a need-to-know basis was paramount.

During the Allied Liberation of Nazi-occupied territory, the Americans got lucky, discovering a series of underground bunkers. One of them had dozens of drawings of disc craft, tunnelling machines, blueprints of underground bases and drawings of The Bell along with notes on a test flight and date for its arrival: Kecksburg 1985. Clearly someone had a hidden agenda. Just who was a complete mystery. More notes revealed that these documents had been gathered together to be transferred to somewhere safe. But this never happened. The bunker had been sealed by shellfire and this, most probably, was the reason the documents had survived at all.

The discoveries were sent back to central government in the US where they resided for many years at Edwards Air Force Base before MJ-12 got their hands on them.

Exhaustive experiments were conducted on The Bell to try and work out how to set the controls along with various atmospheric conditions. It was concluded, in the end, that there must have been some remote launching device that worked with the craft, and without this extra device, the craft would do little more than hover a few feet above ground. To Kessler's knowledge, they were the only ones who had attempted the feat and survived.

So, it would seem that they were not much use to their captors.

Kessler still had an ace to play though, and although he could not help with the science, he managed to bargain their position by revealing undisclosed locations where priceless art and treasures were hidden all over Europe.

With a colossal injection of cash from black market sales, MJ-12 became massively powerful, installing key people in the Senate, the FBI and the CIA, enabling them to enlarge their own army and security. The Dulce base was connected up via a huge tunnel with Los Alamos. This became the stronghold for their organisation's technology. Kessler and the others rose through the ranks, proving their worth and loyalty to the shadow government, and were offered new identities, generous salaries and, of course, a great deal of power.

And now, here he was with the greatest prize of all: the new serving President. This may not have been how he had planned for it all, their early sights set on world domination, thwarted more by bad luck than judgement. The end of the war had come too early. They had simply run out of time. Now time itself had presented them with another chance, even better than before. In this instance, hardly anyone knew of their existence, let alone their plans, and as to the few that did, well, what use were they, and who would believe them anyway?

Consistently, they had seen their submarines and aircraft outperform those of the American government, their weapons putting them in their place, leaving the President and his General Command scratching their heads with concern.

The population demanded an explanation for strange sightings in the sky, details of weird encounters far too frequent to be dismissed easily, testimonials from a hoard of experts citing disinformation from the authorities.

But it was not disinformation. The real truth was that the government elect did not know who or what was responsible, and was very apprehensive to admit it. That would only lead to more probing from the media and more awkward questions with no answers.

And now the shaping of destiny had begun, sealed with plans to overthrow the unworthy. As they broke away, increasing their strength, it would only be a matter of time before the inevitable prophecy was fulfilled. The total world domination by the Bavarian Illuminati was now within touching distance, or so it would seem.

But there had always been rumours circulating within the aviation authority of strange craft, similar to their own but much faster, and far more manoeuvrable, even underwater. They were on radar one second and then gone. They were sometimes reported to vanish before people's eyes. The strange craft had been involved in conflict on several occasions with warplanes, the Americans always coming off second best.

So, the Shadow Government started asking the same questions.

At first, they thought the mystery objects might have been Russian, but as time went by, it became apparent that their capabilities were even less than that of the United States.

So, who were they, and where were they from?

This troubled Kessler. Knowing that this level of science was not in their own hands was the main reason why they had been so apprehensive not to advance into the White House by now. No point in attempting the invasion yet, not after showing so much discipline for all these years. It could be what this unknown force was anticipating, waiting for them to show themselves, to expose their organisation and destroy it before they had time to act.

One of the first tasks in his new role was to make it a priority to get to the bottom of this mystery once and for all.

His mind worked over as he slowly paced the veranda that overlooked Lake Champlain. This was a good place to think: clean air, peaceful surroundings, his mistress, Helena, for company. She appeared with two glasses of Jack Daniels on the rocks, handing one over to him.

They both stood for a while, their eyes trained on the cruiser at the end of the jetty rocking slowly in the water, watching the sun setting, the sky illuminated by the magnificent Vermont colours.

It was at times like these that some answers became quite clear.

For some time, the Dulce base had been in contact with a scientific organisation that had offered them multiple ventilation and magnetic systems of such advancement that it bewildered their own personnel. Closely following this were the sonic correctional breakthroughs made by their two German visitors. Now the same organisation was offering more technology, but this time the terms were different.

They wanted access to tunnelling rights under South America.

That was a long way from Germany. Kessler wondered if it was anything to do with the Odessa Project at the end of the war, when President Peron granted safe passage to over three thousand of the German military into Argentina.

But there was nothing down there. Talk of mounting a New Reich never materialised. The MJ-12 operatives working there had never uncovered anything of interest other than the organised distribution of narcotics that they allowed into the States.

So, MJ-12 was not to interfere with any Southern Hemisphere plans. In return, the organisation was going to reveal unconditional access to their headquarters and more technology.

Yes, it all seemed to fit: that this same group were probably part of a much bigger organisation piloting the craft that they could not catch, and firing weapons that they could not defend against. How they would love to get their hands on one of those craft.

Negotiations were going forward headed by Beiger, or Hebb as he liked to be known these days. Part of the deal brokered included requisitioning the two German scientists back to Dulce for a most important matter.

This could be a real game changer for Dalheim. If they oversaw this correctly, it could be the beginning of the New World Order. Strange to think that a pair of Germans were the ones who could solve their problems; how fitting that seemed to be.

He eyed his companion salaciously as she sauntered into the house. That was enough strategical thinking for one day. What is it these Americans said? Too much work makes Jack a dull boy.

Chapter 27

New Swabia

The Haunebu cruised the short distance along the Wohltat River before submerging into the depths, the auto-correction employed to steer the craft along the riverbed avoiding the rocky outcrops of the steep bankside. The crystal clear water allowed a view of the fantastic array of fish, the bright colours dancing over coral beds, large spider crabs scurrying away from the craft's disturbance as the tidal river gave way to the underwater cavern exit. The auto lights illuminated the blackness, the depths increasing all the time as the occupants readied themselves for the outside world.

The Haunebu picked up speed as the underwater cavern expanded into a perfect tunnel, straight as a die for half a mile until dropping down, following the overhang into the sea bed before emerging into the ocean itself. The craft picked up speed, employing vector technology as it made its way to the surface.

Schumann gave the order to set a heading for Key West, Florida. Kaufmann and Weisse both acknowledged and obeyed without question. Von Getz appeared with the now traditional bratwurst, the homely aroma wafting around the cabin. Schumann took one appreciatively as he searched the data banks for an address.

The first line of reasoning was to look for a place in Germany, but he could not find a suitable destination that he was happy with. He then remembered the intercepted television programmes that he used to watch on scientific phenomena. He especially liked programmes on subjects created in the United Kingdom. They always had very interesting production technique, and he liked their theoretical way of thinking. One particular expert that they always called on for opinions was a man called Derek Mills. He usually made sense and spoke on several occasions about the Dulce base. It was a long shot, but it could be the only way to expose what was going on in there. Schumann certainly could not do it alone. He wrapped the notebook up carefully, writing an address of a UK PO box number on the front.

As soon as the craft was in position, Schumann ordered Kaufmann to activate the cloaking device. They floated silently into the quayside and Schumann slipped onto the wooden dock unnoticed. If he hadn't been so angry about the whole situation, he would have been utterly terrified. As it was, he felt remarkably calm walking into the street of quaint, painted buildings, so different from the desert town of Dulce. The place was positively charming, bustling with activity, and the people seemed cheerful.

Strange, electrically-charged music seeped from various establishments. It sounded odd to him. Clearly, from the cheering, the Terrans were enjoying it, though.

He located the post office with ease, joined the small queue and waited. In no time at all, he was seen by a jovial woman who was extremely helpful, aiding him to send the parcel in the safest manner possible via airmail to England. Keeping his voice low to disguise the accent, he handed over the cash, the woman chatting away non-stop as she wished him good day, seamlessly talking to her next customer.

Schumann made his way back to the dock, taking a good look around before climbing into the invisible hatch and closing it behind him, the Haunebu sliding away from dockside before sinking into the ocean depths once more.

Mission accomplished.

"Everything okay, sir."

"Yes, fine. Set a heading for the Dulce base."

They followed the same lines of protocol as before, keeping to an identical route for navigation. They touched down effortlessly at the base, taxiing over to where they had parked only a short time before. As they stepped onto the Terran soil, Holt marched over to welcome back the two Swabians.

"Back so soon, gentlemen? They must have liked your work."

"Yes, it would seem that way." Schumann and von Getz shook hands with the Terran.

They were led into the base where they underwent the now familiar security checks. Von Getz was to rendezvous with Professor Logan, while Schumann was to meet a group of scientists elsewhere.

There was the same arduous journey into the lower depths to the labs, where von Getz parted company, leaving Schumann with two security guards. The lift continued downwards.

He wondered what the purpose of his escort was as they passed Level Three, then Four, the dread starting to creep into him, remembering the contents of the notebook; the lift descending past Level Five, the voice of Clare Logan in his head reminding him of the revelations that she had entrusted him with; bad enough for a Terran to comprehend, but even worse for someone who barely knew what to make of these surface dwellers. Coming up now ... the lift approaching the next level ... slowing down to a halt ... Level Six ... Oh, no.

Now he knew why he had armed company as the doors opened to a familiar layout, no different at all, the officers ushering him to the left, walking either side of him, silent, looking about as happy as he did.

The corridor widened out, taking on a car width, rooms with glass windows revealing scientists conducting all manner of experiments, signs in English but also with weird script underneath. He saw a sign pointing to another corridor marked 'arsenal'; the opposite way marked 'military'. Further on he saw another for 'DNA labs'.

An electric car met them, the driver nodding officially as they all climbed in. The tunnels were even wider now, yet more labs and large rooms full of metallic containers. They came to a cross-section, the car going straight ahead. A sign on the left read 'cages'. The one on the right reading 'terrible mixture storage'.

Schumann did not like this at all, and the familiar outline of Albert Hebb coming into view did nothing to make him feel any better.

"Ah, Mr Schumann, a pleasure to see you again so soon."

"Likewise, sir." Schumann delivered this through gritted teeth.

"Welcome to Level Six, the most advanced genetics facility on the planet," Hebb scoffed. "Allow me to show you around our fine departments."

They continued on foot, the two security guards now tailing off to a discreet distance, Hebb chatting enthusiastically about the different departments and the work that they did.

The first point of interest for Schumann came when he observed a large illuminated band that went right around the walls and floor. He could tell immediately that it was made of phosphorus, which was curious as there was ample lighting built into the walls. He chose not to ask about it.

Soon afterwards they came across the labs. Hebb pointed out what was happening in each. It was positively shocking from the start. Schumann was shown the biogenetics area, spurring onto tanks full of animal parts, fish, then mammals, birds and mice.

They walked along to the next section where horror truly took on a new meaning. Hundreds of sealed tanks full of human body parts, legs, arms, torsos and heads, all bobbing about in a regulated environment. Schumann was sickened by the sight of it all, but gave out an impression of external calm. Hebb was wallowing in his own world of madness as he excitedly listed the catalogue of medical breakthroughs they had made at Dulce.

"It always amazes me how much the pharmaceutical companies will pay for our medical research."

But at what price? Schumann thought.

They continued to the next department, scientists busy monitoring yet more tanks, but these were animals that had been altered to a level of almost non-recognition. Then more tanks, with humans vastly altered, massively deformed, all floating in a translucent green liquid. Judging by the appearance, this area was set aside for the failed experiments.

Schumann felt his legs turn to jelly. He stole a glance at the security guards behind him. They looked alarmed, one in particular, who met his gaze, widening his eyes.

Schumann prepared himself for the next instalment of this living nightmare. In fact Clare had called this level 'nightmare hall', her notes so far depressingly accurate. Because of this, he knew what was coming before he saw it.

Through the windows of the room he could see vast tanks of more humans, but this time grafted onto animal parts, all floating lifelessly; some horrendous hybridisation of unimaginable proportions. Next to these were identical rows of animals and humans. The extent of the research was on a gargantuan scale, and out here in the middle of nowhere, there was no one to stop them.

"This is the cloning department," Hebb announced proudly. "This type of work will soon enable us to grow spare body parts for those who can afford the privilege."

He smiled, tapping the side of his nose.

"Impressive," Schumann managed.

"Please, if you will." Hebb led the way through a large alcove into a circular room where more scientists were busy poring over computer data encircling a large dark object. Hebb ushered Schumann closer. He noticed the remains of a scorched swastika on the side of a large cast-iron object about fifteen feet high. Schumann knew what it was; the shape was a dead giveaway: Das Glocke.

"Yes, all the rumours are true, it does exist," said Hebb offhandedly. He turned to face Schumann. "We would be most appreciative of your input on this matter."

"How can I be of assistance?"

"It's quite simple. We would like you to find out how it works."

Schumann was surprised. They had The Bell, the legendary craft from World War Two here at the Dulce base, one of the original occupants standing right next to him, and they did not know how to fly it? He chose not to ask why.

"I will have a look of course, sir, but it really is not my area of expertise."

Hebb nodded studiously, plodding along slowly. "I realise that, Mr Schumann, but what harm can it do?" He parted his arms in a conciliatory manner.

Schumann offered up his best smile. "Of course, it will be interesting, I'm sure."

"The rest of this level is of little importance," Hebb declared. "Let's get back now."

Schumann was trying to figure out what all this meant, how all he had seen could be relevant to his visit. The unknown was petrifying.

Back at the car, they all climbed in, the driver taking them back the way they had come, across the phosphorus band to where the tunnel narrowed, and then back to the lift.

Much to the relief of Schumann, they got in and the doors closed up. He did not bother to check the magnetics as the door closed this time, he no longer felt the need to.

The lift descended to Level Seven, familiar territory. The four men disembarked, walking in the direction of the underground docks, the cold dampness in the air reaching Schumann's lungs. So to the sonic testing area, he consoled himself.

They continued to the point where he had witnessed the strange argument. This time, though, it was deserted.

Another driver appeared; they all climbed in again, heading down to the tunnel split. But instead of heading towards the dock, the driver took the opposite direction, continuing on for several hundred yards before they emerged into a cavern.

Now what? Schumann looked around the vast expanse, Hebb instructing the driver to make for the far corner. They all disembarked, Hebb once again pointing out all the not-so-wonderful departments on Level Seven.

If possible, it was even worse than before, the first section once again bustling with activity as yet more experiments were carried out on human embryos in various stages of development. Row after row, a mixture of human remains in cold storage; next to these, the heartbreaking remains of children in storage vats.

Schumann looked on, numbed by the whole sorry spectacle. Who the hell were all these people?

"And over here," Hebb boasted proudly, "are our prize specimens."

Schumann peered into the massive room observing yet more enormous tanks full of liquid substances. The tanks went back much further. Many of them looked empty, save for the green murky water in them.

He strode up to the tanks showing fake enthusiasm. He looked them all up and down, hands on his hips, nodding.

Out of nowhere, and without warning, came a dull clunk as a massive bulbous head, eyes mad with rage, hit the tank glass, causing Schumann to jump back. The head leered at him, sporting a huge grin, a blueish tongue appearing, licking the observation window eagerly, the whole mottled-brown head mass tilted to one side. Then a pair of arms appeared, but not human. These resembled tentacles.

Himmel, what a monster, the Swabian said inwardly.

More of the monstrosity appeared, revealing a human torso and yet more legs, the suckers pulsing as they stuck to the glass. More multi-armed and -legged humanoids appeared from neighbouring tanks, some with octopus heads, others with huge beaks in the middle of their faces, expressions ranging from anger to utter despair. One particular subject, a human squid-like hybrid looked at him pleadingly, an expression that Schumann interpreted as a cry for help, all six eyes blinking in unison, displaying great sadness. The creature tapped gently on the glass with a gigantic lobster-like claw.

"Ah! I see Otto and his friends are introducing themselves to you," Hebb said gleefully, pointing to the mad octo man.

"How old are they?" Schumann spoke quietly.

"The specimens you see here are around two years old, but this is the culmination of decades of work by hundreds of scientists."

Schumann had never seen anything so shameful.

They carried on a short distance to a complex of cubicles that housed grotesque bird hybrids with human heads for bodies, faces contorted in pain; humanoid bat-like creatures up to seven feet tall; and other bird men with multiple bills in the middle of their faces.

He walked along, not being able to look away, overcome with morbid fascination. A bat man eyed him with a look of disdain, the head turning to one side and lowering to take a closer inspection, wings flexing slightly. The creature gave out a long guttural caw. This only served to alert others to their presence.

As Schumann came into view, the occupants of the cubicles became agitated, banging on the square, meshed windows of their prisons, the pain and anguish blatantly evident, others with grins of lunacy spread over their faces ... those that had a proper face.

"And last but not least, allow me to introduce the Goran, the future of land warfare." Hebb pointed to a vast brightly illuminated cavern, the floor covered in sand.

Schumann peered through the steel bars at a herd of around thirty animals, their bodies the size of a rhino with reptilian tails, the flanks with giant green overlapping scales, the heads with a huge bony hood that hung over their small beady eyes, a pair of tusks that swept from either side of the head joining into one massive point in front of their nose.

"Armour-plated," said Hebb. "They're actually bulletproof for the most part. A man can ride them, sheltering behind their heads. They can withstand extreme temperatures and smash through brick walls as if they were never there. The central horn is as sharp as a razor."

They were formidable beasts, that he had to admit. It was a surreal sight to see them just innocently grazing in the middle of their cavern without a care in the world.

"The end result of all the hard work. Now you see why we have to try so many variables, to get these new species to function in the way we need them."

Schumann looked at Hebb, nodding studiously, feigning interest.

"Soon, we will have oceangoing and airborne versions too," Hebb said excitedly. Imagine winged bomb-carrying beasts, and insect-sized creatures with spycams; how we will be able to infiltrate any military stronghold in the world. Just try and conceive, if you will, what this means?"

Schumann could see only too well. "Very impressive, sir," he managed to say.

"It is hard to believe that this is all real, and that despite everything we have reached a great landmark in the history of science."

It was clear to Schumann that Hebb was completely insane. His rhetoric reminded him of the mindset of the high order in World War Two, but that, by all accounts, was where the man belonged.

Hebb led him through the industrial aggression of metal and electrics that adorned the cavern, the upper gantries full of activity as scientists scurried around busily. There seemed to be an almost fanatical work ethic here. As they walked, Hebb explained how he would be spending a great more time at the base.

"I have assumed a far more hands-on role for the lower

levels of this facility. I will still control Los Alamos and Taos, of course, but this will now be my primary interest."

"That is a lot for one man to cover, sir," said Schumann, fishing for information.

'Well, yes, I know it's going to be tough," Hebb replied, full of self-gratification. "But I relish the challenge. No one should be afraid of hard work, do you not agree, Mr Schumann? Especially as I have you to help me now."

"Of course, sir." Schumann was filled further with dread.

"Yes, so generous of your organisation to transfer you here. I have so many projects and so many problems for you to solve." Hebb laughed out loud.

"I look forward to it, sir.' Schumann felt totally betrayed. He had been sold out by the hierarchy of New Swabia, probably as part of the deal brokered by Vessels and Co.

It was at this point that he realised how vulnerable his situation was. He had become a victim of his own success, awards for scientific achievements, a wonderful lifestyle, then being promoted to a level that most could only dream of.

So this was his reward: being sold out to the highest bidder along with his entire country, it would seem.

As they walked the vast expanse, Hebb led them to a doorway where the two security guards were waiting for them. The four men entered a short corridor which changed into a metal bridge allowing them to cross over a man-made canal. He could see up ahead that the body of water terminated in a large, Olympic-sized pool covered by chequerboard meshing. Beyond this was the familiar sight of the dockside in the distance.

"The holding pond is for testing the marine life," Hebb declared.

Schumann could see some steps that led down to an

observation area, the side of the pond with a long glass window.

"Here we can test for extremes in temperature, low oxygen, vision, speed and agility and, of course, efficiency."

Schumann could guess what happened to the specimens that did not reach expectations. For now, he had to play along with the charade until he was able to regroup with the others to figure out what their next move would be.

"So how can I be of service, sir?"

"Well, one of the jobs I need help with is creating a magnetic locking device for the various sections. We are on electric for some of the circuitry and I would like that all upgraded." Hebb pointed to a few examples. "Also, I have a deep exploration team that are going into the lower caverns. I would like you to be part of that team."

Schumann could tell already that Hebb was used to getting his own way, and he did not mind letting other people know about it. The idea of exploring the lower caverns would at least get him away from Hebb and his creations for a while. That in itself would be worth the journey into the unknown.

"Sounds interesting, sir. I look forward to it."

"Good, I will get you inducted into protocol tomorrow morning. That will be all for today." Hebb marched off towards the dock where a launch crew had assembled in waiting.

The two security guards closed in to escort Schumann back to the upper levels. They guided him back along another tunnel, sparing him from what he had just seen, the mundane appearance of polished walls and latex floor a far more attractive option. They came to the entrance to the lift in no time at all, but instead he felt hands steer him further down the tunnel in an authoritarian manner. He allowed this to happen without objection; an instinctive intrigue gripped him inside to go along with the two men.

The guards coaxed him down a right turn, a never-changing landscape only broken by a motif on the floor that he had seen in another tunnel. They passed the motif again, changing direction into another tunnel, this time far more poorly lit.

They stopped, the guards turning to face him.

"Alright! What's this all about?" Schumann demanded.

"We don't have much time. Please listen," said one guard.

"This is Cale. I am Sagen," the taller of the two men stated. "We are taking a great risk in even talking to you."

Schumann relented. "Okay, I'm listening."

It was Cale, the one who had cast him the look earlier, who spoke next.

"Please forgive the theatrics, Mr Schumann, but we have to be careful." He cast a look around to make sure they were alone.

"There is a small group of us here who are aware of your visit; the stranger who improved the sonics, and who has returned to offer his services once again, but who appears to have a conscience, who actually cares what happens down here, who displayed disgust at the experiments that he witnessed. Am I right?"

"Yes, you are right," Schumann replied without hesitation.

"So why are you here?" Sagen enquired.

"I was ordered here by my superiors."

"Alright." Sagen looked at him with eyes of kindness. "Alright. We are on your side. You have to believe that we do not wish you any harm, but there must be someone back in Germany who you can contact and to whom you can expose what is going on here."

Schumann felt his heart sink once more. If only it was true, that would be a far simpler way to expose what was going on down here. But the truth was, even his own government were about to sell out him and their entire nation.

"I cannot tell anyone about this back in Germany," he said. "No one would believe me."

Cale looked crestfallen. "So we are left in our small minority with no one to tell, and no way of stopping this madness."

Schumann looked at them both. "Who are you working for? Have you no allies yourselves?"

Sagen looked at him squarely. "We have allies. Plenty of them, but down here with all the security, getting the intel out has proven to be very difficult."

"The truth is, we thought that you were a contact come to instruct us on what to do next," Cale exclaimed.

"I am afraid that the people I thought I could trust have put me in this position," Schumann replied. "I don't know what I can even do about my own circumstances."

Sagen patted his shoulder. "I guess we are all in the same situation."

Schumann looked at them both. "How many of you are there down here?"

"There are eight of us," Cale admitted.

"We are a mix of infiltrators and sympathisers. Our common goal to end this terrible practice," Sagen added.

Schumann could see the desperation in their faces. "Okay, clearly we can talk freely here. How is that so?"

"You see the insignia on the floor back there?" Schumann nodded. "That is where the microphones and camera monitors end."

That was useful to know, he thought to himself.

"We are seconded to your security detail tomorrow. We could meet up again around the same time," Cale suggested.

Schumann thought hurriedly. His options were few. To forge an allegiance with this group was risky to say the least, though he had no immediate alternative. He would have to take a chance.

"Okay, agreed. We will meet tomorrow."

The two men looked relieved. Cale took a look around.

"We'd better get you back, sir, before we are missed."

The men made their way back to the lifts and up to Level Two where von Getz was waiting in the conference area. Cale and Sagen made their excuses and left.

The two Swabians made their way to the surface, Schumann insisting on a walk to build up an appetite. He led von Getz away from the base up to the cave. Once inside, Schumann recalled what he had seen earlier that day. He could see the concern on his fellow countryman's face.

"So how long are you seconded here under Hebb's command?" von Getz asked urgently.

"I don't know, but I fear it will be for some time." Schumann suspected it may actually be permanent.

"Well, we won't stand for it. We will go back to New Swabia and overthrow those who wish to threaten our nation's security."

An admirable notion by his friend, thought Schumann, but easier said than done. Von Getz looked desperate as he paced the small cave space.

"I won't leave you here with these maniacs. We'll smuggle you out somehow, and hide you away back in the homeland."

Schumann smiled. The same idea had crossed his mind with Clare Logan: to fly off into the sunset. What a notion that was! He had to think fast. They had to have a realistic plan that would buy them time until they could figure out how best to resolve their situation.

"I could get you on the detail. With your experience there would be no objection. I could do with your observations down there."

"Of course, sir." Von Getz did not hesitate. "You are too valuable to the homeland. We cannot lose you."

The thought had not crossed his mind before.

Due to his recent, elevated promotion, he was now in line for the job of chancellor, should the high command be removed altogether. Vessels and his cronies had bestowed such a high level of clearance on him that they would surely not risk his return. This posting was supposed to be his last, he was sure of it; cast out into the Terran world to do the bidding of a lunatic, a nightmarish conclusion to his existence, a life under the command of Germanic heritage. How ironic.

"Okay, let's get back to the base. We can see what happens tomorrow, meet up with Cale and Sagen, and go from there."

"Right, sir. I will inform the flight crew of our plans."

They headed back for base, a brisk jog employed to satisfy the personnel of their intent.

Chapter 28

Cambridgeshire

Marius appeared in the dining room, surprised that he was the last to appear after the previous night's drama. They were all there assembled around a huge William IV mahogany dining table, tucking into an impressive breakfast. Stanley pulled a chair out, ushering him to sit. The waft of bacon confirmed how ravenous he was, and he too tucked in gleefully.

As Martha served him tea, he could see Caroline chatting away to Helen without a care in the world. Mills was reading a copy of the *Telegraph*; H was walking around on the phone, a chunk of toast in hand. It all seemed so far removed from recent events.

"Sleep okay, old boy?" Sidney enquired.

"Yes, I did; like a log actually." The hypnotherapy session had left him drained of energy, and despite his mind being hot-wired with excitement, he had slept right through until the morning.

Caroline looked up, smiling in acknowledgement. Marius was glad she seemed okay. He had forgiven her for the charade at his office. That was all in the dim and distant past.

As he finished breakfast, Mills appeared at his side, *Telegraph* under his arm. "Want to get some air?"

Marius knew there was more to it. "Yes, good idea." He

followed Mills over to the French doors which led onto the terrace. The two men descended a series of steps onto a path that cut its way across the immaculate lawns.

As the two men walked, a pleasant glow from the sun cut through the haze of the morning sky, sweeping across the gardens, offering up a comforting light, illuminating the greenery. The sun felt good on his back, some reassurance of normality far away from the world of weird that seemed at present to lurk around every corner.

Mills was about to deepen the mystique further.

"You did well last night, the both of you. We will take your details and make sure you are paid by the end of the week."

Marius had quite forgotten about the money, and in a way was quite uneasy about it. It seemed a huge amount for what he regarded as a shot in the dark.

"I really must be honest, I don't know why she responded so well. I did nothing out of the ordinary."

"But nonetheless, you and your colleague did manage to unlock her mind and reveal valuable information to us."

"I meant to ask. Who is Enoch?"

Mills' brow furrowed as he studied the ground. "Well," he said, looking up, "it's the name of a deep cover operative that we have in place at the Dulce base, and who has been out of contact for a long time. In fact, we did not know whether his group was still operational."

"But he spoke through Caroline," Marius exclaimed.

"I know, and I have been thinking about that. You see, something is not right about all of this. That should not have happened."

"You're telling me." Marius stopped to face Mills. "What about the child, Bek? You stated that she had no children, yet, apparently, she has a seven-year-old son."

"I know that appears to be the case, but it's the first I have heard about it. I have known Caroline for years. Trust me, she told me herself that she was not interested in having children."

"Am I right, then, in thinking that her recollection under hypnosis is something that you have heard of before?"

Mills nodded. "Yes. I have heard of many cases, but never in so much detail. The thing is, she does not remember Bek at the moment. I don't have a clue how she will react to the news." Mills looked worried.

"Well, we won't mention this for the time being," Marius concurred.

The two men continued doing a circuit of the grand house taking in the sights. Mills turned to him as they were about to go back inside, taking him by the arm.

"Look, you know that you are free to go whenever you wish, but we would be very grateful if you would hypnotise Caroline again."

"I'm not sure ... this stuff, it's pretty heavy. I'm out of my depth here.

"Please, Marius, this is of the utmost importance." Mills looked at him desperately. We have been looking for this opportunity for years. With your help, we can try and put an end to MJ-12 once and for all."

There was no doubting Mills' sincerity. The simmering tension was put to one side as the two men entered the house; he was obviously putting on a front, particularly for the sake of Caroline.

It was agreed by all not to reveal the parts of hypnosis that she did not remember. It was better for her to gradually recollect the memories in her own time.

When presented with the opportunity of another regressive session, Caroline was only too eager to help.

Marius cast a look around the room as he carefully implemented the procedure of the latest leap into the unknown. He had to steady himself as the quiet commands were given to his client. Inside, he was a nervous wreck, only too glad that the others had chosen to stay and watch.

Once again, Caroline drifted into a deep hypnotic state, her vital signs quite normal at this point. He had a few pages of script, hurriedly penned by Mills and H, that he could refer to, but that would depend on where Caroline took him.

She sighed, lying on her back on the chaise, wearing a half-smile, hands resting on her stomach. The tension was almost too much to bear; not a sound in the room. Marius could clearly hear Caroline's breathing, deep and steady. The breathing became deeper, stronger, and more regular. Her arms trembled and her eyelids fluttered. Then a few soft moans, followed by incoherent mumbling.

Marius did not have the chance to speak as Caroline sat bolt upright, arms outstretched, tears welling in her eyes.

"Bek, my son, come to me … I can see him … he is here."

The words came out at high volume making Marius jump, her voice carrying a high level of emotion.

He pulled himself together. "Caroline, describe what you can see."

"We are surrounded by a white light … It's wonderful, full of love … Bek is so handsome."

Marius took a chance. "Has Bek any information, Caroline?"

"Oh, no … No, Bek is my son, he is young, Bek does not carry information … Bek does not do that."

God, now what? This whole thing is a bunch of riddles, Marius thought. He would have to phrase his questions carefully to extract the right answers.

"Does anyone else there wish to offer information?"

There was a long silence, the odd interruption only from Caroline having an inaudible conversation with her son. Then there was a change in mood, a sudden shift in body language from Caroline as she reclined back into the chaise, nodding to another invisible entity as she did so.

"Enoch, German scientists back, working on Levels Six and Seven, assigned to explore caverns. They seem to have advanced knowledge of problem solving."

Marius looked around at H and Mills. They looked like two excited children, struggling to contain their enthusiasm. Clearly, he was delivering financially. They gestured for him to continue the process.

"Caroline, has Enoch more information for us?"

There was a long, drawn-out silence, Caroline breathing steadily, Marius by now used to the unexpected, waiting patiently for a reply. He checked her over for anomalies, but she seemed perfectly fine.

"Enoch, Level Seven has a river that connects to the base exiting in the Gulf of Mexico.

"The same area has human and animal experimentation at a level never thought possible. Looking for allies to strengthen our position … Heightened security make this difficult."

Enoch continued with more locational detail regarding the underground river system, which Sidney duly made a note of.

Marius felt a nudge as H passed over a note. He complied without objection.

"Caroline, can Enoch tell me what date it is?"

There was a pause, the hypnotherapist not quite sure why, of all the questions, this was priority.

Then Enoch was back. "Date is September sixteenth."

H's jaw nearly hit the floor. Mills went as white as a sheet. Marius continued with the questioning, regardless.

"Caroline, can Enoch tell me, is he in direct contact with the German scientists?"

"Direct contact has been made."

"Names of scientists?"

"Schumann and von Getz."

"Okay, good. I have more …"

"Got to go. Enoch out."

Same as before, Marius thought. *Time for a change of tack.*

"Caroline, is Bek still with you?"

"Yes, Bek is here … Bek is here," she drawled sleepily.

"What can you see?"

"I see pink lights in the lab now … Have to be careful … Hebb is in charge. He is here all the time. Security is even greater than before."

"What is Bek doing?"

"He is … He is … He has to go now, they are coming for him … he has to go back … Goodbye, Bek … Good …"

Caroline stopped communicating, her mood darkening, moving to another plane. Her sleep pattern took on a series of changes before she began recovering on her own without the assistance of Marius. That was strange in itself.

She broke out of the hypnotherapy status, and transcended into a state of shallow sleep. He had not seen this before. Sidney gave him a look of surprise; it was all very unnerving. Curious that she did not describe being taken into the craft this time. Maybe they were being spared the repetition.

Or maybe not.

Marius did go through the final stages of recovery as a matter of protocol, but was sure he need not have bothered.

Caroline awoke with a sigh, stretching her arms. "How did I do?"

"Very well, I think," Sidney replied, giving nothing away.

It was clear that she remembered nothing from the hypnosis, which contradicted the earlier sessions where she could recall some of her experiences.

Marius left her recovering with Helen by the fireside.

H led the way to the games room, jostling past the billiard table to a seating area with a drinks bar.

"A little early in the day, but what the hell." H poured out a Scotch from a crystal decanter. They all accepted the offer, including Mills, who was still shaking.

Marius took a big slug and breathed out heavily. "Okay. Judging by your reactions back there, I'm clearly missing something."

Mills did his cursory look at the floor, then after draining his glass, he spoke. "Marius, my friend, that was a most remarkable event that we just witnessed."

"Please elaborate."

"That was no hypnotic regression session," Mills exclaimed.

"What do you mean?' Sidney said forcefully.

Mills put up a hand. He was not playing games, merely trying to come to terms with the events that had just taken place, and to try to put it into words. In the end, he just blurted it out.

"Not hypnosis. It was channelling."

"Holy Moses, are you sure?" Sidney retorted.

"There can be no doubt. The sixteenth of September is today's date, is it not?"

"It could be Caroline adding her own confused thoughts," Marius offered.

"But you don't really believe that, do you? Come on, I know it's hard to take in, but it all fits, the way the censorship was lifted, the communication with Enoch, all of it. You could never achieve that under hypnosis alone."

Marius knew he was right, but how was it possible, and in so much detail?

Mills went on. "This is all connected to Bek, I'm sure of it."

He saw the others look puzzled so he explained his theory.

"As fanciful as it seems, you are all familiar with the numerous accounts of women becoming pregnant after abduction, only to have their embryos removed. There are even accounts of meeting siblings at a later date just like Caroline apparently has."

The others all nodded.

"So the difference here is the detailed regressive account, which I'm sure is in real time, and has occurred when Bek has been in contact with his mother." Mills eyed them all over the top of his spectacles. "We are probably looking at an advanced hybrid being, part human and ..." Mills scratched his head. "Well, I don't know what, but something genetically advanced that would tie in with other documented accounts. My best guess is that he is telepathic, but also possesses a unique relationship with his mother that means he can communicate at great distance, the hypnosis being the portal to trigger the process."

"My God!" H hissed. "That would make him one powerful weapon."

"Yes," Mills replied, with a grave look. "And one valuable commodity. We can only hope that the powers that be at the base do not know the extent of his capability."

"Okay, so what now?" Marius pressed him.

"We need to keep working with Caroline and map out the base, get as much information as possible," H announced.

"Alright, but what can we do about it?" Sidney said exasperated.

"We are going to have to think of something, but this has got to come to an end. MJ-12 must be stopped," Mills retorted.

Chapter 29

Dulce, New Mexico

Schumann made his way to the base entrance. He had liaised with Weisse and Kaufmann, documenting his observations on the lower levels, and left them to read at their leisure. He was leaving nothing to chance. The base could be listening in on their conversations.

Once inside and cleared by security, he made his way to the recreation area.

Clare Logan could not hide her delight at seeing him, but remained stoic in her manner and kept the conversation very business-like. Von Getz also appeared to talk shop with her for a while. They had so much more to discuss, but that would have to wait for the time being. Maybe Schumann could get her on the exploratory detail far below their feet.

Thankfully, Hebb and his cronies were never seen on the upper levels, preferring to take the shuttle back every evening to Los Alamos. That suited Schumann just fine.

He had met Holt on several occasions now, and was sure that he detected a dislike between the two sector heads. Holt seemed like a decent sort that was trapped in between the layers of red tape, entangled in the politics of power on the base. He was a soldier through and through, but Schumann could detect an attitude of objection towards Hebb's involvement. He had to try and exploit the situation for all it was worth.

Chapter 30

London

The intercom sounded in the office of the luxury apartment of Claude Perfekt, his secretary announcing the arrival of two gentlemen in the foyer. He knew who they were and arranged with his secretary to meet them in the hotel bar across the road. He thanked Luciana and dismissed her for the night. There would be no more need of her services today.

He loved the position on Chelsea Bridge, making sure as soon as the development was finished that he bagged the prime location on the top floor. The panoramic three-sixty glass view enabled him to look right across Battersea Park and the Thames beyond; then to the right he could see straight down Chelsea Bridge, the road sweeping beyond past the old barracks in the direction of Sloane Square; and behind him, the old power station restored, the grounds all redeveloped. What a sight that was to behold.

The sun was setting in the distance, the remnants of daylight merging into the transient night-time lights of London. He had stood and witnessed the transformation on many occasions. This time, there were other matters that would take him from his lone vigil.

He grabbed a navy Tom Ford jacket from the cloakroom and entered his personal lift, instructing the keypad to ground level. After a swift descent, the doors opened into a secure parking lot where he strode over to a door with a combination touchscreen. He punched in a six-digit code and was soon inside a discreet corridor of the Hotel Porto, a few strides from the door seeing him briskly emerge into the bar area. He spotted the two men at a table, each with a Courvoisier in hand watching a football match on the television, chatting away without a care in the world.

"Gentlemen." He sat down and joined them. An efficient waitress in smart black uniform appeared immediately. He nodded for his usual; all the staff knew him well.

"Car disposed of as you instructed," said one of the men, distinctly English.

"Good. We don't want any loose ends," Perfekt hissed.

"What are your new orders, sir?" the other man enquired.

"We have an important meeting with the UK fraternity. There have been some interesting developments in America; could be we might all be going on a trip to New Mexico."

MJ-12 had its European headquarters in London, the ideal springboard to hop onto the Continent whenever required, and then on to liaise with the place where it had all begun: the German sector.

Perfekt sensed that something monumental was going to happen. He had a feeling that the time was not far away to make their move at last. And he wanted to be right up at the front when that happened. The time would be right for him to emerge from the shadows, to take what was rightfully his, and to lead the world into a new era. They would all be eternally grateful for that.

"Sir, any news on the Templars?"

"No, nothing, they are not a threat to us."

Perfekt remembered the old guard well, highly trained covert operatives with exceptional combat skills. But over the years their numbers had dwindled, their effectiveness restricted by the American underground strongholds. They had no answer to that. Plus, there was the advancement in military hardware that could not be matched, The Templars existed only in small pockets of resistance these days, more of an irritant than a direct threat. Yes, Perfekt and his brothers would soon realise their destinies. Nothing could stop them.

Chapter 31

Dulce, New Mexico

Schumann found that he could pretty much assign who he wanted to for the exploratory detail. It seemed that Hebb had more respect for him than he realised and had given the Swabian 'Ultra Clearance', the highest level available. This made a lot of sense if he thought about it. His recent promotion back home and the increasing relationship between the two parties had opened many new doors for him, providing he did as he was told, of course.

Cale and Sagen were the obvious choice for security. Added to the detail were Clare Logan and von Getz. The two final members of the team were two scientists well versed in base protocol in the lower levels. Their names were Gallagher and Clunes, coming highly recommended by their security detail. Schumann took it at face value that they were part of the group of sympathisers.

They passed through the usual checks entering one of the lifts and descended to Level Seven. That feeling of dread soon returned like an invisible warning to all on the detail, Schumann reading the uncertainty on the other faces that clearly mirrored his own.

The lift opened with Gallagher taking up the lead. They followed him over to a pair of electric cars. He and Clunes would drive the two groups in convoy.

Before setting off, Gallagher addressed them all.

"Okay, we are about to go deep into the caverns, way beyond the outer boundaries, so please listen carefully." His steady confident voice blended well with his muscular physique. Schumann guessed he was in his mid-thirties. He had a neat brown beard that accentuated his jawline, the hard hat he wore hiding any other hair. His eyes were fixed with an intense blue stare. Everyone was listening, even the baby-faced Clunes who must have heard it all before on numerous occasions.

"We are likely to engage the reptilians or, to give them their official name, the Draco. It is best to allow the Draco to speak first. They converse telepathically. You can respond with speech. Please keep the conversation businesslike and to the point. The worker beings we refer to as the Caste. They cannot speak and are controlled by the Draco."

Schumann listened intently as Gallagher versed them on the entities that inhabited the area they were about to enter; only these were not behind toughened glass, but roamed around freely. He could see the unsettled look on the face of von Getz; Clare Logan did not appear too thrilled either. After what Schumann had recently witnessed there was no telling what they were letting themselves in for.

Gallagher continued.

"They usually keep their distance for the most part, but if you sense them becoming a threat, they cannot cope with nonsensical dialogue and will usually back off. They see us as inferior and of little threat, although no weapons are allowed in the sector ahead." Gallagher started the car. "Everyone good to go? ... Sir?"

He looked at Schumann, who remembered he was in charge. He steadied himself. "Yes, thank you, Mr Gallagher, please proceed."

Gallagher nodded, pulling away with Clunes following behind with the others.

They drove along the centre of the right-hand tunnel, bypassing the area that housed the monstrosities Hebb had so proudly shown him the day before. The cars passed the point where Schumann had witnessed the strange altercation, marked by one of the motifs on the tunnel floor. The walls of the tunnel were the usual shiny petrified rock produced by the boring machine process, the road with a central broken line to identify the lanes stretching ahead as far as the eye could see.

Schumann possessed a great deal of experience on underground environments, but he had never encountered any strange inhabitants on his explorations. He felt a mix of extreme apprehension and curiosity, the scientist in him barely able to contain his excitement, but also tinged with an instinct which told him the whole thing was a very bad idea.

Gallagher caught his eye as they sped along the tunnel.

"There is another entity that we may encounter: the Greys. They can reach a height of seven feet. They are not to be trusted, and work closely with the Draco. They converse in the same way, telepathically. Again, keep it simple and businesslike."

"Anyone else that we should know about?" Schumann enquired.

"Not that I know about. Some pretty impressive sights, though; you will see for yourself soon enough." Gallagher seemed to relax somewhat.

"No cameras or listening devices here. We should be okay before we encounter the Draco and the others."

Schumann could hear the officious tone leave Gallagher's voice, and now realised it was only to appease whoever might have been listening in.

Then came the revelation.

"I will put my cards firmly on the table, sir. We are part of a small group operating in the base with Cale and Sagen. Professor Logan is a recent addition to our ranks."

She nodded in acknowledgement. Schumann was relieved that they were all now clear about where their allegiances lay.

"So, tell me," addressing his question to Gallagher, "what is the intention of the Draco and the others?"

"Honestly? We do not know for sure. What we can ascertain, though, is that the fragile alliance has been forged between the two parties for quite some time, possibly fifty years in the making."

Schumann was intrigued. It appeared, from what he had already surmised, that most of the Terran population had no idea what was going on at these underground bases. Gallagher continued.

"It would appear that the Draco are using any means possible to acquire as much magnetic power from the planet's resources as they can. Almost all their technology involves magnetic field factoring."

Schumann was careful not to let his facial expression reveal anything. Inside, though, he found the news very disturbing. Due to his own expertise in this area, it was no coincidence that he was heading this mission and had such a large free reign in what was such a high security zone. It made perfect sense, now that he had access and powers that most Terrans could only dream about.

"So, what do the other side get in return?" the Swabian enquired.

"The top bods are very secretive about what the deal is, but we have discovered that some of that technology is passed over. We think the leaps in computer, medical, weaponry, avionics and, of course, science-based advances have all stemmed from deals made with the Draco."

Schumann expelled breath heavily, raising his eyebrows. "And all of that you think is in return for magnetic resources."

"No, that's just a part of it. Then it gets much worse." Gallagher was not one to drag out the detail and came straight to the point. "All those humans you saw in the tanks, alive and dead, including children? All the body parts? The whole project is overseen by the Draco." Gallagher kept his voice as steady as he could, but was clearly very emotional. "The authorities turn a blind eye to it, to the victims regularly abducted by the Draco, thousands of them, to end up down here to be experimented on."

"And they create those monsters in there with them?" Schumann gestured towards the direction of the labs with his head.

"Well, not exactly. The knowledge is passed on by the Draco to Hebb and his cronies. They are human creations. The Draco are only interested in the way that humans function."

Schumann was shocked. "Surely this would never be allowed in this day and age."

"It's not." Gallagher went on. "All these experiments are super-secret, only known to a handful of people and funded by the black budget, connected to an organisation called MJ-12 that operates independently from government. Most of the people here have no idea who they are really working for.

"You can imagine how much revenue MJ-12 can generate from what information the Draco give them. They use some of the abductees as live guinea pigs to find cures for serious disease, then charge extortionate amounts for the pharmaceuticals. Imagine how much they have made from microchips alone. The list goes on: missiles, aircraft sales worldwide, all the amazing advances that we now take for granted, all in such a short space of time, can be traced back to these underground bases."

Schumann breathed deeply. His head was spinning. This information was terrifying enough for a Terran, but for a Swabian like himself, sheltered from all of this unspeakable evil, from a world so removed from this utter madness, it was hard not to erupt into a blind panic.

How could Vessels and the others have been so reckless as to jeopardise their whole nation's existence? No amount of power was worth this. He would tear them apart with his bare hands for what they had done.

And when he thought about what they had done to him personally – one of their own, a loyal servant who had never questioned orders – to be betrayed in such a way tore his insides to pieces. He sat on his hands to disguise the fact they were shaking so much.

"But just who is in charge down here? That is very unclear to me."

"And to us, sir." Gallagher shook his head. "There have been many incidents between the two sides, a lot of casualties. Arguments are frequent, tensions high all the time, even occasional exchanges of fire."

"And that is tolerated?" Schumann found the whole thing farcical.

"It is seen as an occupational hazard. The Draco are given what they need in the lower levels, the military control the upper decks. Down here, the motifs on the ground designate the boundaries, but they are often breached by both sides. We regularly negotiate the release of curious workforce members." Gallagher wore a look of despair. "Things are getting pretty desperate down here. One time the Draco and the Greys killed a load of scientists. They had to send in special forces. They lost sixty men in a firefight; the others sustained many casualties too … and, yes, they can die just like us. Took a long time to calm things down after that."

"Seems to me this uneasy alliance needs to end right now," Schumann said.

"I agree entirely," Gallagher acknowledged. "We are certain even some of MJ-12 wanted the exact same thing to happen; not to push their luck, so to speak. They are dealing with something they know nothing about. They are not certain of the motives of the Draco, if they have their own hidden agenda, or if they, in turn, work for some greater power. What is certain is they are not to be trusted at all, none of them whatsoever. They are highly analytical and technology orientated. They are reckless with their experiments without empathy for other living creatures.

"They are interested in our emotions as they have none of their own; no guilt, sorrow, happiness, nothing at all. So you can imagine how unpredictable they can be."

"So what has been decided between the two sides?"

"No one can tell at this point," Gallagher said bitterly. "All we do know is that there is a big visit being planned in the near future, a lot of important investors coming to see what their money has paid for. There are plans to extend the base further, and to increase the shuttle network, linking up more of the cities. The plans all point to a move to take over the regular government. With the underground network, they can operate without being seen. We know MJ-12 have operatives in prominent positions, ready to strike at a moment's notice."

Schumann noticed the walls change to a more natural finish, and start to widen.

Clare Logan had remained largely silent for the journey,

taking in the information dealt out by Gallagher. It was clear from her reactions that the revelations were also new to her. It was her first time in the lower caverns, the area not being in her remit.

"How many Draco are there?" she asked.

"No one's really sure," Gallagher replied. "But it's in the thousands for sure; a carefully maintained population level, I believe."

"And how long have they been on the Earth?"

"That's the weird thing. Both the Draco and the Greys have revealed that they are native to this planet. They have inhabited the natural cave systems for at least 500 years, before we blasted the base out. Of course, we only have their word for that."

"True," Schumann said. "But fundamentally they are similar to us in many ways."

"Yes, the physical similarities are there in parts although, like I said, they have no emotions, so will operate on a far more efficient thought plane."

Clare added her own expertise. "Everything that lives is the same at the most basic level, animal into plant, fish into animal, for instance. We are all made of the same twenty amino acids, but this merging is not precise, and you do not know what you are going to create when you do this. You have to let something grow and then decide what to do next time. The great fear is creating something that would wipe out the human race. Mistakes will eventually happen, you can be sure of it."

"That's why Hebb has so many variants in the tanks, looking for that ultimate species," Gallagher uttered.

"What about the Caste? Tell me more about them."

Gallagher shrugged. "They are a cloned product created by the Greys for doing everyday mundane tasks. They will respond when approached, but they report directly to the Draco, so be careful what you say. Some of them assist in the labs. They are completely separate from the clumsy attempts as in Hebb's emulations."

"So Hebb does not have access to that level of knowledge?"

The big security officer shook his head vigorously. "No way the ETs would reveal too much about their technology. Just enough to get their own way, and to keep the upper hand, of course."

The ETs, as they referred to them at the base, were indeed very smart operators. He would have to steel himself like never before.

The two cars continued on a similar smooth surface of natural stone, the walls opening out all the time vanishing in places, replaced by darkness, natural columns now appearing in numerous groups. Although the light was now decidedly dimmer, there seemed to be a natural glow coming from the light stone canopy.

Schumann guessed they must have been about a half mile from the boundary, the natural elements taking on a more erratic layout, the honeycomb of tunnels a labyrinth of confusion. Which one to take? But Gallagher had been here before, pointing out the etched guidance markers so they could trace their way back. As they explored deeper each time, new markers were added to the route. They continued in a relatively narrow cavern section for another half mile, the roof above them, around a hundred feet high.

"Here we go," Gallagher uttered. "Better stick to official talk from now on. Remember the protocol and we should be okay."

The light improved again, the six of them arriving at a vast opening, the floor falling away ahead of them to a reddish array of rocky apertures rising from the depths like great plant stalks, lozenge-shaped terminals at the top, brightly illuminated.

Schumann could see movement in the shadows and immediately a craft appeared hovering above the human convoy. It was very much like the Swabian craft he was used to, but much smaller; far easier to handle in the caverns, he presumed.

The escort kept its distance as they progressed deeper, Schumann noticing that it bothered him a lot less than the others, probably as they were filled with awe at the advanced craft. For his part, though, it was nothing out of the ordinary. He would like to get a look at the interior, though.

"No need to be alarmed." Gallagher tried to sound matter of fact. "They appear quite often."

Schumann felt strangely relaxed, almost enjoying the sights, rock apertures becoming more artificial where they had been carved more purposefully, massive stalactites and stalagmites presenting a natural obstacle course around the smooth roadway, a lot of them glistening white as scattered beams of light struck them from all directions.

Gallagher brought the vehicle to a halt, the one behind doing the same, their escort still hovering at a measured distance. Gallagher climbed out, beckoning the others to follow. He led them through an opening and onto a naturally formed balcony. Schumann gasped.

Far below in a floating mist was a city, swirls parting occasionally revealing a mass of stone buildings, roadways with numerous vehicles, the upper level a hive of activity as numerous craft identical to their escort went about their business, weaving this way and that. A mass of lights shone from everywhere. Even the walls of the cavern, where yet more multi-layered buildings could be made out in a continuous populated mass, had been used to great effect.

"Some view, eh?" Gallagher swept a hand into the air. "Welcome to Dracoville."

"Never quite get used it," Clunes added. "All this you would never believe was possible."

Schumann knew that it was not so difficult but, nevertheless, from their vantage point, it was an impressive spectacle.

Gallagher led them back to the cars where they proceeded to descend into the mist, lights on full beam suddenly illuminating a group of Caste who paid them no attention.

Schumann realised that one of the figures in the argument he had witnessed was one of these beings. They were a curious sight, in identical light blue jumpsuits, their bodies very spindly, the heads the only skin part showing, a pale grey, the eyes large and shaped like lemons, black as coal, no nose, and the ears were little more than holes on the side of their oversized craniums, the mouth a motionless thin slit.

Schumann could see the look of wonder on the faces of von Getz and Clare Logan as the two cars pulled up alongside.

"They're harmless," Gallagher pointed out.

The Caste walked silently in single file. The two vehicles pulled away, leaving them behind rapidly, the rest of the descent completed in five minutes before the road levelled out once more.

"Okay, we're here, sir," Gallagher announced, parking outside a stone building. Clunes drew up alongside.

Clearly, he was to take the initiative and lead by example. His instructions from Hebb were to explore the caverns, but it was obvious that magnetics were high on the agenda. Schumann had an array of testing gear in his backpack that would enable him to judge how the Draco used the technology.

"We have to state our business here," Gallagher said as he walked through a doorway. Schumann followed, almost floored by a dreadful odour.

"That's them, not me," Gallagher said, trying to sound humorous.

On a wall in front of them was a large circular screen which suddenly came to life. The dark outlines of three figures appeared. The two at the front flanked the one behind who seemed to be their superior. Clearly, they did not deem it worthy to show themselves in person, the odour clear evidence that they could not be far away, though.

Schumann breathed in through his mouth, trying to bypass the stench.

"State your intent," the assumed leader demanded.

Gallagher replied in a mundane tone, and to the point. "We wish to explore the lower caverns."

"For what reason?" They could all hear the voice in their heads.

"To see what the formations are made from."

The Draco leader considered the reply for a few moments, consulting with the other two, then waved a dismissive three-fingered silhouetted hand, clearly not impressed.

"Very well." The Draco then turned and walked off as the screen went blank. Gallagher turned to the others, wafting the foul stench away with his hand.

"We should be okay to take a look around for a while, then we should get going."

Outside, more of the Caste appeared in groups, all of them identical, trudging along at the same speed. It was a pitiful sight, but Schumann was careful not to show any emotion. They made their way along what passed as the main avenue, observing and retaining what they saw should anything be of significance. As far as Schumann could make out, the technology the Draco possessed was kept well and truly out of sight. Occasionally the stench would reach their nostrils, and, as unpleasant as it was, Schumann knew that this was a weakness that could be exploited.

With their morbid fascination at their surroundings satisfied, they made their way back to the cars, aware of the limited time they had left.

This time, Gallagher drove the other group while Clunes took Schumann, von Getz and Clare Logan. The scout vehicle followed them to the outer limits of the settlement before turning back in the opposite direction.

Clunes carried on feeding information as they journeyed inwards, his British accent cutting over the drone of the car's electric motor. He had a cheery lilt to his high-pitched voice which Schumann took for bravado; probably his way of dealing with the intensity of their situation. Gallagher signalled to take a new tunnel, much smaller than the others.

"He's been meaning to explore down there for some time," Clunes informed them.

They entered the 'new' tunnel where Gallagher made markings on the wall. They did this every two hundred yards or so.

The tunnel gradually narrowed on them to little more than a car's width, the floor becoming uneven, until Schumann suddenly called a halt to the convoy. He signalled to cut the engines. He climbed out eyeing the tunnel wall up ahead on the left. Von Getz followed his line of sight, nodding in acknowledgement. The two Swabians led the small team of eight to a point where the wall recessed for about ten feet.

Gallagher looked around him and then at the wall. "So why have we stopped here, sir?"

"Look at the wall. See how it moves like waves in the sea; very subtle, but you can see it."

To the untrained eye it was just part of another natural tunnel system, but to Schumann, who was well versed in these matters, it was all too familiar.

"I don't see anything," Clunes announced.

"Me neither," Cale added.

"Sir, we really should …"

Gallagher was stopped in mid-sentence as Schumann plunged his hand through the wall, his arm disappearing up to the elbow.

The others jumped back, apart from von Getz who smiled for the first time in an age. "Cloaking section, and pretty good too."

Schumann removed his arm from the section. "It's a false wall, very high tech."

"Wait, you've seen this before?" Gallagher exclaimed.

"I have been trained to spot the signs, yes." That was a very modest assessment.

"Wow." Gallagher was gobsmacked. "I mean, I've heard of stealth anti-radar detection, but this …?"

"I too am surprised, even at this." Von Getz pointed to the wall, going along with the ruse.

"I'm going through."

"No, wait, sir. You don't know …"

Gallagher's words fell on deaf ears as Schumann's body sank into the wall before vanishing completely. The area around him shimmered and rippled like throwing a stone into water before settling back down again.

Once on the other side, he was greeted by an intense light as bright as the sun.

Instinctively he ducked down, rolling behind a large boulder. Peering around the corner, his eyes adjusting to the brightness, he could see a huge cavern expanse like the colony they had left a while before, only this was larger, much larger.

A long way below, he could see a city of enormous magnitude. There were craft buzzing around in the air just like last time, but in addition there were bigger models some fifty feet across; and on the ground literally thousands of Caste being directed by taller versions – the Greys, Schumann assumed – and also Draco in plain sight. Even from such a long distance, he could clearly make out their reptilian appearance, a humanoid body but with a lizard-shaped head, the tail of around four feet sweeping back and forth as they swaggered along the cavern floor in between the hundreds of multilayered buildings. Unlike the outpost, this place had a lot more architectural input with metals infused into the designs of some of the structures.

Over to the right, he could make out a large river that cut through the cavern, a hive of activity with numerous vessels going back and forth adding to the imagery of the Hadean nightmare spread out in front of him. He shuffled along for a few feet to a safer position and sank back through to the tunnel.

"Thank Christ. Are you okay?" Gallagher said, running over to him.

"You vanished through the wall," Clare looked alarmed.

"What did you see?" Clunes asked urgently.

"See for yourself." Schumann pushed him through, with von Getz doing the same with Gallagher. After a short time they were all together looking down on the colossal city. Gallagher was shaking his head in disbelief.

"We had no idea this place existed. Look at them all."

And they all looked at the hordes, Schumann trying to imagine what damage the Draco could do mobilising a mass assault.

Von Getz pointed out structures to the south of the city,

warehouses with large windows, hangar doors wide open taking delivery of supplies, large craft that hovered only a foot from the ground, smaller versions that cruised the stone roadways in vast numbers, Caste and Greys bustling in all directions, a few more Draco swaggering about.

Schumann examined the scene one last time before leading the others away, back through the wall.

On the other side he made a decision.

"Okay, that's enough for today. Let's get some distance from this area. That cloaked wall was put there for a reason. I don't want anyone to come through and spot us."

All the reasoning needed to rally the team.

They drove away at high speed, putting plenty of distance between them and the false wall, heading back to the outpost which they now knew was a cover for something far more substantial.

They decided to keep the discovery to themselves for now, for they could only guess what sort of allegiance Albert Hebb might have made with the Draco. Whatever it was, they would not inform him. Instead Schumann would fob him off with some jargon to massage his ego.

They passed the small colony without being challenged, seeing nothing but a few Caste heading towards the base for work detail. They paid them little attention this time, as was reciprocated. 'Once you had seen one you had seen them all' could not have been a more truthful statement.

Up ahead, Schumann spotted the outline of another small figure, although this one had a bit more purpose to their stride. The two cars soon drew up alongside the lone figure, who turned to face them.

"Good afternoon to you all," the diminutive figure said in a welcoming manner.

The figure turned out to be a child Schumann guessed was probably under the age of ten, very handsome, with large blue eyes and blond hair. There was something almost ethereal about him, a maturity beyond his years. But just what was he doing down here?

"Are you lost, little man?" von Getz asked him.

"Oh, no. Nice of you to ask after my well-being, but I know this area well." The youngster chuckled. "I have been assisting in the caverns."

He had supreme confidence and was obviously very intelligent. Schumann had to smile and was grateful for that respite alone.

"Would you like a lift?" he offered.

"Why, that would be much appreciated, sir."

"Please call me Hans."

"Okay, Hans, pleased to meet you. My name is Bek."

Bek climbed aboard with Schumann and his passengers. They continued towards the base with Bek chatting away excitedly about his day full of innocence, just as would be expected of a boy of his age. They were all quite taken with the charisma he oozed, and found his company most entertaining.

"Are there more like you, Bek?" Clare asked.

"There are a few, yes, but I think I am the best one," Bek announced proudly.

Schumann laughed and the others joined in.

"So you mean that you are the most intelligent?" Schumann said, still laughing.

"Oh no, I mean that I am the most advanced of my kind," Bek said, beaming.

All fell silent as the announcement was made.

Surely this was not an advanced Caste model. Please don't let it be that, Schumann hoped ... but the question had to be asked, if only not to cause alarm to their junior passenger.

"So you are the best, Bek, Can you elaborate?"

"Well, I would be happy to, Hans. You see, I am a hybrid, half human using alien DNA to produce a new superbeing, but we are a long way off perfecting this. I am the best version that they have created so far."

Schumann felt a new level of dread rising up inside him. He checked himself, though, knowing further questioning might be useful to him, making sure that his emotions did not unsettle the young boy.

"So how were you created, Bek? Do you know?"

Bek glanced down from the lanyard around Schumann's neck to the ID card, nodding as if recognising the high clearance level.

"My mother was abducted and brought to the base, where she was impregnated. After I was born, I was raised here to work and to aid with research."

Not a care in the world, Schumann observed, as if completely unaware of how wrong this all was.

"And your mother was quite happy to let this happen?"

"Oh, she did not know anything about it. They are very clever here and apply techniques that allow the recipient no emotional distress at all."

"So what is your objective?"

"I am afraid that is classified."

"What, even to me?" Schumann said, trying to persuade Bek.

"Even to you, Hans."

Schumann was puzzled by the sudden reluctance to comply, but he decided not to press the issue.

Bek entertained them for the rest of the journey with his outgoing personality. Schumann picked up on his perceptiveness; he seemed to have a heightened awareness of his surroundings, and of the human aura. They pulled up dockside and disembarked. Bek thanked them for the lift and made off in the direction of the labs.

Schumann felt a mix of intensity and exhilaration, and a change inside him that would challenge his sanity to the utmost. He had been exposed to a series of events that were difficult to deal with. He knew the others were coping as best they could with their own emotions. One thing was certain: the balance of power above and below ground was shifting continually. There was no stability that he could see, and no worthy victor.

They were suddenly aware of raised voices emanating from one of the other tunnels.

Schumann could make out a security detail arguing with two Greys. A group of Caste scuttled by, also in the direction of the labs. Bek, who was nearby, said nothing, but they seemed to respond when he looked in their direction. They met up and continued together. The argument in the tunnel seemed farcical, escalating into angry exchanges from the security men with responses coming by silent telepathy from the Greys.

"Something going on in one of the conference rooms," Sagen muttered.

"Better take a look," Clunes suggested, knowing the cameras were on them. They walked over purposefully in the direction of the fracas, Schumann and the team waiting by the cars.

There was a short, sharp whoosh that made the detail turn just in time to see the blackened windows light up for a brief second; then a scream and confusion ... and shouting in all directions.

"Get down," Sagen shouted as he rolled behind an extractor unit. The two Greys were advancing, the argument over, the security men they were with now lying on the floor, the smouldering aroma of burnt flesh exuding from their bodies.

Clunes picked up a service wrench, throwing it hard at one of the Greys. It was a great shot, hitting the being full in the face. Sagen managed to slide in and rip off the weapon strapped to the fallen Grey's torso. The whole area around him lit up as the other Grey touched his chest, sending a high intensity beam of energy into the other that lay stunned on the floor, still trying to recover from the heavy blow. The beam sent pieces of Grey matter all over the dock area, with the oversized head bouncing violently over to where the cars were parked, landing at the feet of Clare Logan, the lifeless eyes peering up at her, blood, almost black in colour, trailing behind across the floor back to where the remains of the body lay.

Sagen swivelled on his back, managing to lock his arms into firing position, the other Grey coming into view. He fired.

The Grey stopped in its tracks, a black gash appearing, the right shoulder and arm falling away from the rest of the body. Sagen fired again and blasted the stomach away, leaving a huge gaping hole behind. The Grey fell to the floor, lifeless.

"Fall back now," he commanded, running back, Clunes close behind.

From their position near the cars Schumann could see half a dozen more Greys emerge from the conference room, all with beam weapons. A man in a jumpsuit followed, staggering through the doorway, hugging the building as he made his escape.

"They're killing everyone," he shouted over the confusion.

Even though Schumann was focused into combat mode, he could still admire the efficiency of the Greys as they fanned out, their silent communication with each other very effective through all of the noise. The shouting from the 'suit' only served to attract them to his position, one of them peeling off from the unit and engaging his beam weapon. The interior of the 'suit's' head seemed to glow and its skull appear like a red x-ray before exploding, sending brain matter up the window above him, the headless corpse toppling onto the floor.

"Go, go, go," Sagen shouted, running for all his might, Clunes puffing behind.

Schumann noticed the Grey with the human kill now rounding on Sagen readying to turn his weapon on him. He leapt from cover, running directly at the Grey who was levelling the flash gun into position. The Grey turned his attention to the Swabian, who threw himself to the floor, sliding into the legs and, at the same time, pulling as hard as he could on the left arm, sending the being crashing to the floor with tremendous force. The flash gun discharged harmlessly in the air. Schumann grabbed the massive head in both hands, expertly snapping it sideways, breaking the neck.

Relieving his victim of its Armolux, he let go of the corpse and ran back in an arc, drawing any fire away from the main group. He felt the heat of a flash as it seared past his head, smashing into a main servo unit. He turned, dropping to his knees, both hands lowering the weapon, releasing a full power charge at another Grey perpetrator. The creature continued to run several paces before staggering and turning ninety degrees, now missing an arm, dark fluid pulsing from the wound. Schumann could see a spindly hand going for the weapon on its chest, and wasted no time firing again, taking the top half of the head away, before sprinting back towards the cars.

Cale jumped into one car, engaging the motor, with Schumann jumping into the other. The others all piled in with Sagen throwing himself in the back as they made off. Clunes jumped up too, straddling the tailgate only to receive a beam delivery firmly to the midriff, showering the other occupants with blood, tissue and bone as he disappeared from existence.

Von Getz grabbed the handrail as they sped off. "Where are the weapons kept?"

"Not near here," said Gallagher. "At the end of the sector. They're not permitted in this section by the Draco, unless …"

Sagen looked over the dock to the far side where Hebb had his offices, but there was no sign of life and no personnel about. If there was anyone over there, they were staying well out of sight.

"We'll have to try and make it to the checkpoint," Gallagher continued.

The two cars sped away, putting distance between them and the Greys. Sagen let off one more burst from the flash gun, hitting the lead Grey and almost cutting it in two, the others tumbling over in a heap as they ran into its lifeless body. It was all they needed to get out of range.

"What the hell happened back there?" Schumann shouted over the commotion.

"Looks like one of security wandered into the conference with a sidearm and must have forgotten to take it off. I spotted it on the floor near the doorway."

"All because of that?"

"I told you they were volatile bastards. Now you can see just how much," Sagen bellowed.

By now the emergency sirens were sounding, instructions coming over the tannoy.

'Please make your way to the upper levels in an orderly manner. Please go to Recreation and report to your team leader.'

The message repeated itself over and over as a heavily armed detail of thirty men raced by them towards the firefight, paying little attention to the exploration team. They passed more troops going to assist as they reached the checkpoint. Lockdown was engaged and they only just made it through before heavy steel doors started to seal off the sectors.

"Fuck, no." Sagen put his hands in his head. "Steve."

"Even if we wanted to go back and help, it's too late now," Cale spat angrily, looking over at what was left of his dead colleague. "God knows how many they've killed this time."

"Clunes was a good man," Gallagher added, patting Cale's shoulder. "But we need to get out of here now."

There were people running around in all directions, many clutching documents or peripherals, taking the objects with them to the upper levels. Level Seven was in meltdown. By now, there were so many bodies in the way, all scrambling to get to the exits, that the team had no choice but to continue on foot.

"Wait," von Getz suddenly commanded. They all turned to him. "The surveillance is out on this level. The Greys must have damaged the system in the firefight. We could use this situation to our advantage."

"Okay, what's your plan?" said Gallagher, looking confused.

"Just trust me on this, it is very important. We have to get this man out of here and we could do it now." Von Getz took the name tag and ID from Schumann and put them onto the remains of Clunes. With most of the body mutilated it would be difficult to identify him without witnesses.

"That's all well and good, but you will never get out of the upper levels," Cale said.

"Let us take care of that. We have to try."

Even Schumann himself was not sure about this escape plan, but there was no time to argue. They filed through the workforce, electing to take the emergency stairwell that would be activated to be able to cope with the enormous evacuating numbers.

As they climbed the stark grey stairwell sections, Schumann spoke to von Getz in a low voice. "Getting out of here is one thing, but what then? I'm from Neuschwabenland. I've got no idea where to go."

Von Getz considered this as they climbed. "You need to take someone along."

"But who?" Schumann hissed.

"I'll go with you," Clare Logan announced quietly. "Sorry, couldn't help overhearing."

"You sure? There'll be no going back."

"After what I've seen, try and stop me."

"She does know the area, sir. Makes sense," von Getz reasoned.

Schumann didn't have time to dwell on the offer. They were nearly up to Level Six. From this point on, they would have to keep their faces hidden.

They made the slow climb pinned in like sardines, Schumann with a baseball cap pulled down over his eyes, Clare a little way back doing the same, careful not to look up to the left where all the cameras were located.

In truth, they could have pulled rank and taken the lifts the rest of the way, but there would have been the high risk of recognition, so the ascent to the upper levels was a long and arduous climb. Once there, it was easier than expected to remain hidden as scores of personnel hurried along the corridors, too busy to notice them until they reached Recreation, bypassing it with ease, the noise of a manic roll call being implemented; a timely distraction.

"So what now?" Clare asked, trying to get her breath back.

"The air duct on Level One." Von Getz turned to Schumann. "Make your way up to the outer limits, to where the breach is in the cave."

It might work. At least when they emerged, it would be out of sight and beyond the motion detectors, but could they find the breach?

"What about you, Kaufmann and Weisse?" asked Schumann.

"Don't worry about us. With you and Professor Logan here as fatalities, no one will be looking for you. We will report back home and you will be given a burial with full honours."

"Be careful, my friend, and watch your back with Vessels."

"Don't worry, we can handle him. I'll drop a FESS pack for you to pick up, then await your emergency Evac signal."

"Okay, I'll wait for midday a week from now."

"Got it." Von Getz looked at the two of them. "I guess this is it. Better get going before someone sees you." He wore a grim smile as he shook hands with them both. "Good luck, sir, madam." He gave Clare a curt nod.

"You too." Schumann turned, with Clare close by, merging with the confusion in the long corridor. They were gone in an instant. Von Getz stood rooted to the spot for some time, staring through the faces in the crowded corridor, already wondering what would happen when he returned home without his commander. He felt the hand of Gallagher on his shoulder.

"Your friend pulled some pretty good moves back there. That looked like high-level combat training to me. Not what you would expect from a scientist."

"Some of our research is very important. You need to be able to look after yourself."

"And I suppose that includes acute observational skills?"

He knew what Gallagher was getting at: the ability to detect the false tunnel section, and his own assessment of the non-operational surveillance cameras.

"We are trained to be keen observers; it's a German trait." Von Getz smiled. His eyes were still fixed on the corridor.

Gallagher eyed him for quite some time before speaking.

"Just who the hell are you?"

"Nobody important. Just a couple of German scientists."

Gallagher laughed but said no more.

———⋄———

Back on Level Seven, the special ops team had regained control of the area. Albert Hebb was walking slowly across the dock side with the ops commander.

"Current status, if you would."

"Seven ETs, twenty-six civilians from the conference centre, four security, one of my own men and two scientists … all dead."

"Gott im Himmel." Hebb turned to face the OC. "Do you have their names yet?"

The OC looked down at his clipboard. "Mmmm, let me see. Ah yes, here we are. One female, Clare Logan, and a Hans Schumann."

Hebb nodded looking at the ground, hands behind his back, his cheeks reddening with rage. "Are you sure?"

"Body of Schumann is over there, or what's left of it, with the ID. Witness saw Professor Logan take a direct hit from an Armolux charge. Nothing left of her."

"That is most unfortunate. Two of my top researchers." Hebb was beside himself.

"I'd better make a final sweep, sir."

The OC made to depart, leaving Hebb to seethe. "Oh, Captain," he shouted after him. "You know what to put in your report."

The OC knew full well what his superior meant: classified mission in the Middle East. Tragic accident.

"I'll be sure to inform the families, sir."

Hebb was dressed in his favourite khakis, jackboots gleaming, steering them carefully around the cleaning team as they mopped the floors clean of blood and gore.

It was important to restore order as quickly as possible. He had to keep a lid on what had just happened. So much was riding on the impending visit, and he was determined there would be no more incidents on his watch. It was not an option to make him look incapable of justifying a position he had only recently secured.

He was taking no more chances, assigning his own detail to shadow him at all times. He had additional troops posted permanently at strategic positions. He didn't really care about the Draco protesting. Undoubtedly, they would object to the weapons limit extension. Probably the best way forward for the time being was to cut the interaction down to a minimum so as to reduce the risk of another incident.

They had tried exhaustive measures to reason with the Draco; it would benefit both sides to work together. But the Draco worked on their own terms, their methods totally irrational; one day they could be very laid back and co-operative, another day, very hostile and difficult. The latest plan by Hebb to find out more about them had resulted in the death of his best asset. This put him in a very awkward position with the MJ-12 board, and the new alliance forged with New Swabia. He would debrief the surviving members of the exploratory team. Maybe von Getz would have some new findings that would help take the heat off him.

Putting the deaths aside for a moment, it appeared that very little structurally had been affected. That at least meant that work would be able to commence long before the planned visit. Right now, he wanted the name of the guard detail that failed to spot the sidearm enter the restricted zone. Examples had to be made. His neck was on the line and that meant someone would end up as dinner for the ETs.

Chapter 32

Dulce, New Mexico

The base was still in confusion as Clare Logan led Schumann into Level One. She knew where the ducting system was. Progress along the corridors was slow, teams of scientists, military and admin alike all trying to get to their respective assembly points with their salvaged work details.

They used the crowds to good effect, Logan eventually signalling that they were at the service hatch. She loosened the panel and began to climb in. Schumann bent down, shielding her from view until she was out of sight, then waited for the right moment until no one was looking in their direction and swung himself through the hatch, fixing the panel back into place.

Inside, they climbed several rungs before the duct altered by ninety degrees to run along the ceiling. They had to lie down and progress by crawling along the middle of the duct. Clare headed the way using a small spotlight from her backpack.

For a while, they could hear the commotion in the corridors below; hundreds of voices that gradually faded away, an indication that they were heading in the right direction to the outer limits of the base. After about an hour, the duct began to curve, Clare informing him that they had reached the boundary perimeter.

The breach was a lot easier to detect than expected, the sudden chill entering the stifling humidity of the shaft. She pointed the light above her head at the damaged area convexed and twisted.

They were able to sit up, Schumann moving the boulder in the cave out of the way. He climbed upwards, helping Logan out of the duct. He then put the boulder back, taking a few minutes to pile more obstructions on top just to be absolutely safe.

They both waited for darkness before venturing from the cave mouth, Logan with a compass directing them north into the harsh ground, the night sky above them, clear and full of stars. It was a wonderful sight, a first from Schumann's perspective, but he was also acutely aware of the plummeting temperature. Logan seemed to read his mind.

"We'll get some distance between us and the base, then find somewhere to hole up for the night. It's going to get a lot colder."

They broke into a jog. Their own body heat would help them cope until they found shelter, Schumann using a handheld detector to avoid the surveillance devices. They could see the lights of patrol vehicles in the distance, but none came close enough to cause concern.

They covered another two miles before stopping at an abandoned truck. The canvas canopy over the flatbed had long since rotted away, but the cabin shell was intact, glass still in place. Schumann forced one of the rusted doors open and climbed in, sweeping a pen light around. It was dry.

Logan got the backpacks in place. They had no sleeping bags or coats, just jackets worn for the caverns. The desert boots would keep their feet insulated to a degree; but that was it, and they dare not light a fire so near to the base. Schumann pushed with his hand on the rear seat through the covering, quickly opening a pocket knife, cutting the seam open. He felt inside; it was foam filling. Working around the seat, he opened up the interior, then by carefully cutting a cross section, he made a large flap into the foam. He continued until it was big enough to get a shivering Clare Logan inside, whereby he tucked her in to insulate her body. She made a pillow from her belongings. He did the same with the passenger seat in the front, careful again with his work, fighting off the cold until he had the foam strapped over the top of him, weighed down with his own backpack. After a while, he felt the cold subside. It was surprisingly effective, their body heat slowly returning to normality.

"You okay?" Schumann asked over his shoulder.

"Yeah, I am; it's fine now." She had stopped trembling. "Got any ideas?"

"Head in a direct northerly route from here and rendezvous with the FESS pack that von Getz will leave us. Then it's your call."

"Great. No pressure, then."

"Not very good on American geography, I'm afraid. Is there anyone that can help us?"

No answer came. Logan was asleep.

Chapter 33

Cambridgeshire

Derek Mills sauntered down the pea shingle driveway to his post box that was built into the wall near the main gates. He unlocked the back and fished out the contents. Only one item; a parcel marked from the United States.

He frowned as he walked back to the house, tearing open the brown paper covering. He did not even make it to the front door before shouting to Martha for his car keys.

Mills made the short drive to the manor house, bursting in without bothering to knock. Hector Valerian was busy poring over research documents when he heard the commotion in the hallway. He ran through the house finding his colleague almost speechless, holding out a tattered notebook.

"Get the others here at once," he gasped.

Chapter 34

London

Claude Perfekt had just returned from his monthly meeting at MJ-12 Europe headquarters, conveniently situated at the Old Fellows building in Westminster.

A very interesting meeting it had turned out to be: another skirmish at the Dulce base, quite a number of casualties, far too many for comfort, including two scientists, one a German by the name of Hans Schumann. They would have to inform the facility in Bavaria of his passing, and they in turn could inform the family. Cause of death was put down to a shark attack while visiting the Gulf of Mexico. With a few minor alterations, this would suffice given that the body was missing the head, an arm, and part of the torso. Terrible things, these attacks; they could occur when you least expected them. As for the other scientist, a female called Clare Logan, well, they could put her with him, still missing, the coastguard still searching for any sign of her.

And now for Hebb, the head of the New Mexico facilities. True, he had been a faithful and loyal servant to the cause. He would keep an eye on his progress. They did not want any more incidents, that was for sure, particularly because of the imminent visit that they would be attending.

Perfekt looked out over Battersea Park, a glass of Veuve

Clicquot in hand, stroking the hair of his favourite waitress. The smile had never left her face since he slipped the gold and diamond rope bracelet on her wrist. He had picked the item up from Grays Antique Centre on the way home; thought she deserved it.

Perfekt much preferred to graze through the staff pastures rather than saddle himself with a permanent partner. That could become problematic with too many questions asked. No, this was a far more interesting way to fill up the social calendar.

Rosanna was twenty-five, and like the others thought that she was the only romantic interest in his life. Her purpose was to look after things when he was away. He could trust her to arrange cleaning and keep the place in order. The same could be said for Luciana, his personal assistant, but her role was purely administrative. He had never been intimate with her, although the occasional libidinous thought had strayed into his mind as he frequently liaised with her. Sometimes it was just too easy. He knew Luciana liked him and that was no challenge, unlike Rosanna who had taken him five months to lure into the apartment.

Life was good in England, just as the United States had been for his equals. He had always declined the opportunity to take the presidency. That was a role better suited to Heinz Kessler, Perfekt favouring, as always, to operate from the periphery of attention. With the generous black funding that he enjoyed, he could fly over whenever needed.

He was scheduled to see his close friend soon enough, in Washington, for a most important meeting before leaving for Denver airport, where they would transfer for Dulce.

Chapter 35

Dulce, New Mexico

The sun broke over the horizon just enough to cast a glint on the windscreen of the abandoned W-series truck; enough to stir Schumann from his sleep. He shook Logan awake in the back. She stretched and sat up, freeing herself from her foam cocoon bed. Although it was still early, the sun was coming up fast, and it was imperative to escape from the hornet's nest of interconnecting bases that they resided in. From what Logan had told him, they were at the top of New Mexico, about centre left of the base network that stretched further left through Utah, Arizona and Nevada, even onto as far as Western California.

For the time being, they would have to head north over the border into Colorado to enable them to intercept the FESS pack that von Getz would hopefully drop ahead of them. The bases were always situated in the most off-grid positions, placing the two of them in the harshest of environments.

It would be hard going on foot and would take too long; they would never survive the blistering heat for long. They had no time to obtain food and water as they fled the base. What they had would soon be gone.

They decided to move off before the temperature rose out of control. Schumann straightened out the cab, disguising any sign that they had been there, closing the door with a firm push.

He jumped down off the step to ground level, giving the truck a respectful pat. Logan took a compass reading and they headed off direct north over nearby rocks, careful not to leave footprints near the truck. They kept this tactic up for about a mile before daring to drop onto the dusty earth, moving steadily but not so fast as to expel too much energy.

"So, Professor, where are two dead people going to go now?" Schumann's question had a serious meaning to it.

Logan had been thinking about that. If they did seek out an ally, the chances of being found out were high; too many questions for a start.

Their only real chance of survival and anonymity was to seek out the very organisation the others had spoken of at the Dulce. Sagen had revealed coordinates to all the group, a place of sanctuary controlled by the sympathisers. Right now, it was their best shot.

"We head for New Jersey, and please, it's Clare, remember?"

"Okay, Clare, what's in New Jersey?"

"People who can help us," she said, desperate to be right.

They walked on for several more miles, their destination the area of Las Animas, Colorado. By keeping on a heading between Trinidad and Springfield, this would eventually bring them onto Highway 13 in the direction of Yuto, where they should be in position at the drop-off point.

The terrain was uneven and hard going, the temperature rising steadily by the minute. The only sign of human activity was a light aircraft which buzzed over them ahead at a safe distance. There was a natural beauty to the ruggedness of the countryside that Schumann appreciated. For him, it was like being stranded on another planet, curiosity aiding him to deal with the concern for their safety.

Their options seemed to be minimal. Even with his vague

grasp of their current geographical position, he knew that New Jersey was a mighty long way from here. They needed to get out of their combats as soon as possible, and get hold of some transport, and blend in. It would be another night without supplies before the drop. It would be wise to find shelter and wait it out. Whatever the outcome, they had to survive for a week before he could send out the pickup signal for exfil and then he had to hope von Getz could find an excuse to leave New Swabia.

They heard a rushing noise just over the brow of the hill ridge, getting louder all the time, and then the drop-off down to rapids of a river, coming into view as they peered over.

They carefully picked their way down the side of the ridge, descending sideways for several minutes before arriving at the river's edge. The temperature here was significantly lower, aided by the shade of the trees and vegetation. Clare knelt down, pushing her face under the water, letting the coldness into her body, hands sweeping back her hair as she surfaced. She filled up two water bottles, while Schumann drank directly from the river, the relief incredible. They both sat back, staring at the lava-capped uplands in the distance, regaining their strength.

"I've been meaning to ask you," said Clare. "Where is Neuschwabenland?"

Schumann remembered, as they were escaping the lower levels of the base, he had blurted it out to von Getz: very careless of him. In all the turmoil of what had happened, he had let his guard down.

"It's an old nickname for an area of Bavaria." Which was not actually a lie.

"Oh, I see. Is there anyone back there who could help us?"

Schumann thought for a moment. There was an installation

there that dealt with intelligence and covert operations, but they reported back to the homeland, and that would mean Vessels would get to hear that he was still alive. It would be best for the time being to remain deceased.

"No, it would not be safe to go to Germany."

"Guess we'll just have to try and make it east then," Logan sighed.

Schumann looked at her as she gazed into the distance.

"How did you get mixed up in all of this?"

"The promise of unlimited funding and access to advanced technology. I suppose curiosity got the better of me," she replied grimly. "How could I have been so naive?"

She turned to him. "What about you? How did you get assigned to the base?"

Schumann pouted, throwing his hands apart. "Money, I suppose. I mean, my company were approached due to my knowledge of sonics and magnetics." Which was again not entirely untrue. "None of us had any idea what was going on down there."

"I wish there was something we could do to put an end to the experiments," Logan sighed again.

Schumann had no solution to that. He was in a world where he could barely function, in the middle of nowhere and without supplies. He would have to rely on basic reasoning until an opportunity presented itself.

"Right," she said, "now we need to look after ourselves and get to your rendezvous point. Come on."

He stood up, dusting himself down. "We should get moving."

The duo collected their few belongings, Logan once again leading in a northerly direction.

Progress became slower, the relentless heat becoming too

strong, before long forcing them to seek shelter. Luckily, Logan spotted a shallow cave which offered respite, the natural overhang offering sanctuary from the sun's aggressive rays. They gathered a healthy supply of brush and firewood, working hard in readiness to stave off the drastic drop in night temperature. Keeping a fire going throughout the night was a priority; they were miles from the base now; plus, the cave would serve to mask the flames in the darkness.

When the night finally came upon them, they took shifts of two hours each until daybreak offered enough natural heat to break through, allowing the fire to die out of its own accord.

They set off at a steady jog, making the most of the early morning conditions, the terrain reasonably flat. Schumann had tried the tracker a couple of times without success, too early to expect anything yet perhaps, but it broke the monotony.

Their spirits were raised, though, as they found the main road, buoyed even more by the fact that a truck came by a few minutes later. Schumann noticed it had an old-fashioned look, the loud engine noise informing him that they were still using fossil fuels as it came to a halt beside them. Once inside, Logan gave the driver a tale that they were part of a National Guard unit making their way into Colorado on exercise. In truth, the driver was not the inquisitive type, just pleased to have company.

"Don't see many folks out this way. Pretty remote round these parts," he said through a wheezy drawl accentuated by too many cigarettes. "There's a gas station and diner 'bout twenty miles up. Stop there and get breakfast."

Schumann nodded, enjoying the climate-controlled air on his face, realising how long it had been since they had last eaten. "Sounds good," he replied in his best American accent.

"Be good to recharge the batteries before linking up with

the unit," Logan said.

"How long you guys out there for?" the driver asked casually.

"Just for a few days," she said in a non-committal fashion.

"Not got too many supplies there with you." He pointed at their rather empty-looking knapsacks.

"Part of the training. It's all we are allowed until rendezvous point."

"So you might be bending the rules taking a lift from me, then?"

"A bit, maybe, but we won't be having anything but water at the diner to keep within the rules."

"Well, up to you. I won't say nothin'." He cackled. "Me, I'm gonna have myself a mother of a pile of pancakes, bacon, eggs an' all. Yeehaah."

They all laughed, Schumann guessing that Logan had got them out of an awkward spot. They had no money.

The truck left the road, pulling into a designated compound, the tyres sending plumes of dust into the air. They said their thanks to the driver, whose name turned out to be Hank.

"Sure you folks don't want to join me?"

"Better not, Hank. We're going to freshen up a bit. Enjoy the pancakes."

"I surely will. Take it easy now." He locked up and headed for the sizeable diner. The gas station was next door, also serving as a mini-mart. The whole place was alive with activity, plenty of vehicles parked out front in neat rows.

Schumann kept out of sight while Logan used the restrooms, staying in the shadows until she reappeared looking re-energised. "Your turn." She smiled brightly. For a while, the world seemed just a little more inviting.

He found the restroom and proceeded to refill the water

bottles. He washed his face and hands then filled a sink, submerging his head, rubbing water through his hair. It felt wonderful.

Logan was milling around the car park at the rear where it was much quieter. She did not want to get into any difficult conversations.

A patrol car crawled by a rusty pickup she was using to shield herself behind, the officers giving it the once-over, the driver almost stopping. The two men exchanged words, the passenger pointing in Clare's direction. She ducked down behind the rear wing, the radio in the patrol car crackling to life. There was a lingering look from the lawmen before they headed back onto the highway, making off at high speed, their priorities re-directed. She watched from around the rear fender, making sure the car was well into the distance before straightening up. She breathed a sigh of relief, stretching her legs.

"Well, what have we got here?" a gruff voice announced from the direction of the diner.

She turned to discover two men, one spitting heavily into the dirt then sidling up to her. The other who had spoken blocked her exit, trapping her between him and the truck.

He was big, about six-four, reeking of stale sweat, his unkempt beard with all manner of food stuck in it. He removed a tatty cowboy hat that sat awkwardly on his moon-faced head, smoothing his greasy hair with his hand before replacing the hat. The other man looked around anxiously, alerting Clare that she was in trouble.

"Lost, are you, little missy?"

"No, just waiting for my boyfriend," she replied as calmly as possible.

"Whatcha doin near our truck? Not planning on stealing it,

were you?" The other man leered.

The big man laughed. "Naw, she's a lady. You can see that. Real pretty," he said as he grabbed her by the upper arms. "Now we all gonna take a little ride together," he hissed, his mouth an inch from hers, oozing its foul breath, almost causing her to choke. He had her pinned against the pickup, his partner's scouting eyes making sure no one was around.

"Get in the truck. Any trouble and I'll introduce you to my little friend here." His glance indicated a large hunting knife strapped to his belt.

She had no choice but to obey, the passenger door opening with a noisy creak.

"Get the rope from the back there, Deke," he said. "Deke, hurry up now; we gotta go."

Deke did as he was told, putting chewing tobacco into the front pocket of his grubby overalls, fishing a coil of tow rope from the clutter-strewn rear.

Almost immediately, Deke jerked upwards in a sudden motion, landing heavily, his head smashing into the rusted bodywork. There was a crack and a slight yelp as he felt his back give way.

"Deke, what are you doing back there? Hurry up now, dammit." The big man was getting impatient. He couldn't wait to get his hands on his prize.

"Listen, my boyfriend will be back soon," said Logan, "and he will kick your ass."

The big man laughed. "Are you kidding me? Nice try, lady, but I'll take my chances. Deke, dammit, give me that rope." He shouted now, overcome with excitement.

The rope appeared at the window dangling from the roof, the big man grabbing the end with a feverish excitement.

Schumann dropped the other man's body to the ground,

cartwheeling over the trailer, landing neatly in front of the big man, at the same time kicking the door into his side. The big man grunted and staggered back out, walking straight into a tyre lever that caught him square on the side of the head sending his stupid hat spinning into the dust. He shook his head, sneering.

"That all you got, huh?"

Schumann was surprised, but never complacent. He easily avoided the lunge, sidestepping the big man's blow as it met thin air, ducking down, whipping the knife from his belt. He rolled forward sending his hand locking up in an arc as it hit the top of the back, the knife finding its target. The man grunted, staggering around trying to reach the handle protruding from his body.

"I'm gonna kill you, and then I'm gonna kill her …"

Schumann swung the tyre lever again, this time finding the nose, smashing it to a pulp, sending the victim spinning away but still standing. The next blow caught the handle of the knife, sending it crashing through the sternum, the point now visible at the front from his chest. Another similar blow and a gaping hole appeared, blood spurting in all directions, the big man managing to expel a gurgling gasp before falling over the tailgate. Clare retched at the carnage as Schumann grabbed the big man's legs, tipping him into the back. He ran around the other side of the truck, hauling Deke's corpse onto its feet before tumbling it over to join his dead colleague. He kicked the dust with his boots, covering up any blood on the ground.

He fumbled in the pockets of both men, finding a set of keys. They had to fit. "Here, you drive," he commanded as he threw the tyre lever in the back, and jumped in the passenger seat. "We need to get these bodies out of here right now."

Clare obeyed without question, turning the ignition,

crunching the gears until she found first, the truck spinning wildly before she eased off the throttle, trying to calm her senses.

They headed up the highway, Schumann looking back. No one had seen what had happened. Logan did her best with the truck, her knuckles white as they gripped the wheel, her whole body shaking.

"Are you alright? Did they hurt you?" Schumann asked.

"Oh, I'm just fine, thanks." She was trying not to cry.

"I had to eradicate them. They were going to hurt you."

"Eradicate them? What are you, the goddam Terminator?"

Schumann was unsure how to respond. Who was the Terminator? He would not risk asking the question, but it was clear he had fallen foul once more of his poor choice of words to match the situation.

"It was unfortunate but necessary," was all he said by way of reply.

They drove in silence for a few miles before turning off the highway onto a dirt track. They could see a deep valley to their left; a river flowed angrily far below, probably the same one they'd seen the day before, he guessed. At any other time, he would have thought the sight spectacular.

Schumann could see that Logan was in shock and eyeing him with suspicion. Maybe he scared her. He hoped that was not true.

He knew that they could not risk being pulled over with the vehicle in case they were caught out by the authorities, so his idea of abandoning the truck seemed like a logical option. He tried to help Clare out of the pickup; she brushed his help aside, heading over to a large boulder where she sat staring into space.

Schumann left her to her own thoughts, busying himself

with the two bodies. He hauled them out, prising the hunting knife from the big man's body, returning it to the sheath on his belt, positioning him in the passenger seat. He hoisted Deke behind the steering wheel, then doused them with a can of petrol from the back. He doused the rest of the truck before releasing the handbrake. The truck was on a downward slope about twenty yards from the edge, just enough for the truck to pick up enough speed. Schumann pushed on the tailgate to aid in the delivery.

The truck rumbled down the track, crashing through bushes and scrub before pitching over the side. It was a long way down, at least fifty feet. The prolonged silence hung in the air for an age before the kaboom of impact, the whole truck becoming a colossal fireball, plumes of smoke rising up into the air, the two occupants incinerated.

"We'd better get going; catch the rendezvous point," Schumann said, eyeing the burning wreck.

Clare nodded warily, donning her backpack and following behind as Schumann led her back to an area near the highway where they could cross the river and continue north. They walked out of sight of the traffic for several miles, saying little before the Swabian tried the tracker again. He switched on the device, the screen black and motionless, searching for a reading. Then a dull ping. LOCATION IDENTIFIED, followed by coordinates.

"He did it." Schumann turned to her.

"What, von Getz, you mean?" she said brightening slightly.

"Yes, he made the DOP up ahead, about a mile away." He punched the air triumphantly. "Well done, Klaus," he said out loud.

They found the drop-off point in amongst some trees, the FESS pack resting neatly in a clearing with a handwritten note.

'Awaiting signal, good luck, Klaus'.

Schumann started checking the contents. He sensed Logan's closeness.

"I suppose I should thank you for rescuing me," she said shakily.

"I am only sorry you had to witness that."

Clare looked at him closely. "Where did you learn to do that? You took those guys out like they were nothing."

"I was enraged that they were going to harm you. I had to act fast."

Clare looked at him for a while longer but then dropped the subject, far from convinced.

Schumann continued examining the contents. There was a number of electronic gadgets fixed to a utility belt, a hunting knife and some food rations. He delved in further, discovering two sleeping bags, coats and light clothing. It appeared that von Getz had attempted to accommodate Logan's size, as there were also some smaller garments, including leisure shoes. It was still military issue, but a lot less conspicuous than their current attire.

He checked the side pockets, packed with useful items including six thousand American dollars. Von Getz had stripped the craft of all the survival supplies, including the last item. He had to smile as he opened the packet, offering Logan some of the contents.

"Here, try one of these."

She took the object as she watched Schumann munching away, a big grin on his face.

Logan was too hungry to ask questions. It tasted like a chewy hotdog, cold but not unpleasant. She devoured the bratwurst in no time.

"I see you approve of German cuisine," he tried. "Got some

more here if you want."

She had three more before she came up for air, sitting back against a tree, a look of mighty relief on her face.

"God, I never felt so ravenous," she sighed.

Schumann finished the last one, feeling energised by the protein, and it gave him a big confidence boost having the FESS pack in his possession. Now they had options.

"My God, look at all that cash. Your friend rob a bank or something?" Logan said suddenly, spying the wads.

"We owe von Getz a great deal," was all he replied.

Schumann gathered up the supplies, donning the new backpack. They had changed into their new clothes, Logan fashioning a pair of shorts out of one of the pairs of trousers. With shirt sleeves rolled up and the fish tail knotted at the front, she looked every inch the hiker on vacation.

Her demeanour had softened towards Schumann, although she was still suspicious of him; he could tell that much. He was trying to cope with this new and very large surface world, rather like a man who had just been marooned on another planet. It was bad enough having to continually think of the right thing to say, but the few Terran situations he had already experienced had left him more confused than ever.

Why would those two men back at the diner want to attack Clare Logan in that way? It was true that he had reacted very aggressively towards them, ending in the worst way possible for Deke and his friend. But to even conceive of that behaviour in New Swabia was illogical. So was Logan's reaction. She obviously thought that he had gone too far.

Maybe she had a point. It was not a pleasurable feeling taking someone's life, but his training offered him only one outcome. They could not leave them alive to talk; that was the way he saw it. He had eliminated the threat and had saved her from a terrible fate. Perhaps he would have to accept that he might never understand the surface world.

"We'd better get going; get as far away from here as we can."

They hiked along the highway, avoiding human contact as traffic passed infrequently in the distance. After an hour, they came across a patch of woodland and a large slab of rock that would serve well for base camp.

As dusk descended upon them, Logan started to gather firewood.

"No need for a fire." Schumann took a device from the utility belt, signalling Logan to sit near him. She did so reluctantly, looking confused once more.

"Listen, we're going to get cold out here in the open, even with these …"

There was a faint hum as the device activated, enclosing the pair in a transparent bubble.

Logan frowned heavily, as she gingerly touched one of the sides. It had a warm pleasant glow, yet she could see through it perfectly. Her scientific brain kicked in.

"This is … it's remarkable." Her voice filled with emotion. She could feel her cheeks glowing as the temperature rose.

"I can alter the temperature."

"No, it's fine," she gasped. "Okay, Mr Schumann, I want some answers now."

"I will try to help."

"Let's start with the FESS pack. What does that mean?"

Schumann looked her in the eye, realising that he could not deceive her. He would just have to be careful.

"It is short for Fully Equipped Survival System."

"The sort of thing a scientist would have at his disposal?" Logan arched her eyebrows.

"We have one in the jet; it's part of the itinerary."

"Okay, I could buy that part, but this?" She pointed to the transparent bubble. "What is it?" She was exasperated.

Schumann could not talk this down so he tried another tack.

"Back home, we have made some amazing advances in DPM survival technology, incorporating magnetics." Logan was listening. "We have to be careful that this technology does not fall into the wrong hands. As you have recently witnessed, the results could be disastrous."

"So how does this thing work?" she marvelled, turning her attention back to the shelter.

Schumann explained the jargon to her: the shield emanating from a device in the corner no bigger than a phone, incorporating cloaking technology, soundwaves and air. This was the disruptive pattern material used to create a very sophisticated science that even Logan had trouble keeping up with. The shield also insulated the occupants, but was at the same time breathable.

He explained a few finer points to the design, then felt Logan's head slump onto his shoulder. She was asleep.

Schumann nodded to himself. Perhaps he had stumbled on a cure for insomnia, his own voice, but then realised how shattered he was himself, the intense hiking over, the uneven terrain taking its toll on their bodies.

They awoke to the sound of rain tumbling in a surreal manner all around them. Logan watched, mesmerised, smiling with wonder. She had never seen anything quite like it, the ground surrounding them bone dry and in a perfect square.

For Schumann, he had never been exposed to the rain. The closest he had come was flying through storms in disc craft. There were no storms in New Swabia, ever.

"Better wait it out," Logan said, her voice slightly raised.

He used the time to programme their position into another device, an ordnance satellite navigation system that could pre-warn them of what lay ahead in extreme detail. He put in the coordinates for New Jersey. The readout showed it was over two thousand miles from their position and would take thirty hours to get there.

That was in a vehicle.

He could hear the rain ease off, time to remedy their transport situation.

They walked along the deserted highway for several miles, watching the sun come up, the heat reacting with the sodden ground, creating steam through the long grass. The road had dried out by the time they arrived at a small town called Jansen on the outskirts of Trinidad.

They started the day at a diner, Schumann on high alert after what had happened at the last one. Logan had spotted a car lot further down the road.

By the time they had finished breakfast, the owner was opening the shutters of his showroom.

Schumann eyed the gleaming cars with schoolboy admiration. A convertible BMW M6, all in black; that would do nicely.

Logan had to smile as she pulled him away. "A little out of our range, I think."

He realised that he had no concept of value here, and he would have to learn fast.

She led him across the lot to a neat diagonal row of parked vehicles. She patted the hood of an old Jeep Renegade, probably the last vehicle he would have selected.

"Can do you a good price, mam," the owner hollered over. He hobbled towards them with the aid of a walking stick. "Low miles for the year; these things were built to last. Won't let you down." He puffed. "Name's Lenny, Lenny Masters as the sign says." He pointed over his shoulder.

Schumann was amazed at the variation of regional accents, this particular Terran having a thick southern drawl. The man was short and portly, greying hair thinning on top, a neat moustache parked under a broad nose.

"Take two thousand for it?" Logan asked casually.

"I'll take two four if it's cash," he said more evenly.

"Two two, and you've got a deal," she said, looking him straight in the eye.

Schumann watched in fascination as the bargaining played out. It seemed you could negotiate your own price.

"Hell, alright. You got my day off to a good start. You got yourself a deal, lady." They shook hands and went inside to do the paperwork. "That's a fine Jeep, mam. Knew the old owner personally. He had it from new."

"So he upgraded, then?" she said, smiling.

"Well, that's the darnest thing ever. Cory (that was his name), he just went and vanished one day, never came home. That was over a year ago. I'm selling the Jeep for his wife. She ain't got no use for it now."

"He just disappeared? No trace at all?' Logan enquired.

"Not the only one either. Been several over the years. Some say it's just people moving on to Denver and such, on account of us being off the beaten track, so to speak. But I knew Cory for many years. Completely out of character. Didn't have a worry in the world. Worshipped his wife and his two kids."

Schumann looked at Logan uneasily. He could guess where they may have ended up.

"Right. That's it. Ma'am. Here's the keys," said Lenny.

They followed Highway 25 for two hours before exiting, then headed for the eastern Colorado border. The roads were becoming busier. Schumann enjoyed the antiquated mode of transport; it was certainly better than walking, and meant that they could now stock up with a lot more supplies.

They decided to use some of the cash to pay for a motel room, Logan craving a proper bed for the night. It would mean that she could also charge a burner phone that she had purchased.

The Harrison was on the main drag and would suit their needs perfectly, laid out in the usual practical style. It made sense to Schumann to have the vehicles parked outside their respective rooms. He surveyed the area. Not too much to see, a gas station across the road, a liquor store beside it. He took in the night air as Logan checked them in. It was a moment for him to reflect on recent events.

Here he was in a very vulnerable situation with only Logan for company, whom he relied upon heavily. He thought about the two men he had killed, how he took their lives as if it was a regular occurrence, the act made slightly easier by knowing that they meant harm to his companion. He surprised himself at how little guilt he felt, instead taking comfort in the fact that his military training had surely saved Logan from a terrible fate.

He was staring up at the stars in the clear night sky as she appeared with the room key.

Inside, the room was basic but clean. The fixtures and appliances had seen a few presidential changes, but were all in working order.

Logan was the first to commandeer the shower room, leaving Schumann to browse the TV channels. He settled for a news channel that was in the middle of an article concerning weather warnings for the east coast of America. A series of bad storms was responsible for minor damage around South

Carolina. He watched, fascinated by the devastation in the footage that the film crew had captured. It reminded him of how the natural elements could be so very destructive on the surface world. Back in New Swabia there was no bad weather.

Logan emerged from the shower room in a bath robe, opening drawers until she found the hairdryer. Schumann smiled as he was robbed of the television volume by the deafening sound of the ancient technology. The Terran world was like a living museum to him, witnessing, as he was, a catalogue of things playing out in real time that had been obsolete in New Swabia for many years. He could relate to what Hebb and the others had accomplished back in 1985 going forward in time by forty years. For Schumann, it was like going back the same distance, both men being catapulted into strange new worlds.

He thought about Hebb a lot, and who had been behind the origins of their machine. The fact that the technology was not available now, let alone at the end of the Second World War, intrigued him. What else did they know? he wondered. And what had his superior, Vessels, revealed to the Terrans already? Hopefully not too much. Whatever the case, he knew that Albert Hebb was mad and would stop at nothing to release the horrors of the lower levels of the Dulce base onto the Terran surface world.

Based upon what Clare Logan had told him, the Illuminati-backed organisation had been in existence for over a thousand years, evolving from a secret, deeply religious arm of the church into a corporate superpower, hell-bent on overthrowing other governments. Schumann knew that it all came down to power in the end, a lust that had vanished decades ago in his homeland ... until now.

Something had driven Vessels and his henchmen to strive for the same goal. He knew this could only end one way, though, and that was badly for all of the citizens of New Swabia. The pressure was on to find an answer to their desperate predicament, every second of his time on Terra a test of his mental strength.

He had to break down the puzzle into stages and try to persuade Logan's contacts to help them. It could be his only hope to stop his homeland being devastated. At the same time, the threat from the Draco and that from Hebb was a concern that could end with the destruction of the whole planet.

Chapter 36

Dulce, New Mexico

Albert Hebb was pleased with the repairs to the Level Seven dock area. He strutted past the laboratories and conference rooms, hands behind his back, nodding his approval. The head of his personal security detail came smartly over, stamping his boots together, followed by a crisp salute.

"Ah, Rascher, what did the DNA tests reveal?" he said with disinterest.

The tall figure of Rascher stilled himself before delivering the news. "Sir, the results show that the remains of the body identified as Hans Schumann ... they are ..."

"Well, spit it out, man, I haven't got all day." Hebb's voice raised an octave.

"The remains match that of a Steven Clunes. He was on our database. There can be no doubt ..."

"And he was part of the exploratory team, was he not?"

"Yes, sir, he was one of the security detail."

"One of General Holt's men?"

"Yes, sir, I believe so."

"I see." Hebb went quiet, nodding for a few moments, his left hand shaking as he removed the small round pair of spectacles he was wearing. He folded them up and put them into his pocket, his face reddening all the time. Rascher waited nervously to take the brunt of the inevitable volley. He knew his superior well.

"I want to see all of the CCTV footage when the evacuation took place," Hebb shouted. "And I want you to get hold of General Holt at once, code red."

Rascher knew not to object to the demands. It was not an exaggeration that questioning his orders could result in what the personnel had termed as tanking: ending up in the experimental labs. The code red priority would spell out in no uncertain terms the gravity of the situation.

"I will inform him at once, sir." Rascher clicked his heels, spun around and marched off to find General Holt.

Hebb watched Rascher board an electric car, the driver taking him in the direction of the lifts. He eyed them until they were out of sight.

He remained rooted to the spot for some time, digesting the bewildering facts.

So it was likely that Hans Schumann was still alive. Why else would someone put his ID on Clunes body? Furthermore, he must have had help to escape.

But just who were his accomplices?

Hebb made his way up to Level Three, a rare ascent in the Dulce base. He preferred to leave the mundane tasks to others, but on this occasion, it was a task that he must oversee himself.

He met General Holt in the surveillance hub, and wasted no time telling him what he thought of his upper level security measures. Holt, of course, had objected, citing unique circumstances, the confusion of the evacuation creating the perfect diversion should someone choose to escape unnoticed.

Hebb weighed up all the facts. He would go easy on Holt, but only because it suited him to do so. He could always change his mind, have him mysteriously vaporised without a trace, just like some of the others in recent times. He was a high ranking office with connections; it would not be so easy to explain. Holt was of some use, at least for the time being.

They were looking at the evacuation footage very carefully, painstakingly going through slow motion frames one by one. Hebb could see how someone could have reached the upper levels undetected. All the security checks had been abandoned due to the massive volume of people trying to get out of the lower areas.

He observed the shift of personnel making their way slowly up the staircases. Most would look up occasionally, some out of habit, others glancing at the bulletin boards to see if there were any notifications posted up that would update them. He looked on in silence, Holt doing the same, neither really sure what they were looking for.

Hebb's eyes were drawn to a couple, standard issue peaked caps pulled down low just like many around them, only these two had not looked up once, not at all.

He found their behaviour strange so stuck with their progress as they climbed upwards. Another level, and still they did not look up at all. On to Level Three, and an endless series of video frames looked over, then one of them looked up just for a second as the crowd around them thinned momentarily. He clicked on the face and brought it up magnified by twenty.

The face belonged to a woman, but a face that was also supposed to belong to the dead: that of Professor Logan. There she was climbing the stairs, very much alive. That made him concentrate on the other figure travelling close to her.

It was not until Level Two that he finally caught sight of his face. There he was, turning to say farewell to persons out of camera shot, but unmistakably Hans Schumann.

He worked the camera footage with Holt assisting, the two

of them tracing their targets through the hordes of people. It was hard to track them even with all of the cutting edge technology at their disposal. Hebb checked the footage a few times away from the population build-up. That was where he lost them. Holt could not find them either. They switched to the motion sensor placements, calling on anomalies that may have occurred in the base's outer limits, but still nothing. This scientist was very good, somehow managing to get out of the base without detection, for the sensors proved that he and his companion, Clare Logan, were not on the upper levels.

"So what now?" Holt asked.

Hebb just looked at the monitor screens for a while, thinking. They had to move fast.

"Send up the drones ... all of them."

The smart drones were the latest advancement to come out of the Dulce base. With the knowledge given over by the Draco, they were able to develop a network to cover most of America, with sensory zones that could send up vast numbers of stealth drones, armed with onboard computers, that would have enough information on the two fugitives in question to be able to pick them out on the ground and send back their exact position to the base. They could then send agents in to deal with them.

The Draco did have their uses, although their hostility was surely trying his patience.

And Hebb did not like to be made a fool of.

Having two people escape the base was unthinkable. The knowledge that they possessed must not fall into the wrong hands. He could not be sure who their allies were, but based upon what he had seen Schumann already achieve on the base, he could not afford to take chances. They had to be eliminated.

Chapter 37

Eastern Colorado Border

"I can't believe, in this day and age, that you don't drive," she said over the noise of the Jeep's engine.

"It's one of those things I never got around to doing."

Schumann had stopped short of telling her that he was only qualified to operate mag cars. In truth, the petrol vehicle was quite easy to master, but he had no ID or licence. If the police pulled them over, it would be difficult to explain that he did not exist. Just as well that Logan kept her personal details on her at all times at the base. She would have to do all of the driving, which would mean stopping more often to let her rest.

They had the roof down in the Jeep making the humidity of the afternoon bearable. Logan seemed reasonably at ease with the situation, keeping to a steady fifty miles an hour. They had made good progress, and could see rivers to the left and right of the highway, the city of Lawrence coming into view up ahead.

As they entered the outskirts of the college town, they spotted another motel, and elected to spend another night of comparative luxury. They were about a third of the way to New Jersey and, as far as he knew, they were not being followed. It looked like they would be okay so long as they avoided any trouble.

Chapter 38

Dulce, New Mexico

Hebb was now back on Level Seven, overseeing other essential duties. He had the ARF drones up in the air, the control room carefully monitoring them all, supervised by Holt. He had better find them, should he value his life at all. Hebb eyed the tanks in front of him, concluding that Holt would be on the other side of the glass should he fail.

The creature Hebb called Otto came into view, leering at him through the green murky fluid in the tank, tentacles flailing, sporting the mad look that Hebb found so appealing.

He inspected the new magnetic lock on the tank's hatch before walking further along to watch a team of engineers as they performed the upgrade. At least he had secured that information from Schumann before his escape. Maybe he would spare his life; tranquillize him when they tracked him down. As for Logan, she would be executed in front of him, whatever the outcome.

He walked into the section with the dry tanks, walking slowly along the compartments until he came to a whimpering human individual. Hebb knew who he was. They made it a point of getting personal information soon after kidnapping.

"What's the matter there, Cory, are you hungry?" he sneered as he threw a hunk of bread. The object hit the half-naked man's side, making him recoil. He was no real exception. Even the strongest of wills soon succumbed to him after a short time. One look at some of the wonderful creations in the other tanks soon had them cowering before him. What a pathetic sight Cory was, and not much use to the breeding programme. He was too frail, but would suffice as a body part donor. Hebb liked having him around so had delayed his fate, preferring to humiliate and torment his subject. It made him feel good about himself.

Satisfied that the upgrades were on schedule, he prowled around the dock area for a while putting the fear of God up everyone before heading off to Level Three.

In the control room, General Holt was feeling the pressure, frantically getting his crew to scan the respective towns and cities, starting with Dulce and broadening the search as the results returned negative. The trouble was, the states were vast, some of them bigger than countries, there was a lot of ground to cover, and there was no way of telling in which direction the pair was headed.

They had two hundred drones in the air backed up by dozens of agents positioned all over the country, able to respond to a sighting. Holt could not be faulted for effort. But that would go unrecognised if he did not produce some results.

Chapter 39

Kansas

It was just after five in the morning and the Jeep Renegade propelled its two occupants through Kansas City, affectionately known as KCK to differentiate it from the city of the same name in Missouri. Even at this time of the morning, the heat from the sun's rays were strong and the temperature would exceed ninety later in the day. The hot climate in the area was notorious for colliding with the cold air from the Rockies up north, and could result in some spectacular tornados and storms. Thankfully, the weather today seemed pretty stable.

Schumann marvelled at the size of the waking city, taking in the Terran architecture that seemed far more impressive on the ground than from the sky. They took great advantage of the fact that the streets were quite empty, Logan keen to get to their destination as soon as possible.

By the time rush hour occurred, they were far from the city, continuing on Highway 70 through the forested hills and rolling prairies where the Ozark Mountains transformed into plains and savannah, the landscape of rugged limestone rising up from the numerous angry creeks that surrounded the Midwestern college town of Columbia.

Logan took a side road into the Rock Bridge Memorial State Park. She parked the Jeep near a glade where she proceeded to cook breakfast in a purpose-built barbecue area. Schumann was impressed with her culinary skills, the aromas reaching him quite irresistible as he took in the view from a nearby bench.

There was a noise in the undergrowth, some twigs snapping, the sound of foliage being parted. Schumann wheeled, tense, ready to respond to any danger. He watched the bushes move, hand moving for a sidearm as the head of a white-tailed deer appeared before him.

He laughed to himself as the animal came into full view no more than ten yards away from him. Logan turned to see the deer wander off. She smiled at the sight, a moment of normality, and in those few forgotten seconds they were just like a couple out for the day, taking in the sights. She watched Schumann, who had a child-like fascination for the simplest things. A ladybird landed on his arm; he showed an intense enthusiasm for the creature. The woodland area was alive with the sound of activity, chirping, shrieking and buzzing all around them as they ate. At times, the noise was surprisingly loud from the après-dawn chorus, Schumann taking in the sights and the smells of al fresco dining. An Eastern grey squirrel broke cover running up one of the mighty oak trees. It reminded him of a rat with a big tail, followed by two cotton tail rabbits chasing each other through the undergrowth.

He watched it all unfold, leaving him more confused as to why the Terrans would want to embark on their path of destruction. Why risk their fragile ecosystem? They did not know how fortunate they were.

Chapter 40

Dulce, New Mexico

Hebb returned to Level Seven from the control room a very frustrated man. It was early days, that much was true, but his desire to locate the two targets was top priority. He could tell Holt was under intense pressure, but then that came with the job. He would give him a while longer to prove himself. He decided to take his mind off the matter by inspecting some of the laboratories.

He amused himself by taunting Cory once more before moving on to the abduction labs. The first seven rooms had women abductees in them, all terrified. Luckily, the rooms were soundproofed so he was spared the screaming. The science teams worked their expertise, extracting what they needed, then the abductees were processed into categories of reproduction, research, or recycling. The last three labs had no subjects in them, just human staff and a few Caste working on various duties. He could see down one of the tunnels, a long way in the distance, one of the Draco conversing with a couple of Greys. Even from this position, he could make out the look of disdain on the face of the reptilian. Hostility between the groups was still very evident.

Hebb suddenly realised how far away he had strayed from the security of the brown shirts. The Draco, seeming to sense this, turned to face him full on, revealing an amulet around its neck, an amber-coloured mineral glowing brightly in the gloom of the tunnel. Hebb backed off, walking briskly along the side of the labs, signalling for an electric car. Once on board, he was taken back to the safety of his launch and the offices across the underwater lake. He told himself these inspections would have to be carried out more formally from now on.

―――※―――

The four of them had seen Hebb pass the window. Bek could sense the danger pass, his mind processing the various levels of information available to him. Two scientists prepared him for the 'visit' as he conveyed to the one they called Enoch that the leader of the Draco had been identified. Enoch duly noted this, along with some security information, before getting to the task in hand.

Bek could hear the female voice as plain as day and yet there was no one else in the room. "Mother is here," he announced.

The conversation started with terms of endearment from Caroline, Bek reciprocating before the subject turned to more serious matters.

Enoch opened the channelling.

"Leader of Draco identified; has been seen in the dock area ... another skirmish, civilians killed, German scientist and Professor Logan have escaped the base and are on their way to rendezvous point ... the base commanders are trying to track them down ... it is vital that they are not captured."

The chanelling ended. Bek looked up at him, smiling. "Try not to worry, Enoch, we will prevail."

The man patted the blond head of the little boy. Really it was his duty to reassure others, but Bek was exceptionally advanced for his age. It was equally essential that they got him out of the base to safety.

The dialogue continued with Bek and Enoch sending out as much information as possible. The unique channelling ability would help the information reach the right people. Enoch still withheld a lot of intel from Bek for his own protection, just in case the Draco became suspicious. Likewise, some of the rebels did not know of his involvement. He would keep the protocol the same until the time was right. At least his contacts would be kept as safe as possible in this way.

They were relying heavily on the Germans, too, desperate that Schumann and Logan would reach the safety of Paramus. Their intel was invaluable.

The hostility between the Draco and the humans was getting worse. They could not allow either party to gain control. But how long would it be before the next conflict?

Chapter 41

Cambridgeshire

Marius backed away from his patient, giving her room to recover. The dialogue was more perplexing than ever, and he could tell by Mills' expression as he looked at H that this was getting out of hand. The base was now in danger of becoming lawless, with many innocent lives being caught in the crossfire.

Mills picked up a phone, securing a safe line before informing their forward operations base in the USA of the new information. H was organising flights, sending out signals to various sleeper units to get ready for an assault. The question was, how were they going to get near the base to enact the plan?

Marius was on one of the Adam sofas when Mills came over and sat beside him.

"I won't bugger about with small talk, my friend." He sighed heavily. "We would like you to join us and help bring an end to all of this."

"What do you want me to do?" Marius asked.

"Well, it's a non-combatant role, of course, along with Sidney and Helen if they are also in agreement." He tapped the notebook that Schumann had posted to him. "Look, we've all seen the contents of this book. There is no point in excluding the rest of you now. You know as much as we do about the Dulce base, and it is terrifying." He looked at Marius squarely, his face grim. "It is no exaggeration that if MJ-12 are allowed to continue, they could take over the USA and ultimately wipe us out."

The others had all gathered round listening intently. Mills continued.

"There are creations on that base that must stay there. They must be eliminated at all costs, and with the information we now have we just have to work out a strategy and an MOE to infiltrate the base. Trust me, we have the personnel. We only need to say the word."

H was now off the phone. "I will lead the assault myself. I leave for the States tonight."

"But what use are we?" Marius asked. "We're not soldiers."

Mills said, "I too have no military training, but can be of use running the war room."

"War room?" Marius looked at Mills in disbelief. "Just who is this organisation?"

It was a fair question, and warranted an explanation.

"Okay. We are part of an organisation known as the Lords Of The Black Stone or, to give it its real name, Die Herren Vom Schwarzen Stein."

Marius had not heard of it, although it was attached to something he was much more familiar with.

"The society was formed in 1220 by a Templar knight called Hubertus Koch, who created a foothold in Germany, their base being built in the Untersberg mountain where they created temples and galleries. The highly principled Teuton movement grew over the years, even gaining knowledge of long forgotten powers. These practices and knowledge have been passed down over the centuries, the movement dedicating itself to combat the evil that we now see around us in the world today."

Mills paused, letting Marius and the others take in all that had been revealed to them, and continued.

"Our main adversary that has existed alongside our own society for many centuries is the Illuminati. I'm sure you have heard of them." Marius nodded. "Their American sector, MJ-12, are the board members that run the order. They have become extremely powerful since entering into this alliance with the dwellers of the caverns of Dulce, but at the same time are gambling with the existence of the human race. They are prepared to take these risks in return for the technology that is given to them, but we know that knowledge will not be for the benefit of humanity, but will profit the few and leave the rest of us vulnerable."

Marius took it all in. "Go on," he encouraged.

"Well, now is our chance to strike and destroy the base."

"You really think you can do that?"

"We will never have a better opportunity. Think about it. We have inside intelligence on the layout, and we have knowledge of the visit to the base that will put the top delegates of the Illuminati all in one place. It is too good an opportunity to pass up. This could devastate them, even wipe them out altogether."

Marius could see why they were so keen to act. "So what would our role be?" he enquired.

"Help me run the war room. You can continue working with Caroline, too. Her information will give us real-time intelligence through Bek as to what is going on inside the base. It could make a real difference to us."

The whole thing seemed insane to him: secret armies fighting with each other for hundreds of years. It was yet another layer of absurdity. But it was real. It could not be anything else.

Marius exhaled heavily. Sidney and Helen looked at him in acknowledgement.

"Okay. We're in."

Chapter 42

Indiana

They sped along Highway 70 with the roof up, the sun at this point of the day just too hot to tolerate. Logan looked at the OS satnav on the dashboard.

"There's a gas station just up ahead. I need the restroom."

Schumann nodded as he stretched in his seat.

They had crossed the border some four hours back, and were now in the state of Indiana, about twenty miles out from the manufacturing town of Terre Haute. Logan parked up at the pumps, leaving Schumann to gas the car as she strode across the forecourt to the restrooms. The canopy over his head gave welcome shade as he worked out how to fill up the tank.

Logan, out in the open, broke into a jog to get under cover, but it was still enough time for an assessment to be made of her from the sky above. It was only an instant, but enough for the drone to reference the onboard data, relayed from the base, on her height, facial structure and photographic recognition. The drone pilot shouted to the team leader that he had a possible match. He banked the drone around, careful not to go too close. He did not want to spook them. The drone hovered just below a tree line of ferns on the other side of the road and waited for Logan to emerge from the building. The pilot did not have to move from cover as he trained the camera and zoomed in on the door just as she emerged. The drone was able to process more recognitional points to confirm the target was positive, one hundred percent.

The control room became a hive of activity as the team leader informed mission command of the find.

At the Dulce base, Hebb ordered agents to intercept on the ground. They had three units that could be there in half an hour.

Logan wandered into the gas station. She picked up a few snacks and, looking out of the window, saw that Schumann had finished with the fuel. She paid her bill, emerging outside under the pump overhang and climbed into the jeep.

"Drone fourteen, do you have visual?" came the harsh voice from base Net.

The drone remained in position, unable to find its target.

"No visual. The place is full of people and vehicles; canopy obscuring view."

"Drone fourteen, can you move in closer?' came the voice again, more impatiently.

"That's a negative. Electrical wires around the building. Will have to wait for visual."

The oblivious Clare Logan had to weave the Jeep through the packed forecourt, filtering behind a white Mustang and a silver Dodge Intrepid. It took a while to pull out on to the highway, the traffic quite busy in both directions. Eventually, they were once again heading along the highway.

The pilot jumped as the voice barked through his coms. "Drone fourteen, do you have visual?"

"Command, there are cars everywhere. Could not see occupants clearly. Am heading northeast on Highway 70 suspecting non foxtrot. Have deployed other drones southwest. Request more drone cover."

Hebb seethed at base command. At least they had a confirmed sighting, that was very fortunate, but he did not want them to slip through the net now. 'Non foxtrot' told him that they were not on foot, which he suspected due to the distance that they had managed to cover already.

So, they had a vehicle. Very resourceful.

He deployed more drones to cover all the roadways in the area. "Drone fourteen, keep on your northeast heading." He tapped his thighs with his fists nervously. He knew that once they reached the built up areas, it would become difficult to find them.

———⟫•◆•⟪———

Schumann checked their progress. Not long before they reached Terre Haute.

He could already see the Wabash River to the east. Logan had found a local radio station, WXXR, specialising in rock and alternative music. He found it quite bizarre, but did not protest. More objectionable were the endless interruptions from advertisements. One they seemed to keep repeating had silent gaps during its one-minute duration. He sighed at the repetition as the advert came on once more but, during the lull in noise, he detected something familiar. It was the same buzzing he had heard in the national park earlier, only this time much louder. He glanced out of the window up at the sky, spotting the black outline of a large drone. He started to pay more careful attention after he spotted another to the west.

They were following the road.

Schumann leaned over to the back seat, fumbling inside the

FESS pack until he extracted a pair of red lens field glasses. Clare glanced at him as she drove.

"What the hell are those?"

"They're called rangefinders, self-focussing digital binoculars."

"Another of your company inventions?" she laughed. Schumann laughed as well, casually.

He put the glasses to his eyes and zoomed in on the drone. It was about six feet long and shaped like a stealth craft to disguise it as much as possible. He could clearly make out the cameras fitted on the undercarriage, and also, more alarmingly, an RPG flanked by two machine guns. The other craft checked out the same.

As they rounded the bend, up ahead he saw the nose of a black Lincoln Navigator parked up a track. He knocked both their sun visors down to obscure their faces.

"Hey, what …?" Logan stopped. The look on Schumann's face told her not to question him.

"Put this on." He handed her a baseball cap and pulled his own peak down low. The tinted side windows would help shield them as they passed by.

Yes, there was no doubt someone was looking for them, Hebb must know they were alive. He had to think fast.

They passed the Lincoln feigning laughter; it was the last thing the assailants would expect. Schumann checked the rearview mirror. The car did not move out of position.

They came to a canopy of woodland, the sky blocked out for a few hundred yards, the drones having to climb above the treeline, unable to follow. They seized the opportunity. He instructed Logan to floor the accelerator.

When they emerged from the canopy, the two drones had fallen behind. She eased off the gas, bringing the jeep down to regular speed once more. Schumann trained the glasses on the drones for some time; they seemed preoccupied with other vehicles on the highway.

"Maybe you're getting paranoid," Logan suggested.

"You don't believe that, do you?"

"Well, we don't seem to be attracting an interest," she added hopefully.

Schumann had the glasses trained on the highway behind them, examining all the vehicles in turn: Ford pickup, Nissan SUV, an eighteen-wheeler, Isuzu Trooper, and then a black Lincoln … the Lincoln. They were being hunted alright, the vehicle about a half mile back closing fast.

He spied a side road a short distance up ahead. "Pull in there, quick," he ordered.

Logan obeyed without question, sending a cloud of dried earth into the air as the tyres hit loose ground. The Jeep came to a sliding halt with Schumann simultaneously grabbing the FESS pack once more. He fished out another device and switched it on.

There was a humming sound as the item powered up, settling into a quiet purr. Schumann punched in some instructions. There was a whizzing sound, the screen on the device reading DPI ACTIVATED in large red lettering.

The stream of traffic passed them by, including the Lincoln. Schumann clocked the driver, male, short hair, tanned, military type, wearing a black suit. His gaze did not deviate.

A gap in the traffic enabled them to re-enter the highway. They could see the Lincoln with the drones flying abreast, some ten cars up ahead.

"Be careful to keep your distance from the car in front. We are now fully cloaked."

Logan frowned. "What the hell does that mean?"

"No one can see us."

Logan cast him a glance. "You have got to be kidding me?"

"I would not joke with you at this moment in time."

Logan looked stunned at first, but then her expression darkened.

"Another technological advance that your company has made, I suppose?"

"Yes, we are fortunate …"

"Look, cut the crap, Hans, okay, I've had enough of this." She had to brake as a car nearly hit them side on. "What the hell? … Open your eyes, hammerhead."

"They can't see you. I told you to keep your distance," Schumann tried to say quietly.

Logan was losing patience. "Look, I've seen some pretty weird things recently, but that is just impossible. You seem to forget I am a scientist too. I know that technology just does not exist."

"The Lincoln passed right by us, Clare. They did not see a thing."

"But I can see you, all of this stuff in the car." Clare was getting upset.

"It's not that hard if you understand that we are not really invisible; it's an illusion."

She was not angry any more, but a little scared. Schumann picked up on this, realising that as much as the Terran world scared the hell out of him, his advanced equipment probably had the same effect on her. Because of her high-level clearance, there was not a lot that existed that she did not know about … until now.

"It works by reflecting the images around us back on themselves."

Logan digested the information, her expression revealing a

mind trying to comprehend the rationale.

"Okay, then, just suppose it could be possible, it distributes false images where our real location should be?"

"That's part of it, yes," Schumann said enthusiastically. "But the process is so effective because of managing air flows and light."

"But we are still here?"

"Oh, yes, in every physical sense, but we are in essence. Disruptive Pattern Imagery: camouflaged."

Logan mulled over the information for some time, then surprised Schumann with her acceptance.

"How the hell did you do it?"

"A lot of trial and error, and some brilliant minds." Which was true.

"Hans, this whole thing, the gadgets, your visits to the base, the way you dealt with the sonics, it's way ahead of anything I've seen. Who taught you all of this?"

"A large team of scientists have been collectively working on these devices for many years, but one man was instrumental in several breakthroughs. His name was Kammler; he was a great man," Schumann said without hesitation.

"I don't think I know the name," Logan replied.

"He was very under the radar, very secretive; only a few people were allowed to access his information. He was adamant that his findings should not fall into the wrong hands."

"Well, looks like he got his wish." Uttered with more than a hint of sarcasm. "So, this is only known to your organisation?"

"That is correct. This is super-secret and is unknown to Terran science." Schumann winced at the Freudian slip, but Logan seemed too preoccupied to notice.

"And we can stay cloaked for as long as we like?"

"Well, in theory, yes, but when we get near a built-up area, it will be too dangerous to travel in this mode."

Logan nodded. With vehicles everywhere, they were bound to be involved in a traffic accident.

Located seventy-five miles west of Indianapolis was the town of Terre Haute. With a population of over 60,000, they had no choice but to de-cloak in the suburbs. After snatching some supplies from a grocery store, they headed back out to the bluffs on the east side, just before the start of the historic flood plain, parking up in a sheltered area far away from prying eyes.

They cooked over a campfire in the late afternoon, Schumann demonstrating the cloaking device for her. He cloaked the car and then himself, both instances drawing a gasp from her as she came to terms with the technology. Schumann could tell that she doubted him before, maybe going along with it as part of her coping mechanism.

There was no doubt to be read on her face now.

She touched his head and the air seemed to quiver around him, then settle again. She could feel him as normal, and the Jeep too. But it was as if they were not there. All she could see were rocks and trees.

"I would never have believed it possible," she whispered, taking her hand away.

He switched off the mechanism, and reappeared from a mere shadow into solid form within a matter of seconds.

"You must wear the portable unit to make it work." He showed her how to operate the device. They were circular and about three inches in diameter. The controls were built into the side.

"We have two devices so can split up if necessary." He put his own device away and set about making camp.

Logan loosened up a little as they talked. It had been a

far from straightforward escape, and her nerves were near shattering point. Up until a few days ago, she had never seen anyone die, since then only to witness one gruesome death after another, transforming her workplace into a battle zone.

She has lost her job, and left the only friends she had ever known behind at the base. Now all she had left in the world was her wallet and the strange Schumann with his out-of-this-world gadgetry for company. But he had saved her life and she was grateful for that. She knew that she could trust him.

All her work and research was gone, hijacked by Hebb and his organisation. She knew that did not matter now. They had to be stopped, if that was at all possible.

Right now, as darkness began to fall, it was important to get some rest. They would make an early start tomorrow when the traffic was light and they could cloak the car in more safety.

Schumann activated the shelter and they settled down for the night.

He was restless, totally wired, his mind full of uncertainty, the strange environment still unsettling him, the quiet woodland enhancing all senses. He had started the evening chatting casually to Logan, making small talk laced with tactile questions before realising that, exhausted, she had fallen asleep leaving him alone with the sounds of the forest and the thoughts in his own head. He had been mulling things over for a good hour when he heard something unusual.

A snap of a branch, almost inaudible but amplified by the stillness of the night; his eyes flicked open, greeted by a view of the stars in the clear night sky. He held his breath, waiting for another sound, training kicking in once more, telling him to be on high alert.

There it was again. His eyes moved instinctively around to the left to be met by a face bearing down on him, eyeing him with curiosity. He stiffened, taken by surprise, completely caught off guard.

It was another white-tailed deer, the barrier of the shelter offering the animal enough of a shield to come closer to the man without inhibition. The deer could probably not pick out the scent. Schumann breathed a sigh of relief as his faculties cleared; nothing to worry about. He watched the creature for a while, a wonderful looking beast, as it munched on some nearby grass.

The deer continued grazing for a short while before its head suddenly snapped up, looking away into the gloom towards the highway in the distance, distracted by something unseen, frozen in the moment, the sophisticated senses detecting movement way beyond human capability.

The animal bolted into the undergrowth and vanished into the darkness.

Something was out there. Body on high alert, he rolled over to the FESS pack, his hands moulding around a modified Glock Armorlux handgun. A few seconds later, there was a sound Schumann knew well from military training, as two short chuffs from a silencer firearm were dispatched.

The shelter was not bulletproof by any means, but offered enough protection as the two bullets were slowed down by the barrier, giving sufficient time to react. He deactivated the shelter; it would be futile to return fire with it in operation.

He prepared to stand to.

Logan was now awake, disturbed by the commotion and the sudden chill that came over her. Schumann silently signalled for her to take cover under the chassis of the Jeep as he rolled away behind the trunk of a giant oak.

The assault team fanned out, bearing down on them fast, the commander barking out orders. Schumann had to think fast. He donned his night-vision glasses which immediately exposed the reason for their compromised location. He spied the drone above them which he guessed was probably using infrared scoping. It was probably relaying footage back to the assault team. He took the safety off the Glock, rolling over on his back, locking both hands together, and let out four bursts from the gun. With his own night vision, it had been easy to hit the six foot long drone along its fuselage. The craft's engine pitch changed from a steady hum to an erratic scream before the smoking drone made off some hundred yards, then hitting another of the mighty oaks in the wooded area, followed by a deafening explosion.

The assault team paused as the noise reached them, Schumann risking breaking cover to scan the darkness with his glasses. Two of the unit came into view, caught off guard by the commotion. He dropped to one knee, squeezing the trigger steadily.

The first man shook as he was struck in the neck and head, the splinter impact shells sending a spray of blood over his colleague and his helmet spinning into the undergrowth, the other not even able to respond as a bullet went through his thigh, shattering his upper leg. He screamed as he dropped his weapon, clutching his leg, Schumann taking advantage, running over to him, double tapping him at close range. As his lifeless body slumped to the floor, Schumann grabbed the assault rifle and a couple of magazines before skulking away and dropping down behind another tree out of sight.

He could hear shouting as the OC instructed his team. Schumann gained in confidence all the time as he assessed their strategy. They had no drone cover and were two men down. He had the upper hand.

By carefully making his way through the undergrowth, he was able to pick his way in a circle through the foliage until he was behind what remained of the assault team. With the aid of the NVGs, he could make out the remaining three members of the unit. He tracked them from a safe distance until he had enough clear space to take them out. The commander kept his men low, trying to pick him out of the gloom using their own night vision to pinpoint his position. But he was too good for them and stayed well hidden.

It was then that Schumann realised his mistake.

True, he had circled his prey in a perfectly trained Swabian move, but had overlooked the fact that Logan was not a soldier. He was naïve to think she could react to the situation. Instead, she had stayed put under the Jeep as instructed, but was now being roughly manhandled out of her hiding place by the unit commander.

"Mr Schumann, I have Professor Logan. Come out and show yourself if you don't want her to start losing her looks." The commander produced a large hunting knife from a sheath, placing the blade under her chin.

Schumann assessed the situation. Three men and a hostage; the odds had changed.

"Mr Schumann, I'm an impatient man. I haven't got all night. Ten seconds … nine … eight …"

"Okay, don't hurt her." He broke cover about thirty yards from them.

"You sound concerned, Mr Schumann. I didn't put you down as the caring type." He gestured over to where his two dead men lay. "Pretty good for a scientist, I must say, but not good enough. You are far too trusting, Mr Schumann."

The two other troops brought up their weapons, training them on the static figure up ahead in the clearing, and opened fire. The men were calm and methodical, spraying the figure with bullets.

Clare Logan screamed at the gunfire. He stood no chance. She sobbed, preparing herself for her own fate as the commander turned her away, relaxing his grip on her. At the same time, she witnessed a confusing scene as the two other troops jumped and convulsed as jets of blood and gore ripped their bodies apart.

It all went quiet, Logan turning to see the commander standing behind her, remaining impassive for about ten seconds before eventually tottering forward, taking a couple of steps; and then falling face down into the dusty ground, a large mass of blood pooling around the head of his lifeless body.

Logan remained rooted to the spot, whimpering in shock. Schumann emerged from cover, running over to her.

"Clare, are you okay? Did they hurt you?"

She was not quite able to comprehend what she was seeing and could barely speak. It was then that she spotted the figure in the clearing up ahead and started to scream. Schumann covered her mouth, stifling the noise.

"Clare, take it easy. It's me, it's alright. Keep it down; we don't know if anyone else is out there."

It seemed to do the trick, Logan nodding her head, sobbing, pointing at the figure still holding the same position.

Schumann fumbled with controls on his utility belt; the figure vanished.

He held her tight for a long time, held her head to his chest, reassuring her for what seemed like an age before she eventually spoke.

"I thought you were dead. I thought you were gone."

"I'm here, it's okay."

It took several more minutes before Schumann smiled at her, revealing the device's extra feature. It was the cloaking device again, but on a setting which allowed the pre-recorded image of him to be replicated, meaning that the men had been firing at a projection, the perfect distraction as the real Schumann took up position elsewhere, eliminating the remainder of the unit.

"I can't take much more of this," Logan said softly.

"Neither can I," he replied, with an ironic expression.

She took it the right way, smiling faintly, averting her gaze from the carnage around her.

"We'd better get out of here. The incommunicado drone will tell them that something is up. They are bound to send another unit."

Logan did not need to be told again, and to Schumann's surprise, sprang into action, helping him to pack up the campsite while he disposed of the bodies.

It was not long before they were once again on the highway, Logan using the NVGs to avoid using the headlights, the cloaking device also activated securing full covert protection.

They looked at each other, Logan elbowing him in the upper arm, unable to understand why she was even laughing. Schumann, with his knowledge of such things, knew it was a release of emotion due to the close proximity of close combat that they had experienced.

"Thank you for saving me, Hans," she said with candour.

"You are welcome. You may yet have to return the favour."

Chapter 42

Dulce, New Mexico

Albert Hebb was still staring at the static on the screen, his whole body shaking, the rage once again building within him. Quietly, he instructed the team on his next move.

"Dispatch another drone to the coordinates. I want the area scanned over with a fine toothcomb."

They complied, the control room a hive of activity as the assault team members were each radioed in turn.

"Team commander, come in. Do you read? Over … Team commander, please respond. Over …'

But it was like the other four coms; they all came back with the same result: not responding.

"We've lost contact, sir. What are your instructions."

"Send everything you've got, and cartwheel the area in a fifty-mile radius. They must not escape again."

Hebb turned on his boot heels and marched smartly out of the control room, down the corridor to one of the private conference rooms. Once inside, he punched in a phone number. The phone rang at the other end a couple of times before answering.

"Albert, old friend, I trust you have matters in hand."

"I'm working on it, sir, as we speak."

"Oh?" There was no disguising the disappointment in the

tone of Dalheim's voice.

Hebb started to fill with dread. What was he going to do? The High Command did not tolerate failure. Indeed, they were not used to it, such was their level of achievement.

We have them somewhere on Highway 70. They will not get far."

"Good, good. I knew I could count on you to clear this little matter up, especially after the little incident on the base."

"I can assure you, Mr President sir, that everything is under control."

"That is very reassuring, area base commander. I will tell the rest of the board that all is under control, shall I?"

"Absolutely, sir."

"Very well. Keep me posted, won't you?"

"I'll be sure to do that.'

Hebb put down the receiver, sweating profusely.

Chapter 43

Indianapolis

Schumann had taken to driving the vehicle and, as he suspected, it was quite straightforward. As they maintained cloaking mode, he was quite secure from being pulled over by the police. In any case, at this time of night, the powers that be were more likely to be dealing with unruly behaviour in the inner city. Logan was trying to sleep as he took the route through Indianapolis towards Columbus, which he estimated at their current speed would take them another half an hour. He scanned the clear sky above for drones. He was taking no chance, guessing that the craft were armed with advanced motion detector devices. Any sightings and he would bring the Jeep to a halt and wait for the danger to pass.

He let Logan sleep, a private escape from the stress of their current situation. He could see the outskirts of Columbus coming into view now; a mass of lights as far as the eye could see. This was by far the biggest Terran settlement he had encountered to date. The place had a special interest for New Swabia, in that it was the home of the biggest private research and development foundation. The twenty-two thousand employees worked on metals and material science, instrumental in the Terran space programme. Their titanium alloys were used in many scenarios all over the world, and although basic by Swabian standards, it was still interesting to observe what they were up to.

The city was massive, home to nearly a million people. He de-cloaked the vehicle to avoid an incident. Logan took over the driving from this point, steering them through the city centre, past the business district and into the commercial sector. She picked up Route 76 and headed for Pittsburgh. The end of the journey was now in sight.

Chapter 44

Dulce, New Mexico

Albert Hebb had calmed down enough to go back into the control room. He was going over the last few minutes of drone footage before they had lost contact.

The night vision from the camera gave a daylight perspective of the ground below. He could see the remains of a campfire, the thermal imaging exposing the heat signal with ease. Not far from this was a blue Jeep Renegade, parked under a large tree.

Good, they now knew the vehicle type. That would make tracking far easier.

But there was something of far more interest. Two bullets hitting a shimmering square bubble, and inside the bubble were Schumann and Logan. He shook his head in amazement as the rounds slowed before falling harmlessly to the ground. He had seen some pretty advanced technology, but this was something quite unexpected; and at the centre of it all was that German scientist. But he was more than that, a lot more. Hebb watched in secret admiration as Schumann deactivated the shelter, rolled onto his back and sent a volley of gunshots at the drone. The footage became shaky and blurred before being permanently replaced by static. The brief video went dead, leaving Hebb shaking his head. God, how he would love to find out what other tricks Schumann had up his sleeve. One thing was certain: his adversary was a highly trained combat operative.

"I'm sure we could have become friends, Mr Schumann," he muttered to himself. "How unfortunate that I must now kill you."

Hebb marched along past the labs escorted by two brownshirts, turning right to where the pens were located. He spent a while with his ritual teasing of Cory, laughing at the volley of abuse returned in his direction, before moving deeper into the sector. There was a newcomer for him to examine, oldish, distinguished-looking, obviously educated by the way he carried himself. That was of no consequence down here, though. Hebb eyed him, sizing him up. Would he be as much fun as Cory? Only time would tell. He prodded him with a baton.

"Well, who have we got here?" The captive man swayed from the blow taking a step backwards, his eyes rolling upwards. "Of course, my friend, you can't talk, can you? Too high on the conditioning at the moment. Well, no matter, the drugs will wear off soon and we can have a talk. Then you can tell me all about the life that you used to have." Hebb cackled. "Oh, how I love this job. Well ... goodbye for now."

The imprisoned man looked straight through him, oblivious of his predicament. Hebb sauntered off, tapping the baton against the side of his boot, the two brownshirts trailing in his wake.

His mood had brightened considerably, buoyed up by the confidence that the teams were closing in on Schumann and

Logan. All of the highways were now covered, and he had eyes in the air for three hundred miles in all directions. Unless they ditched the Jeep, it would only be a matter of time before they identified the vehicle. Even if they did proceed on foot, the drones could easily pick them out from a crowd. And when they did locate their target, they had a protocol to follow.

Chapter 45

Kansas

They were being followed again, the headlights behind at a steady distance, the giveaway coming from the accompanying two drones he could clearly make out through the NVGs. They had been behind them for around twenty minutes.

Dawn was breaking, the sun's brightness illuminating the trees on the horizon. Logan remained calm, the relatively busy highway providing obstacles for the assailants, preventing them from making a move before now. But Schumann knew that they would not wait forever.

They pulled out, overtaking an old Buick, a mix of oxidised red and rust. The driver, grizzled, with a full beard and a ruddy complexion, gave a wave of his left hand, a silent message of 'You go on ahead, I'm in no hurry'. They pulled back in, blocking the view from the Lincoln, Schumann knocking off the headlights, Logan switching on her own night vision. He wasted no time in activating the cloaking device. He looked behind to assess the situation. He could see old grizzly in the Buick do a double take as they vanished out of sight.

As predicted, the Lincoln glided out and overtook the car behind them. He could see the two occupants become highly animated as they looked all around, clearly perplexed as to where their quarry had gone. The Lincoln rocked forward as the driver accelerated up the highway, clearly of a mind that the Jeep Renegade was further ahead, out of sight.

The Jeep's soft top flapped as the Lincoln passed them, only a couple of feet away in the other lane. Logan reacted by slowing down, tucking back in behind the confused Buick driver. The drones flew away to join the Lincoln. They had lost them.

"That was close," she exclaimed with relief.

"We'll be safe enough until we get to Pittsburgh," said Schumann, "but they are sure to be waiting for us in the city."

"Right, and even if we take another route, the other roads are bound to be full of traffic," Logan added.

They considered pulling over and waiting it out, but they were only too aware of the danger of being cut off as the search for them intensified. The cloaking device would only be effective for so long. They made the decision to push on before rush hour.

They passed McKees Rocks, taking the road that ran alongside the great Ohio River. A Lincoln and two hovering drones manned the highway slip road before they hit the city proper; then another parked Lincoln before Logan turned off the main drag, taking the Smithfield Bridge over the river and into the North Oakland district. Here, the roads were smaller and far more plentiful; it would be far more difficult to monitor all of them at once. They managed to drive through Squirrel Hill North still cloaked, and also most of Frick Park before the traffic became too heavy.

Logan pulled behind a building where they de-cloaked. She then decided to head southwards for a while into Wilkinsburg.

The congestion thinned as they entered the Pennsylvania Turnpike. They had been fortunate with the city having 446 bridges – an absolute nightmare to monitor all of them at once – offering them a myriad of alternative routes. Logan's decision gave them a clear run away from the outskirts with no more sightings of the enemy. The turnpike ran for 360 miles, and provided it did not become too dense, they could cloak up again.

Schumann was beginning to think that they had outsmarted their pursuers, the traffic strangely accommodating compared to previous routes that they had travelled on.

"Oh, no," Logan suddenly uttered. "I should have known."

"What is it?" he asked anxiously.

"Toll booth up ahead, and no way around it."

That was very bad news. The turnpike was so quiet because you had to pay to use it. The cheek of the Terrans, as if it was not antiquated enough, Schumann complained to his inner self. But that would not help him at present.

Logan parked safely to observe the toll up ahead. She could see several pay-by-card lanes, followed by cash lanes, pre-paid lanes, HGV lanes and then a service lane right on the end, manned by highway patrol officers. She could also see a black Lincoln parked on the other side of the barriers. Four drones were buzzing around in the sky.

They were trapped. There was no way that they could pass through without de-cloaking.

They were certain that the police were not looking for them. They would have seen motorists pulled over and questioned. Which meant, if they paid and drove through, the Lincolns and the drone back-up would have to let them go without giving chase until they were well clear of the toll.

It could be their only option.

Logan crept the Renegade into the far cash payment booth. She waited as long as she could, signalling to Schumann to stand by. She got to within a few yards of the booth, the toll buildings structure offering them just enough cover to switch off the cloaking device.

Logan threw the coins into the collection basket, the barrier lifted automatically, and they drove through slowly. A pair of patrol cars were parked up either side; their occupants gave them the once over; neither crew seemed interested. Logan allowed herself to pick the pace up as they homed in on the two black Lincolns up ahead.

By the time they levelled up with them, she had got the Jeep's speed up to fifty, merging with a few other cars as the road lanes narrowed. They were three vehicles ahead when the Lincolns pulled out. At least they were at a safe distance for the time being. Schumann kept a close eye on them as Logan drove as fast as she dared. They were still in sight of the patrol cars, and they were short on options. It was too risky to activate the cloaking device in full view, although he would consider it if there was no other alternative. It was important to keep the Lincolns behind them.

Then, unexpectedly, the two SUVs exited the highway via a slip road.

Schumann was waiting for them to reappear on the entry road, looking all around for a reason why they had turned off the highway. Maybe the Lincolns were not looking for them after all. Logan was equally mystified by the manoeuvre. Nevertheless, they were gone, leaving them a clear run towards Morgantown.

The morning sunrise brought with it a pleasant glow, and a new sense of hope that they could actually reach their goal. As the sun climbed higher, the traffic bulked out, becoming ever heavier as rush hour peaked. In truth, they were both thankful for it; safety in numbers.

Schumann gazed out of the window to the left, taking in the

wondrous beauty of the landscape. The sky was a brilliant blue and cloudless; visibility was very good. That was the reason he could see the black shape homing in on their position. He looked over to the right, and there was another. More drones, closing fast.

It was strange that the road pursuit had dropped away, leaving only eyes in the air. It was a new tactic that he did not like. His worst suspicions were confirmed as an RPG left one of the drones with a flash. He saw the weapon ignite, then the fiery trail coming straight towards them.

"Incoming missile ... incoming," he barked to Logan. Immediately she reacted by pulling into the overtaking lane, then braking sharply, surprising a driver in a Sudan as he flew past them.

The RPG flew over the roof of the Renegade, exploding on the highway in front of them, causing Logan to swerve to avoid the smouldering crater.

A woman in a yellow Taunus looked in amazement as concrete and roadway fragments flew in all directions. When she looked back ahead, she was too close to the lorry in front of her. She panicked and hit the brakes, at the same time swerving to avoid the edge of the crater, sending the Taunus in a one-eighty arc. The wheels locked, the car pitched and rolled over. The woman screamed as the roof hit the highway, the airbags unable to stop the metal decapitating her, sending her head rolling down the road like a bowling ball. A pair of men in the car behind shouted to each other at the horrific sight, the driver unable to avoid the Taunus, now sideways on in front of the oncoming traffic. There was a deafening smash on impact; their red Chrysler somersaulted over before coming to rest on a VW Beetle, killing the female occupant instantly. Amazingly, the men were still alive. Behind them, Schumann could see a multiple pile-up as vehicles ran into the accident, fuel igniting causing a massive chain reaction of explosions, the two men engulfed in the fireball.

The drones homed in on their position, the machine guns working overtime, the onboard computers calculating their target. Bullets streamed down the highway, hitting the number plate, then the left rear wing, clipping the soft top and framework, forcing the Jeep to veer sideways. Logan wrestled with the wheel, at the same time having to negotiate the actions of shocked motorists as they, too, tried to avoid the incoming volley of fresh gunfire.

She hit the gas, taking the Jeep up to eighty, Schumann managing to reach the cloaking device that he had hidden away at the toll point. There was nothing for it. They were trapped.

The cloak took only a couple of seconds, several motorists looking wide-eyed as they vanished into thin air. He worked furiously recalibrating the cloak's mechanism to compensate for the tear in the projection fabric which now exposed part of the Jeep. It would suffice for the time being; it would at least mask the visual contact from above. He looked skywards, noticing that the drones were now flying erratically. With the visual lost, they would only have limited motion sense.

Schumann shouted out instructions over the noise, Logan complying with a nod of the head. She dropped the speed, cutting in behind a blue Nissan to confuse the detectors.

To the pair's horror, the two drones randomly opened fire, machine guns indiscriminately chugging out hundreds of rounds in controlled arcs across the highway. Bullets carved out a line, narrowly missing the invisible Jeep, the trail continuing into a camper van. The couple in front shook like rag dolls as they were struck by multiple rounds. The riddled camper meandered harmlessly off the road, coming to a halt on the grassy embankment. Logan was still following the Nissan, going flat out, but the steep incline of the road slowed the Jeep's progress. They started losing ground on the car in front.

More machine gun volleys followed, spraying a black lorry cabin, the driver's head almost split in two as a spray of blood hit the windscreen. The lifeless body slumped forward, sending the cab crashing into a family of four travelling in a Ford Pinto, both vehicles exploding into a ball of fire.

The drones were still firing, the sound of police sirens now audible within the chaos.

Logan was now passing a row of traffic as more and more vehicles pulled over, some people running back to the carnage to help. Others, not so willing, took cover underneath their own vehicles.

The drones were adding to the body count as several more drivers were caught in the random gunfire, creating a third multiple pile-up, this one completely blocking the highway. People ran in all directions, out into the open, making easy targets for the drones. Schumann could see through the rear-view mirror as the guns opened up, making short work, as dozens were mown down indiscriminately.

He could hear the sirens growing louder as the police from the toll responded to the incident, then the thumping sound above him, two large black shapes coming in from the west. The drones were still trying to find them, the traffic now almost non-existent. Random gunfire scythed zigzag lines around the cloaked Jeep, a trail of bullets hitting the rear tyres of the blue Nissan in the distance, slowing the vehicle dramatically. More gunfire blew out the back window as the Nissan came to a halt, the sole female occupant scrambling out of the driver door as more bullets smashed into the cabin, and before the drone corrected the trajectory of her movement, striking her in the midriff multiple times, ripping her chest apart and killing her instantly.

Logan took evasive action, avoiding the carnage by swerving instinctively onto the hard shoulder and back onto the highway with a left-right of the steering wheel.

The sky was now filled with the sound of two Black Hawk helicopters. The drones broke off, arcing round to engage just as Logan took a slip road off the highway, a wise move before the police closed off the road ahead and trapped them.

As they rounded the camber, they both witnessed the two drones being shot out of the sky by the Black Hawks. Logan slowed down to a reasonable speed. The Jeep remained cloaked, Schumann scanning behind them for more danger. The whole incident had lasted no more than three minutes.

"Can you believe that? They just opened fire on all those people," Logan said shakily.

"It is clear that they want to stop us at all costs," Schumann replied grimly. "We are facing an enemy that are willing to kill anyone to get to us."

The stakes had changed.

The person that knew this more than anyone else was none other than Albert Hebb. Staring at the two screens of static, he realised that there was no going back now. The death or capture of his quarry would satisfy his state of mind, and nothing less. True, the trail would soon run cold when the investigation into the source of the drone attack was averted. They had the capability to cover up their tracks. But the board would be far from happy with him authorising the decision to open fire on a highway full of civilians.

He reviewed the carnage just before the drones were lost, the scene playing out before him, Hebb himself acknowledging the skill of the drone pilots as they navigated their way through the transport to get to their desired target. He felt no emotion as the body count rose to an alarming level in a matter of seconds. He had a mission to fulfil, history had taught him the reality of collateral damage.

But once again, the prey had eluded him.

He watched in admiration as the Jeep vanished into thin air on the highway, the technology once more in naked conformity. The shelter was one thing, but this was even more impressive: a cloaking device so advanced it left the area base commander almost breathless. Despite all the urgency, maybe it would be a better idea to capture Schumann alive and extract the technology from him.

Chapter 46

Pennsylvania

They had managed to find refuge in a side road that led into a wooded area close to Highway 68, both of them relieved to take a rest from the frantic recent events. It was horrific, the local radio abandoning the regular schedule to broadcast exclusively on the horrendous carnage on the toll road. Many were suggesting a terrorist attack, such was the blatant disregard for civilian life. Others were struggling to explain what had happened at all. There was no shortage of people coming forward with their theories, trying to make a name for themselves.

There were only a few people who actually knew the truth. Schumann and Logan were only too well versed in the knowledge of Hebb and his cronies, a world that was unknown to all the self-appointed experts that now crowded the airwaves.

Much to the relief of Schumann, Logan had found an extra resolve, and far from caving in to the pressure of the recent massacre, she seemed to accept their circumstances with a level-headedness that had to be admired.

They studied the road map of the surrounding area. Because of their sudden detour, they were now headed for Johnstown on Highway 76. If they continued up to Carlisle, they could get back on track and onto Highway 78 which would take them directly into Paramus, New Jersey, not such a bad position to be in. Their shelter was based under a rocky outcrop, no fire and no thermal print. They would camouflage the Jeep, and then wait for the early hours to make their move; then proceed in cloak mode for as long as possible. From now on it would be vital to avoid another Turnpike incident.

Schumann had a restless night, more intent on making sure that Logan got her sleep. He was mindful of another night assault by Hebb's men and kept vigil until the early hours. He enjoyed the peace and quiet, a chance to think about their situation, some time to think about how he was ever going to get back to New Swabia. He looked over his shoulder at the sleeping Logan. She looked so peaceful, the innocent look on her face a strange source of comfort to him.

The chances of von Getz executing an Exfil mission were slim. The Swabian High Command would be wary of his intentions. Then they would have to survive the hostility element of Hebb and his men on the surface world.

He had been taught never to trust the Terran population, and for reasons he could easily relate to. But there was a certain collective that chimed with his own values, the likes of Gallagher, Clunes, Cale and Sagen, and the numerous other voices that needed to be represented. He promised himself not to be so pre-judgemental again, and to make sure he would return to repay that group who had aided his escape and remove the base command. But the more he thought about it, the more that seemed to be a long shot. Right now, just to stay alive was the primary objective.

Daybreak found the two of them and the cloaked Jeep on the road once more. Logan had managed a fair amount of sleep and was now swigging a can of Kickstart as she turned onto Highway 76.

They had to move carefully, choosing to tailgate an eighteen-wheeler to avoid motion detection. They could see drones come and go like flies, their flightpaths selected to keep out of the way of helicopters that randomly policed the skies, making sure that another bloodbath was averted.

The Lincolns had been replaced by random vehicles, Schumann noting that they maintained their conspicuous positions at the side of the road. A couple of cars had passed them, the occupants trying to blend in with civilian attire. But there was no doubting by their facial expressions who they worked for.

They drove without incident to the outskirts of Carlisle.

"We should swap the car if we can, then as we get closer to New Jersey we can negotiate the traffic de-cloaked."

"Agreed." Schumann knew that made sense. Every time they were visible, they could be identified straight away.

"Keep an eye out for a car lot."

"Will do."

Schumann held onto the roof rail, the view ahead still blocked by the HGV they were following. As they entered the built-up area, they found a discreet place to de-cloak. After continuing for a mile or so, Logan spied a large sign on the left of the main drag for Jed's Car Sales. She parked up on the forecourt.

The two of them got out, wasting no time in selecting an SUV realistically priced at three thousand dollars. A man that just had to be Jed appeared, wiping his mouth, belching quietly to himself as he extended a hand of friendship.

"Howdy. Lookin' for a new set of wheels?" he said with a chirpy Midwestern accent.

"I like the look of the Sportage," Logan mused, hoping it would be an easy negotiation.

"Lookin' to trade up the Jeep there?"

"Yeah. What will you give me, straight swap?"

Jed stared for a few seconds then let out a guffaw. "Hah Haar, tell you what I could do; take a thousand off the Kia, make it two thousand."

"No way, buster, this car has done eighty thousand miles." Logan paused; she was keen to get going. "Make it fifteen hundred, no test drive, we'll drive it out of here no comeback."

Jed gave the Jeep the once-over, examining the damage to the rear passenger side, muttering calculations on the repair bill to himself. Eventually, he straightened up, wearing the look of a man who had got the best out of the deal.

"Okay, lady, put it there. I'll go get the papers for you and you can take her away."

Schumann smiled as he once again witnessed the bargaining skills of his companion.

They settled up in cash, parking the Jeep up into one of the neat rows of vehicles so it would not be so easy to identify. Jed handed over the keys to the Kia.

"You folks take good care of her now. Everything works, just been serviced."

What on Terra did he mean? The cars had sexes? Surely not. Schumann dared not ask.

They pulled out onto the main road without incident, the traffic quite busy. The SUV boasted air-conditioning, and as the temperature rose alarmingly by the minute, they were relieved to discover that it actually worked. The cabin soon became bathed in a cool blast of air as they proceeded along the main drag, passing the large army base that was a main feature of the town.

Logan pulled into a gas station to fill up the Kia. Schumann elected to do the duties while Logan made her way to the kiosk.

A patrol car eased onto the forecourt, the two men giving him the once-over. He had seen this before; the sort of Terran authoritarian showboating he had become accustomed to. The car parked up nearby and the two men got out, the driver stretching theatrically, the other rubbing the back of his neck in a pointless manner.

Schumann continued gassing the car, watching them from the corner of his eye.

The police driver ambled over. "Looks like it's gonna be another hot one." He pointed skywards.

"Yeah." Schumann kept it brief.

"Where you folks headed?" The patrolman's beady eyes narrowed.

"New York." A good answer that was feasible.

He finished filling the car and signalled to Logan inside. She waved and proceeded to the checkout.

The cop was kicking the ground with his boot, looking up and down the street. His whole manner put Schumann on edge. He could see his partner by the door to the kiosk. There was no one else around.

There was the click of a handgun as the safety was disengaged, the barrel aimed at the middle of his head.

"Don't move, don't even breathe. Do exactly as I say." The patrolman turned him around and patted his torso for concealed weaponry. He closed his eyes, cursing himself for being so complacent. The patrolman put the cuffs on him behind his back. He then ushered Schumann into the back of the patrol car.

Logan appeared from the kiosk, the patrolman keeping his distance until she was next to the Kia. She looked round to see where Schumann had got to, the patrolman breaking cover, repeating his procedure, placing the revolver to the back of her head.

"Get in the car now." He pushed the gun roughly into her neck, guiding her into the back of the patrol car, her body falling heavily into Schumann. The patrolman shut the door ordering his colleague to drive away. The other man jumped into the Kia, following the patrol car out of the garage. He looked over to the kiosk. A man of Hispanic origin behind the counter, reading the morning paper, had seen nothing.

"What is the meaning of this? I demand to know why we are being detained." Logan said.

"Shut up, lady, we don't need to give you a reason," the driver remarked over his shoulder. He picked up the radio. "Okay, we've got them. We're bringing them in."

Schumann cast a glance at Logan. He had no idea about Terran police protocol. It was clear from the look on her face, though, that something was very wrong. She gave a slight shake of the head which he took to mean that these were not real patrolmen. How could they be? They had broken no law.

He looked around in the back. The doors were locked, and there was metal meshing separating them from the driver. The cuffs were uncomfortably tight on his wrists; no way of working his hands free.

"You've no right to do this," Logan continued.

"Keep quiet back there," the driver hissed. "Now what?" He hit the steering wheel with the palm of his hand as he slowed down.

They could see a roadblock up ahead. A patrolman held up an arm, signalling the car to pull over. The Kia pulled in behind them.

The patrolman walked over to them.

"Hey, neighbour, what brings you out this far?" he said to the driver, noticing the plates from out of state.

"Just delivering a couple of suspects for questioning. It's an ongoing enquiry; pretty hush-hush so they tell me." He winked at the other officer, sporting the nametag Jackson.

"Right, well, road's blocked up ahead with an RTA. It's not too bad; should have it cleared in no time."

"Alright, we'll wait it out," the driver said, casting a look at his two prisoners. Officer Jackson sauntered off to join his colleagues.

From his position, Schumann could see a discussion going on by the roadblock, a lot of pointing further down the tree-lined road beyond where he could see. He could tell the driver up front was twitchy, nervous as hell, just looking for an excuse to make the job a whole lot easier and execute them at the next opportunity.

Jackson walked casually back over to them, smiling at the driver. "Shouldn't be long now. Sorry for the delay."

"No need to apologise. These things happen," said the driver.

Jackson looked the car over for a while, nodding a few times, and then remarked, "Colorado plates, I see." He pointed.

"Yeah, bit of a way from home, Central Denver."

"What station are you based? Hope or Langdon?" Jackson enquired.

"Hope," came the reply.

"Right." He paused for a moment. "Say, you must know Sergeant Chapman, Red Chapman, been there for years."

"Sure do; see him from time to time," the driver retorted.

The other man gave a smile. "I better get an update; see how they're getting on clearing that road." He walked off casually over to the roadblock and beyond before disappearing out of sight.

The driver got out of the patrol car and made for the Kia. Logan and Schumann could see both men deep in conversation.

Left alone, they took the advantage to speak freely.

"If I can reach the FESS pack, I can get us out of these restraints," Schumann exclaimed.

"But how will we get near it? The pack is in the trunk of the Kia," Logan replied desperately.

"We need a distraction. Once we are away from this roadblock, it will be too late. We have to act before we start moving again."

Their driver, whom they only knew as Bud, made his way back to them. He had a slightly bandy walk and a habit of hooking his left thumb on his belt. He wore a continuous unpleasant scowl on his face. He climbed in, turning around to face them.

"Just remember what I said: we can hand you over unharmed or shot up. It's up to you, and don't think that we won't hesitate to kill those men out there." He nodded over his shoulder. "Just make sure you both ... Hey, what's up with him?"

Schumann was shuddering in the back seat, his eyes rolling. He started making noises with his throat, and then suddenly slumped into Logan's shoulder, unconscious.

"He's going into shock through lack of circulation. He has type one diabetes; he needs his medicine." Logan delivered this in an emotional panic.

"Where is it?" Bud growled at her.

"It's in the other car. There's a backpack in the trunk."

"Okay, I'll get it. What's the medicine called?"

"Just bring the pack. There are several different bottles, and they're all in German. I need to choose the right one." She increased the intensity in her voice.

"Alright, alright, dammit." Bud got out of the car and walked purposefully back over to the Kia, careful not to attract unwanted attention to his actions.

Logan could see the whole thing playing out as Bud explained to his colleague what was happening. The other man they heard addressed as Karl opened the trunk and pulled out the backpack. There was a short and quite abrupt conversation before Bud came back over with the pack, Karl left looking around nervously in the background.

"Okay, I've got it," Bud barked as he climbed back in.

"Okay, get the cuffs off him," Logan demanded.

"Hey, no way I'm doing that."

"His circulation is compromised," Logan said. "Look at him. He's going nowhere."

Bud cast an eye over Schumann, whose body was now twitching, his mouth wide open. It didn't look good.

"Okay, I'll remove the cuffs, but any funny business, you'll get a bullet in the kneecap, gottit?" Bud hissed.

"Yes, okay, okay, anything. Just help him, please," Logan begged.

Bud opened the back door and removed the cuffs from Schumann's wrists. The Swabian did not respond.

"Okay, the cuffs are off. What now?" Bud said, adding a slight concerned tone of his own.

Logan could only indicate at the side pocket of the FESS pack, but it was enough.

"In there; some bottles of tablets. Get them all out so I can see," she pressed him.

Bud had now let his guard down fully and had bought the ruse completely. Logan had to admit to herself that Schumann's fake performance was worthy of an Oscar.

With her own hands restrained, she had to use her head to nod at the correct bottle. There was a selection of drugs for allergy, some antibiotics and anti-inflammatories, along with supplements. Being in a foreign language meant their captor would be none the wiser.

She helped Schumann with two capsules, rubbing his arms to try and revive the circulation.

"Hurry; that damn officer could be back any minute," Bud interjected, looking at the roadblock. Schumann used the opportunity to delve into the backpack, wedging several items into the seat behind him. Bud looked back behind him as Schumann closed his eyes once more.

"Is he responding?" he said in an almost humane manner.

"He's stopped convulsing. At least that's something."

"You some kind of doctor?" Bud asked with a frown.

"I have medical knowledge, yes," Logan replied, not looking up.

Bud started to say something, but stopped as he spied Officer Jackson walking around the roadblock towards them.

"Okay, let him lean on you as if he's sitting up straight," Bud rasped.

Jackson came over, looking more serious. He put his hands on the driver's window ledge. "Accident's all cleared up now." He signalled to several other cars that had joined the queue to proceed. He, however, did not move.

"Okay, guess we'll be on our way; get these two into custody," Bud said cheerfully.

"You're not going anywhere." Jackson drew his handgun, levelling it squarely at Bud's head.

"Hey, easy pal, what's all this ...?" said Bud

He could see another patrolman armed with a shotgun herding Karl over to them with a third armed officer covering from a distance. A fourth man was by the other patrol car, calling the situation in.

"Okay, Mr whoever-you-are, Red Chapman never worked at Hope Station, or any other place for that matter. In fact, he doesn't exist." Bud frowned even deeper as Jackson continued. "I knew something wasn't right with the way you were acting. Just seemed strange to transport two suspects in such a way, so I tested your story." Jackson relieved Bud of his firearm. "You see, my brother-in-law works at Hope so I gave him a call … No one heard of you there, Bud." He turned to the other man. "No one heard of you either, wise guy."

Karl rolled his eyes looking skywards.

"Okay, cuff 'em," Jackson ordered.

Schumann could hear it all playing out, but kept his eyes closed. He had used the opportunity to slip his concealed items into his pockets.

The argument became heated as Bud protested, trying to front it out, but Jackson was having none of it. The two men were handcuffed and guided over to the other patrol car.

When the footsteps faded, Schumann opened his eyes, fishing out the cloaking device. Within seconds, they were invisible.

He clicked open the door and got out, closely followed by the still cuffed Logan. They crept away, leaving the argument to ensue, over to where the Kia was parked. Schumann peered through the glass. The keys were still there. The Swabian got Logan inside and de-cloaked, adjusting the mechanism to accept the car. He climbed inside and turned the switch back on. The Kia cloaked and vanished from sight.

The police had Bud and Karl in their car now. Jackson turned to walk back over.

Schumann started the Kia, slowly reversing from the scene. It took Jackson a few seconds to register the anomaly fully before shouting wildly, "The other car. Where is it?"

He ran over to the patrol car, glanced in the back, wheeling around looking in all directions. "Where did they …? What the hell is going on here?"

Schumann allowed the car to reverse for a further hundred yards before turning to drive off, leaving Jackson to scratch his head. When they were a safe distance away, Schumann gave out a large whoop.

"I do believe I am slowly turning into a Terran."

"What the hell are you talking about now?" Logan looked bewildered.

"Just an old saying." He would really have to be a lot more careful.

"Never mind about that," she protested. "Get these cuffs off me; they're killing my hands."

He brought the Kia to a halt and got out. Inside the FESS pack he found a small device, then ordered Logan to sit forward, holding her arms out in front of her. There was a hum and a high-pitched whistle that lasted about ten seconds before the cuffs fell away onto the seat.

Logan rubbed her wrists, picking up the cuffs. A neat black scorch mark separated the two halves. She stared in wonder.

"Don't tell me ... "

"Well ... it's ..."

"Hans, spare me, I don't care at the moment. Let's just get going." She gave out a short laugh. "Oh, and thanks." She jangled the cuffs and threw them in the back.

He shook his head smiling as they made off once more.

He had to admit they had been fortunate. That was a very close escape. It was nerve shattering to say the least, and not over yet. Their assailants had motion detectors in operation and could lock on to their coordinates without visual recognition. The best way to stay hidden was to stay close to other vehicles and built-up areas. They had to stay smart at all times. There would be no more second chances.

Chapter 47

Dulce, New Mexico

President Dalheim was not a man to be kept waiting, and Albert Hebb knew that fact more than anyone. As he stared incredulously at the screens, trying to keep his temper at bay, he got the call; they had got them at last. All those men, all that technology at their disposal. About time, too. Then came the sheepish voice delivering the update ... they had lost them again.

Never before in his long and distinguished career had he ever witnessed such monumental incompetence and careless acts of complacency. The pressure was mounting. There was only so long he could delay talking to Dalheim; break yet more bad news to him.

It would not have been so bad had the drone attack been a success, but now the fingers from MJ-12 would be pointing in his direction ... Bad call, Albert ... What did you think you were doing? All those civilian casualties, all that work to cover their tracks, stop the trail leading to the organisation. How some in certain places would love to seize the initiative and take his place; others, always eager to please, to creep their way in with their wealth and flimsy heritage connections.

How dare they? He, Albert Hebb, had been there; he had seen the atrocities first-hand, the meaning of power, the honour of being part of the original plan.

Even in those pre-war days, they had seen something in him: leadership qualities that would long outlive the war, that would see him hand-picked for the most important mission of all. Yes, it was true that lesser men with a weaker lineage would have been eliminated for their incompetence. The organisation had not grown stronger for making allowances. But he had been a loyal servant way beyond the command of the Führer, securing his place in The Bell for the next mission that would secure the existence of the Reich. That was probably the only reason that he had not been relieved of his command at the base.

But even Dalheim, or Kessler as he knew the man, would eventually run out of patience with him.

Hebb had changed the large armed drones for more discreet miniature models that were only six inches long. By doing so, he could carry out aerial surveillance, reducing the chance of detection. He would then have to rely on the teams on the ground to intercept on detection.

He stared at the various screens feeding back footage from each camera housed on the small drones, none of which was yielding anything interesting.

The phone sounded in the control room, Commander Holt picking up the handset and turning to Hebb. Hebb took the phone, knowing who it was already.

"Mr President, how can I be of service?"

"Albert, listen up, and don't answer back." Hebb balked, but did not protest.

"The targets are to be pursued discreetly from now on. If they are dealt with, that is all well and good, but we are not concerned with them disclosing information to the authorities. The consensus of opinion is that their accounts will not be relied upon."

Hebb listened, intently nodding to his superior on the video link.

"There are far more important things at stake here. As you know, we are due to visit the base with an extensive contingent of investors who are keen to see where their money is going. It is imperative that this visit is given the utmost priority." There was a lengthy pause at the other end. "I cannot stress how important this visit will be for the organisation, Albert. Your priority is to make sure the base is ready for the large contingent that will be with you soon."

Hebb could feel the tension leave his body at the news. But there was always a sense of duty and pride in apprehending the two fugitives. This had become personal and he would endeavour to complete the mission regardless. That would look good when the dignitaries finally arrived at the base. It would also vindicate him before the doubting Toms who eyed his position as their own.

"Everything will be in place for the visit, sir. Trust me."

"Oh, I am trusting you, Albert. You can be sure of that."

Chapter 48

Dulce, New Mexico

Enoch had worked at the Dulce base for all his adult life. He was a trusted member of the security detail, and was cleared at Umbra seven level which gave him access to all areas.

He began his career on the upper sections on a need-to-know basis, attached to the military personnel dealing with the more mundane tasks before gradually being promoted into base liaison as a senior security technician which took him down into the furthest depths of the base and into contact with the Greys and the Draco.

At first it seemed surreal to see humans working alongside these entities on a daily basis. Once he had learned to fight the fear and thoughts of panic, a morbid fascination grew within him. There were so many questions that he wanted to ask his superiors, but knew better not to approach the subject with anyone.

Enoch was tasked with checking security cameras at the extremities of the base. Quite often, one of the personnel would stray off limits, the ETs would seize them and he would have to negotiate their release. He became very skilful in these communications, and although the entities treated him with disdain, it was always Enoch that they asked for when there was a problem.

In the early days, like many on the base, he had been completely unaware of what went on in the lower levels. They were told it was a 'tri-bio transfer facility' doing advanced methodology for medical and mental gains. It was only when he witnessed the entities and the experiments first-hand that he realised the real reason why they operated in the middle of nowhere. The place was a crime scene, using human lives to see what would happen to them. Even more horrific were the rumours of spare human body parts being used as food for the Draco. Then there was the Vivarium that housed all the horrific crossbreeding programmes. Enoch hated that place most of all, but there were levels of high security in these areas that also had to be maintained. He had no choice but to go in there from time to time. For the most part, he kept his eyes away from the tanks and cages, trying to mask out the screams from the monsters as best he could.

Some of the other workers embraced the work ethic, the end goal seemingly plausible to them. So they carried on with ever more enthusiasm, loyal to the cause. But for Enoch, the magnitude of the situation weighed heavily on his conscience. He soon learned that there was no one he could tell or confide in, and that once you were institutionalised into the base, there was no way out until they said so. Family members were watched, and files collated about private lives. They knew everything.

Enoch had taken an oath under the penalty of death. No matter what was seen or heard on the base, to divulge the information to the public domain would mean he would be executed, guilty of treason. The regrets were obvious. How he hated his existence at the base. The situation seemed hopeless.

Then one day, while on Level Seven, Enoch found himself yet again negotiating the release of another curious soul from the Draco. After the human was released, he was reading him the riot act when the offender, who was called Sagen, made an unexpected revelation.

It emerged that within the base was a small group who Sagen belonged to who were totally against the experiments and certainly did not agree with the alien alliance. When Enoch met with the others, he recognised most of them as offenders from the forbidden zones. Straying off limits was an excuse to try and gather intelligence on the ETs.

It was at this meeting that he decided to join them, to form a rebel alliance with the intention of either sabotaging the base, to escape if possible, or both. His connections with the entities, the Caste and the hybrids made him the obvious choice for leader. His close friendship with Bek brought the boy into the fold who in turn could offer up the allegiance of the Caste and Aral numbering around four hundred. Their numbers would be of huge benefit, but they were still short on firepower.

Then came the recruitment of Clare Logan, and the visits to the base by the Germans. It would still be a long shot, but now they also had contact from the outside world thanks to the channelling talents of Bek.

They were all assembled deep inside tunnel three; the Greys and Draco had long since retreated to the lower depths until the next day. The early evening was always a good time to meet just before they ascended to the surface at the end of shift. The point of no return had arrived. It was time for Bek to be introduced officially, and other parts of the plan to be initialised.

Enoch gave a courteous nod to all before him, appreciative of how difficult and dangerous it was for all to attend. Now was the time to execute his instructions. There was a quiet stillness in the tunnel, the awareness of a new chapter in history evident to all attending, only serving to enforce the importance of why they were all there.

"Thank you all for coming at such short notice." They all nodded in compliance. "The visit from MJ-12 is nearly upon us. It is imperative that we are ready to strike. We will never get another chance like this."

"Do we have a date yet?" Cale enquired.

"It will be soon, but they are keeping the exact date under wraps."

"What about the channelling?" Gallagher turned to look at Bek. The boy looked up at him and smiled.

"We have sent all the information to the source. We can only hope that they can do something to help," Enoch answered. "I do know they have military capability. There is a long history between them and the base command."

"Have faith, everyone, we will prevail," Bek exclaimed.

Enoch nodded in appreciation. "Yes, we will indeed, we will find a way." He paused, looking at them each in turn. "We must be ready."

Chapter 49

Pennsylvania

They passed through Allentown without incident, and Easton soon after.

The Kia Sportage remained cloaked, nestling comfortably into the bustling traffic. Logan had become quite adept at anticipating other drivers' manoeuvres, judging her distance perfectly between vehicles, just enough to avoid the motion detectors from the miniature drones that they spotted in the sky from time to time. They had seen cars parked up at intervals, some of which were sure to have been looking for them, but none gave chase.

"Not long now, Hans," she said with a bright lilt.

Schumann was enjoying the sun on his face, and the relief of outsmarting a very capable enemy had invited a good few hours of sleep. Logan, for her part, had declined a rest, preferring to push on to their end goal, adrenalin and nerves keeping her wired to the task.

Schumann looked around, stretching his arms. "What is this place that we are going to?"

"It's a building in the middle of a town called Paramus," she responded.

He could see another large settlement coming into view.

"That's Newark up ahead of us. Not long now," she

announced.

The area became increasingly more dominated by residential dwellings, mainly farmsteads at first, but then eventually replaced by clusters of modern developments, suburban bolt-on sprawls to accommodate the demand to live within striking distance of New York, either side of the highway a giant building site.

They started to encounter a lot of traffic and had no option but to de-cloak the Kia, only too aware that the miniature drones were never too far away.

It was as they approached a major junction that Logan spotted a terminal in the distance.

"It's time to ditch the Kia, Hans."

"Why?"

"The traffic will only get worse and we are likely to get caught in congestion. We would be sitting ducks."

Schumann understood. "Okay, what's your plan?"

"It's public transport from now on."

Logan found a quiet side street and parked up. They took out the backpacks and made their way back to the bus terminal. She studied the timetable for a while, working out a route.

They could take a bus through to East Orange and then change to a Greyhound that would take them through to central Paramus, and ultimately on to their final destination.

Chapter 50

Washington DC

The two bodyguards checked out the aircraft hangar. When they were satisfied with the sweep they signalled the all-clear. Claude Perfekt descended the small flight of steps from the jet, and within seconds was inside the limousine, which took him away at high speed towards the busy city.

President Kessler, or Dalheim as he called himself these days, was waiting for him in his study, admiring his latest acquisition. It was a large oil on canvas by Fritz Wagner: three men in eighteenth-century dress, sitting around a table, laughing as they plotted together.

"If only you could talk to me," Dalheim said quietly to himself as he examined the jovial expressions in detail. The picture fitted snugly between the two windows behind his colossal partner's desk. He had managed to secure it over the phone from auction for $15,000, a bargain. He turned his gaze in another direction several times before reverting back to make sure he had got it right; and of course he had ... as usual.

The intercom sounded. "Sir, Mr Perfekt is here."

"Thank you, Jack. Send him through."

Perfekt glided into the room. He had a swaying movement that disguised the built-up shoes that he wore to compensate for his lack of height. This, in his own mind at least, reduced everyone, and stopped them towering over him as much. But he could do nothing about the President who, at six-four, looked down on most people that he met.

"Claude, dear friend, good to see you," extending a hand.

Perfect gave a firm handshake and took the chair that was offered to him. He noticed the canvas. "Ah, Fritz Wagner if I am not mistaken." Perfekt knew what to say.

"Why, yes, just arrived actually. It could be us with Bieger in another time," Dalheim retorted.

Perfekt forced a smile at the figures in the picture, although he did not feel the same humour at present. "Everything alright at Dulce?" He raised his black eyebrows.

"A few minor issues, but nothing that we cannot handle." Dalheim cleared his throat. "The ETs are getting ever more demanding. Caused quite a lot of trouble recently, but Commander Bieger, I mean, Hebb, has dealt with the issues."

"Which brings me neatly on to the next subject." Perfekt shifted in his seat. "The two people on the run," he probed. "Are they going to be a problem to us?"

"They are not a threat. They will be dealt with soon enough." Dalheim poured out two generous brandies, handing one to his guest. Perfekt accepted gratefully, turning the crystal balloon glass into the light.

"I am intrigued by the scientist. I take it Vessels was not too pleased to hear about the shark attack?"

Dalheim felt his face begin to redden. "We have yet to inform him of the situation."

Perfekt took a swig of brandy, pausing for a while, sensing his colleague's discomfort. Although the two were great friends, there were standards to be met at all times. The President took advantage, filling the silence with an explanation.

"Once we have him back in custody, dead or alive, it will

be easier to decide how to proceed. If he is captured alive, Vessels may be grateful of the opportunity to deal with the man himself."

Perfekt softened a little.

"The technology that has been offered to us by Vessels has been analysed. It is most impressive. No wonder his man Schumann is so capable."

Dalheim understood only too well what was at stake: access to the legendary New Swabia and all of its advances; the chance of an alliance that would see them rise up once more, the ultimate war machine, the ultimate Reich.

The Swabian leader had become a major player. Vessels had been invited to the meeting at the Dulce base, and it was becoming increasingly more important to welcome him into their future plans.

"You can see why he has become a key player," Perfekt continued as he stared into space. "With Vessels combined with the Draco alliance, there will be nothing to stop us." Perfekt stood up smartly, arms behind his back, examining the Wagner painting in more detail. He then turned to face Dalheim.

"Just imagine what news this will be to our investors," he said with glee. "A new impregnable superstate for us to springboard our operations from."

He slowly adopted the Nazi salute. "Heil the new fatherland."

Dalheim complied. "Heil the new fatherland."

Chapter 51

Cambridgeshire

Derek Mills led them back to the secret entrance in the hallway. Soon, they were assembled in the underground research facility, surrounded by the vast bookcases. Mills waited for the door to close, and only then did he operate yet another hidden lever. The centre section of mahogany from the breakfront slid to one side, revealing the shiny metallic doors of a lift.

"To the war room. Please follow me."

They all filed in behind Mills, the lift doors closing, the mechanism taking them downwards, the journey brief.

The doors opened into a room, unexpectedly large, a bank of five screens with digital readouts covering the far wall. Only one was currently in operation displaying a world map, and at least twenty workstations had computers powered up, at the ready. It had the appearance of Mission Control at Cape Canaveral ... minus the staff.

"Normally this room would be fully manned, but because of the extenuating circumstances, we will be running affairs ourselves." Mills eyed them all in turn. "Every available combatant has flown out under the command of Hector Valerian. It is up to us to provide the intel."

Marius looked at the others wide-eyed, and then back at him. There was no need to state the obvious. No one knew what the hell they were doing.

Behind the work area was a large digital table map of the United States. Next to this was a screened-off area with a large couch in place.

Mills showed them to their respective areas, explaining each role to them in turn. Helen was to monitor airborne activity; Sidney, ground activity. Mills took charge of logistics while Martha arrived to handle comms. She gave Marius a wry smile. As for his own role, he would work with Caroline extracting information from the Dulce base and relay the intel real time.

Mills got everything on line.

"Okay, you will all be drilled over and over again until your positions become second nature. There are hundreds of lives depending on us, and when the time comes, we must be ready."

Chapter 52

New Jersey

They were on the Greyhound now, on the Garden State Parkway. It was a popular route and the bus was full, forcing some of the passengers to stand in the central aisle. These included Logan and Schumann. They chatted to each other with a casual air, looking every inch the happy couple out for a day's shopping at one of the numerous large malls that lay up ahead. They passed Montclair, then Clifton Passaic before nearing Garfield. The highway was busy, the bus interior alive with multiple conversations as the large SUV levelled up with the Greyhound.

The occupants carefully studied the passengers one by one until their eyes rested on the centre of the bus.

Logan could not help feel the tension of anticipation as they neared the end of their journey. She felt exhausted and concerned with the responsibility of what faced them in the near future. She looked at Schumann who was gazing ahead, taking in the sights, with that childlike naivety he showed about everyday mundanity. *What secrets do you keep, Hans?* she thought to herself.

She happened to cast a glance out of the window, her drowsiness suddenly clearing as she met the steely glare of the man she only knew as Bud. She could also see Karl in the seat next to him.

The SUV dropped back behind the bus before operating the electric tailgate. The door swung upwards enough to release the drone, Karl expertly guiding it into the open air. The drone swung around before banking to face the bus sideways on.

Logan alerted Schumann to their plight. He looked over her shoulder, out of the window, at the now familiar sight.

"Gott im Himmel, will these people never give up?" he muttered.

Even with the naked eye, it was clear that there was no rocket launcher on this model; luckily it was too small for that. But it was big enough to carry machine guns. That was bad enough, being wedged in by a wall of people with no escape.

The drone moved in, bright flashes and a heavy thumping sound as the guns engaged.

"Get down, now," Schumann managed to say as the rear windows gave way with a deafening roar.

The pair hit the floor, others sensibly following their lead, while many filled the bus with screams of panic, pushing each other in all directions, the gunfire sweeping down the bus taking out all standing.

On the floor, the pair could see bodies jumping and convulsing as they were struck multiple times, the gunfire unremitting, ruthlessly efficient, taking out men, women and children mercilessly. The gunfire arrived at the front of the bus, reaching the driver who, in a mixture of shock and disbelief, was unable to react as he was riddled with bullets, his body a lifeless ruin within seconds, the bus meandering into a shocked motorist coming the other way, smashing head-on into his Cadillac, killing him instantly. The bus continued, the weight and speed of the vehicle pushing the Cadillac to one side, the drone moving back up the bus searching for Logan and Schumann.

They could not survive for much longer as more bullets breached the bodywork below the now shattered windows. The inside of the bus was a mass of dead bodies and smashed glass; the few that still survived huddled below the seats into what cover they could find.

The drone moved in as the bus drifted from the highway onto the loose verge, sending large plumes of dust into the air, onlookers in other vehicles coming to a halt, watching in disbelief at the carnage unfolding before their eyes, other drivers swerving to avoid the out-of-control Greyhound wreck.

Schumann took advantage of the billowing dust and broke cover, reaching for his back pack. Using a pillar to hide behind, he caught sight of the drone trying to locate its prey.

All the time, a live feed was broadcast back to the Dulce base where Hebb was watching in excited anticipation as the drone scanned the sliding bus for survivors.

"Come on, come on, where are you?" he hissed in a tone of fever-pitched lunacy. He switched to the SUV. "Karl, where are they? I can't see them. Are they dead?"

"Unconfirmed, sir, but they are going nowhere; it's only a matter of time now."

The bus came to a halt diagonally across the highway, letting out one last defiant blast of dust and gravel. It was all the opportunity Schumann needed; as he appeared in the middle of the wrecked bus, the drone immediately registered its target, firing relentlessly.

Hebb jumped up and down in his seat like a hyperactive child, unsettling the others in the control room, watching as bullets rained into the bus.

Then something curious; a familiar sight, a bright flash, and the live feed was gone.

"Karl, what the hell is happening? I can't see ... Karl, tell me ... confirm ... why can't I see anything? ... Karl ... talk to me."

It was getting tense in the control room. Karl was looking on in astonishment, not quite able to comprehend what was happening.

Schumann had used the remote projection again to full effect. While the drone fired at the false target, he had bought just enough time to respond with his Armolux. At close range, it had a devastating effect, the drone exploding in mid-air, crashing onto the highway in a ball of fire.

Schumann wasted no time, rising into view through the shattered rear window of the bus, the two occupants of the SUV still shocked by the demise of their prized possession, caught completely off guard, the Armolux firing off two more beams through their windscreen.

Bud and Karl had no time to react as the glass shattered, spectacularly lighting up the car's interior as the weapon delivered two direct hits on the occupants. The smoke cleared, leaving two smouldering charred bodies, their heads smashed out of shape, coils of smoke billowing from their vacant eye sockets.

Schumann stayed just long enough to check the kills, the only remaining sound a familiar voice on their comms demanding an update. He allowed himself a grim smile and left the man to ramble to nobody, hauling Logan to her feet and leading her down the centre of the bus past the groaning survivors.

They passed the remains of the driver, squeezing out of the buckled doors and onto the highway. They used the cover of the thick smoke pouring from the drone to sneak away from the carnage to a group of nearby trees, down an embankment, and out of sight.

They could hear the sound of sirens as they headed for Rochelle Park.

Hebb was still bellowing at the static on the screen.

Some members of staff had managed to excuse themselves. Holt had not been so fortunate.

"Have we got a damn visual yet?" Hebb demanded.

Holt searched for a backup. Eventually he found one, bringing the miniature drone on line. Even from a distance that they were forced to operate to avoid detection, it was clear what had happened. Holt skilfully operated the joystick and zoomed the spycam onto maximum.

Hebb could make out the smouldering drone on the highway, and the SUV with its two dead occupants, not to mention the numerous other corpses strewn around. He brought his fist down with a loud thud.

"Damn," he seethed. "This is getting tedious." He looked at Holt for a long time before speaking. "These people are making a fool of me. I don't like that. I will be contacting the President later. Just how am I going to explain this to him?" He cast a hand in the direction of the live feed on the screen. "I want those two eliminated at all costs. Do I make myself clear?"

"Yes, sir. I will do my best."

"Are you hit?" Schumann checked with Logan as they walked briskly along the embankment.

"I'm okay. Just a bit shook up, that's all."

"That was really close. We were lucky to get away," he replied, dusting himself down.

"I can't stop seeing those two faces looking at us; that sheer look of hatred."

He could sense that Logan was again in shock. He took her by the hand; she responded accordingly. Most people would never go through the catalogue of recent traumas in an entire lifetime.

They passed through the park area using Highway 17 as a reference point. On foot, it would take them half an hour.

There were police everywhere, responding to the incident on the Garden State Parkway, helicopters offering aerial support, forcing the pair to mingle with the many people using the pathways that snaked through the park.

They struck up a conversation with another couple, Logan asking for local restaurant recommendations. The other pair were only too happy to help with suggestions as they walked along together for a while, until it was time to part company at the Arcola Country Club.

As the other couple said farewell, Logan noticed the road sign.

"Look, Century Road. We're here."

They wandered down the road for a short distance until they arrived at number 120. Logan studied the building next door owned by the same company, number 140.

"Over here, this way."

She led Schumann to the main entrance. They entered the main hallway. There was no one around. The only other doorways were two steel elevators in front of them.

Schumann turned to her. "What do we do now?"

Logan's eyes were wide. Her mind trying to think straight. Even inside the building, the sirens of emergency vehicles could easily be heard increasing in their numbers. She pressed the only two arrowed buttons on the left door. The lift opened. They stepped inside. She breathed heavily as she studied the keypad.

"Okay, Level Thirteen."

Schumann could see the floor levels on the keypad. They started from one, as you would expect, going all the way up to the twentieth floor.

"But there is no Level Thirteen. Look." He frowned pointing to the keypad.

"Yes, that's right." Logan gave out a smile. "A lot of companies do not have a thirteenth floor. It is seen as a sign of bad luck."

"But we need a floor that doesn't exist." He was exasperated.

"Have faith, Hans."

She remembered now. She put her fingers over the one and three buttons and pushed them both twice simultaneously. She breathed a sigh of relief as the lift activated. Schumann gave her a look of surprise, which was reciprocated as the lift unexpectedly headed downwards.

There was no indication as to what the building was used for, and nothing inside the lift to indicate where they were headed. All Logan had was the verbal instructions stored inside her head.

The lift continued downwards for less than a minute before gliding to a halt, the doors opening into an area similar to the one they had just left.

Just one pair of doors in front of them.

"What now?" Schumann whispered for no apparent reason.

Logan studied the door. There was a small button below a meshed speaker. She pressed the button. There was a brief silence and then a voice.

"Code, please," an abrupt female voice announced.

"Enoch nine."

"You may enter."

The doors opened, bright lights making them flinch as their eyes adjusted to the reception area. The female smiled warmly, rising from behind the solitary desk. She was perhaps mid-forties, dressed elegantly in black, her fair hair tied up in a ponytail. She walked over, embracing Logan like a long lost sister.

"You are the ones with Enoch from Dulce?"

"Yes ... yes, we are." Logan relaxed a little.

She gave Schumann a firm handshake. "Welcome, both of you. I am Dana Redmond. Please follow me."

They walked along a functional corridor of metal cladding, Redmond leading the way. Schumann suspected by the way she carried herself that she was connected to the military in some way.

"Not far now." She smiled over her shoulder. "You did remarkably well to get here."

The corridor came to an end, terminating at a steel door. Redmond placed the palm of her hand on a wall screen to allow her fingerprints to be checked.

"Retinal scan," a metallic voice sounded.

Redmond stood in front of the screen, a neon vertical line passing her face. There was a low bleep and the door opened with a hiss.

They entered onto a balcony surrounded by metal railings, a flight of steps at each end descending below into a large room full of personnel, all in identical black uniforms. It resembled a huge newsroom with people running in all directions, interacting with colleagues, seated at computer terminals, a tannoy barking out updates.

Redmond led the way down the stairs to a long store room. "You can leave your things here; they will be perfectly safe."

Reluctantly, the pair took off their backpacks. Redmond looked them both up and down and pulled out two uniforms from a rail.

"You can freshen up over there." She indicated some shower cubicles. "Boots over there if you need them. Just pick your size.'

"Thanks," Logan mustered.

Redmond nodded. "I'll be outside when you're ready."

Schumann had a quick scan using a device from the FESS pack. There were no cameras or listening devices present. The room was full of equipment, the walls decked out in gardenia eggshell paint, the floor a grey resin. There were no windows. It was smart and functional.

He stepped in the shower, letting the hot water jet over his head, the feeling wonderful and revitalising. It was actually just what he needed, soaping away the dust and grime and the horror of their journey.

He emerged wrapped in a towel, facing Logan who was already dressed. Her uniform fitted perfectly. He noticed the red cross insignia on both upper arms.

"It's the Knights Templar emblem," she explained.

Schumann remembered reading about them extensively at school, about the connections with the old fatherland, the old folklore emanating from ancient Germany. How strange that all roads seemed to lead him back there in some way.

He got changed into his new clothes, the pair emerging to be met by Redmond. "Very smart," she chirped approvingly. "Please follow me." She led the way courteously.

They walked past the busy hive of activity, passing several other rooms, uniforms with headsets, air traffic control and operations on the ground being readied. It all looked pretty heavy duty to Schumann.

Redmond stopped at an office and stepped to one side. "Please go in. He is expecting you."

They were met inside by a large man who gestured to them both to sit. He wore a look of grim determination that broke into a slight smile as he introduced himself.

"So glad you made it out of there. Welcome to Paramus base. My name is Hector Valerian, Leader of the Black Stone."

The Lords of the Black Stone. Schumann knew the story well, of the breakaway Templar group that developed great power and wisdom, only to vanish around the fourteenth century.

"I thought the Black Stone were extinct," he uttered quietly.

"I'm flattered you know that, Mr …?"

"Schumann. Hans Schumann."

"Pleased to meet you, Mr Schumann." Valerian removed the reading glasses from his large authoritarian head. "True, our numbers were greatly diminished. We were almost wiped out completely but for a few stoic individuals who passed down their knowledge.

"Slowly, over the centuries, our numbers recovered along with our power to what you see today here at our American headquarters a half mile underground." Valerian cast his arms around. "We need to get your intel as soon as possible; all you can tell us about the Dulce base." He looked at them both in turn. "This place was built for a purpose. It's not for show." His expression darkened. "Your information could be vital to help us rid the world of a terrible enemy once and for all. Are you willing to help us?"

The debrief took more than an hour, the questioning relentless and exhaustive. At the end of it, they were taken to the map room where the two escapees pinpointed locations of defences and possible breaches to the base including the GPS coordinates for the sea entrance located in the Gulf of Mexico.

Valerian had been methodically digesting all the information presented to him, recording it all posthumously, showing little emotion up until this point.

"And you're sure of this location by sea?"

"Yes, absolutely sure," Logan stated.

Valerian looked satisfied. "You pair should get some rest. You look like you need it." He smiled, buzzing the intercom. Redmond appeared almost at once.

"I will show you to your quarters. Please follow me." She had a pleasant, reassuring tone in her voice, chatting casually to the pair, putting them at ease.

It was the first time in a while that Schumann felt he could relax, strange that it should be in yet another underground facility. He certainly felt more at home here than on the surface. But he would have to return to that Terran realm sooner than he would have liked.

They arrived at their quarters, rooms in a neat row along a corridor. Logan said goodnight, retiring to the first room. Schumann spied a bookcase further along. He pointed to it.

"Mind if I take something to read?"

Redmond smiled. "Help yourself. That's why the books are there. See you in the morning." She retreated down the corridor, out of sight.

Schumann entered his room: functional, sturdy bed and furniture that could be dismantled and moved easily; typical military issue.

He climbed into the bed and put on the reading light. He felt tired, but at the same time totally wired, and concerned that he may not be able to settle. The book may be just the answer. He looked at the hardback he had chosen from a shelf full of similar related subjects. The book was entitled *Paperclip and the New Age*. On the front cover was a picture of the German scientist Baumann, the man responsible for the V-rocket development during World War Two. He, along with thousands of others, had been granted safe passage to the USA to carry on their work, but this time they would be disclosing their findings to the Americans and working for them instead. In return, their past involvement with wartime atrocities would be conveniently overlooked.

The Germans were given prominent positions in the scientific community, Baumann himself becoming heavily involved in the US space programme.

Schumann became engrossed in the reading. It was interesting to get the Terran perspective on such matters. He was familiar with a lot of the projects from his school years, but then he came to a section on advanced technology and experimental craft. He read with interest the blueprints of disc craft captured by the allied invasion, the experiments with torsion physics, the strange structure in Poland called the Henge, supposedly connected to The Bell in some way. Yes, there it was; the picture of Die Glocke, the craft that had mysteriously appeared in 1985 in Kecksburg, and the craft that he had seen for himself at the Dulce base, supporting the theory that Hebb and the others had managed to travel through time, a concept that even the scientific world of New Swabia had never been able to achieve. He flicked back a few pages to the disc craft pictures. They were similar to one he had seen at the military base in New Swabia, the forerunner of the craft they flew nowadays, although they were a little crude in design and the weaponry antiquated.

He read on.

He came across a chapter on secret bases and the theory that these vast underground facilities existed without public knowledge, harbouring today's top secret technology. His eyebrows raised as he read about German investors before the outbreak of the war buying up land in the middle of nowhere, partnerships forged with the Americans on joint project ventures.

With his own knowledge, it suddenly dawned on him that they must have been involved in the construction of the bases. It was no coincidence that a lot of the breakthroughs made in Germany between 1939 and 1945 were never made operational. They were probably working with a secret American organisation all along, but when war broke out, the two sides were cut off from each other. But still the work went on until the time was right. The war ended and they were transferred to places like Dulce to continue that work. But who were they working for? Certainly not Hitler. It would seem that they kept a lot of information from him and his SS henchmen, the so-called true believers in the new world order. Schumann did not blame them. As the war was lost, they saw many of their colleagues executed and their work destroyed. As a scientist himself, he knew how that must have felt for some of them; to have their life's work decimated before their eyes. The Führer had murdered so many brilliant minds, and with them wiped out huge amounts of scientific knowledge ... but not all of it.

The Allies advanced into Berlin before he could execute his plans in full, leaving only one option open to him.

After Hitler's suicide, Operation Paperclip was implemented.

There seemed to be much confusion within the ranks of the western powers as to how the Germans had managed their advancements in such a short space of time. One prominent defector scientist called von Braun even answered the question at Wright Patterson Air Force Base in 1970, stating, 'We had help from them', gesturing skywards, suggesting that alien technology was involved.

Schumann's mind wandered back to an incident he recollected in 1936 in the Black Forest region of Germany, when a mysterious craft had crash-landed there. That could have been the help von Braun was referring to.

Given his own recent encounters with beings on the lower levels of Dulce, he was willing to bet that the Greys were the ones who had helped his ancestors in return for safe passage. But von Braun would have been more accurate to have pointed below his feet rather than up into the air. It would also explain why the Greys had the good sense not to reveal too much knowledge so as to retain the upper hand in negotiation.

That all tied up very neatly and was the most plausible explanation.

Schumann was enjoying adding his own truths to some of the myths and theories in the book, and it went a long way to explain how his own leader, Jan Kammler, had masterminded the construction of the advanced land of New Swabia. The only difference was that Kammler had a lot of the answers to the technology that no one else in Germany had, taking all of the best scientists for himself during the evacuation. There were even a few names and numbers of U-boats and ships listed in the book as missing along with key personnel. Schumann knew where they had all ended up. And so they had advanced in New Swabia at an even greater rate, dedicating their efforts towards the perfect society rather than that of the constant hostility of their Terran ancestral existence.

The modern day German involvement in America was a concern. There was no escaping it. There seemed to be a move, the largest since 1945, to launch an assault for world domination, but this time using covert tactics more akin to espionage. There was no blatant enemy on view as before, and no country to attack. This was a new era in tactical warfare from within. This enemy lurked underground and used very powerful figureheads. Armed with his own information, he knew it to be true. The impending meeting at the Dulce base seemed to point toward this. Vessels was a fool to get involved in such reckless pursuits. It could mean the ruin of New Swabia and the end of all its people. He had to help Valerian in any way he could to stop this madness.

Chapter 53

Paramus, New Jersey

He awoke with a start, the alarm on his watch unbearably loud in the confined space. He stretched out of the short sleep after reading nearly all night.

His mind was buzzing with theories, the puzzle revealing more clues to him, the same country figuring in all of it; the secret organisations, the languages, the science, the legends and the ultimate goal, all emanating from his own heritage.

He was met by Logan in the corridor, and almost immediately after by Redmond.

"Hope you both slept well," she said. "Please follow me."

They followed her along a familiar route full of people already hard at work to where Valerian had his office. This time they were directed to the room next door.

"Come," delivered by the booming voice inside.

Redmond retreated as Valerian invited them into a boardroom and to breakfast. There was just the three of them, Valerian showing them over to a trolley of bacon, eggs, pancakes and toasted bread.

Valerian filled the air with the aroma of strong coffee as he did the honours. Schumann and Logan needed no prompting, much to the great man's expression of approval. The room was a fair size, a large campaign table with twelve chairs the only items of furniture. Valerian sat opposite them, feeling no need to take an official position at the far end. He smiled tightly as he eyed Schumann with a glint in his eye.

"So what's your story then, my good man?"

"Just a scientist caught up in the wrong place at the wrong time, I guess." His dialect was coming along nicely.

Valerian's gaze became a little more intense.

"You see, we know about Professor Logan here and her work at the base, but you, Mr Schumann, are a bit of a mystery." The Swabian tried to remain calm, keeping his expression steady as Valerian continued. "This is a powerful organisation with huge resources. We have to be very careful, you understand."

"Of course. Naturally." Schumann was getting hot under the collar.

"We checked your background in Germany. It all checks out of course; your credentials are very impressive. But it is like you appeared out of nowhere." He waved a hand above his head in a circular motion.

"The sort of work you are involved in does not go unnoticed, and you just show up, waving a magic wand, fixing problems that people have been trying to solve for years. A little convenient, yes?" Valerian still had a casual air about him, although it was clear Schumann's cover was being tested to the limit.

"We have made some significant advances recently," he said.

"That is possible, of course. You must accept, though, you choose some strange bedfellows to share this knowledge with." Valerian raised his brow slightly.

"I can assure you that if for one minute I knew what was going on down there, I would never have agreed to this assignment." That part was true.

Valerian sat back looking into space, Logan was now eyeing him with renewed suspicion. Schumann took the opportunity to carry on.

"Look, my organisation sold me out. I fear that they are about to hand over all of our research."

"But why would they do that?" Valerian's expression softened.

Schumann seized the moment. "Money; a lot of it. And power." He knew this was plausible in the Terran world.

"Nevertheless, these are national secrets. I would be surprised if the German government were complicit."

"That's true, they know nothing about it."

Valerian nodded, leaning forward, the glint back in his eye.

"So your country knows nothing about your work: a top secret facility, with groundbreaking technology, making deals with the Illuminati?" The big man looked doubtful.

"My countrymen have no idea what is going on at the base. They have been fooled." That part was also true.

"Am I to believe that you are caught up innocently in all of this, Mr Schumann? I mean, from where I am sitting it does not look good at all."

"He did break out of the base. He had no idea about this place or your existence. It was I who volunteered to go with him." Logan looked at them both in turn.

Valerian processed the words from the professor, weighing the situation up as he crunched his way through a chunk of toasted bread. He leaned down beside him, retrieving several objects which he placed on the table in front of him.

"And what about these?"

Schumann could see his image projector, the shelter device, and his gun all laid out in a neat line.

"Excuse the intrusion, but we had to check, you understand."

Valerian's eyebrows were raised to a record height. "The flash gun I could just about accept, but these ..." and here he pointed to the other devices, "have been examined by our top scientists right here. They have never seen anything like them."

The game was up. Schumann would have to offer something to satisfy his interrogator, otherwise ...

"We are a completely off-grid organisation with cutting-edge technology, selling to the highest bidder."

"And ...?"

"I just work for them. I have nothing to do with the deals made."

"So that would account for why your government has no idea that this is going on. Is that what you're telling me?" Valerian persisted.

"Yes, it all changed after the war. Many secrets were kept hidden from both sides."

Valerian could see the logic in the explanation, but remained unconvinced. Schumann could sense that he was a threat to them. He had to think fast.

"The notes that you have on intel?"

"What about them."

"I sent that information to someone in the UK, so you must know them."

Valerian became slightly less officious. "Who did you send them to?"

"Derek Mills."

Valerian's face remained frozen for a few moments, before breaking into a large smile. "That was you?" He laughed. "We wondered how they got to Florida."

"Florida? How did you get them there?" Logan looked surprised.

"Had to take a detour for security reasons; had to be careful."

He was solving one problem and creating another. He would be caught out eventually if he kept this up. She was about to say something when Valerian beat her to it.

"That notebook has been key to our preparations." He nodded at Logan. She reddened slightly. He adopted a conciliatory attitude as he continued. "So what about these two devices; what do they do?"

Schumann had Logan's eyes burning into him. She had already seen for herself what they could do. He had no choice.

He got her to sit on the floor and activated the shelter. The air shimmered around her as the membrane materialised, leaving her in a translucent cocoon.

Valerian rose slowly from his chair, mesmerised by the demonstration. He prodded the side with his finger, which rippled in response before settling back down again. He poured some coffee from his cup, watching in amazement as it left Logan untouched, running either side of her to the floor. Schumann deactivated the device.

"And the other?" Valerian tried to sound unimpressed.

Schumann activated the projector, his own image appearing ten feet away from his real self.

"Well, will you look at that." Valerian nearly fell over. He waved his hand at the image. "It's so real you can't tell the difference. How did you …? I mean …" He fell back into his seat once more.

Logan relented, softening to Schumann's cause, joining his side in a small defiant protest.

"We did not risk our lives to come here to be insulted. We have told you everything we know. Mr Schumann here has revealed technology way beyond protocol. I hope he has satisfied your curiosity?"

A gobsmacked Valerian gave a shake of the head in disbelief.

"I ... I don't quite know what to say, but please understand that there are enemy spies everywhere. We have to be very careful." He spoke almost pleadingly.

Schumann gave a big sigh of relief inside. Logan's appeal seeming to assuage Valerian's manner somewhat. In fact, he became awestruck.

"Would you be willing to share these items with our team?"

"I would be only too willing to help." Right now, Schumann had to secure a way to get back to New Swabia, and if there was a chance, he had to take it.

"Very well. Welcome aboard, Mr Schumann."

Chapter 54

New Swabia

Klaus von Getz stepped out of the shuttle, his journey from New Berlin terminated. He had his pass checked by security before being waved over to the mag car hire point for New Bavaria, his peripheral view allowing him to witness the other passengers being jostled in a rather undignified manner to the main checkpoint. New Swabia was now a police state, its population under strict control from Vessels and his henchmen. They had taken to wearing swastika armbands, the eagle flags flying high over all of the cities, martial law now in place.

Von Getz eased the mag car onto the main highway and was soon speeding towards the military base, repelled by what he saw. He and many others had been careful to suppress their feelings should the same fate befall them as it had others who had dared to challenge the new regime. This was surely not what their forefathers had intended.

He passed several new military checkpoints before reaching the base, whereupon his credentials were once again checked at the main gate.

He glided past the plethora of military hardware now displayed with intimidating might, eyeing the saucer fleet that seemed to have expanded at an alarming rate, before arriving at the main entrance. The female escort met him with a formal nod and a face that could not hide its despair. She guided him down the heavily guarded corridor to the great doors that were parted for his arrival. Inside were two figures, seated behind a grand bureau plat. The man von Getz knew to be Vessels rose smiling, welcomingly.

"Oberstleutnant, please be seated," he oozed in a sickly drawl.

"Thank you, sir," he managed, trying to avert his eyes from the iron crosses both he and the loathsome Great General Brunner were sporting around their necks.

Vessels sat back down and wasted no time getting to the point. "So, Herr Schumann, I trust he is well?"

"Yes, Vice Chancellor, they are very pleased with his work at the base."

Vessels gave a wry smile. "It is Chancellor now."

Von Getz hid his feelings as best he could. "Forgive me, Herr Chancellor, I did not know …"

"Why would you, indeed? You have been away on operations so I fully understand. Chancellor von Gellen met with an unfortunate end."

"That is terrible news, sir."

"Yes, a fatal heart attack; most unusual. He had a very modest funeral at the request of the family."

Von Getz felt his stomach churn at the sudden realisation that the two men in front of him were now in charge of the country. He kept his face expressionless. He had gambled on Hebb not wanting to disclose the fact that one of New Swabia's top scientists had escaped the Dulce base. They would also want to keep the skirmish with the ETs quiet before the visit.

"We have your observation notes here. They are very informative. You have done well." Vessels looked directly into his eyes. "When will you be ready to return to Dulce?"

"Tomorrow, sir. I have informed my crew; that is, if it meets with your approval."

Vessels' chin jerked upwards. "You show great enthusiasm for your work. I like that, Oberstleutnant, I like that a lot." He looked aside to Brunner who nodded his approval. "It would be useful to have you there before my scheduled visit to Dulce."

"Of course, mein Führer." Von Getz could see the look of pleasure on the man's face at the mere utterance of these words. "When do you plan to visit? I can be in place for when you arrive."

Vessels' eyes narrowed at the request as he mulled over the question. His left hand fingers drummed the desk for thirty seconds at least. Von Getz could hardly breathe.

Then Vessels' shoulders relaxed and he broke into a smile.

"It would be good to have a familiar face at my side, especially one who is proving such an asset. I can see why Mr Schumann selected you as one of his personal staff." He stared at the wing commander intently. "I will arrive at Dulce the day after tomorrow at eleven in the morning their time."

Von Getz was almost bursting inside.

"Understood, I will make sure I am nearby to meet you when you arrive. I will be sure to inform Commander Schumann."

"I appreciate your support. Not all in New Swabia are so patriotic in this time of mourning." Vessels put on his best look of sorrow. Von Getz did the same, bowing his head to avoid eye contact.

"Good luck on your research mission," Brunner grunted.

Von Getz stood, giving the new Nazi salute that he knew would be respected. As he turned to leave, Vessels fired off a passing shot.

"All of this, need I remind you, is top secret, not to be

discussed with anyone. Understand?"

Von Getz turned back with a solemn gaze. "Absolutely, of course, mein Führer. In the strictest of confidence."

Chapter 55

Dulce, New Mexico

Enoch had finished his rounds, and with most of the personnel gone for the day, he took the advantage to meet up with Bek in one of the labs. He was conversing telepathically with three of the Caste and a member of Aral. The Aral were far more human in appearance than the Caste. They were often used to calm abductees in the ships as they were transported to the base for experimentation. Additionally, they provided the same role in the labs. Aral could be described as a hybrid of a level directly between the Caste and Bek himself. They had a high level of intellect that interacted with the Greys and Draco that had become a vital route for mediation, quite often being the only possible way to communicate as the alliance became ever more fragile. The role of Aral was becoming very important. Just where their own loyalties lay was uncertain.

Enoch observed as Bek conversed silently with the other beings, an occasional nod the only recognisable gesture. The dialogue continued for a few minutes until Aral and the Caste filed out in a neat line and headed down one of the tunnels.

Bek look pleased with himself as he turned to Enoch.

"Have faith, my friend, the time is near."

Chapter 56

Paramus, New Jersey

Schumann studied the electronic imagery maps that seemed to hang in mid-air. There were four in all, depicting various parts of the US, one of them being a map of the Dulce base, the seven levels having additional information added to the layout constantly. Logan was there beside him. He had a hand in his left pocket protecting the cloaking device. It had never left his person. He felt by covering it he was shielding its existence. It made him feel even better that Logan had not felt the need to mention it to Valerian.

As if on cue, he entered the room, nodding officiously.

"We have word from the base. Rebel team is ready and are waiting our instructions. Black Stone Force are on standby."

"How many men do you have?" Schumann asked.

"Two hundred special forces for the ground assault, five aircraft, eight helicopters, and one sub."

Schumann knew it was not enough. The aircraft would never make it without help. The ground assault team could, in theory, penetrate the base, but to make it all the way to the lower levels was unlikely.

"You think that's enough?"

"It will have to be, but we're heavily reliant on help from the inside."

"Who is your assault commander?"

"You're looking at him."

Schumann could not help but admire the optimism this man had; their commander-in-chief, leading the assault himself.

"I know it's a long shot, but we have to try. There will never be a better opportunity than this." Valerian enlarged the image of the Gulf of Mexico. "The entrance by sea will, unfortunately, take too long to navigate, and I fear our Gemini craft would never be able to bypass the security."

"That could be a way to get directly to Level Seven though," Schumann observed.

"That may well be true, but we do not have the capability."

"I would like to join the task force."

Logan looked at him and nodded. "And me too."

Valerian smiled admiringly.

"You are scientists. I may be short of troops, but these are highly trained combat operatives. Thank you, but the answer has to be no."

"I must be able to help here somehow," Logan said forcefully.

Valerian put up a conciliatory hand.

"Please, I mean no offence." He looked through the observation window at the people rushing around urgently, preparing for the inevitable, a lot of familiar faces that he had known for years, all with personal accounts from the past connecting them to the enemy in some way.

"Look, we made it this far, didn't we?' Logan insisted. "We want to help."

Valerian was humbled by the gesture. "Your efforts to reach us have not gone unnoticed. The intel that you gave us is invaluable. But this is a combat operation."

He looked at them both for a few moments. It was an unprecedented moment where the rules did not apply any more.

"Very well, you can both help out here. You can give intel regarding the base to the comms team."

Logan looked to Schumann, expecting him to protest, but instead he made a request.

"I have a contact who may also be able to help. I am expected to meet with him later today."

Valerian looked surprised. "Where is the rendezvous point?"

Schumann was impassive. "Not far from here. I could walk there."

"So you do have a network in the States."

"I do, sir; a very small network, but very loyal to me. I would like you to meet them."

"Why would I want to do that?"

"My contact was with me at the base."

"And you think he got out of there?" Valerian barked.

"It is my belief that he did, sir, yes. He would have been expected to report back to my organisation."

"I'll think it over."

"Trust me, sir, after witnessing what we saw down there, we do not need to be persuaded to comply. My contact will be carrying more intel from the base, and that could make all the difference."

Valerian mulled it all over.

"Even if I agree, it will take a lot of organising, and remember they are hunting you out there. Step out of this building together and we both become targets."

"I am willing to take the risk, sir."

"I believe you." Valerian smiled. "I don't want to elevate my level of importance here, Mr Schumann, but it would be like the president going out alone to do a spot of shopping at one of the malls down the road. It just would not happen. The security risk is too high."

Schumann thought this out logically. His idea of meeting von Getz in the park was a no go. He would have to think of something else that would satisfy Valerian.

"Sir, do you have a helipad on top of this building?"

"No. Comms antennae and back-up generators are on the roof. No room, I'm afraid." Schumann looked disappointed. "But our other building next door has."

They walked down another underground corridor that connected the two buildings and entered the elevator. The two men ascended to the top level whereupon they used Valerian's pass to access a stairwell that led up to the roof. Schumann fished out his Tacbe and activated the signal.

He was five minutes early for the rendezvous; the signal from the tactical beacon would take time to be encrypted. Then if it all went to plan, von Getz would home in on the ERV coordinates.

A few minutes passed. Valerian shielded his eyes from the sun, taking a panoramic view of the sky, looking for the craft to come into view.

"No sign of your friend yet," he muttered.

Schumann did not reply, his eyes constantly monitoring the comms.

Far below, he could see the occasional flash of a mini drone as they buzzed around the buildings still trying to locate Logan and himself. From his vantage point, he had a spectacular view of the city. He spotted the highway where the bus was ambushed. Lights were flashing from emergency highway vehicles making road repairs, the area still closed off. A helicopter with markings belonging to a TV station was hovering above the scene, giving the viewers an update. He wondered what their explanation would be.

The comms sounded. Schumann's heart missed a beat.

Possibly the most important message in his life.

"Identify yourself," came the officious voice.

He nearly shouted for joy. "HSNS3842NB requesting evac."

"Code confirmed. We are at emergency rendezvous point. Please take cover."

"They are here." Schumann beamed at his companion. He ushered him over to the stairwell.

"I can't see anything." Valerian was scanning the empty sky.

"They are here," Schumann repeated.

They stood for a few minutes, Valerian looking impatient until a voice sounded. "Sir, we are powered down. It is now safe to board."

Schumann led the way; the other man dumbfounded, as a set of steps appeared from nowhere.

Von Getz appeared from inside the craft.

"Apologies, sir, we are only programmed to shift to a private jet, and that might look a little strange on top of a building, so we had to stay cloaked."

Schumann laughed as he hugged his compatriot. "You made it. You actually made it."

"Of course, sir. Did you really imagine that I would let you down?" Von Getz laughed too.

Kaufmann and Weisse appeared, shouting wildly, joining in the celebration.

Von Getz took a breath. "Look at you." He had Schumann by the upper arms. "You made it all this way. I can't believe it."

Valerian was looking around the interior of the craft. He gazed at the unusual layout and then stepped outside, scratching his head. "What the fuck is this?" he asked.

Schumann checked himself, remembering his manners.

"Gentlemen, this is the leader of the good guys, Hector Valerian."

"You have some explaining to do," said Valerian, rather bewildered.

"Ever tried Bratwurst before?" von Getz offered.

Valerian stepped gingerly back inside.

"Please take a seat," Weisse invited him.

He sat looking around nervously in wonderment. Schumann thought he almost detected a juvenile-like persona. He would spare him the discomfort. He took a large bite of Bratwurst; he swore it was the best he had ever tasted.

"Forgive me, sir, but I could not be sure that they would find me. These are my team." He cast an eye over them. "They are my friends."

Valerian was still wide-mouthed. "What *is* this? I mean it's like something from *Star Trek*. This is a spaceship."

"Not exactly, sir."

"This is a flying saucer, is it not?" he said flabbergasted.

Where to start, Schumann thought.

They started with a tour of the craft, showing Valerian around, keeping the propulsion, weaponry and cloaking technology to a level that he could process. Too much information could overwhelm even a man as important as the leader of DHvSS.

Valerian was like a child. "What does this do? Wow, what's that?"

They accommodated his naïve knowledge by managing to not offend him. This was clearly a very important man, and a key player in attaining the end goal that would mutually benefit all of them. They had to keep him onside. The strategy, if played out in the right way, would not only rid the world of a terrible threat, but would also ensure the safety of their own nation.

By the time they had finished the tour of the craft, Valerian was subservient to all of them.

It was not Schumann's desire to overshadow the status of the Black Stone Society, but he did see the benefit of influencing the outcome. Now he had surely secured a pathway back into the Dulce base on his own terms, which meant that he could manipulate how to breach the defences to his own advantage.

Valerian was still in a daze as he gave all the crew access to the base.

They entered his office, were issued passes and processed as AAA which gave them the highest security level.

Logan could not contain herself as she was reunited with the crew. Any doubts that Valerian had about loyalty were evaporated in an instant as he witnessed the genuine emotions. It was combat allegiance that could not be faked. Logan hugged them all in turn as they made a fuss of her like a long-lost sister.

Schumann shut the door on proceedings as Valerian squared up to him.

"Alright, mister, you have me at a disadvantage. What do you propose?"

"We have the craft you have witnessed plus another smaller vessel. This can be used to navigate the underwater system in the Gulf, and could infiltrate the lower levels of the Dulce base. The other craft could help in the aerial assault."

Valerian processed the information carefully. "I'm not altogether happy with your explanations, but ... I do not have any better options, that's for sure."

Schumann decided to level with the other man even more. He used a Terran metaphoric explanation to give it more credibility.

"Look, we were sent to the Dulce base to stabilise their sonic weapons. They were in danger of wrecking the whole ecosystem in the Southern Hemisphere. Our unit is deep cover, totally off-grid."

"But you're operating out of Germany, right?"

"It would be more accurate to say that we operate from an underground facility not too much different from this." Schumann indicated with his hands.

"Out of sight and out of mind, right?"

"Something like that."

Valerian paced the room for a while and then looked up.

"Okay, we'll keep this conversation between us for now. You had better get Mr von Getz in here, if that's his real name."

"It is, sir."

Von Getz entered the room. It was mainly full of filing cabinets aside from a map table with four chairs. They all sat as von Getz delivered what intel knew.

Valerian sat astonished as he was given a tour of the lower levels of the base courtesy of von Getz's captured footage from the camera hidden in his spectacles. The film had come out remarkably well, exposing a huge amount of information to them.

"It's even worse down there than I thought." Valerian looked downbeat.

Further footage showed the research facilities, the dockside, the massive caverns that led to the Draco cities and the vast armies, along with the scientific laboratories. Valerian watched wide-mouthed at the hordes of Caste, the Greys directing proceedings, human body parts, and worse still, clearly captured in the film.

"It's like hell on Earth," Valerian uttered, still staring at the projection. "This is going to be an impossible task. There are just too many of them."

"Sir, if I may." Von Getz switched off the device. Valerian

looked up at him with a defeated expression. The Swabian glanced at his leader. Schumann gave the go-ahead with a curt nod.

"As already pointed out, we have the Haunebu Dora 20 and also a Flugelrad 20 on the seabed near the Gulf of Mexico ready to go."

"What equipment did you manage to get?" Schumann asked.

"We have two image projectors, one portable cloak and six Armolux."

That was not a lot of gear. Gaining aerial superiority would be relatively straightforward, but taking control of the inside of the base with such a small armoury would be difficult. Schumann had to remain upbeat for the sake of the others. Von Getz continued.

"If you took your men and mounted a four-pronged attack." He pointed to the Dulce perimeter and looked at Valerian. "And if we time our assault correctly, it could catch MJ-12 cold. Remember, they will not be expecting us to attack."

"I hear what you're saying, I really do, but we need more intel before we can mount a strike," Valerian said wearily.

"There is no more time, sir," von Getz announced. "The meeting is tomorrow."

"Are you sure?" The big man recoiled at the revelation.

"We have people from our own facility in attendance. There is no doubt."

Schumann sighed with a grim determination. "We will target the delegation and inflict as much damage as possible."

"You mentioned obtaining more information. You have contact within the base?" von Getz asked Valerian.

"We do. A unique system. We have an individual down there, a hybrid boy who can get information out to one of our contacts. His name is Bek."

The two Swabians looked at each other.

"We have met," Schumann revealed. "He seemed wise beyond his years."

Valerian acknowledged the fact. "Yes, I witnessed first-hand as he channelled information out to us. Truly amazing."

"I had no idea he was with the rebels," von Getz stated.

"I think contact with his mother gave him a sense of purpose." Valerian brightened. "He could be a valuable asset to us."

They studied the updated layout of the lower base. They still had the rebel unit in place who could, if notified, be in position to ambush the delegation. Bek would be able to inform them that a strike on the base was imminent. If they could get inside, they could coordinate together in a pincer movement that might just work.

Schumann suddenly remembered the sonic weapon in the middle of the underground harbour. Thanks to his recent adjustments, the device could be used against the occupants of the base. It would be a far more effective method than explosives. That would eliminate the need to smuggle them in and to plant them in key areas.

He ran the idea past the others.

"What sort of damage are we talking here?" Valerian said quizzically.

"If I can power the sonics up enough, it could take out everyone on the lower levels."

Valerian nodded slowly. "I like those odds better." He looked into space wide-eyed. I guess this is it, then. I'll inform everyone to stand by."

Chapter 57

Denver, Colorado

The real president-in-waiting swished his crystal tumbler around in his hand, making the ice tinkle with the generous measure of Scotch inside. Claude Perfekt mimicked the motion. It made a pleasing sound.

"You are enjoying my Macallan?"

Perfekt took a large swig and let the whisky burn pleasantly down his throat. "A very fine choice. I hope to return your hospitality back in the United Kingdom."

"Why, I look forward to it, my dear friend. It's been a while since I was last in London."

The two men chatted for a short while before being interrupted by the pilot. "That's Denver below us, gentlemen. We will be landing in a few minutes."

The two men looked out into the night. Far below, they could make out the lights of Denver airport: a strange choice of location, actually being some considerable distance from Denver itself.

It was always thought odd to build a second airport here, but even so, Dalheim and the others had managed to develop the 35,000-acre site into the largest of its kind. It had run ridiculously over budget, mainly down to the underground bunkers and rail system that, built off-plan in a fiendishly elaborate plot, they had convinced the freemasons to contribute in return for some flimsy, jumped-up prestige which included an impressive capstone located inside the airport sporting the synonymous all-seeing eye logo. Underneath was the completion date, and the accredited organisation going by the name of The New World Airport Commission.

On the subject of commissions, they had approved a set of murals that depicted some rather confusing scenes of an apocalyptic nature. There was quite a lot of objection to the upsetting scenes, resulting in their eventual removal altogether. Dalheim smiled as he thought about the games they had played with theoretical minds trying to come up with various conspiracy theories to explain their meaning, completely off the mark, of course.

Perfekt nudged his arm as the private jet taxied down the runway, another controversial landmark coming into view: the famous blue stallion statue rearing up in the air, the eyes glowing red in the night, yet another symbol of power for all to guess the meaning of and, of course, to get completely wrong. Many had arrived at the conclusion that the sculpture was based on the fourth horse of the apocalypse which represented death. But even the Majestic 12, with their wicked sense of humour, would not have been so foolish as to suggest that connection with flying. That would not be a very good advert. It was actually a Lipizzaner, commissioned in memory of the Führer, a breed used in the war by their leader in an attempt to develop a master horse race.

Unfortunately, while creating the masterpiece, the sculptor was informed of this connection and strongly objected to continuing on the project. Luckily, he had completed the majority of the work before he met with a very unfortunate accident. How ironic that his own work managed to fall on him, severing a main artery. It only served to add to the mystique of the magnificent sculpture. The two men gave it the respect it deserved as the jet slowly came to a halt. Two suits appeared from a hangar securing the area before waving the two MJ-12 members from the jet.

They chatted casually as they were steered to the cover of the hangar before the large electric door closed behind them. A short while after, the door re-opened just enough to allow a blacked-out limousine to speed away towards the airport exit.

Inside the hangar, Dalheim and Perfekt watched from a window as the lights from the decoy car disappeared into the distance. They exchanged a knowing glance as they were shown to a secret trapdoor. Once inside, they climbed down a short flight of stairs to an elevator. The steel doors shut, taking them down for thirty seconds to a tunnel way below the airport runways. They exited the elevator and were promptly greeted by two armed guards who took them by electric car to an underground shuttle. They boarded the spartan but functional carriage, the only passengers at this point. The shuttle pulled away and was soon speeding underground in the direction of Dulce.

Chapter 58

Cambridgeshire

UK command burst into action, Derek Mills orchestrating his small team.

At first it had seemed odd to Marius not to join the others at the main control room in Paramus. But as Mills pointed out, they were the subsidiary unit, and should the main control be discovered, they would still be operational. They were leaving nothing to chance, however unlikely. This was a mission like no other, the unique inside information presenting them a one-off opportunity to wipe out the MJ-12 organisation. Mills had commented on more than one occasion that most of the secrets held within the higher echelons were passed down traditionally by the spoken word. Very little information existed in hard copy format. Wipe out the leaders, and the whole organisation would fall apart.

Sidney joined Marius as he proceeded to put Caroline under. They could then open the channel with Bek and relay the information real time. The others started to monitor the assault.

"Here we go. Eyes on, people."

Chapter 59

Paramus, New Jersey

Paramus control waited for the screens to light up.

Redmond had changed into combats and was now manning a terminal herself. Every spare pair of hands was given an operational purpose. She took up position next to Logan. They would relay intel from the UK.

Valerian had joined the ground assault on the boundary of the Dulce base. He had split the men into an arc with the two main units at either end. Positioned in between were ground-to-air artillery, drone support and remote controlled all-terrain scanning vehicles. The frontal assault teams were kitted out in Camo body armour, armoured helmets, abseil and radio harnesses, and carried NBC suits with respirators. Weapons were MP5 machine guns and M4 carbine rifles with a grenade launcher which sat neatly under the barrel. Others in the teams carried Heckler and Koch rapid-fire grenade rifles. For close quarters, the favoured choice was a Sig 226. Should the primary interior assault go to plan, hopefully a lot of this weaponry would be surplus to requirements.

Schumann had flown out cloaked to rendezvous with the Flugelrad.

The four-man team changed into dive gear, black lightweight drysuits with hoods, black boots and second skin

Viper waistcoats. Attached to these were Armolux weight belts to keep them under the surface. The chosen dive mask was a customised Dager model that incorporated a closed-circuit rebreather attached to a black oxygen canister. This would enable them to swim shallow without leaving a trail of giveaway bubbles. To aid them through the water at speed, they would be using mag swim boards with built-in depth gauge and GPS.

Once kitted out, Kaufmann activated the Stingray on the Haunebu. The device worked in a similar way to a flatfish using its body on the seabed to camouflage itself in sand. The process operated until the top hatch was the only part of the ship that remained visible. The team then transferred over to the smaller vessel for their method of entry.

They all climbed down from the foul weather hatch and took up their respective positions. Weisse checked the position for the cave opening. It was about a half-mile north from their current location. He fed the coordinates into the computer and the screen lit up the short route.

The Flugelrad glided away, sending a gentle cloud of debris into a coral bed, a shoal of clown fish spooked back from the disturbance, but within seconds returned as the sand settled as if nothing had been there.

Schumann peered through the observation window as Kaufmann manned the scanners. It was not implausible that the entrance would be protected with motion detectors.

The short journey revealed nothing of concern as they arrived at the entrance. It was cleverly hidden under an overhang, in true Swabian fashion. The men looked at each other suitably impressed. The channel between the rocky seabed and coral outcrops narrowed, allowing for little error. The Terrans had been meticulous, and without the reference point, no one would find the place by accident. Weisse reduced the speed of the craft to dead slow as they passed under the overhang. Schumann activated the infrared revealing the black walls which narrowed, forming a tunnel. They proceeded up a steady incline before Schumann was satisfied that no defences were present. He nodded to Weisse who increased the speed. They continued for an hour before they breached sea level, Weisse taking the Flugelrad to the surface. Schumann opened the hatch.

Although they were now in an underground river, the air was still heavy with salt and it made him start. The craft's magnetic propulsion made very little noise. He cleared his throat, the sound echoing around him, reminding him that they would have to assume absolute silence as they neared the base.

Bek should have been informed of their mission by now, so would hopefully be in position for when they arrived. A lot of the operation came down to guesswork. Schumann did not like the odds or the uncertainty. A lack of information reduced their chances of success significantly.

This would be their first conflict with the Terrans, forced into a perilous mission by the greed and recklessness of their own leaders. Schumann knew that if he failed, it could mean the end of New Swabia, or civil war at the very least.

If they could prevail, he could retain the secrecy of the nation, they could go back to the old traditions and prevent any chance of the same thing happening again. There was a lot of supposition in his thoughts; the only real advantage was the element of surprise. He had studied many campaigns where armies, vastly outnumbered, had emerged victorious. To make this possible, it was vital that they strike fast and decisively. They had superior firepower and would have to use it wisely. He climbed back down into the craft. It was time to go over the plans one more time. There could be no room for mistakes. His men were counting on him.

Chapter 60

Dulce, New Mexico

Albert Hebb jumped out of his chair as his intercom sound. The voice of Commander Holt filled his office.

"Two visitors for you, sir. They will be arriving by shuttle in five minutes."

"Very well, Commander. I'm on my way."

Hebb checked himself in his wall mirror. He straightened his tie and donned his cap. He was jumpy, the recent events making him unusually nervous, and now two visitors to deal with. They were probably a forwarding security contingent, a couple of BGs doing a pointless sweep just to appeal to their boss's egos.

He met Rascher at the dockside, who ordered two of his men to fire up the launch. They made the short crossing over to where the shuttle terminated just in time to spot the train coming into view. Hebb stood on the platform impatiently. He could do without this. He had to finalise everything before …

The doors opened and a number of support staff from Los Alamos disembarked, ready to start their shift. As they thinned out, making their way to their departments, two figures appeared from the furthest carriage. His heart sank as he recognised them.

Claude Perfekt and Heinz Dalheim were early.

"Gentlemen, welcome." Hebb stifled his surprise as best he could.

"Albert, good to see you again. I guess we are the first to arrive, are we not?"

"You are indeed, Mr President." He gave the other man a curt nod. "Good day to you, Mr Perfekt."

"Why don't you give us a guided tour before the others arrive?" Dalheim knew he had caught Hebb out. First the skirmish here on Level Seven, resulting in multiple casualties, and then the bloodbath, instigated by machine-gunning his way across five states. And to cap it off, his two targets were still on the loose. It would do Hebb good to be put on the back foot.

Dalheim would make him sweat for a while.

"So here we are in Level Seven. This is where the firefight took place, I believe."

"Yes. All the damage has been repaired, and relations are resolved with the ETs."

"That was fast work." Dalheim looked him over as they made their way past the labs. "You liaised with them yourself?"

"We have a man called Enoch who takes care of that sort of problem."

"Impressive work. I would like to meet with him."

"Of course, Mr President. Consider it done." Hebb glanced at his second in command, Rascher. "Give Commander Holt a call. See if he can track Enoch down."

The tinted windows in lab three masked out the hive of activity within. Bek was sitting calmly as Aral and the Caste monitored his vital signs. Although he showed no sign of anxiety, the channelling did require some considerable mental strength.

For this reason, there was only so long that he could safely maintain full contact with his mother. They could clearly see the shuttle platform in the distance, and had a panoramic view of the dockside. From one end they could see the tunnel entrances, and at the other, the exit that led to the elevators. Behind them were the archways that led to the experimental sectors.

Bek relayed the information to his mother that two important-looking men were now being shown around by Hebb. They had to be part of MJ-12. He also confirmed that he was expecting the arrival of a four-man team via the underground river. He would watch out for them. The rebels had their own teams in place. These included loyal Caste and Aral that Bek could control and the small human unit led by Enoch.

He was keeping a lookout from his vantage point when his comms sounded.

"Enoch, it's Commander Holt. Hebb is looking for you."

"Do you know why?"

"No idea. Watch yourself down there, okay?" Holt sounded anxious.

"I can see him from here. I'll see what he wants. Out."

Enoch cut the comms and looked over at Aral. "Something's up. We have to suspend the channelling."

They stopped, the Caste finding menial chores to do while Aral started working on a computer. Enoch took a deep breath, stepping out from the lab, walking over to the three men.

"Sir, I believe you asked to see me."

"Ah, there you are, Enoch. Yes, I have someone here that wants to meet you."

Dalheim smiled warmly. "I hear you are the one to thank for brokering a peace deal with the Draco."

"I have met with them on many occasions, sir. I think that

counted for something," he replied modestly.

Dalheim's smile broadened. "I'm sure there was more to it than that. They tell me you know them better than anyone."

"I'm just glad I could be of service, sir."

"Please, would you walk with us? We are just about to go on a guided tour and I may have some questions."

"Of course."

Albert Hebb expelled a long, silent breath as he led the way to an electric car. There were brownshirts everywhere, with some of them providing escort front and rear in convoy.

Perfekt spoke for the first time. "Glad to see you have security prioritised."

"We are leaving nothing to chance," Hebb remarked.

Enoch sat in the back with Dalheim beside him. "We'll start with the labs, I think," Dalheim ordered.

As they drove around the perimeter to the main lab area, Dalheim chatted informally to Enoch. "So tell me, what do you think the Draco want from us?"

Enoch was surprised at the candid questioning, but saw no harm in voicing his opinion.

"They are a very secretive race, sir; they give very little away. But I suspect they tolerate us as we supply them with humans and other commodities for their work."

"And do you think that the information they give us in return is worth the risk?" Dalheim pressed him. It was a very good question, Enoch thought.

"I do not think that it is a price worth paying, sir, no."

"Oh, come now," interjected Hebb from the front. "There may have been some difficult times, but look at what we have learned from them." The convoy came to a halt at the advanced lab section. "See for yourselves."

They climbed out, the two visitors gazing in wonder at the

spectacle in front of their eyes.

Scientists were working on a variety of human subjects, the observation windows allowing them to view the struggling victims as they were injected with various substances. Enoch tried to avert his eyes; he hated this area.

"So what are they doing to them?" Perfekt spoke for the second time, with a genuine interest.

"They are being trialled to see how they react to various diseases."

A man foaming at the mouth broke free from his restraints and started to bang on the glass, his blistered face contorted in pain.

The scientists sprang into action, injecting their 'patient' in the neck. His expression relaxed as he slid down the glass. They watched as he was dragged back to a gurney and strapped down securely.

"Come now; we have more to see," Hebb said cheerily. Enoch hid his disgust behind the back of a hand.

They came to more human abductees in various states of mental disorder; the hybrid section which Perfekt found particularly entertaining; and then onto the holding area where Hebb introduced them to Cory.

"This is the holding area we use before deciding on the best process for them. In his case, because of his mental condition, he has limited use. He will probably end up being trialled for dementia or something." Hebb spoke casually as if it was nothing. The two visitors nodded enthusiastically. The next cage along was occupied by another male standing perfectly still, a vacant expression on his face, looking malnourished.

"Here we have a relatively new arrival," Hebb ranted on. "We condition them to start with, to prepare them for the experiments. This one is due to participate in a programme starting tomorrow. Isn't that right, Fred?"

The man blinked once slowly, and continued to stare into space. Hebb led the group away with Enoch at the back. As he passed the cage of the subject called Fred, he heard a whisper; only a murmur, but it was audible enough to be heard. Enoch did not react or divert his gaze as he followed the others to the hybrid section.

At this point, Hebb pointed out the multitude of creations that stretched for fifty yards in either direction, tank after tank, cage after cage, the scale of the operation quite bewildering. There were hundreds of them.

"What's this for?" Dalheim asked, pointing to a canal flowing gently in front of the tanks, random bridges uniting the banks, allowing for closer inspection.

"Ah, a new addition. The water course is used to empty tanks and their contents when they are of no more use. It is an easy way to dispose of them." Hebb took delight in attracting Otto into view through the murky green contents of his lair. There were the same demented grin and mad eyes, the distorted bulbous head floating in front of them all, tentacles stroking the thick glass as an enormous tongue appeared and proceeded to lick in circular motions. The visitors were mesmerised as they crossed the bridge for a closer look. Enoch stayed where he was. The guided tour was taking too long. He needed to get back.

"So this is obviously a failed experiment. Why keep it alive?" Perfekt asked.

"Ah, here's the thing." Hebb was relaxing somewhat into his role, the tension of the VIP presence melting away. In fact, he was beginning to revel in the occasion. "We can still learn a lot from our rejects, and can use Otto here to extract his DNA to crossbreed with other specimens to improve the product."

Hebb chatted away as if it was a cake recipe. The whole scenario was insane. Enoch wanted to run.

They were shown more octo men as they joined Otto in unison. The squid man was there, the six sad eyes blinking together. For the first time, Enoch felt compelled to touch the glass. The squid man brought his enormous claw up and tapped where the human hand rested. Enoch gave out a secret smile that only the creature could see, then retreated not wanting to provoke conversation from the others. There were more nautical nightmares, most impossible to put a name to. Enoch guessed they originated from seals and walruses, drastically altered by crossbreeding.

"You see, we would never have come this far without the help of our green friends down there," Hebb blathered. "They gave us the ability to merge species together, recoding their genetic structure. It really is quite amazing, don't you think?"

"Fascinating," Dalheim purred. "Very impressive, Mr Hebb."

"Yes, very impressive," Perfekt added. Enoch just gave a polite smile.

Hebb was now well and truly melting into his own egotistical world. "Well, it's not all down to me. We have a very good team here at the base; some of the finest scientific minds in the world, all working for the cause."

"Good job they have no idea what that is," Perfekt quipped.

There was a brief silence before he burst out laughing. The others joined in too, filling the cavern with echoes as their voices rang out all around them.

The noise set off the birdmen in the next section. They cawed noisily as the tour continued. It was going better than Hebb expected. Perhaps another promotion might be on the cards.

They were shown the towering birdmen and introduced to

the real batman, his wings folded up eyeing them with disdain.

"And these must be the new magnetic locks?" Dalheim examined a four-inch-square panel on the cage door.

"Yes. Good to know Hans Schumann was of some use to us."

"So he was responsible for all of the upgrades? He did all this?" Dalheim looked impressed.

"He did indeed, making it far easier to secure the lower base on lockdown. The locks feature all over Levels Six and Seven."

"I wonder why he decided to go on the run," Perfekt mused.

"And that female professor, too," Dalheim added. "Did either of them show any sign of discontent?"

"None at all. Their escape coincided with the skirmish with the ETs," Hebb stated.

"We still have that other chap. What's his name? ... von Getz, a good scientific brain in his own right, I'm told."

"Yes, good on the sonics." Hebb had quite forgotten that he was due to return to the base. "He could be an ideal replacement."

"Right, that's settled, then. You can inform him when he arrives," Dalheim confirmed.

They continued past the Goran pens, Hebb delighting in explaining the terrible mixture section that was used to deliver sustenance to the Draco on a regular basis.

The final sector housed the new arrivals. There were dozens of drugged-up abductees ranging from toddlers through to the elderly.

"They will be assessed and prioritised by the science teams," Hebb said with glee.

The two visitors nodded studiously as the lab visit came to an end. The convoy came to collect them. They circled back, observing the rest of Level Seven by car. Enoch was desperate to distance himself from the others, and clear his mind of the recent horror show. He was shaking with rage inside, not helped by the suggestion that came next.

"I would like to see the Draco sector. Enoch could show us around," Perfekt suggested.

"Why, I'm sure Enoch would be only too pleased." Hebb gave him a look, raising his brow.

Enoch was in shock. "I will have to talk to them. They can be difficult."

"Well, if anyone can assure them, I'm sure it's you, Enoch." Perfekt patted his arm.

Dalheim looked at his watch. "It's getting late. Our tour took longer than I expected. With the others arriving soon, it might be an idea to postpone going into the lower levels." He looked at Perfekt. "Don't worry, my friend, we can go tomorrow morning."

Perfekt pulled a sulking face, then smiled broadly.

Hebb breathed a huge sigh of relief. A journey into the Draco sector was never easy at the best of times, and would be a logistical nightmare trying to keep the president safe. He would try and talk the men out of it later. No point at the moment with them behaving like excited children.

Enoch had been saved by the clock; Hebb and his colleagues had to meet with the other visitors.

"You can stay a while with us, Enoch. Some of the others would be fascinated to hear all about the ETs," Dalheim said.

His heart sank again. "Of course, sir. I would be delighted to."

They arrived back at the dockside where even more security was in place. One of the large conference rooms had been given over to host the reception, the area transformed for a five-course banquet. Catering staff appeared with trays of canapes and champagne.

Hebb cast an eye over proceedings. There were bodies everywhere. To make matters worse, the brownshirts near the tunnels had to remain unarmed as part of the new treaty agreement with the Draco. He steered his guests through the crowd towards the shuttle platform.

Enoch kept back as the shuttle glided in to a halt. The doors opened and out stepped a group of smartly dressed men. They all shook hands, exchanging pleasantries. Dalheim greeted them all warmly in turn. They repaid the welcome, addressing him as 'Mr President'.

Enoch took a sharp intake of breath. Just a short while ago he had been sharing a car with the president of MJ-12 himself. He could feel his cheeks flushing with anger.

The chatter carried on for several minutes, the group sauntering across the great expanse toward the conference room. The brownshirts stayed close by as Enoch held back. With so much to preoccupy them, he managed to slip away without being seen. He skirted around the gathering and navigated his way back to lab three. Once inside, he gasped his apologies.

Wasting no time, the Caste and Aral got Bek ready as Enoch helped the boy to re-connect with his mother. He had to gamble that the people with her had kept her under, otherwise it would be a waste of time.

A knock at the door. Enoch froze as it opened an inch. Gallagher, Cale and Sagen entered the room, wearing black security uniforms. Enoch let out a sigh of relief. He could not take much more of this. He returned to the delicate task of channelling with Bek.

For a long time, there was nothing, Aral and Caste all offering silent conditioning. Gallagher and co. waited patiently, keeping a watch as the dinner conference got underway. Enoch was counting on the occasion buying him time before he was missed. He could make an excuse that there was some security issue to attend to. It would not be difficult to believe, the way things had been recently.

Bek murmured as he connected; contact with the outside re-established. Enoch relayed the new intel on Dalheim, a good description of the president, an update of security and where the conference was being held. He let Bek converse with his mother. Any intel she had would be recorded for him.

"I had the President right next to me," he said. "I can't believe it."

"Don't be hard on yourself," Gallagher replied. "All our weapons are in the armoury. Besides, if you had have killed him, it would have warned the others. We must make sure that we get them all." He nodded over at the meeting room.

Enoch tried to calm himself. "You're right, of course."

"Are they all in there?" Sagen asked.

"I think so, but I don't recognise that guy in the doorway." Enoch indicated a thin officious-looking man, champagne in hand, talking to Hebb.

"Name's Vessels. We had to escort him down here. I guess he is one of the investors," Gallagher spat.

Enoch conveyed the information to Bek, who channelled it out along with a name one of the captives had uttered to Enoch.

"We had better get going," Cale pointed out.

"You and Sagen go ahead. I had better stay here and help Enoch." Gallagher took up the lookout position.

"Very well, we will go on patrol for a while, until the time comes."

"Okay. Good luck."

The two men left the room, merging into the crowd.

Chapter 61

New Mexico

The ground assault team had flown down to a private airstrip fifty miles north of Dulce. It was as close as they dared to get before switching to road vehicles. They were dropped off two miles from the boundary, then the team hiked their way to the edge of the restricted zone that surrounded the base.

At this point the team divided into four. Valerian would take red team and breach the cave. Blue team would assault the mine shaft, while green and black would take the central ground.

It seemed like an endless wait before the radio crackled into life. The comms man next to Valerian relayed the new intel.

"At bloody last. Where have you been?"

"Sorry, sir. Nets been down with the base. They want to know if von Gellen means anything to you."

"No, nothing."

"Okay. Stand by, sir, rebel unit is now in place, members of MJ-12 have arrived and are currently on Level Seven."

Valerian growled. He could hardly believe it.

They carried out last minute weapon checks and a final sweep of the area. He could see an army APC led by a Jeep on the dusty road in the distance. He had the movements of the patrols from Gallagher and his men. Although he could not be sure of the accuracy, the patrols had been regular enough to signal the advance.

The rovers moved ahead, probing for hidden devices, the men following at a steady pace, the teams fanning out.

Progress was slow. They had to be sure that Cale and Sagen had managed to disable the motion detectors and microwave security. They skirted around three gunnery placements with ease. At this point, the terrain became more even and stable, good enough to switch to longboards fitted with large off-road wheels, the powerful dual brushless sensor motors built into sleek carbon fibre camo decks, delivering 6000 watts of power.

The caterpillar rovers carved a safe route for the boards to follow. It was a little risky, the teams exposed out in the open before they reached the cover of the scrubland, but it was the only way. They could have increased the rate, but the element of surprise was paramount. They had to remain patient.

Chapter 62

Dulce, New Mexico

The Flugelrad was now cloaked, its speed reduced to a crawl, the jammers allowing the craft to slip into the dock area unnoticed. Weisse had them hugging the harbour floor as they cruised across the expanse of water until they reached the jetty where Hebb had his offices. From this point, they followed the bankside the short distance to the huge cavern where the submarine base was situated. Schumann sneaked a look through the periscope, scanning in a wide arc from left to right. There was no one around. The place had been shut down for the officers to join the others on the dockside. He spotted the sonics weapon where he had last used it. He signalled Weisse over to it.

The Flugelrad came to a halt as Schumann had another good look around before signalling the craft to the surface.

The sonic unit was easy to power up; the adjustments took only a short time to reprogramme. The more difficult task would be to activate the receptors in the dockside so that the disparity of the soundwaves would cover the lower caverns and Level Six. They could engage the sonics remotely, but the receptors would have to be positioned and armed manually. That would take a two-man team to do the job. The other team were to make contact with the rebel unit and get them back to the Flugelrad.

Schumann used a pair of rangefinders to examine the roof of the cavern high above their heads. He nodded to Kaufmann who released a small drone, the size of a matchbox. He used a remote unit to steer the tiny flying machine up the side of the cavern and along the roof until it was directly above them. Kaufmann then increased the height until the drone stuck to the ceiling, then powered the device down.

They got back inside the Flugelrad and headed back to the dockside, Weisse tucking the craft neatly into a recess twenty feet down. The small recess would allow them to find the cloaked craft with ease.

Von Getz knew all of the rebel team. He would take Kaufmann with him to the rendezvous point. Schumann and Weisse would deal with the receptors.

They left the hatch in a line, the boards powering them through the water, all of them cloaked, using the rebreathers to full effect.

The best MOE was under the dock front. Here, a meshed grill around four feet wide covered a short tunnel that led to the canal on the corner of the experimental labs. They hid the boards up and removed the grill.

They swam the short distance to the canal, easing slowly from the water. They climbed out between two gantries that Schumann remembered led to the large pool with the observation window. The team carefully folded the drysuits up, wedging them out of sight underwater. Von Getz put the tanks together and attached an adjustable detonator. He let the tanks slip from his hands to the bed of the canal. They clipped their waistcoats back on, making sure not to splash water on the ground – not an easy thing to do when everything was cloaked – but they could not take the risk with all of the CCTV around.

They split into the two groups, and headed off in opposite directions. Schumann led Weisse away from the labs to start their task. They would have to go in there eventually, but he would start with the less stomach-churning areas first. They kept to the buildings and walls for cover where there were less people. They nearly collided with a man carrying a tray of champagne as he rushed towards the banquet, muttering about coping with the demand. The pair proceeded more cautiously, checking open doorways before crossing the threshold.

As they passed the last block, they turned a corner into another sector. At this point, Schumann fished a receptor from his backpack, placing it into a gap behind some pipework. There were miles of pipes branching out in all directions, offering plenty of hiding places for them. They advanced quietly until they reached another set of labs. These, Schumann recognised as he led Weisse to the third room along. He took a good look around and gave the order to de-cloak. He tapped on the door. It opened only an inch, and then fully as the two men were bundled inside lab three.

Gallagher stifled an outburst as he recognised Schumann. He and Weisse were introduced to Enoch, who looked up in astonishment.

"My god, you made it ... but?" He suddenly checked himself. "No time for that. We have to inform the others right away." His voice quivered as he spoke to Bek, who was reclined in a chair, his eyes closed.

Weisse gave a gasp of disbelief as he watched the Caste and Aral monitor the boy's progress. Schumann had never seen Aral in close proximity. He was very human in appearance although it was clear that he was different. Dressed in one of the lab coats, and at a distance, it would be hard to tell, though. It was eerie watching as Enoch's solitary voice communicated with the mixed telepathy, conveying the intelligence from the two Swabians through Bek and back to his mother.

"Enoch, river team have made contact, sonics operation in progress, MJ-12 are still with Hebb along with Vessels."

Schumann stiffened at the name. He had hoped Brunner would be with them, but it looked as if Vessels had left him in charge back home. No point in worrying about that now; they had to get the rest of the sonic gear into position. Gallagher checked for the all clear. As they were leaving, Enoch looked up and spoke.

"Does von Gellen mean anything to you?"

Chapter 63

New Mexico

Green team reached the marker, a series of abandoned rusted military vehicles, parked into groups, shell craters all around them.

"Green leader, we are at the range."

"Red leader, okay, split the team and proceed. Over," Valerian's boomy voice ordering half of green unit to advance ahead to the rendezvous beacon while black unit would head to the main entrance of the base.

It took green another twenty minutes to reach the GPS coordinates, green leader checking with his GPR reader. The signal was strong beneath his feet – not a doubt that it was the right place – but there was nothing to see. If anything at all, the area became even more flat; there was no vegetation at all for a hundred yards in all directions, the only deviation a slight trough that ran in a straight line. He pulled the team back to the cover of some large boulders where they primed surface-to-air and disposable 66-rocket grenade weapons.

Valerian moved red team forward, boarding behind the rover, finally reaching the tree line. Black team were level with them a mile away to their right, blue team another half mile beyond that.

The comms sounded again. They had found the entrance to the mine shaft.

Red team continued on the boards until the ground became too steep and uneven. They continued on foot, following the GPS coordinates, eventually arriving at the concealed cave entrance. They rolled the brush vegetation aside, entering in a line.

It did not take long to clear the rocks, exposing the air con duct breach. The last man brushed the footprints from the dirt track before camouflaging the cave entrance. He would stay behind, making his way to the base entrance and join up with black team.

Just inside the cave entrance, the comms sounded the final message that all teams were now in position. Contact was now terminated with all teams as they entered the base.

Chapter 64

Dulce, New Mexico

"Chancellor von Gellen is alive?" Weisse gasped.

Schumann could barely comprehend it himself. Vessels had abducted his own leader and shipped him to the base, condemning him to a fate worse than death.

They were crouched behind two huge nutrient tanks, facing each other as Weisse clipped another receptor into place. Enoch had told them where von Gellen was. Schumann could not bear to think what they had done to him. Thankfully, he could not have been at the base long enough for the experimenting to start on him. But could they help him at all?

"How many receptors are left?"

Weisse looked in the backpack. "There are four left."

Schumann checked the layout on his tablet. "That's not enough." He pointed to the far cavern with its many rooms and corridors. "This area here; we just do not have the receptors to cover it. We need an extra one."

"What are our options?" Weisse asked.

Schumann thought for a moment, scanning the plans carefully. There was only one solution. "The gas tanks that run behind the experimental labs; we can set a charge on the valves and detonate the area."

Weisse took a closer look. "Yes, that would work, I think.

The explosive spread should cover it."

"Okay, let's get the rest of them in place. We don't have much time."

They cloaked up and continued around the base perimeter.

Von Getz and Kaufmann had reached the armoury. They were pleased to see the new locks in place, courtesy of their commander. Von Getz tried the handprint key pad; the door slid open. Inside were forty Armolux, a couple of ancient grenade launchers, some hand grenades and about a dozen Glock handguns. Kaufmann picked one up, turning it over in his hand.

"Not fired one of these in years."

"Let's hope you don't have to."

They loaded up their backpacks with weapons and stepped out, securing the door. Von Getz put in a jamming code and they made off to meet up with the rebel unit.

Chapter 65

Albert Hebb was in his element. His concerns about Schumann and Logan were diminishing, and even the Draco were keeping a low profile. That suited him just fine. They were unpredictable at the best of times, and he would have been as nervous as hell with them walking around, stinking the place out.

He would try and put a spanner in the works regarding Perfekt's visit to the lower caverns. That had disaster written all over it. He looked at the man sucking up to the president. In truth, he hardly knew Claude Perfekt. Dalheim had always kept him in the background and well out of the conversation. They seemed to be getting on very well now, though, quaffing the champagne he had supplied.

Dinner was nearly over. It would soon be time to take them all on a guided tour. He knew what Dalheim's game was: arriving early, trying to catch him out, then relaying information to the others about the research as if he was some kind of expert. The truth was, Dalheim visited the bases quite infrequently, choosing to stay in Washington DC, staring longingly out of the window at the White House. The real work and the real money was made down here, and real risks were taken to make that happen. And as for Perfekt, people like him made him sick, with his five grand suites and his penthouses. Things would be different if Hebb was in charge.

"Albert, dear fellow." Dalheim snapped him out of his daydream.

"Yes, sir, Mr President."

"Where's Enoch disappeared to? The others want to meet him."

It seemed that everyone was more popular than himself at the moment. He drained his glass of champagne.

"I'll see where he's got to." Hebb took a walk, plucking another full glass from a waiter's tray.

Gallagher saw him coming from a long way off, the khaki uniform almost glowing next to the brownshirt entourage, never too far away.

"Hebb's heading this way."

Enoch looked up sharply. "I'll have to go with him, otherwise he might become suspicious."

"Alright. The intel has been sent out anyway. Better wake Bek up."

"Oh, I am wide awake, Mr Gallagher. Everything going to plan?"

Gallagher smiled. "Yes, Bek, so far so good."

The Caste and Aral busied themselves as Hebb approached. Bek resumed his duties. It had to look as normal as possible.

Enoch stood in the doorway so Hebb could see him.

"Ah, there you are. The others are asking for you," Hebb slurred. "Come and have some champagne. This is a cause for celebration."

"I take it the visitors are pleased."

"Indeed they are. We are about to take a tour." Hebb indicated with his hand. It was more of a silent command than an invitation. Enoch was used to his ways.

"I would be honoured, sir."

Gallagher ran a scanner over a few peripherals for effect,

trying to look innocuous. It didn't work.

"Mr Gallagher, you come too. I could do with some extra muscle around. These damned Draco, so unpredictable these days."

"I could do with a weapon," Gallagher muttered.

"No can do. The tour takes us into the treaty area; no weapons allowed. Better off shouting a load of obscenities at them anyway." Hebb gave a low belch.

Gallagher did not reply as Hebb led them away back towards the banqueting area.

Chapter 66

Schumann and Weisse entered the experimental section with the last receptor, where the first block of labs was situated. Schumann had already told his friend what to expect, but no preparation was ever enough. He reacted like most would in his position. Schumann allowed him a few moments to come to terms with what he saw. They had entered from the opposite direction which meant the first area they saw was full of birdmen.

Schumann could hear the cawing start up and signalled to back away. Even though they were fully cloaked, the creatures knew they were there. Weisse, like all the others, was almost hypnotised by the monstrosities before him. Schumann grabbed his arm and led him over to the pens.

Further down the cavern was an area where the human abductees were kept. They made their way past numerous subjects, keeping their nerves in check until they came to pen 29.

The man inside was sitting on a bench, motionless. He looked malnourished and somewhat dishevelled, but better than they expected. It was unmistakably Chancellor von Gellen.

Schumann checked the motion cameras. They did a very large sweep which meant they had a couple of minutes before they completed their cycle. Clearly, security were not concerned with issues in this sector. He examined the locking mechanism; no way they were getting out.

They de-cloaked, checking over the gear before looking up at the man in the pen. He rose from his seated position and let out a low audible gasp. He staggered over to them, his hands gripping the bars tightly.

"Schumann, it really is you."

"Herr Chancellor, we have come to get you out of here. Please be patient. We will return as soon as possible."

"Please hurry. The brownshirts will be doing their rounds soon."

He gave his leader the thumbs up, leading Weisse away into the gloom at the rear of the cavern. They found the gas lines and set the explosive charges.

"That's it. Once we connect the sequence, the sonics will activate," Weisse confirmed.

"Okay, so far so good. Now we can …'

Something caught Schumann's eye. He was about to draw his Armolux when his eyes adjusted just enough in recognition.

"Das Glocke."

Weisse could also see the object glowing under the soft lighting in the distance. Hebb had moved the craft to coincide with the guided tour route. He could waffle on about it to his guests before he took them into the chamber of horrors next door.

"I thought it was destroyed." Weisse walked closer, mesmerised.

"Me too, until I saw it for myself."

They cloaked up before the cameras made their sweep, Schumann allowing Weisse a moment to get a close-up examination.

"Magnificent," was all he could manage.

Schumann looked at the craft. He never did get a chance to

see how it worked.

"Sir." Weisse shook him from his reverie. "You said we are going back for the chancellor, but how are we going to get him out of there?"

It was a good point. The mag locks that he had improved had the codes stored in the main control room on Level Three; no way of getting in there. But he did have one trick up his sleeve.

"I installed a secret manual override at the end of the sector."

"But you still need the operation codes, surely," Weisse quizzed him.

"Not if I throw all three switches at once."

"That's brilliant." Then Weisse went quiet before stating the obvious. "But that would mean opening all the locks at once."

"Yes, it would."

Chapter 67

Albert Hebb decided to start the tour at the docks, leading a small armada of launches up to where the submarine command was based. The visiting group looked in awe as they saw the sonic testing cavern for the first time, its immense ceiling illuminated to full effect; the gunnery placements now manned with brownshirts; the sub command in full ceremonial dress as they greeted MJ-12 at the quayside. It was all carefully coordinated to impress, and Hebb had made sure that all the military hardware they had was out on display for their guests for full effect.

Gallagher took a good look around. There were some serious defences here. There were nine nuclear-powered subs all in a line, each one with a small detail standing with their hands behind their backs on the weather decks. The gunnery placements he knew carried live shells at all times, but he had never known them all to be manned at once. If Hebb had stationed the rest of the route in the same way, it would make the assault far more difficult.

Enoch was busy answering questions on the Draco. He had pulled in a small audience by now, led by Perfekt, who seemed to have a morbid fascination with them. They would both have to go along with the charade for as long as it took, to buy the rest of the team time to get into position.

However, this inclusion on the guided tour was not part of the plan. The rebel unit was now splintered, leaving Bek on his own in the lab area. They would also have to rely on Cale and Sagen disabling the auto-flash response units they knew would activate in the event of an attack.

The ETs were still very quiet. For the first time in his life, he wished that they would appear to give Hebb a problem to deal with, which would free up Enoch and himself to go and calm things down. But the visit held no interest for them whatsoever. They had a specific work ethic which did not involve human social interaction. The Draco and the Greys would make an appearance in the next two minutes, or maybe not for days. That was how they were.

Gallagher took a discreet glance at his Omega Seamaster. All units should be in place by now. One good thing was that they had made it this far without being detected. That filled him with a modicum of optimism. Right now, they had to play along with Hebb and his cronies so as not to arouse suspicion. More champagne and canapes were offered to the guests. That was good. The more alcohol they all consumed, the more their judgement would be clouded. Gallagher and Enoch joined in with the high-spirited gathering, veritably encouraging yet more consumption of alcohol, while at the same time tipping their own contents into the water when no one was looking.

There were a few minutes more waffling before the guests were encouraged to board the launches back towards the main dock area.

Gallagher took a good long hard look around. A lot of the informal entertainment had been stripped away, replaced by a more aggressive military presence. This was clearly a tactic of Hebb's to put on a show of strength. Gallagher could sense the approval on the faces of MJ-12. Hebb was winning them over. He sidled up to Enoch who gave him a look of acknowledgement.

"So how long have you worked here?" came a sudden enquiry from a champagne flute-wielding visitor.

"Longer than I care to remember, sir," came Enoch's reply.

"Vessels, Gerhard Vessels. Pleased to make your acquaintance."

"Likewise," Enoch replied cautiously. He felt the hairs prickle on his neck as the words of Hans Schumann resonated in his head. Another primary target. This man was top of the hit list, although he did not know the reason. But he did not have to. He trusted his friend and that was all the intel that he needed.

Gallagher could feel the magnitude of the whole situation coming to fruition. All the key players now in position right next to them, how he would readily have sacrificed himself to take them all into oblivion with him right now. But Hebb was more cautious and paranoid than he had expected. There were no weapons to hand to execute the endgame, no improvisation to engage the plan. They would have to be patient and follow protocol, and trust in the man called Hans Schumann.

Chapter 68

The receptor chain was in place. Schumann was now looking at his compatriot as they waited for the next stage of the operation. They both knew that the chances of escape were not that good, but the chances of stopping MJ-12 were possible. The fact was that they were the only hope, although mankind could have no idea what the threat was.

It suddenly dawned on Schumann that this was yet another mission carried out that the human race was so ignorant of; yet another warped organisation that managed to operate undetected, profiteering from ignorance and greed. Now it was up to him to take the lead, to find a solution to all their causes. And to wipe out the threat once and for all.

Schumann knew what was at stake. If he eliminated MJ-12, it could mean world peace for all races, and it could secure the existence of New Swabia for hundreds of years to come. That was easy to think, though. The execution would be another matter.

They took refuge behind the air conditioning unit, where the experimental labs started. This was a three-way juncture, giving them options depending on what happened when the assault was activated.

It was always going to be guesswork if and when the surface teams infiltrated the base. Schumann knew they would have received the last transmission from Bek about an hour ago. He had allowed for another thirty minutes, and then it would be a case of coordinating as best he could.

He heard the sound of footsteps shuffling towards them and instantly he knew who it was. The figure de-cloaked in front of him, declaring his security clearance. There was no need.

"Klaus, over here." Schumann and Weisse revealed themselves to their colleague, Kaufmann also appearing from the shadows.

They kept the repatriation to a minimum as they concentrated on the task at hand.

"They're just starting the tour by car, sir," Kaufmann stated.

"Okay, we have the charges and receptors in place. When the initial charges blow in the sub cavern, we will only have a few minutes to free the chancellor," Schumann said hurriedly.

Von Getz shared out the Terran weapons while Kaufmann laid out the mini rocket launchers and the hand grenades. They affixed the grenades either side of the lab entrance with mag chargers, and pointed the launchers with a trajectory of three feet off the ground. These were attached to mag remote detonators. If they timed it right, it should be enough to take out the whole convoy.

Schumann looked at his watch. It would be too much to ask the convoy to pass by as the surface units entered the base, but if the opportunity showed itself, they had to take it.

At some point before the ambush was executed, they had to get Enoch and Gallagher away from the rest of MJ-12. That would not be easy.

Bek was also looking at the clock. It was time for the Caste and Aral to return to the lower caverns. They would merge with the other workers as they descended before planting the last of the receptors. Bek had spent a long time conditioning them against susceptible telepathy. They should be able to withstand the probing. He took a look outside. There was a lot of security around, but they seemed preoccupied with the visit. His acute vision also spotted two Greys with a Draco milling around, half a mile down the right-hand tunnel. He gave the signal, and his mini unit made their way toward the ET group. He watched as they closed in on them, simultaneously observing the convoy leave for the first stage of their tour. It was ironic that many MJ-12 members had hoped to see the ETs for themselves, and now were moving off in the opposite direction just as they were coming out of hiding for the first time.

A few minutes passed. Bek could see the Caste and Aral pass the ETs without incident.

Cale and Sagen returned in readiness for the next stage of the plan. They slipped inside the lab. "Here, take this." Sagen offered a flash gun to Bek.

Bek smiled. "Thank you for the offer, but I will not be needing that."

Sagen looked confused but did not challenge the refusal.

"Just spoken to von Getz," Cale stated. "They are ready."

"That is very good. Now we begin."

Chapter 69

There were two rows of six cars, a mix of guests and security. They pulled away together. Hebb had assembled the top echelons at the rear of the convoy, choosing to let the frontal entourage inflate his ego with their shower of compliments that were sure to follow.

Perfekt looked behind him as they pulled away just in time to see a Draco appear from the gloom of the tunnel. "Wait, wait, the ETs are here," he said excitedly.

Enoch looked around too. "So they are." He looked at Gallagher who returned a 'so what?' expression.

Hebb, though, did not want to miss an opportunity to score yet more favour. "Let's get a closer look," he said. He could see the glee spread all over Perfekt's face. He still had to be careful, though. The Draco could become difficult and spoil his agenda.

Hebb was not taking any chances. He split the convoy in two, sending eight cars ahead, while the remaining four with Perfekt turned around.

"We can meet up with the others later," he said, silently congratulating himself.

The cars slowly made their way to the tunnels, Perfekt with a pair of field glasses trained on the figures ahead. Dalheim looked interested too, Enoch observing that their attitude toward the entities was as if they were on some African safari. These animals though, he knew only too well, were far more dangerous.

"Can I say hello to them? Will they understand me?" Perfekt asked.

"Best not to, sir," Enoch advised. "They can be unpredictable."

"This is near enough." Hebb halted the mini convoy. He was not going to gamble by being reckless.

They were about a hundred yards away, near enough for his guests to easily study the two species. He would give it about a minute before taking the convoy away. He looked at the faces of the guests, which included the German, Vessels. Like the others, he seemed mesmerised by them. Hebb could relate to this; everyone was the same the first time on close encounter.

He remembered his own first time with affection, newly promoted at the Los Alamos base. It was like something out of a dream, all the rumours, all the conspiracy theories, and the hordes of so-called experts claiming that beings like the Greys and the Draco simply did not exist. Even with his own inside testimony from the Black Forest crash in 1936, it still came as a massive shock when he saw the ETs for the first time, interacting with the humans on the lower levels as if it was an everyday occurrence. Now he could see that first time excitement play out once again in front of him, which he could harness into an advantage.

They kept their distance, allowing the guests to have a good view of the ETs through field glasses. Hebb could see Perfekt firing questions at Enoch, Dalheim joining in excitedly as they looked at the group ahead, the single Draco representative looking at them with disdain. Occasionally he would converse telepathically with his two Grey companions, but Hebb knew that the visit was of no interest to them.

"Come now, gentlemen, we must proceed." There was a great deal of audible protest. He could have hugged the ETs for their impromptu appearance. "I know, I know, but there is so much more to see." Hebb was in his element, although he was aware that the other half of the tour also demanded his attention too. The convoy moved off towards the advanced weaponry and bio-genetics departments.

Chapter 70

The four Swabians were in position, the rendezvous point agreed, the convoy approaching. Schumann checked his watch. It was as close to synchronicity as he could hope for. There was always going to be a guided tour of some kind. He would have expected Hebb to flaunt the base for all it was worth in exchange for praise heaped upon himself, even more so after the skirmish with the ETs and his own escape with Logan.

It would seem that Hebb was back in their good books again. But he would see that smug look on his face evaporate as they took out the convoy. He could hear them approaching, the murmur of conversation echoing around the tunnel. He signalled for the others to stand by.

The first car came into view and then the next ... no sign of Hebb ... he must be further back. Schumann looked through his rangefinders. There were only six cars; the convoy was incomplete. They were closing in on the ambush point. What to do? He had to make a decision. As soon as the charges went off, there would be security everywhere. They were expecting that, but the plan was to draw the brownshirts into one main area. Hebb and the others were now sitting on their exit route, and they did not have enough devices to cloak all the rebel team. That was a major problem.

Von Getz had the charges primed. The others knew of the

problem by now. They were waiting for him to give the order.

The convoy moved into range. He had to think logically, trying to draw on his combat training. It was now or never. He could see the centre of the convoy levelling up. He put his hand up to give the silent order, then stopped. He gave the signal to cloak up. The others did so without protest, and the convoy slipped past, the occupants blissfully unaware of their near death experience.

When the convoy was a safe distance away, Schumann de-cloaked. The others did the same.

"Change of plan." He looked at them all in turn. "Weisse, you are with me again. You two are to get the rebel team back to the Flugelrad and standby to evac."

"What about you, sir? How will you get back to us?" von Getz asked.

"We get the chancellor out, then ... I don't really know."

"But, sir ..." Kaufmann looked worried, but Schumann talked over him.

"No time to argue, we have to act right now. You wait for us at the dock until five minutes before the sonics activate. If we are not there, then we will have found another escape route."

The two other Swabians did not look at all comfortable with the plan.

"That is an order, Klaus."

"Well, get going, then," Weisse demanded.

Von Getz gave a curt nod. He and Kaufmann cloaked up and moved off towards the dock area.

Schumann looked at Weisse. "I have no right to ask you to do this. You could go with them."

The other man was no fool. He knew their time was running out. He gave a slight smile. "Lead the way, sir." He cloaked up.

Schumann made the short journey back to the experimental

labs with Weisse close behind him. As expected, the convoy had parked up and the guests were being shown the tanks and pens. They walked right through the middle of the crowd to a point where the floor had a built-in ramp that sloped up to a hydraulic platform which was about ten feet by six feet in dimension. At this point they de-cloaked behind a barrier which screened them from detection. Here, they assembled a two-pronged remote Armolux station. When the time came to move off, the weapons would become visible, but amongst the mechanics and pipework, they would not be detected until they were activated. Schumann checked the mag override and gave the signal. This time, he would initiate the strike. They waited in hiding for as long as they dared; time was running out. Schumann gambled on the distraction tactics being enough while they tried to spring von Gellen from his confinement. He was determined not to let the chancellor die alone.

The big dilemma with this plan had always been the staged segregation which would seal off a lot of access points. This would allow security to post sentries in far fewer stations and make their response far more effective. How long it would be for these to activate was unknown to him, but he knew the longer the alert went on, the more sections would be locked down. He also knew deep down that on foot, and with von Gellen in tow, it would take too long to get back to the Flugelrad.

He cleared his mind of that problem.

One final check before cloaking back up. Another few minutes passed.

The straight run of the department offered him a good view for a considerable distance. One reason he had chosen their position was to enable them to see activity at the other end of the labs. He used the rangefinders for identification, studying the gloom beyond the excited guests who were being lectured to on the contents of the rooms in front of them.

The glint of white coming into view, and then more movement, was Hebb and the others. He now had the four cars in focus. Dalheim, Perfekt and Vessels; all present.

He nodded to Weisse, who reciprocated. They cloaked up and made their way down to ground level and then silently over to where von Gellen was situated. He was sitting up, which was a good sign. With a bit of luck, they would not have to carry him out.

Schumann flicked the switches. There was a loud clunk followed by hydro-mechanics, then two seconds later, the locks blew out, setting off the alarms.

At first, Hebb ran towards the commotion, then thought better of it and turned on his heels, signalling wildly with his arms. The others nearest to Schumann jumped back in shock as the doors opened in unison.

Murky green water exploded from tanks, sending all manner of creations spilling out onto the grey shiny surface of the floor. The pens with no water content that were nearest to Schumann clicked to the 'unlock' position, although the doors remained closed.

They wasted no time rushing into von Gellen's cell, de-cloaking before his very eyes, taking him by surprise, the man not quite comprehending what was happening.

"Chancellor, it's us." Schumann barked above the din of the sirens. "We are getting you out of here."

Von Gellen, although worse for wear from being drugged, summoned up enough energy to stand, the two Swabians grabbing an arm each before cloaking up again. They made their way over to the raised area just before a miniature tidal wave hit the wall behind them.

There was total panic in the cavern, people running in all

directions, some being engulfed by the escaping water, and a couple of MJ-12 even managing to climb clear up some steel works as the living hell massed around them.

Brownshirts did their best to reverse the cars away from the danger, but the surge of the water moved at an astonishing speed, engulfing the six vehicles near to where the Swabians were holed up. It threw the brownshirts violently against a wall and back into the frothing turbulence. A fin broke the surface, and then tentacles, followed by mutated shapes of all kinds. They seemed to recover from the force of the blast and were now forming into shoals. The fin moved into the two brownshirts. There was screaming as the water around them turned crimson. A head surfaced with an arm in its mouth; it was impossible to say what the animal was. Schumann could make out an eye, a gill and a human face. Beyond that, it was a tangled mess of twisted limbs. Another creature broke the water, this one standing, a long tail swishing around sturdy legs, green in colour, the humanoid torso with the face growing out of its chest. Its mouth opened wide, releasing a tremendous roar as it pulled a dead body out of the water and threw it a good twenty feet into the wall, sending it back into the depths for a shoal of mini fish with oversize heads and teeth to rip it pieces, stripping flesh off at an alarming rate, sending yet more creatures into a feeding frenzy.

Octo men were appearing now in various guises. One thing that Schumann became acutely aware of was the intellect that they displayed in organising a lot of the other mutations into groups. He looked at von Gellen, who was groaning a little and rubbing the side of his head. Weisse retrieved his water bottle and got him to drink. Von Gellen gulped it down. Clearly he had been starved of rations to keep him weak. They also fed him a glucose bar while they waited for the water to subside. To venture out at the moment would be suicide. They spotted three suits wading across the torrent, trying to keep their footing. Immediately, they were set upon by seal and octo men, flippers and tentacles encircling them, suckers engulfing their faces, pulling them under, blood exploding like a fountain into the air. The men did not come back up again.

Schumann could see the unmistakable huge mottled brown head of the creature called Otto appear further downriver. Now it was free, he could see just how massive it was, the thick powerful tentacles spanning over fifteen feet, the human torso growing as the water receded. Another member of MJ-12 came into view, trying to run through the water. Otto gathered up his body, shooting through the water at lightning speed. He was on the suit in an instant. Even from this distance, Schumann could see the distorted face sneering at his victim as a great arm tore the head off and tossed it nonchalantly into one of the now empty tanks. Another exhausted suit managed to reach the ramp below the Swabians. He hauled himself up to chest height, clambering at the guard rails, just as a huge swirl appeared behind him. Schumann could see a large glowing white eye the size of a dinner plate blinking without emotion just under the surface. About twelve feet in front of this was a boiling mass of activity where two enormous arms with suckers emerged from the water, enveloping the suit's body. He screamed as he tried to struggle free, yet more arms attaching themselves, thousands of tiny hooks digging into his flesh, the beak finding its target, slicing efficiently through bone and cartilage. Blood spurted out of the man's mouth, his face contorted with pain, the water around his body turning red. The squid hybrid retreated with its quarry safely secured. The suit managed to haul himself up just above the waterline, the lower half now gone, a mass of internal gore dripping from his tattered waist.

The Swabians watched in horror as the man bled out in front of them, slipping back into the water, the mini fish shoal moving in at once, stripping the torso with the same ruthless efficiency, cloth and all.

Casualties were now mounting up in all directions. The tanks that held the pickled body parts had given way, their contents spilling into the crimson river, bobbing about, the monstrous creations attacking them in a boiling feeding frenzy, humans knocked off balance by the colossal volume, and in turn being picked off easily. Schumann could see the body count rise alarmingly, their job being done for them by the mass killing machine.

He forced his gaze away from the carnage to the task in hand. He helped Weisse to check the gear over. It would soon be time to make their move.

Chapter 71

Valerian shuffled his large frame along the remainder of the air duct, slowly lowering himself down to the service hatch. He eased the panel away just enough to get his first glimpse of the inside of the base. He checked it was all clear in the corridor before pushing the panel to one side and clambering out, signalling for the others to follow. They filed into a small office as indicated on his diagram, pausing at the sound of footsteps followed by shouting. They all waited in position as six men in US marine uniforms rushed by, radios crackling with activity. Valerian could tell something was up. It could only be the underwater team. It was now imperative to get the upper levels secured as fast as possible.

Blue team had reached the bottom of the mineshaft and were now making their way along a man-made tunnel. The powerful electric boards moved the team swiftly along the smooth roadway for about a mile until they came across the first control point. They were now at the opposite end of the main entrance. They had met zero resistance.

Back on the surface, green leader gave the instruction to stand fast until the order came through.

Black team were also in position, the leader studying the main entrance through a spare set of rangefinders supplied by Schumann. He ordered the advance, using the treeline and scrub to get close before setting up the stun mortars.

As soon as they closed in on the entrance, he would signal for green team to join up with them.

Chapter 72

The water had now receded into the canal, leaving a boiling angry mess that flowed in the direction of the dockside.

It was at this point that Albert Hebb was barking out orders, directing brownshirts to arms, guiding the remaining MJ-12 members away from the mayhem. They had managed to get back to the cars, outrunning the torrent and its contents. The water had started to appear around the lab areas as it found its way down the tunnel, the canal forcing its course like a waterfall over the side of the dock. There were millions of gallons to run off resulting in half of the level being periodically plunged underwater.

Schumann climbed down looking over at the two remaining MJ-12 members from the six car convoy. He and Weisse both de-cloaked. It was sometimes far safer to be seen, especially when using firearms in groups. Schumann kicked a flapping creature to one side. There were large numbers of them now, gasping for air. They had done their job for him; their use was over. He walked over to the two suits still clinging to the steelworks, firing twice. Both men jerked as the Armolux found its mark. Schumann felt no emotion as their bodies were struck in the chest, opening them up like a tin opener on a can, great walls of flesh tumbling away, smouldering at the edges. They should be thankful for their swift death, he thought as he looked over at his own leader. He went back over and helped Weisse lower him down. They had fed him another energy bar, and he was able to move a little better.

They had just made it down to ground level when a team of brownshirts came around the corner in two cars. Without thinking, Schumann activated the remote gun that was trained in their direction, adding his own firepower at the eight men, Weisse dropping onto one knee, squeezing off four charges of his own. The brownshirts were taken completely off guard. They were not expecting resistance, only responding to the lab disaster. The beams hit almost simultaneously. There was no time for shouting or screaming as the eight men were blown a short way backwards. Weisse advanced, checking over the bodies, four now headless, the others with mortal upper body shots. He extracted two Armolux weapons. The rest were handguns; they wouldn't bother with them. It did, however, inform the Swabians that the main armoury had remained inaccessible. That was good. Whoever was left trapped the wrong side of the emergency lockdown would have limited firepower.

Schumann looked back down towards the dockside. There were three octo men and a deformed walrus-type entity slithering about, feasting on body parts. One of them had a whole dead child in the area where its mouth should have been. He activated the second remote weapon, blowing the beasts to pieces, leaving the tunnel in a lifeless, stinking mess.

The path ahead was clear for the time being, but a long difficult journey on foot. He looked behind him at the tunnel in the opposite direction where the brownshirts lay. The cars were undamaged.

They got von Gellen to his feet, cloaked up, and picked their way over towards the two vehicles. They had only advanced about twenty yards when they heard a tapping sound. Schumann scanned the tanks further down. They looked empty. He looked at the pens nearby, his hearing zoning in on a series of identical holdings. The tapping was getting louder.

Although he knew they could not be seen, he erred on the side of caution, pulling Weisse and von Gellen behind a large generator point just in time to see a door swing open. He could hear a scratching sound, and then a feathery head emerged, followed by the body, the whole form standing twelve feet high. There was a low intense caw, soon followed by more doors swinging open. Schumann watched amazed as the creatures appeared in a regimented line.

Even though they had been released, they had remained where they were until the water had dissipated. A bird with a humanoid head and double wings took off, flying around the cavernous tunnel making excited squawks, its massive wingspan casting long shadows on the roadway below, followed soon by others emulating its actions. In no time at all the area was black with giant bird hybrids taking up formation, cawing instructions to each other. The three men watched in awe for some time, keeping as still as they could.

It was then that Schumann remembered what Hebb had said about some of the creations. It made a great deal of sense to him, but at the same time caused him grave concern. The programme was to create hordes of hybrid animals that could fight like armies in combat. Like the octo men, they seemed to be organised and were able to mount an assault with ruthless efficiency. These creatures could communicate at a level he had never encountered. That was why many had dolphin DNA, because of their known intelligence. It was a frightening prospect playing out in front of them.

The last cage in the section opened and out stepped the

batman, the tallest of all, the contorted human face encompassed in a black real-life leathery suit, complete with bat wings. He walked out using his human legs onto the gantry, scanning left to right, looking rather pleased with himself. He flapped his wings a few times before taking to the air. It was at this point that Schumann could see a dew claw at the top of both wings, each one about a metre long. What a nightmare creation, he thought to himself.

Batman swooped down, picking over the dead carcasses about ten feet from them. He looked over directly at them, a puzzled look on his face. He seemed to stare right at Schumann for an age before making a low growl and taking off once more. He circled over them a few times before joining the lead birdman, the two of them directing the flock towards the dockside.

The three Swabians eased their way down the tunnel, keeping close to the wall for cover. They had reached the cars when they felt the tremors.

At first it was quite subtle, Schumann mistaking it for another creature tapping its cage door, but the noise got louder and louder until he realised what it could be. He looked around, the only shelter behind the sides of the cars. He pushed the other two inside and joined them just in time see the herd of Goran come into view stomping their front feet, herding up, picking up festering body parts and animal remains as they grouped together. They showed no interest in feeding at all, their focus, thankfully for them, on the direction of the dockside.

The huge beasts began grunting and squealing loudly, cantering slowly before picking up speed, thundering down the centre of the tunnel before disappearing from sight, leaving Schumann and the others the only survivors in the lab area.

They had lost a lot of time waiting for the danger to pass.

The alarms were still sounding as they climbed into the nearest car, Weisse pushing the one remaining brownshirt from the interior onto the cold, slimy floor. Schumann got the car moving just as a loud clunk sounded ahead of them, followed by another and another further down. Secondary lockdown had started.

They had no choice but to head in the other direction taking them away from the dock. Even though Schumann knew that the levels were circular and that they would eventually reach the same point, it would take too long to go all the way round. The tunnel would also be sectioned off further ahead.

Weisse was studying the embossed layout on the dashboard in front of him, tracing routes with his finger.

"Sir, if we can reach this terrible mixture section, those tanks will now be empty. We may be able to cut through the back wall and take a shortcut."

Schumann glanced over. It was only a short distance ahead; they could examine the tanks anyway.

"Okay. Let's take a look."

Chapter 73

Von Getz looked over nervously at the canal, which was now teaming with activity, as he witnessed a suit being ripped apart by two squid men. Another MJ-12 operative down. A gilled man sat gargling seawater, the fish part of him covered in hoof marks where the Goran had stampeded past them a few moments ago. He was pretty smashed up. Von Getz dispatched him with his knife, nice and quiet.

He led Kaufmann down the tunnel until more noise reached them. This time it was a mixture of birdscreech, gunfire and human screams. They were nearing the dockside entrance.

Still cloaked, they advanced to the rear of the cavern where lab three was located. They tapped on the door and backed away.

Bek's face appeared. "Mr von Getz, so glad you made it. Inside, quick."

They bundled past and shut the door.

"How did you know it was me?"

"I can see you; well, your aura anyway." Von Getz de-cloaked, shaking his head in disbelief. Bek smiled, continuing, "You must be Mr Kaufmann."

He extended his hand. Kaufmann shook it. "Pleased to meet you, young man," he managed, exhaustedly.

Through the windows, they could see the carnage. In the

middle of the cavern towards the water lay feathery bird parts. He spied a unit of brownshirts reloading an artillery gun as troops ran into position. Further down lay two men that had been caught in the Goran stampede. One had a perfect semicircle hoof mark crushed into his head; the other had deep imprints to the body. The animals were so heavy that they impacted the ground with the force of a steel press.

Gunfire was trained on the swooping birdmen, their speed making them a difficult target, the teams firing from left to right and back again which had the effect of catching the odd creature with impact shells as they flew around their heads. But it was impossible to avoid casualties.

One particular specimen dived downwards using its six beaks to pluck its prey from the ground, leaving his colleague open-mouthed as he watched the man carried through the air, then scythed to pieces, the blood-curdling screams ringing all around as his arm came spinning to the ground followed by his head, which bounced across the floor before hitting the wall, splattering brain matter in all directions.

From his own position, von Getz witnessed something extraordinary as the birdman changed direction, swooping over the artillery placement, letting the headless body go with pinpoint accuracy. From such a great height, the body hit the other brownshirt with such force that he was killed instantly.

With one of the gun placements out of action, they were able to fly past the dock area into the other sections, following the direction of the Goran.

While all of this was happening, the numbers of Grey and Draco had increased significantly as they watched the battle ensue. They remained in the tunnel at a distance as Aral and Caste trudged by, their work over for the day. The ETs seemed to be studying the human response to the danger, silently conversing as if it was a spectator sport.

Albert Hebb had two lines of security armed with the only weapons left available. Even Dalheim and Perfekt had armed themselves with Glock handguns from his own emergency supply. The president was shouting at Hebb over the bedlam.

"Where the hell's that damned shuttle?"

"It's getting here as quick as possible, sir. Most of the lines have been sealed off automatically."

"Well, just get on to Taos and get reinforcements down here."

"Right away, sir."

Hebb picked up the radio and called Commander Holt. Holt answered right away.

"Commander, it's Level Seven. Where's that backup security?"

"Sir, we are having trouble gaining access."

"Well, override the mechanism. You have the codes?"

"Sir, codes have failed, repeat, codes have failed. They will not respond."

"Listen, Holt, we are being wiped out down here and ... wait a minute." Hebb stopped ranting. He thought about it for a few moments; the locks all blowing open in the labs, the main weapon store inaccessible, and now the lockdown that could not be overridden. "Put the base on red alert. We are under attack."

"Under attack from who? Are you sure?" Holt replied incredulously.

"Get those doors opened. I don't know how you do it, just get them open now." Hebb halted communication and picked up another device. He punched in a four-digit code and waited. "Come on, come on." No response. He dialled it again.

Nothing.

The comms to Los Alamos were down.

Chapter 74

Valerian led the red team down the corridor past the mess room. As they proceeded, they checked the layout. The maps married perfectly, making it a simple task to navigate their way through the base.

They made it to the lift area where they were challenged for the first time.

"Special unit sent in to deal with the trouble below," Valerian boomed.

"I'll need the code, sir, and your passes."

"Of course."

He punched the guard hard in the face, who went down heavily. They secured him, holding the unconscious body upright.

Valerian fished out a code written on paper. This would take them down to Level Three and no further. That should be far enough, though.

He punched in the code and then pressed the guards hand onto the print pad. The lift activated. Half of red team entered the lift while the rest remained on Level One. They would now assist black team in the frontal assault from inside the hangar.

The lift came to a halt on Level Three, the troops with Armolux exiting first to be greeted by four marines. Before they could even challenge the intruders, they were hit with tight taser fire to their chests. Again, they were restrained and hidden away. Valerian took up the lead again. They worked their way through the sector unchallenged, finding the control room. They burst in, surprising the two men inside. They ordered them onto the floor and tied them up.

Valerian looked at the screens. They showed the base was quiet. None of the images showed any problems. He frowned. That was odd. Maybe Schumann had failed and had been captured. It was impossible to contact him at the moment.

There was a commotion in the corridor outside. Valerian turned as the doors either side of the control room flew open. Troops moved in fast. Valerian shouted for his men to stand down. They had the drop on them. No point in getting them all killed for nothing.

He was angry. He had been caught out at his own game. In the corridor outside he spotted a high-ranking officer. "You in charge here, old boy?" Valerian asked politely.

"I am Colonel Holt. Who the hell are you?"

Chapter 75

The dockside area was still in chaos. Gunfire mixed with Armolux as the brownshirts struggled to contain the birdmen. Some of them had retreated to the top of the submarine base where the roof was at its highest point.

But now there was a new issue.

The cells with the abductees had been open for some time. Now the dock was filling with men, women and children, in various drug-induced stages, that had wandered down following the commotion created by the hybrids. The Goran had dispatched some of them, as had the octo and squid men, but their numbers were so vast that they had managed to force their way through the carnage.

It was a pitiful sight. Security were trying to keep a clear path to the dangers that had once resided inside the tanks. They were now mingling with the hordes.

"My God, look at them all," Perfekt uttered, peering out from the conference hall.

Hebb's radio sounded. It was Rascher. "Sir, we can't cope with the influx. Permission to open fire?"

Hebb mulled it over but thought better of it. He did not want to jeopardise his own position any further. There was a lot of money walking around out there. At the moment, his colleagues thought it was just a malfunction within the base.

He had the threat of the assault under containment. Holt would deal with that for him.

"Save your ammunition. We can herd them down into section six, near the shuttle station, and keep them there until we get the lockdown lifted."

Security were now regaining control as the ETs remained in the same position.

"Nice of you to help us," Hebb muttered to himself, shaking his head. "Where are those damned reinforcements?"

The brownshirts were now supported by two launches in the middle of the harbour, both with M2A1 heavy machine guns on tripods trained on anything that did not look human.

The gunfire became less frequent as the threat diminished. Enoch came up from his crouched position. Gallagher was by his side. They scanned the area. They could see Cale and Sagen approach lab three as the dock became even more crowded.

Hebb was busy pacifying Dalheim and the others as Enoch nudged Gallagher's arm and signalled to follow him out. They slipped out into the masses, keeping their heads low, shuffling along, weaving their way to the rendezvous.

Up ahead in lab three, Bek checked his watch once more.

"The Caste will be back in the Draco city by now." Bek had given two of them receptors to plant in the centre of the populace where they would do the maximum damage. He looked at Aral. "We are ready."

Von Getz could see Enoch and Gallagher appear outside. All present for evac.

"We had better get you all to the extraction craft. Let's go."

They were grateful for the cover offered by the swelling masses. They kept close to each other, making their way to the water's edge aided by the total lack of organisation that the abductees displayed. Most of them were so out of it that they kept walking into each other, which meant the path von Getz carved when leading the others was less obvious.

They reached the dock railings. There were so many people it was shoulder to shoulder. The team crouched down as von Getz operated the cloaking device.

"Right, listen up. I'll take the front, Kaufmann at the back. We all shuffle along in unison, nice and steady. Use the rails as a guide, keeping hold of the man in front of you. If we keep in formation, the cloak will cover all of us ... just."

They nodded that they understood as they faded away.

The team moved along the left side of the dock, nearing Hebb's offices, the six-man guard detail in place staring ahead, ready to react if the area was breached. They inched past, keeping pace with von Getz who made them go even more slowly to keep the noise of their boots to a minimum. Their cause was assisted by the disturbance as the odd gunfight erupted behind them.

There was a screech high above. Von Getz focussed on the task in hand, leading on, eyes front. Suddenly the noise increased to the volume of a hundred crows as a huge shape soared towards them. The brownshirts reacted at once trying to aim at the target.

The birdman swirled and darted with amazing agility as he homed in on the prey below. The brownshirts opened fire in a panic, bullets flying through the air. Instinctively, the cloaked group ducked to avoid the crossfire, breaking the human chain. Cale and Sagen appeared first, then Bek, Aral, Gallagher and Enoch.

"What is this?" one of the brownshirts gasped.

They could barely comprehend what their eyes could see, but it was enough of a distraction for the team to react. Von Getz and Kaufmann still remained cloaked, drawing their

Armolux, firing at the six men.

Two of them were killed instantly as beams passed through their heads, with a third losing his right arm at the shoulder. In the blink of an eye the birdman swooped down, talons extended, finding their mark as they raked into the three guards left standing. It was over in an instant as the two Swabians continued to fire in a controlled arc. The brownshirts had only got off a single shot between them.

Only one guard was left standing. He tottered away, arms by his sides, blood jetting from a huge hole in his back, adrenaline keeping him functioning. He managed a few more steps before he gave out, falling flat on his face.

Von Getz sprang forward, checking the victims over. The first was a head shot, dead. The second and third had two identical grooves gouged out from the base of their backs to the top of their shoulders; victims of the birdman, also dead. The fourth man was face down, dead, the fifth was still alive and in shock, his arm over near Hebb's office somewhere. The last man, head shot, dead. Von Getz could hear the birdman circling round once more. They would have to make a run for it.

"Okay, let's move."

"What about him?" Enoch pointed to one arm.

"We'll leave him for that thing up there. Come on." Von Getz started off, but then stopped. Gallagher was on one knee, holding his side.

"I'm hit."

Kaufmann grabbed hold of him and hauled him up. Gallagher winced, blood pouring from the wound. Enoch grabbed the other side of him and they moved off, Gallagher loping along as best he could.

"What's going on over there?"

Hebb reached for a pair of field glasses. He trained them on the dock, but there were so many abductees milling around he couldn't see a thing. He ran outside and climbed up a service ladder that led onto the roof of the conference room. From his new vantage point he had an unobstructed view. He focussed the glasses on the dock, moving down the left until he came across the dead brownshirts. The hackles went up on the back of his neck as he traced on ahead until he found his target. He fine-tuned the focus, bringing up the faces clearly: some of the base personnel; Gallagher, who was injured, then Sagen with Bek and Aral. What on earth were they …? Then he spotted von Getz with another man he did not recognise, then more of his own men … A breach.

"Gott im Himmel," he hissed.

He turned back toward the ladder. The world turned upside down as a badly-gouged body with an arm missing smashed into the roof with such force that Hebb was thrown into the air from the impact, coming back down hard on his side, bouncing off the building and landing heavily on the floor below.

The birdman circled round, cawing loudly, high in the air, a gunboat trying in vain to bring it down as it glided away towards the sub base, machine gun fire rattling around the huge cavern.

Dalheim, Perfekt and Vessels were now on their own, armed only with Glock pistols. Dalheim pushed the door open, sending several abductees staggering away. He looked around and found Hebb near some aluminium framework beside a mutilated corpse. He was out of it.

Dalheim ran back inside, activating the comms.

"Control," came an official voice.

"This is Heinz Dalheim on Level Seven. Our group is in

danger. We are cut off from security. Send in QRF."

"Did you get that, sir?" Control lead turned to Holt.

"I did."

Holt knew Dalheim. He was the main benefactor of the base, a man not to be crossed, even worse than Hebb by all accounts. He hit the comms.

"This is Control. We are working on the lockdown override. The base is on high alert, sir. Please stand fast, we are deploying Level Seven quick reaction force to your position in the dock area. They should be with you in two minutes. Please make yourself known to them."

"Okay, they had better be. And chase that shuttle from Taos. That's an order, soldier."

"Yes, sir, will do. Stand by ... out."

Holt cut the comms and turned to the man opposite as he put down his cup of tea.

"You didn't tell him. Why not?' Valerian asked.

Holt ordered the guard to lower his weapon. He wasn't going anywhere and he had his men locked up.

"Let's just say I have concerns about what has been going on down there."

"Do you know who they are, these benefactors?" Valerian leaned forward.

"I assumed they were government officials and wealthy investors," Holt said slowly.

"Let me tell you, they are far removed from that. The government have no knowledge regarding the lower levels. It's completely off-grid. Surely you must have suspected something stinks here."

"Okay. Just suppose you're right. I can't keep them down there forever. They will get out eventually, and then ... well, you hear things. People go missing."

Valerian could not waste any more time.

"What if I was to tell you there was a way out of this that could be beneficial to all of us?"

Holt shrugged. "Go on."

"The two lower levels are set with sonic charges. It will wipe out everything down there, massive tragic accident. All the illegal practices, all those horror experiments you know about, will come to an end."

"And what's in it for you, Mr Valerian? Why are you here?"

"I get to wipe out all the bad guys from MJ-12 that are down there. We bring an end to this ever happening again."

Holt paced the room deep in thought for a while before letting out a deep sigh.

"Okay, what do you need from me?"

Chapter 76

Schumann was standing in the area signposted 'Breeding Tanks'. The tanks ran in a huge row with interconnecting pathways. But there was no way in from here. He looked at the plan in the car once more with Weisse. They looked at the options, none of which made sense ... apart from one.

"If we blow an entry point here" – Weisse pointed to the tank – "we can get through to about halfway, blow another section out and keep going until we come out on the other side about a hundred metres from the dockside."

Schumann looked at the plans. It could work. It was the only way they could get to the dock from here, so what had they got to lose? They walked back to the car where von Gellen was waiting. The backpacks on the rear seat had the cutting gear and charges in them.

Without warning, there was a loud rumble as a huge steel section dropped down from above, sliding neatly into place before coming to a halt with a dull thud just where they had been standing only moments ago.

"Himmel, that was close," Weisse exclaimed.

The three of them looked on in dismay as phase three of lockdown was implemented, the thick steel divider leaving the breeding labs on the other side of the tunnel and out of reach.

"No way out," von Gellen said ominously.

He was right. They were trapped, and they were out of time.

They drove back to the labs until they reached the steel door at the other end. It was the same, sealed securely.

The sonics would activate soon and there was no chance of cancelling the explosive charges in time. Schumann turned the car around and took the route past von Gellen's cell. He allowed a glance at it, with vitriol in his eyes.

The lab area ended and was replaced by air con units and generators, then nothing but the shiny walls and floor of the tunnel. They came to the end. A metal staircase appeared, leading to a gantry built to observe the object that now came into view. The soft lights seemed to make the metal glow ethereally.

Weisse was smiling. "They don't make them like they used to."

Schumann laughed, turning to von Gellen in the back. He had fallen asleep, a peaceful look on his face. Schumann turned back around, glad that his leader was oblivious to their situation.

"Can we keep driving for a while, sir?"

"Sure we can. We can do whatever we like."

Chapter 77

They hauled Gallagher along as best they could, taking it in turns to hold him up. His legs had gone now and he was dangerously weak. Von Getz checked the time; they had to get a move on.

"I'm slowing you down. You'd better leave me," Gallagher rasped.

"What is it with you Terrans? We don't leave anyone behind … ever." It came out more harshly than he meant, but Gallagher was in no shape to object. He cringed as Kaufmann glanced, wide-eyed, at him. For all his wisdom instilled into others, he had been careless. Still, no one picked him up on it; a lucky escape for the Swabian nation. He laughed inwardly, and then his mood changed as he thought about his two colleagues. They were still nowhere to be seen. He was aware of their exposure without the cloak activated, but being mobile with one of their number wounded; that was not an option.

A gasp from Gallagher broke his reverie. Not far now, but they were cutting it too fine. He had to think about the end goal. It was his job now to get them all out.

"You two grab his legs, we've got to pick up the pace."

They ran as fast as they could with Enoch and Aral supporting the middle of the injured man. Even Bek helped out by dragging a backpack along the ground. It was exhausting work, but they made good progress. Von Getz took a look at Gallagher; his face was drained of colour, but he was still conscious.

"Hang on in there, soldier. Not far now."

Albert Hebb stirred, trying to clear his faculties. His head was ringing, hundreds of voices chatting loudly. He felt immense pressure, he was hot, he needed some air.

He awoke, the voices suddenly fading.

He was on a table, Dalheim and Vessels looking over him, Perfekt tapping his face.

"He's coming round."

Hebb slowly opened his eyes to strip lighting and metal framework. His mind was somewhere else in a dreamlike state. It was making him hallucinate; the ceiling was distorting, changing shape. He groaned then sat up, wide-eyed, immediately regretting it as a sharp pain stabbed through his temple.

"Christ, my head."

"Take it easy." Dalheim said. "You fell, do you remember?"

He did remember now; the ceiling was not distorting at all.

He stumbled off the table and hit the comms. "Rascher, we have eight intruders on the dock. Engage at once."

"Right away, sir," came the reply.

Hebb turned to the others. No point in stalling any further.

"The base is under attack. Comms are down with the upper levels, and we are sealed in here."

"You must have an emergency exit, surely," Dalheim responded, with a look of shock.

Hebb rubbed the side of his head. "The locking mechanisms have all been jammed."

"Then how are the intruders planning to escape?" Perfekt stated.

"Maybe they have no escape plan." Hebb looked at them gravely. "They were personnel who worked at the base, but they had to be incredibly well organised." He checked his sidearm, and continued. "The technology required to do all this ... they had outside help." Dalheim looked directly at Vessels, who had remained quiet up until now. "Your men, von Getz and Kaufmann, are among them." He directed with his head towards the dock.

"But they are with me. We were supposed to meet up before all this happened." He parted his arms.

"Then what are they doing over there murdering my men on the dock?" Hebb's voice was rising. "This flimsy agreement between our organisations, getting us all together down here to take everything for yourself."

Vessels remained calm and measured. "I am as mystified as you are, but I have nothing to do with this." He looked at them all in turn. "I could have shot you all in the back at any time."

Dalheim held up a hand. "That is true. But maybe we are still of some use to you." He drew his Glock.

Vessels jumped back. He was in trouble. He would have to prove his intentions were honourable beyond any doubt.

"Don't forget, I have given you the location to Newschwabenland. That was part of the agreement."

"But until we get there and see for ourselves, you could have invented those coordinates." Perfekt was now joining in.

"Alright." Vessels had to offer something else. "The craft I arrived in. It is a disguised Haunebu."

The Haunebu. Dalheim was familiar with the project. "So what? We also have a saucer squadron."

"Not like this. It can shapeshift and is capable of outrunning anything."

That did jar in the president's brain.

Those mysterious craft that kept buzzing the bases. Even the Greys could not keep up with them. He could be telling the truth. But could they be using that advanced technology on them right now?

"Convenient that we cannot get to the surface to examine this craft of yours," Hebb added.

Vessels was losing their trust. The Glock was wavering in Dalheim's hands. One last effort …

"I think I know how they got round the base undetected." Vessels began to regain some composure. "Have you any cameras on the dock?"

Hebb puffed out some air. "Yes, there is surveillance everywhere."

"Alright, where was the last place that you saw any of this group?"

"Over there in lab three." Hebb's eyes narrowed. "What's the point of …?'

"Please." Vessels put up his hands in a peaceful gesture; the gun was still on him. "Can you find the footage?"

They went into the next room which served as a mini control hub. From this point it could enable Hebb to see what was going on if he was away from his dockside office.

Their own brand of sophistication aided Hebb in locating a camera still of Gallagher's head looking out of the doorway. He fast-forwarded until he saw the man and the rest of the group start weaving their way through the hordes of abductees.

"So they sneaked out through the crowds. Big deal."

"Wait until they reach the open space on the other side." Vessels was gambling, but the odds were good. Hebb kept the film running as the group reached the dock railings. There was a brief conversation between the group.

Then they vanished.

Hebb looked closer at the screen, rewinding, then back again. "What the ...? They're gone."

The others looked, wide-eyed too, as the film kept running. There was no sign of them.

"It's called a cloaking device. We can use them on ships, too, in fact any vehicle." Vessels saw the gun lower to Dalheim's side.

Hebb recalled the same devices implemented during the pursuit of Schumann and Logan. Maybe he would get his hands on that technology sooner than he thought. "But that does still not explain what your men have done to this base," he levelled accusingly.

"The tanks were opened deliberately?" A shocked Perfekt pressed the point.

"Yes, they all blew open at once. The locks were upgraded by Vessel's very own head of science, Hans Schumann."

Vessels went white. A high-ranking officer from New Swabia involved in a covert mission against the Terrans? It was hard to believe.

"Well, let's get him in here and see what he has to say for himself," he said defensively.

Dalheim looked at Hebb and then at Perfekt. No point in holding out any longer. "Hans Schumann broke out of the base six days ago with a female scientist called Clare Logan."

"Why was I not informed of this?" It was Vessels' turn to be angry.

Hebb's demeanour softened. "We thought we could get him back. He turned out to be quite resourceful." He almost smiled.

"You've no idea where he is?"

"We lost him somewhere on the outskirts of New York," Hebb admitted sheepishly.

Vessels had obviously convinced them of their capabilities.

But it was still a mystery why Schumann and the others had gone rogue.

The Swabian suddenly knew the answer. "It was my idea to assign Hans Schumann to the Dulce base."

"Okay, I can see why you did that, but why betray you?" Dalheim asked.

"He clearly did not agree with our plans to expand into South America."

"Or telling us the location of your country," Perfekt added.

"Precisely."

"Some people have no ambition." Hebb sighed.

"You said that all the cells and tanks opened at the same time," Vessels said, suddenly frowning.

"Yes, all of them," Hebb replied.

"Including the cell where von Gellen was being held?"

"Including his, but no one has seen him. He was probably killed by the hybrids."

"Or maybe not." Vessels began to feel very concerned.

"Do not worry," Hebb said reassuringly. "That old war criminal of yours is in no state to do anything. Even if he is still alive."

Vessels' mind was ticking over; his own men rebelling against him, collaborating with an unknown force, Schumann escaping.

It was true that not everyone in New Swabia was comfortable with the regime change. This was no time to be complacent. He knew there were people who thought the 'death' of their old leader suspicious.

Was there really no desire for their great nation to rise up again and take what was rightfully theirs? There were many conspiracy theorists, voicing their opinions to support this. He would single out the ringleaders. They would be severely dealt with.

He took comfort in the fact there was no way Schumann and the others could get back into the country without his authorisation. They would be outcasts on Terra; they were welcome to it.

He snapped out of his thoughts, looking out over the cavern, the abductees thinning out as the brownshirts rounded them up. More reinforcements had arrived from the other end of the sector; about sixty in all. He knew they all felt better about that. A few more gunnery boats had been called up from the sub base too, carrying yet more troops. They moored up in the middle of the harbour.

He could see the ETs still there in the same place.

His curiosity had worn away. He was glad to leave that part of the operation to the Terrans. The less he had to do with them, the better. He could not wait to get out of their godforsaken base.

Now all of the commotion had died down, Perfekt's morbid fascination had returned. He was the opposite of Vessels. He found them quite remarkable. He could see one of the group with a large glowing medallion around his neck. He could be the leader.

He watched for some time as they pointed and nodded, communicating silently.

Perfekt still had the burning desire to meet them close up. Perhaps when they had got the base repaired, he would do just that.

The comms sounded. "Go ahead, Rascher," Hebb barked.

"Backup units in position, sir."

"What about the rebel faction?"

"Launch closing in now, sir. We have the dock blocked off. They are going nowhere."

"Excellent." Hebb turned to the others, his headache subsiding. "Gentlemen, order has been restored."

Vessels looked doubtful, but said nothing.

Chapter 78

On Level Three, Control had finished patching in the new camera loops. They also patched Valerian onto his desired frequency.

"Any luck with those locks yet?"

"Your boys did a pretty good job. Might be a while yet," Holt replied.

They studied the screens as they came back on line. The quality was not great, but good enough to see what was going on. They had about a quarter of the lower level in view, which included part of the dock area, the labs, armoury and some of the tunnels. They could see the damage where the tanks had blown. There were dead bodies scattered all over the place amidst twisted metalwork and scorch-marked walls where small fires had broken out. All the scientists in the terrible mixture storage area were dead, either floating in half-empty tanks or in small heaps on the ground.

As the cameras scanned towards the dock, the damage became even more widespread, with evidence of gunfire exchange and structural destruction. The dock itself was a hive of activity. It seemed that all the survivors had regrouped in this area. Holt saw for himself that all of the tanks had blown, their contents gone. He spotted the unmistakable outline of Albert Hebb with a small group which looked like it included

Heinz Dalheim. They were observing the cleanup operation.

"Looks like a lot of them escaped the main tank blast," he observed.

"They won't survive the next one," Valerian stated categorically.

"When does that take place?"

"From the time the switch is thrown, they will have two minutes." Valerian looked at his watch. "That will be in a very short time." He hit the comms. "Blue team, respond."

"Blue team in position, sir."

"Black team?"

"Here, sir. In position."

"Green team?"

"Standing by, sir."

Holt looked wide-eyed.

"Couldn't open the front door could you, old chap?" said Valerian.

Chapter 79

Von Getz dropped to his knees trying to catch his breath. He took a good look around. It was all clear save for a low hum in the distance. He gave himself around twenty seconds before placing his spectacles into a hard pocket of his chest rig, passed his cloaking device over, then dived into the water.

It was cold without the drysuit, the water deeper than he remembered. Without the aid of a rebreather, his lungs strained from holding his breath. He was not used to it. Thankfully, the water was fairly clear and he was able to find the top hatch quite easily. Once inside, he grabbed two weight belts, two breather tanks and the only remaining cloaking device.

He slipped on a pair of flippers and let himself out of the hatch. It was a difficult kick upwards with the belts weighing him down so much, but at least he had oxygen this time. As he neared the surface, he caught something in his peripheral vision. It was some distance away, but he could make out a strange shape, white with an arrowhead ... a squid ... or like a squid, but not quite right. It had human parts to it, appendages like claws ... and it was massive.

Himmel. Some of the creatures had got into the harbour.

His mind became a blur of panic as another monster came into focus. A walrus, its back twisted and gnarled, merging into three forked tails, the solitary eye seeming to see everything at once. That must have included him.

He broke the surface, hauling himself onto the dock. He wasted no time explaining the situation to Kaufmann.

"We will all go down together. Safety in numbers," Kaufmann suggested.

Yes, it was a good idea. The continual singular vibrations of the team were bound to attract the creatures over.

There was a hiss that became a roar, then a deafening explosion, as fire and rocks showered onto the dock to their right. They crouched down as shrapnel filled the air around them.

Von Getz got them all on the deck. "Keep still. They can't see you," he shouted. "They are sealing off the pedestrian exits."

Everyone remained motionless, the boat scanning the shore for any sign of movement.

The Commander picked his way along the cavern wall with his field glasses. "Can't see a damn thing. They must have doubled back towards the dock." He ordered the boat to continue dead slow as he scanned further along.

———⋙⋄⋘———

Hebb could hear the shellfire from his own position. Satisfied that matters were in hand, it would only be a matter of time; then von Getz and the others would be right where he wanted them. Even if he could not see them, they were stranded now.

Hebb walked around freely, the others following behind him, adopting the role of inspection as they observed more of the cleanup operation. Security were dispatching the few creations that were still slithering around. One particular octo man was making his way down one of the tunnels toward the ETs. A brownshirt trotted down, drawing his weapon to dispatch the monstrosity. In all of the confusion that had proceeded, he had quite forgotten protocol as he excitedly blasted the animal in the head. The octo man slid lifelessly into a heap at his feet, where a motif could clearly be seen on the ground.

A sudden sense of horror filled him as he realised his mistake. He dropped his weapon as he raised his hands, trying to find some mutual understanding.

Too late.

The Greys stepped forward, nodding at the sidearm, firing Armolux beams into him, opening him up like a fish. He was dead even before he toppled into the massive crustacean in front of him, their two bloods mixing to create a small stream of discharge.

The Draco gave a series of silent orders as more of his kind and dozens of Greys appeared from further down the tunnel.

"What now?" Hebb turned to see the guard fall, and knew what had happened instantly. "Return fire, code Red," he commanded, waving Dalheim and the others to take cover.

The brownshirts reacted immediately, the gunboats in the middle of the harbour responding by firing up their engines, the artillery posts swinging across to engage the ETs. More troops took up position along the dock, but not before a number of the ETs broke out of the tunnel, fanning out, firing their weapons as they ran with surprising agility.

Several beams hit a unit crouched by lab number one, sending body parts spinning into the unit behind. A Draco touched his chest and a large beam shot across the cavern, blasting into the artillery on the rockwall shelf, incinerating three men and shattering the gun. Several brownshirts responded by directing their weapons at the Draco's chest area. It staggered forward a few paces, its body glowing, before smashing lifelessly to the ground.

Above the commotion, Hebb shouted out the orders. Dalheim could not help but be impressed by the man's organisation. Deep down, he felt the thrill return from years of combat dormancy, those memories of campaign warfare washing into his brain like a drug, driving him into action. He came out of hiding, leaving Vessels and Perfekt behind, drawing his pistol, running across the expanse of the cavern until he reached another small unit of men.

He stood up behind them, one knee on a concrete step, shouting his own set of commands as he fired his Glock steadily into a group of Greys. They jerked and twisted as three of them fell, black gloopy fluid ejecting from holes in their bodies. The unit let off controlled volleys of fire, one after the other, taking out the enemy efficiently. Beams from Armolux lit up the cavern as Draco blasted their way out. Hebb could not remember such a sustained and aggressive assault as this one.

More and more Greys poured out, the brownshirts cutting them down in numbers. But the other side were also taking casualties.

Dalheim reloaded. He was enjoying himself, marvelling at the tactics of the enemy. They were testing the defences, sacrificing themselves knowing that eventually, they could overwhelm the firepower. In this current situation, that was certainly true.

Dalheim spotted the medallion-wearing Draco skulking about, organising his own troops. He stared at him defiantly.

How he wished it was like the old times; he could mount a steed, draw his sword, and charge him down. The Draco caught the human stare. He looked back only for a moment before sending two lines of Greys running out of the tunnel in formation, Armolux flooding the cavern. Their accuracy was compromised somewhat by their movement, but brownshirts still fell all around him with gaping Armolux wounds.

Another observation that Dalheim had made was the disregard in dispatching their quarry. They seemed quite content to maim and injure, a kill being a bonus. This was probably because of the severity of the wounds. Dalheim could see a nearby brownshirt whimpering, an arm and a leg from his right side about ten yards behind his body.

Dalheim ran over, picking up the man's Armolux.

More Greys assembled in front of the canal, several Draco joining the front line assault. This was the first time Dalheim had seen them up close. He fired his weapon in an arc, the beam falling short by two feet. Clever, he thought to himself, they were just out of range. They returned fire, their own weapons smashing beams into the wall behind him.

He then instructed his small garrison to fire their weapons at forty-five degrees. The beams fell agonisingly close, but the ETs retreated back, just to be sure. He ordered another volley a little higher; again, short. Mockingly, it seemed to Dalheim, the Draco retreated their troops another short distance.

Then the water in the canal behind them erupted as tentacles, beaks, and huge pairs of jaws plucked the unwitting beings from the gantry. Bodies of white and green were torn apart as the water turned black. Dalheim punched the air. He had seen the creatures moving about earlier, waiting in ambush until someone or something came into range. They had wiped out all of them; about fifteen ETs in total.

More Greys appeared from the tunnel, opening fire on the canal surface, ignoring the beams from Dalheim and his men as they landed near their feet, unfazed as they kept blasting until the water was glowing with a white mist. The canal was left with a mass of mutilated flesh bobbing about on the surface.

Nothing had survived.

The gunboats had reached primary position, the drivers keeping the engines idling in the turbulence. The two gunners lowered their sights until they could see down the left tunnel; and then fired.

The two missiles travelled a few hundred yards, following the guidance system, until the order was given to detonate. There was a rumble as the tunnel illuminated. The gunners loaded again and waited.

The influx of ETs stopped, the clouds of dust in the tunnel cleared and the remaining beings ran aimlessly, losing their command directive. The brownshirts cut them down ruthlessly.

Dalheim could see a huge glowing machine come into view, and behind that a fleet of small disc craft levelling into formation.

The gunners took up the machine in their sights ... and fired. The two missiles went whizzing across the cavern, expertly guided down the tunnel.

"Twenty seconds to target impact ... fifteen ... wait." The gunner looked at his screen, then made the announcement. "Missiles intercepted, sir."

"Status?" barked the ammunitions technical officer.

The gunner looked through his glasses at the billowing smoke down the tunnel.

"Missiles have detonated, sir, but short of the target, the tunnel is blocked, I repeat, the tunnel is blocked."

"Did you get that, dockside?"

"Yes, commander, received and understood. Stand by."

Hebb stood with his hands on his hips, surveying the damage. The ETs had really done it this time. The only saving grace was, they were sealed up on the other side of the rockfall.

What a mess. He was hoping to salvage some of the

experiments from the canal. Now he was looking at a worthless, steaming pile of charred body parts. Even worse, the holding area where the abductees were being held had been destroyed. The whole section had been incinerated, hundreds dead. That was a lot of time, effort and money down the drain.

Dalheim jogged over to his side. "That won't hold them back forever. I saw the size of that Armolux."

"Well, we will be ready for them. I have a sub on the way with bunker buster missiles. They won't shoot those down." He gave out a silent laugh.

"Do you think we can straighten this out with them?"

"Not this time." Hebb shook his head. "What little trust there was has gone now. Still, we do have all of the DNA strands and biogenetic notes to be able to carry on where we left off."

"But what about all of the new technology they would give us?"

Hebb smiled, much to Dalheim's surprise. He did not seem at all bothered.

"It was bound to end like this one day. Be thankful, at least for the time being, that it is on our terms." He pointed using his head in the direction of the labs. 'That makes our friend Mr Vessels all the more important. As one door closes, another one opens."

Dalheim looked on, now smiling too.

Yes, Vessels had only been too eager to spill the beans on what they had tucked away in New Swabia. If they were careful with him, it might work out even better than they could have hoped for. Far better to deal with human beings than those awful creatures.

Hebb made off to his office. He wanted everything in place before the ETs broke through. And when they did, he would have a nice surprise waiting for them.

He met Rascher conversing with three brownshirts. "Any news from the upper levels?' he cut in.

"Still nothing, sir, although we are making headway unlocking the emergency exits."

"Good, very good." He would have Holt's guts for garters.

"We got through to Taos," Rascher continued. "The shuttle will be with us in three minutes."

"Excellent." So it was all coming back on line. Whatever the rebels had planned was now well and truly dead in the water.

He leaned with his back on the waterside railing, looking over at Dalheim in the distance walking across the cavern. He wondered how this would affect their relationship. He would have to be careful not to get on the wrong side of him again.

Especially if he was to get his hands on the presidency.

Chapter 80

Von Getz got the team organised. They had to remain cloaked through fear of detection, which had made the whole process much slower. Thankfully, the disturbance back at the main hub had stopped the launch firing on them. But there were security gathering on the dockside, and the water was becoming busier as more craft made their way to the fracas.

They put Gallagher in the centre of the line with Sagen and Enoch keeping hold of him. Very slowly, they lowered him over the side, the cloak breaking open at times, but not enough for concern.

They were all at the edge, von Getz knowing that they could jump straight into the mouth of some escaped creation, but this was no time for hesitation. He opened the catch on the switch of his remote and flicked it up. Four red lights came on simultaneously and the small screen below illuminated the word ARMED.

He jumped in, followed in quick succession by the others. As the bubbles around them faded, his vision began to clear. He kicked downwards, looking into the depths for company.

They had descended about halfway when he spotted a glowing white disk, the orb moving at a speed keeping pace with them.

Von Getz had elected not to announce what was in the

harbour. Only Kaufmann knew. He saw no advantage in panicking them. He had to keep the dive as controlled as possible. He could see Gallagher's blood leaking from the confinement of the cloak boundary. That was not good.

As if sensing this, the orb changed direction.

It was strange; there was only one orb, or eye as he knew it was. It was face on and homing in on their position fast. Von Getz kicked harder, forcing the pace. He guessed that Kaufmann must have seen it too by now.

Not far to go.

He could make out more of the creature as it closed down the distance, the grotesque contorted leer, the huge brown mottled head, the torso with arms aiding the propulsion system of the beast. Its tentacles were tucked in behind for this operation. Von Getz knew that when it reached them, they would be deployed.

It was an awkward descent with shared rebreathers and tanks, the weight belts at either end. It was made more difficult as he felt the resistance of the people behind him. He glanced over his shoulder at the wide-eyed Cale pointing into the expanse as more detail of the octo man was revealed to them. Von Getz got his hand on the hatch, the others massing around him.

He pulled the lever, signalling Kaufmann to get Gallagher in first, then raised his Armolux, firing directly at the underwater target. The beam slowed down significantly, allowing the octo man time to react, but not time enough. Although the great beast veered to one side, the charge still found its mark, ripping into its left shoulder. There was a flurry of bubbles followed by a distorted roar, but the creature kept advancing. Von Getz cursed to himself.

Another charge of Armolux by Sagen that missed, and the creature was on them.

Just Bek, Sagen, and von Getz were left in the water. They waved their arms frantically as the Swabian fired again. This time the beam ripped off a tentacle, the octo man glancing at the appendage as it sank away into the depths below, leaving a stream of blood clouding the water. The creature turned its head back to them, sneering with supreme ugliness, a tentacle shooting out, grabbing Sagen by the waist. There was an eruption of bubbles as he was pulled away from von Getz's side, more tentacles taking hold, shaking its prey like a rag doll. Von Getz was helpless as he saw the look of horror on the other man's face, the Armolux cartwheeling from his hand, sinking out of sight. The octo man was darting about, playing with its victim like a dog with a ball.

Sagen's mask and tank had been ripped off in the struggle. His face remained fixed in the same desperate expression. Von Getz had to be accurate; he did not want to hit the other man by accident. The Armolux beam was a lot stronger at the reduced distance, octo man swimming straight into a timed shot to the head. The creature bucked from the impact as a glowing hole appeared on the top left side. It responded by jerking Sagen's head to one side, snapping his neck with such severity that half of the head came away from the body, bloody gore clouding everywhere.

Von Getz levelled the weapon again, clearing his mind of Sagen's body as it sank lifelessly into the depths, octo man moving in for the kill. He fired another shot, this one hitting the creature in the human part of the body. It slowed, drifting in, plucking the weapon from the Swabian's hand.

In a final defiant move, von Getz jammed the remote unit into the beak.

The octo man drifted in front of them for a few moments before moving in for the kill.

Chapter 81

Perfekt came out of hiding, looking out at the dust hanging in the air from the missile blast. He found Dalheim outside. They started chatting, body language very animated.

Vessels was not interested in what they were saying. The intercom had just sounded, notifying him that the emergency lift would be operational in a couple of minutes. That was far more interesting.

He had combat training, like all Swabians, but had no taste for it. There were plenty of bodies to do that job back home. He had not fired a gun for years, preferring to concentrate on a role of directorship. True, he was fortunate to have family members in the right places to open the right doors at the right time, but when opportunities presented themselves, who was he to shut himself away from the responsibilty?

Then another door conveniently opened near to where he was hiding. In all the confusion when the fight broke out, he had ducked into lab three where the rebels had met up.

Vessels had crept along below the line of the workstations to the rear of the lab where a row of cupboards used for storage were situated. He noticed a backpack pushed into a recess that looked very familiar. On closer inspection, he realised that the item was Swabian, regulation issue, probably hidden up with rebel gear as a fallback should their initial plan fail. He looked inside, eyes widening as he retrieved a mini cloaking device, an image projector and an Armolux sitting on top of eight Glock handguns.

Ignoring the guns, he stuffed the other three items into the pockets of his tunic before pushing the backpack into the recess. He watched as Dalheim and Perfekt wandered over toward the shuttle terminal. They were preoccupied by the ETs, monitoring their progress, as they bored their way through the rockfall, almost, seeming by their body language, to invite more confrontation.

Vessels had other ideas.

Chapter 82

Up on the surface, the hangar was open. Black team had entered the base and made contact with Valerian and Holt. The entrance where blue team had massed was also open, and they were making their way to Level Three.

"Any luck with the overrides yet?" Valerian asked over his third mug of tea.

"Not long now. Should have access in a few minutes," Holt replied. "The lift is coming on line now."

"Good, I'll send a team down."

"Okay, but you'll have to wait for the reset. The lift froze down on Level Seven."

"Will do." Valerian leaned back in the desk chair he occupied, butterflies in his stomach.

No point in rushing it now. Control had been notified by code of their progress. It was just a case of waiting.

Holt had assembled his senior officers and informed them of the stand down. It seemed to Valerian that they displayed signs of relief that activities on the lower levels were coming to an end.

Chapter 83

The hatch slammed down and the wheel spun into the locking position as Kaufmann jumped into the cockpit, initiating the propulsion system. The craft fired into life, the Swabian running brief diagnostics before easing the Flugelrad out of hiding.

They had Gallagher on a gurney, Aral, Cale and Bek working on the bleeding as Enoch ripped open a medi pack.

Von Getz was shaking as he pulled off his diving suit, hardly able to comprehend what had just happened. He remembered the octo man on him. He could feel the tentacles coil around his body.

He watched as they tried to stabilise the injured man, Bek an integral part of the makeshift MERT team, the Swabian still shaking from his own stay of execution.

The recent events played out to him in perfect video imagery. He shivered at the recollection as he struggled to get the team into the Flugelrad, his mind rewinding to the impossible conclusion that it was unable to cope with.

And now he remembered: Bek, fixed in concentration, both hands outstretched, aiming at the octo man, a low rasp coming from its mouth. The creature was suddenly catapulted backwards in a stream of angry turbulence. It recovered, coming back at them again, but they were safely inside the craft by the time it reached them.

Bek glanced over, smiling, before turning his attention back to Gallagher.

Whatever explanation for what Bek had done out there would have to wait as von Getz picked up two packs of adrenalin and plasma, bringing them over to the patient. They fired two lines into him before putting him on oxygen, rigging him up to a monitor, the pressure stabilising, heart rate slowing. Gallagher was holding on for the moment.

Kaufmann hugged the bottom of the harbour as a myriad of distorted shapes danced above them; survivors of the tank blast, no doubt.

They made it to the harbour entrance and crawled out into the concealed tunnel. They kept the speed at dead slow, passing the holding pond, the area with the charred abductees, then the shuttle link, eventually passing the rockfall point. Even underwater, they could hear the ETs busily cutting their way through the blockage.

When they reached the desired marker point, Kaufmann engaged the mag drive and the Flugelrad shot off at high speed.

Chapter 84

Vessels picked his way through the carnage of the battle zone, occupying the safety of the Swabian cloaking technology. He passed in between a pair of prefabricated buildings, catching sight of the elevator across the hall. It was at this point that he realised he was being followed.

It was Perfekt, stumbling over the wreckage, sneaking his way toward him.

But that was impossible. He was invisible.

He looked down, checking that there was no malfunction. It seemed to be working fine. But there he was, following the same route he, Vessels, had just taken.

Perfekt ran to one side, ducking under a series of metal struts. That was when the terrible odour reached him, almost unbearable, making his eyes water.

He suddenly saw the reason.

The Draco came into plain sight, looking directly at him, the huge green body turning face on, Vessels mind suddenly filling with strong vocals.

"I can see you, Terran. Your device is of no use."

"How can that be possible?" Vessels was stunned.

"I can detect the aura around your body," Draco delivered telepathically.

"What do you want with me?"

"Why, I am going to kill you, of course. I am going to kill you all." The Draco gave a snort of superiority.

"I can hear someone. Is that you, Vessels? Where are you?" It was Perfekt. Of course. He was following the Draco all along, and not himself.

The Draco looked behind him as Perfekt moved closer.

"Stay back, Claude," Vessels instructed.

"Where are you? Ah, there you are." He spotted Vessels in full view to his left.

The Draco looked with disdain at Perfekt, who stopped in his tracks, staring in awe at the being. The yellow reptilian eyes were darting around, assessing the situation, the Swabian standing defiantly with Armolux in hand. The Draco seemed genuinely surprised at the audacious behaviour of his foe; then the ruthless efficiency returned as it touched its chest, firing its own weaponry into the midriff of Vessels.

Perfekt gasped as the beam cut right through his fellow human, just as Vessels drew his own weapon up to aim. The Draco fired again, this time at the head just to make sure, Vessels advancing defiantly, stumbling, holding his head as he fell to his knees.

The Draco moved forward, securing its weapon, its face now wearing a satisfied grin.

A beam smashed into the head of the reptile creature, sending it spinning 180 degrees, its expression one of surprise. Perfekt looked astounded as Vessels leapt from behind him, shooting two more charges into the Draco's chest. It stood staring into space wide-mouthed, before smashing lifelessly into the ground.

Vessels walked over and kicked the great creature's side. "Well, you wanted a close-up view. Here you are."

Perfekt approached gingerly, still in shock. He looked

down at the Draco, its body curled up, the great tail between its enormous powerful thighs, the pointed mane of concurrent triangles now limp and folded over on itself, massive claws rigid and protracted, the expression on the lipless mouth one of evil tranquillity. Perfekt could not help but admire the incredible animal sprawled on the floor.

He suddenly came to his senses, spinning around to face the other man. "How the hell did you do that? There's not even a mark on you."

Perfekt moved closer. "Is it you?"

"It's me." Vessels could see the other man's confusion. "It's an image projector. Clever little gadget, really. Replicates me in another position."

"That's amazing. Is it another Swabian invention?"

"Yes, and it can be yours too if things work out between our nations." Perfekt relaxed, giving the Draco a kick of his own. "Not so tough now, are you?"

"Come on. The lifts should be working now. Let's get out of here and get some real air."

"I heard that."

They walked over to the lift. Vessels pressed the buttons, then placed his hand on the pad. They were all cleared through the system on Umbra seven. The lift responded as the doors opened immediately. The two men climbed in, and the lift glided upwards towards Level Three.

Chapter 85

From dockside, Hebb observed the blocked tunnel, a glow appearing behind some of the rocks. The ETs were nearly through. But they were ready for them. The battle had been intense, many casualties sustained on both sides, but in the eyes of Hebb, it had been a sacrifice well worth making. He felt invigorated; vindicated, even, by events following the threat posed by the Draco assault. In his opinion, the Draco's alliance was now a ridiculously dangerous treaty that was no longer worth the risk.

He relished the moment that the Draco broke through the rockfall.

"All weapons in place and standing by, sir." Rascher announced.

Hebb nodded. "On my order."

Rascher spun on his heels, suddenly alerted by a noise behind him, the dull cough of a side arm being discharged.

As two of his team dropped to the floor, he felt a fiery ache as a bullet entered his stomach. Another smashed into his shoulder before he could react, then returning fire, shooting the assailant at point blank range, who let out a stark grunt before firing again into Rascher's chest. Rascher staggered backwards, clutching at the wounds, trying in vain to stem the bloodflow.

Hebb responded wide-eyed as the attacker homed in,

Rascher separating the two men. The assailant fired five times in quick succession, the bullets shaking Rascher like a rag doll, exiting his back and striking Hebb's portly frame. Hebb returned fire, more bullets flying out of Rascher's chest, striking the other man.

It fell silent as Rascher went down, leaving the two men facing each other.

"Cory," Hebb whispered in surprise, hanging on to the metal railing.

Cory said nothing, just staring at the other man.

It was strange. The layers of drugs administered over the weeks had made him immune to pain, and therefore still able to function, even though he had been hit seven times. Hebb had no such pain threshold, much to Cory's satisfaction. He watched as Hebb gasped, turning away, the back of his khaki uniform now a tattered, deep red.

Cory's memory fought through the conditioning, allowing him a window of memory back to when his cell door had sprung open and he had wandered out in a daze of confusion, stumbling down the cavern, eventually reaching the great illuminated cast iron hulk of The Bell. He had stared for quite some time at the old craft, the swastika clearly visible, aiding him to a sense of purpose.

And then he had it.

That night all those years ago, by his father's side, the glowing craft wedged into the ground, the troops peeling out, the strange but now familiar insignia on their arm only serving to make his mission all the more poignant. He pieced together all the small parts of information that Hebb had bragged about to others while outside his cell. This gave him all the guidance he needed to stagger through the watery roadway, the floundering creatures ignoring him as if they had taken him in as one of their own.

He fought the nausea off as he bent down over a mutilated brownshirt, the same insignia on his uniform, triggering yet more memories of the life he once had. He relieved the man of his sidearm, and continued on until he found the dockside cavern. With all the other abductees milling around, it had been easy to slip unnoticed over to the dockside office marked 'Lower Base Commander'.

It had just been a waiting game until Hebb appeared.

He was grateful for the strength to carry out the end task. It seemed a fitting end, for he knew, even before the injuries inflicted upon him, that he was beyond mental repair. The hidden instinct that had rallied itself to enable him to act out the final scene was only a temporary respite to avenge his father, who had been found shot dead in the forest near to the family home, and all the other lost souls imprisoned in this underground madness.

His adversary was floundering on the dock railings, wearing a look of puzzlement as he looked down.

There was a commotion in the water, almost surreal. The commander stared harder, his head becoming fogged with dizziness, but still able to compute what he saw.

The great head broke surface just in front of him, tentacles flailing, trying to reach him. Hebb gave out a short laugh, coughing blood.

"Otto ..." he managed.

He watched as the large, horribly injured, mottled head tilted up. Underneath, where the tentacles met the body, the beak was now visible.

Hebb could see the remote still jammed in place by von Getz, and knew instantly what it was. Otto rose up as high as possible, but the strength needed was too much.

Hebb gave out another bloody cough. "Nice try, Otto. Looks like the sonics will take us both."

There was another great rush as water flew in all directions, six eyes of sadness all blinking together in the middle of a conical squid-like head, a great claw following, reaching up, the lower base leader unable to move through injury as the claw found its mark, grabbing his torso, pulling him over the side into the foaming mass of Otto's tentacles.

Hebb had no strength left to respond as he hurtled down into the great arms, vanishing as he was engulfed by a thousand sucker pads.

Otto slid away toward the harbour bed, the prey firmly in place, life ebbing away rapidly from both of them. Cory watched as the water's surface settled, as if it had all been a dream. The play was finally at an end.

The dock was silent now as he gazed over the great cavern, the white glow increasing from the tunnel, the troops in the distance at the ready. Still he felt no pain as he watched the scene play out, although he felt his legs start to give out on him.

The timer came round to zero on the sonic hub, the mechanism activated and powered up in a matter of seconds, shooting its wave around the huge expanse, darting into every crevice. At the same time, a series of explosions detonated, sounding at the extremities of the lab section, melting the white electric cars, twisting metal stair treading, fusing glass into giant rippled distorted shapes.

Cory felt the pressure just for a second, and dropped dead.

The Draco had broken through with their great Armolux aglow to be met by the sonic waves igniting the cavern, eliminating every living thing in its wake.

The explosions subsided, the sonics terminated.

There was absolute silence.

Chapter 86

Vessels and Perfekt felt the impact of the explosion rock the elevator shaft. Their heads were left ringing. They felt nauseous as the lift reached Level Three.

The doors opened to a group of heavily armed troops all dressed in black.

Vessels grabbed Perfekt by the arm, pulling him into the corridor before they were blocked off, the cloaking device doing its job. They scurried away from the oblivious unit entering the lift one by one. They saw the doors shut as the combat detail were taken down to Level Seven.

They were alone now, left in eerie silence as they crept along the corridor, eventually reaching the second lift section. It was unmanned, probably because of extenuating circumstances. Security would not be expecting anyone from beneath.

Vessels punched the button for the surface, again granted clearance through the handprint scanner. The lift glided upwards, a weight of tension gradually leaving both of them. Vessels kept the cloak activated as the lift came to a halt for the last time. The doors opened once more. This time there was no one waiting for them. They walked in silence past grey walls and floors to the hangar door. There were four guards on duty and a few more troops milling around outside whom they easily bypassed without detection.

Vessels led Perfekt up the ramp of his aircraft, the door wide open, the crew relaxed, awaiting their next orders.

They jumped up to attention as Vessels switched off the cloaking device.

Chapter 87

The water lapped the edge of the dock, each wave becoming weaker, the surface settling down as the gunboats drifted aimlessly into the quayside, crew members slumped in the footwells. An underwater service vessel lay on its side, no one left alive to right the ballast, the ropes halting its progress.

The canal contained nothing but death, the panoramic scene a display of awesome life-sapping destruction.

Moving away from the visual damage of the conflict, the tunnels and labs took on a surreal viewpoint, all the infrastructure untouched. Some of the brownshirts remained positioned behind the wheels of vehicles, manning computers, some assembled in lines ready to join the firefight further down, others frozen in their last posture before the sonics had hit.

These were the scenes that met Valerian's team as the lift doors opened.

They fanned out, taking no chances, keeping to hand signals as they moved into the first service area. The troops advanced, spotting a group of electric cars. The men yanked the brownshirts out of the vehicles and dragged them out of the way. There was a ruthless efficiency within the unit as they climbed aboard, spotter in each car beside the driver, MP5s trained ahead.

Two men would jump down occasionally, jogging beside

the convoy, peeling off to check over buildings. They had gone the long way round. It made sense to make the outer perimeter safe first before calling in the rest of the troops.

They circled the boundary without incident, the silence making Level Seven seem even more sinister. Structural damage up ahead for the first time, now; a first glimpse of the remains of dead experimental bodies that littered the cavernous lab section, the cars required to weave through the carnage, sometimes stopping to allow troops to clear the way; rows of empty tanks and cages, many caught in the explosion, the damage increasing as they moved deeper into the section.

The lockdown was over, the emergency sections had retracted, offering Valerian a good uninterrupted view of death and destruction all the way down to where the dock started.

He broke the silence. "We'll finish checking this area then head down to the main hub."

"Okay, sir, all sectors are open and on line again."

"Good, that means we should have camera backup." Valerian patched in to Commander Holt.

"I have visual on the team now," Holt confirmed from the control room.

"Okay. Begin scanning if you will."

"Affirmative."

Holt brought the visuals into play, combing the levels for any activity. There was no movement aside from the team in the lab area. He started surveillance beyond them, in a protracted area. The sector beyond them had extensive damage, leaving one solitary camera in operation. He brought up audio.

Holt could hear Valerian's voice booming commands to the team as they moved down the section. They were on foot, the damage too severe to proceed any other way. Valerian could hear the camera whizzing around above his head as he stepped over what was left of a metal staircase. He waved the team ahead, camera safe.

"No, wait. Hold position," Holt shouted through the comms.

Valerian halted his men. "Advise?"

"Just stay quiet. Nobody move."

Holt zoomed in on high resolution, scanning the wreckage extensively, trying to work the area for danger. Was it his imagination? He was taking no chances.

The microphone was up to maximum, the signal weak, Holt had his hand up in the control room. Nobody made a sound.

There it was again: a dull thumping, a short distance ahead.

So he wasn't going mad after all. "Team leader, I have sound ahead of you, about forty yards."

"Control, roger that," Valerian whispered.

"Audio is poor; just a dull thumping sound, intermittent. We are trying to narrow the source."

"Proceeding with caution."

Valerian waved the team ahead. They kept the noise down to a minimum, illuminating the cavern with mag lights on their assault rifles. There was a lot of dust still in the air; visibility was not good at all.

The thumping came again. It was not rhythmic like a machine would make, more sporadic, in bursts about one minute apart.

The team arrived to more tangled wreckage. They navigated their way through until they could see the rear wall. Valerian looked around. There was a lot of debris mixed in with piles of rock that had been blasted down from the canopy.

There it was again. The team primed their weapons, while others pulled away at more twisted wreckage.

Valerian ground his great jaw, his eyes forming a frown as he caught sight of something very odd. More banging.

"Okay, we have a visual. Patching you in now." Valerian's headcam scanned over the scene; Holt's team pored over the footage.

"Do you know what it is?"

"Negative. Don't have a clue." Valerian's voice, now higher. "Wait I … I have something … it's … "

There was screaming, confusion, followed by shouts of hysteria from Valerian. The headcam was shaking about.

"What the hell's going on? Respond."

Chapter 88

The Flugelrad glided through the tunnel as they worked on Gallagher. He was stable, but weak from blood loss. He urgently needed a medical facility.

"Exit point ahead, sir," Kaufmann announced from the flight deck.

Von Getz looked at the injured man.

The Haunebu hidden up ahead on the seabed was faster than their own craft, without a doubt. But to try and move Gallagher at this point could be fatal. They would have to make do with the Flugelrad. He cancelled the transfer.

"Set a direct heading for Paramus."

He was standing amidships, hands clasped behind his back, as the brightness of the entrance to the gulf came into view. The craft entered the ocean, banking left, a course set heading north.

Bek came up to join him, adopting an identical pose. Von Getz smiled down at him.

"Care to tell me what happened back there?"

Bek knew what the Swabian was referring to. "It's called Vril, a way of harnessing the energy around you into a sound frequency that can be used as a weapon."

"Who taught you how to do that?"

"I'm not sure. My genetic makeup has very ancient DNA

strands. I believe that, combined with my human side, I am able to awaken long-forgotten skills."

"You are saying that this practice existed in ancient times?"

"Yes. You are familiar with ancient structures in Bolivia, Puma Punku for instance?" Von Getz nodded. Bek continued. "Those temples found at a high altitude were built with the aid of Vril. There are many more that were built in the same way all over the world."

Von Getz knew his history well. He also knew that a lot of ancient building techniques were a complete mystery.

Bek had the additional capability of absorbing hereditary knowledge. In short, he was born with information to aid his learning ability. Von Getz was of high intellect himself, which equipped him to comprehend just how exceptional Bek was. It made him appreciate the unique abilities that Bek possessed.

"I trust this is a sufficient explanation?"

"Yes, Bek, thank you." He laughed inwardly with admiration.

It did not take long to reach Paramus and to initiate the docking onto the second building. Fully cloaked, they were granted permission to land and safely offload the personnel.

Cale, Enoch, Aral and Bek were welcomed into the complex. Gallagher was rushed down to the medical facility.

Redmond was pleased to see the Swabians again. She looked tired. "Communication with the lower base should be back on line in a few minutes."

"I hope so," Kaufmann managed to say.

"We'd better get going," von Getz announced.

"Of course. We will patch you in when comms are back on line. Good luck, gentlemen. Stay safe."

The main assault on the base was over, but there were still recon sweeps to do in case MJ-12 had any hidden airborne surprises waiting for them. Kaufmann banked the Flugelrad down to a thousand feet as they reached the border for the state of New Mexico, and cloaked up. They cruised at the fixed altitude, starting with the perimeter of the base. It was quiet. The ground patrols had been called back by Commander Holt.

As they moved closer to the base itself, they saw numerous vehicles parked on the high ground to protect the entrance and runway. There were a few personnel milling around the hangar, the Templar flag now flying from the top of the building. The two Swabians exchanged solemn glances as they banked around for one last check.

The comms sprang to life. "This is Commander Holt. Are you receiving, Flugelrad craft?"

Kaufmann jumped slightly as the silence in the cabin was broken. "This is Flugelrad to base. Receiving you loud and clear," he replied, rather bewildered. Von Getz also looked puzzled.

"This is Base. Control of the lower levels is confirmed, mission a success, enemy eliminated."

"Glad to hear it, Control," Kaufmann replied.

"Flugelrad, we can confirm that we have full comms with the lower base. Patching you through now."

"Go ahead, Control."

'This is Base lower level to Flugelrad. Is that section six concluded?"

Von Getz grabbed the comms in shock. "Who is this?"

"It's me, Klaus. Who else would it be?"

Kaufmann looked up in surprise as von Getz fell back in his seat. "Hans, we thought you were dead," Kaufmann gasped. "How ...?"

He burst out laughing, von Getz joining in. New Swabia still had no losses in combat.

Schumann explained how Weisse had come up with the

idea of climbing inside The Bell to shelter from the blast. As suspected, the sonics were too weak in that section to do them any real harm. Valerian had heard Schumann banging on the door which had jammed after the craft had been thrown fifty feet by the impact of the blast.

"We got the shock of our lives when we fished them out of that thing," Valerian suddenly boomed through the speakers. "Got your scientist friend von Gellen here, too."

They got him out? That was unbelievable.

Von Getz could guess why Schumann had chosen the cover story; much better than trying to explain who the leader of New Swabia was.

"That's great news. We owe you a drink."

"I'll hold you to that," Valerian chuckled. "Be aware, we are breaching the top of the cavern."

"Okay, we'll do one more sweep and come in to land."

"That's an affirmative, Flugelrad, over and out."

Von Getz was still laughing, shaking his head. He could see Kaufmann smiling as he looked at the green team on the ground below setting the charges around a hole of approximately four feet, made by the drone that Schumann had sent up from inside. From a safe distance they could see the team retreat as the charges were detonated.

More charges, quite a way back, created a fire wall for a hundred feet, Armolux beams hitting the ground, tracing the men as they ran in all directions.

"What's going on down there?" Kaufmann brought the craft round for a closer look as another cluster of beams came at them. He pulled the Flugelrad out of the turn, throwing them sideways as a searing light flew past them.

He quickly accelerated them away from danger, taking the craft to incredible speed in a matter of seconds. In no time at all they reached the coastline, the broad expanse of the Atlantic Ocean gaping in front of them. Von Getz got the scanners running as he strapped himself into the co-pilot's seat.

"Powering up weapon banks." He flicked a series of switches, a panel lit up, and then three screens with 3D digital maps, including a mag radar system.

"Weapons on line and ready." Von Getz looked at Kaufmann. "Who the hell was that? And how did they know we were there?"

"I don't know, but my guess would be a cloaked Haunebu. Only a craft like that has the capability of detecting us." Kaufmann looked worried. "It also has starfish Armolux weapons."

"You said that like it's really bad."

"It is, Klaus."

"But we have Armolux too, and the nation's best pilot," von Getz encouraged.

Kaufmann could not help but laugh within the gravity of the situation. "Praise indeed. I thank you, but I suspect that they are in an H-10."

"So what are our chances?"

"In a Flugelrad, none at all. We are slower, our weapons are inferior, and they will probably have a full crew to track us with geotherm tracers."

Kaufmann took them underwater, forcing the craft down to a thousand feet, idling the drive on the seabed before cutting the power. He turned to his compatriot, whispering, "We need a plan, and fast. We can't stay hidden for long."

"Alright, bring up a contoured map of the seabed."

The Haunebu skimmed the surface of the Atlantic looking for activity, the broad span scanners working efficiently as they covered the ocean.

The Haunebu commander took up the central position where he could oversee the operation. Upfront he had the pilot and navigator, to the left and right two pairs of gunners, and behind him a rather bewildered-looking civilian.

"So how do you like our ship?" Vessels asked over his right shoulder.

"Quite remarkable," Claude Perfekt replied in absolute amazement. "I can't believe how fast it is."

"Yet another asset we are more than willing to share." Vessels gave a large wink.

They were circling Cuba, conducting an SPS sweep, the speed of the Haunebu covering a huge area of water in minutes.

"Last known vector trail of bandit craft?" Vessels demanded.

The flight crew checked their detection records. They showed a positive wave pattern entering the sea a few miles off the Caribbean.

"They hit the ocean just off Bermuda," the pilot informed him.

"Good, we have an entry point."

"Sea-penetrating sonar will only allow us limited depth capability, sir."

"Yes, but combined with the motion detectors, we should be able to track them down." Vessels interjected. "The Flugelrad is no match for us."

Kaufmann kept the craft on the seabed, weaving through the coral reefs, parrot fish darting around acrobatically, oblivious to the mechanical disc that drifted through their playground, the natural structures offering the Swabians limited protection from the detectors above.

The geographic area of the seabed had yielded little in the way of cover. Von Getz scanned the 3D screens for inspiration, looking for anything that would help them. He threw the rollerball director around, working through the underwater terrain until he found some contour.

The Taino Ruins were well known to New Swabia, a reference point when taking the sea routes. There was nothing secret about them, but von Getz knew the layout better than most, studying the ruins in great detail as a young science officer.

The great temple was at the centre of the sunken city. It was situated off the Western coast of Cuba in 132 feet of water. Behind the temple, the seabed fell away dramatically where the top of a cavern had collapsed, exposing a series of caves. There were a few that interconnected, leading to a single exit point half a mile down the coastline.

They continued along the coral reef for several miles before von Getz reacted to movement from above them.

Kaufmann looked over anxiously. "It's them."

"Activating image projector," von Getz responded. It would work for a short while before the dual course became obvious. He set the widest parameter he could: eight hundred feet. He also varied the projection height and size to add to the confusion.

Kaufmann could tell they were close. He tried to fight off the trackers, but it was difficult with the superior technology installed in the latest Haunebu model. The enemy were going to get a lock on them any second, and when they did, it would be game over.

They could almost feel them breathing down their necks as they accelerated away from the reef into open water. At least here the depth increased to about five thousand feet and with the sudden speed increase, it gave them a head start as the island of Cuba came onto their screens.

The water became shallow again, an alarm sounding. Kaufmann stared at the cross hairs on his left-hand monitor, the sight agonisingly close to their magnetic vector drive system output. "We're not going to make it," he hissed.

Von Getz studied his readouts. There was nothing out there, but … "I have something. Change course thirty degrees left."

Kaufmann complied, accelerating once more. Both men looked through the observation hatch. About fifty feet above them, the water was alive with numerous large objects. Von Getz used the viewfinder to zoom in.

Fish of a strange appearance, some of them fifteen feet long, were shoaling up, forming a large spiral shape as they swam: hammerhead sharks, known to occasionally form huge gangs. No one really knew the reason for this. Right now, it was not important.

Kaufmann took them up from the seabed to twenty feet below the shoal, terminating the image projector. He looked at the crosshairs. They had strayed from the middle to the far right of the sight screen. The alarm had stopped.

Random starfish Armolux bursts were discharged, striking a few of the hammerheads, sending clouds of blood around the shoal. This only served to intensify the mass as the other fish turned on their own injured, the blood a trigger, to home in for the kill.

Kaufmann could see their detectors behaving erratically. It

was working, the signal temporarily scrambled by the massive shoal.

Von Getz spied the ruins up ahead. They took a chance, Kaufmann throwing the Flugelrad into maximum power, sending huge plumes of bubbles from the rear of the craft. He could see a starfish burst hit the disturbance only thirty feet behind them. He directed as much power to the propulsion system as he dared, squeezing an extra few knots out of the straining craft.

Over the temple, between the massive columns that lined the sides of the building, another starfish slammed into the seabed to their right.

They could see the glow from the Haunebu above, the cloaking device deactivated. There was a flash; another starfish, this one searing through the depths, clipping the entrance to the cavern as they entered, sending a shower of rocks crashing into the fuselage, throwing the Flugelrad into the cave wall; followed by the loud sound of scraping as the hull struggled to free itself.

Kaufmann wrestled with the controls as the rocks tumbled into the blackness. Von Getz checked for breaches; compensating the drive system for the damaged sensors. Thankfully, they were still watertight.

"We've lost magnetic inertia boost," he announced. He jettisoned anything that was surplus to requirements, along with a mag charger. "That's all I can do."

Kaufmann tried the back-up drivers. "It's improved a little, but not enough."

Von Getz knew they were in trouble. They arrived at the split, four entrances all of identical dimensions. "Take the far right," he instructed.

Kaufmann did not hesitate, using the infrared to light their way, the visibility now down to zero. They travelled for two hundred yards until the next command.

"Now, slow her down and take us through the gap in the left wall."

Kaufmann had to stop to turn the ship 180 degrees, the new entrance barely wide enough for the Flugelrad. Kaufmann was able to manage the feat by angling the craft through the widest point.

As they disappeared, von Getz caught a glimpse of the Haunebu closing fast.

The decision to uncloak was now apparent as their pursuer probed the depths with the high-powered beams of motion light in the hope of revealing their position. Von Getz dared not take the risk of allowing the Haunebu too close.

They drifted back on themselves, the adjacent tunnel taking them away in a half circle. It was now a game of cat and mouse as Kaufmann looked at the comms signal flashing.

"They want to open up a channel of communication," he announced.

Von Getz thought it over for a few moments. If the two ships were quite a distance apart, it might not be a good idea. But this close together, it would not make a difference in detection terms.

"Okay, let's hear what they have to say."

"Herr von Getz, Herr Kaufmann, I hope you are pleased with the devastation you have caused."

"You?" Kaufmann gasped at the sound of Vessels' voice.

"I might have known," von Getz added.

"You and your band of renegades have caused us a great deal of inconvenience."

"I am pleased to have stopped you," von Getz responded flatly.

"You cannot stop us. We have the superior craft. It will only be a matter of time before we catch you." Vessels sniggered. "In all honesty, by destroying the caverns, you have done us all a favour. The Draco were getting out of control anyway. We will rebuild somewhere else with MJ-12."

"You are a traitor to your nation."

"Nonsense. This is the dawn of a new era, a chance for us to rise up and to take what is rightfully ours. You clearly do not share that viewpoint."

"You would risk our existence for that?"

"I think you have a very negative opinion of our country. There is no risk. With our technology, we could wipe out the Terrans in a week."

It was true. Von Getz was aware that they could abuse their position. But New Swabia had prospered because of its anonymity. The nation was no longer a war machine. He wanted no part of this grand new plan.

"You're insane. The people will not stand for this."

"The people will do as they are told. They always have."

Von Getz knew what he was trying to do: buy some time while the Haunebu detectors did their job. But Kaufmann had superior tactical knowledge, and was disrupting the signals, probably a good reason why they were still alive.

"It is such a waste to have to destroy a Flugelrad. Why don't you just surrender? I'm sure we can all come to some arrangement." Vessels was trying the nice guy approach now. Kaufmann was working hard, frantically checking calculations. He turned to von Getz and nodded.

"We have decided on an arrangement," said von Getz.

"Ah, that is good. I knew you would see sense."

"If you would look ahead of you, Haunebu crew." Von Getz cross-referenced the mapping route. He could hear the crew talking to Vessels, and his voice rising to hysteria.

"Get us …"

The comms went dead. "They've cut the link." Kaufmann smiled looking over his shoulder.

"Activating now." Von Getz smiled back.

"Full reverse now." Vessels barked.

"What's going on?" Perfekt demanded.

"The cavern narrows up ahead. The ship's too large," the pilot shouted back.

"Check their position," Vessels demanded.

"Flugelrad is still in the area, sir."

"They must be in the next tunnel behind us, damn them." He slammed his fist down on the back of a chair.

"Comms are requesting a link, sir," the helmsman shouted.

"Denied! I'm tired of this. Take us back to the main entrance." Vessels turned to Perfekt. "We have them now."

They could see bright lights dancing through the turbulence as they reversed. But they were not the navigational lights; they were Armolux beams.

Vessels watched, tutting to himself. They were way out of range to do any harm to them.

The beams hit the roof of the tunnel ahead, splintering rocks tumbling away harmlessly and sending thousands of air bubbles into the water. Vessels watched them dissipate onto the tunnel floor, the rocks coming to rest in small plumes of silt.

"Lock on to those coordinates."

The Flugelrad powered up, moving swiftly away from the cave entrance, von Getz glued to the cockpit screens. The Haunebu reached the point where the cave was wide enough to turn around.

"Full speed ahead," Vessels shouted like an old sea captain.

The cave entrance came rushing up towards them. Vessels realised too late that they had been led into a trap.

There was a tremendous roar as the mag charger detonated the Flugelrad's jettisoned ballast. The cave entrance collapsed on top of the Haunebu, pushing the craft downwards, pressure mounting, engines screaming as they fought to break free as yet more boulders crashed into the Haunebu, pinning the craft to the seabed, sand and silt billowing, clouding the water, engines failing, leaving the sound of dull thumping combined with creaks and groans.

The sounds then became drowned out by hysteria from panicked voices as the hull breached, sending water rushing into the interior, flooding it in an instant.

Kaufmann banked the Flugelrad around to face the cave network. They hovered for a few moments as the cameras scanned the damage. They could see the metalwork and two observation windows peeping out from behind the rockfall. The lights inside the ship flickered as the power failed.

Von Getz set off a series of Armolux charges that brought yet more of the cave mouth down until the entrance was sealed up with hundreds of tons of boulders.

Aboard the Haunebu, Vessels had managed to grab a rebreather and oxygen tank. He lay trapped in the watery wreckage, the lifeless body of Claude Perfekt wedged next to him. He felt the porthole with his hands trying to force the glass open to create an escape route. The rocks were still falling where there were still gaps for them to fall into. The panic was rising inside him. His leg was caught fast in the tangled wreckage. He started to shout for help for all the good it would do him. He tried to wrestle free, twisting his body backwards and forwards, shouting louder.

Von Getz and Kaufmann watched the wide-eyed face

impassively, pressed up against the glass, the lips mouthing pleadingly.

Like a dramatic theatrical scene, the electrics finally gave out, plunging the Haunebu into darkness, Vessels' pathetic image disappearing from view.

The reply came in a creaking rumble as the drive system cracked open, the chemical reaction igniting the weaponry. There was a dull *whump*, only audible to Vessels himself as the ship imploded, condensing it like aluminium foil scrunching into a fist, more rocks occupying the void, thousands of tons of them, the ship fracturing into pieces as the metal was pummelled relentlessly.

The Flugelrad hovered as the rocks settled, searchlights scanning the entrance. Nothing was getting in or out of there in a hurry. The entrance was now completely blocked.

Kaufmann checked for any vital signs. All negative. The craft was dead, and so were the occupants. Von Getz breathed a sigh of relief, patting his colleague's shoulder.

"Well done, my friend, get us back to Dulce."

Chapter 89

Dulce, New Mexico

Green team had abseiled through the breach and onto the rockface below them. From here it was a case of making the short descent to the observation platform and climbing down the man-made stone steps, then taking the cage elevator down to where the submarine base was located.

They came across numerous casualties en route, before commandeering a launch, removing more of the dead from inside, then driving the vessel to the dockside. Valerian was waiting with red team, surveying the damage. They had rounded up all the electric cars that were still operational, using them for recon.

Schumann sat in one of the cars rubbing the side of his head, still feeling the effects of the sonic blasts. Weisse was sitting next to him. Von Gellen was in the sick bay, a medical team working on him, rehydrating his body after the effects of his imprisonment.

Valerian alerted Commander Holt to their situation, and ordered the team to advance. He jumped into Schumann's car. "That's the whole of Level Six and Seven checked. No survivors."

Schumann nodded. He knew how lucky he was.

As they descended into the tunnel, the devastation

continued: the giant Armolux burnt out, the small saucer fleet behind on the ground still sizzling, the circuitry fried. There were bodies of Draco sprawled and twisted, with Greys and Caste resembling fragile puffs of smoke, their faces with not a trace of emotion, not even in death.

The cars wove a path by the carnage and descended deeper.

A red mist hung in dense patches, the micro-atmosphere turning the air damp, the absolute silence around them making the electric motors in the cars sound deafening.

They arrived at the slope that led down to the first city. Dozens of Caste lay on the side of the route.

No one had uttered a word for twenty minutes. For some, this was the first time that they had set eyes on the lair of the Draco. As they neared the crimson architecture, there was a feeling that a curfew had been lifted, whereby the forbidden was now uncensored.

They arrived at the building where they had conversed with the three Draco. This time it was empty.

Like many of the structures, they were partially natural, with many still lit by the Draco's own power source. They made the place feel even more unsettling, casting vast shadows around the massive expanse of the cavern.

The cars turned onto what passed for the main street, which was again littered with bodies. Draco and Greys were slumped in doorways, face down in the road in various poses, attending to their tasks before the sonic wave hit them, freezing them to the spot.

They toured the area for some time checking for survivors. There were none.

Many of the buildings were locked. Doubtless, H would order cutting gear down and open them up at a later date. He gave the order to advance into the next section, through the natural obstacle course of mineral and stone to the tunnel where Schumann had discovered the cloaked entrance.

The camouflage had disintegrated due to the failing infrastructure. It was now visible for all to see. They followed Schumann through the opening onto the rocky outcrop offering the breathtaking view of the massive second city.

But the view that met the Swabian was far different this time.

The Caste had carried out Bek's instructions to the letter, delivering the sensors into the heart of the great settlement, wiping out everything with ruthless efficiency. Huge numbers of ETs littered the streets, disc craft lay motionless, many embedded in buildings where the pilots had died instantly and lost control. The river that snaked its way across the once bustling empire carried expired crews of vessels that meandered by the bankside in disorganised flotillas. The small team observed the wreckage from multiple vehicle pileups, lines of Caste, fifty strong in deathly heaps, and Draco that once commanded them by their sides.

"I've got a reading," Weisse exclaimed suddenly.

The others looked shocked at the announcement as they waited for the Swabian to disclose more information. He looked at the screen, at the flashing images, pulling the rangefinders up to his eyes. He scanned the vastness, the digital counters ticking over as they probed through the red mist, the auto-locate homing in on the target.

"There, beyond the river to the north."

They could just make them out with the naked eye, taking it in turns to look through the rangefinders. The herd of Goran were grazing on an open plateau, appearing to be unaffected by the sonic blast.

"Not a care in the world," Schumann said in amazement.

"They really are the ultimate war machine if they can withstand the sonics," Weisse remarked.

Schumann had to agree. They were like cockroaches after a nuclear attack, innocents caught up in events that were nothing to do with them.

They agreed to leave them there, isolated from the surface world. "They could do no harm.

"Well, I don't know about you lot, but I could do with a beer," H exclaimed, leading the way back to the cars.

The Swabians collected von Gellen from the sickbay and said their farewells to Valerian, Holt and the rest of the base teams. It was time to collect the Haunebu and head for home.

Schumann looked up at the brilliant blue sky. The sun was shining brightly on his face, and a moderate breeze blew the dust from his tattered uniform. He gratefully lapped up the atmosphere.

He walked across the runway, beer in hand. Weisse had one too, pushing a wheelchair with his spare hand, von Gellen on board. He was emotional, the outside world difficult to come to terms with after his nightmare confinement far below his feet. He knew that they were lucky. It could have ended very differently for all of them.

The Flugelrad was parked up near to hangar one, the ramp open, Kaufmann busy checking the hull over. Von Getz stuck his head out of the door at the top of the ramp and shouted. Both men came running over.

"I still can't believe you made it out." He shook hands vigorously.

"I hear you had a few issues yourself," Schumann replied.

"Look at the state of your ship, man. You should be ashamed of yourself." Von Gellen smiled weakly. They laughed as the Chancellor held von Getz's hand.

"What of Vessels?" he asked.

"He's gone, sir, and his crew."

Von Gellen sighed heavily. "Okay, we have work to do. Someone help me out of this damned chair."

Chapter 90

Cambridgeshire

Marius rubbed the bridge of his nose as he sat back next to Caroline. Mills removed his headset, looking around the small control room at the rest of the team. He wore a look of contentment, born of years of inherited struggle against an enemy now heavily defeated.

The twentieth century had been a difficult struggle for the Templars, the seizure of power by the Kaiser followed closely by Hitler, had enabled the Illuminati to gain a stronghold over Europe which had then seen the power migrate to the United States after the war. It had always been a great mystery how they had exploited such a position, until now. Their repulsive alliance in the underground base now exposed, it all made sense how they had managed to retain the upper hand, how they had been able to operate so efficiently, prospering from their spoils, the information gleaned from the Draco used to extort vast wealth from the world population.

He would get the full lowdown from Valerian soon enough. There was so much research to do, so much to absorb. For an academic scorned by many for his beliefs, this was vindication on a grand scale, and the reward of knowledge way beyond any 33rd degree mason.

Mills shook with excitement as he replayed in his head the

footage that he had witnessed. He fumbled with the coffee that Martha had prepared as she handed him a cup. It was all too much. Perhaps a walk around the grounds would do him good for the chance to breathe in some fresh air and look up at the sun.

He was still shaking as he reached the large French doors that led onto the terrace. There was the sun, high in the cloudless, brilliant blue sky, shining brightly above him. He sighed as he sat down on the step, resting his elbows on his knees as he felt the first tear run down his cheek.

His head fell into his hands as he wept uncontrollably.

Chapter 91

Gulf Of Mexico

The cloaked Flugelrad cruised at an altitude of ten thousand feet, the coastline of the United States giving way to the ocean expanse, the course set to rendezvous with the craft hidden away on the seabed.

A commercial aircraft in the distance, a container ship cutting through the moderate swell of white caps and several smaller boats skirting the harbour, all of them bathed in bright sunshine, were all oblivious of the invisible space they shared with Schumann and his crew.

It truly was a glorious day for the Terrans to enjoy, completely unaware of the battle that had taken place beneath their feet. There had been many unsung heroes over the centuries, and although he did not count himself worthy of the title, he had played a major role in ridding the planet of a terrible threat. The circumstances that brought him to the Dulce base may have been unconventional, but it was clear that fate had played a major hand in placing the Swabian directly where he was needed.

Just what the future held now was anybody's guess.

They entered the water, cruising steadily to the seabed before de-cloaking. Weisse guided the craft through the reefs and contours until they reached the coordinates. The Haunebu was waiting for them like an old friend, the foul weather hatch the only part visible above the sand. Schumann smiled as they closed in, on 'dead slow'.

Kaufmann made a sweep of the area. "Unidentified object closing in from the east, sir."

"How far out?" Schumann demanded, taken aback.

"Object is six hundred yards from our position, measuring perhaps fifteen feet in length."

"Alright; trackers out, and get me a visual as soon as possible."

Schumann was perplexed. There surely was no way that they could have been followed. An equally puzzled Weisse was busy calibrating, conveying information to Kaufmann. He brought the screen to life; a view of the ocean, visibility around a hundred yards, as he ran diagnostics to determine the threat.

Schumann sounded battle stations. They all took up their respective positions, von Getz powering up an Armolux cannon. He drew the cross hairs down into the centre of the ocean expanse, and waited.

"Object is still closing," Kaufmann announced.

"Cloak us up, please, Mr Weisse."

"Affirmative."

Weisse activated the controls. They watched in silence as the object closed in, the crew on high alert. Schumann's eyes were trained on the screen. He could hear his heart beating loudly as a shape appeared out of the gloom.

Weisse was still running diagnostics. "Object is organic, sir."

They watched as the image became focussed, Schumann relieved that the object was not man-made, but at the same time concerned that the creature was on a direct heading for their position.

They had visual now, and reasonable magnification. Kaufmann enhanced the imagery and there it was.

"A squid," von Gellen exclaimed in puzzlement.

"I have the target locked on, sir."

Schumann stalled himself to give the command. They still had a few moments before the creature struck the hull.

They watched as the form became more detailed. The creature slowed, tilting its body vertically, now drifting, the tentacles flailing gently to aid buoyancy, as if to display a show of might. But Schumann could sense no threat. It appeared the mollusc was examining them out of curiosity as it drifted ever nearer.

"Sir, what are your orders?" von Getz asked nervously, the creature now only a short distance away.

"Do not fire. De-cloak and stand down." He gave his friend a glance.

It was true that they had seen numerous squid before, but none as bold as this example. They were normally shy and elusive, avoiding their crafts, staying very deep.

This one was very different.

Schumann walked onto the flight deck, next to Weisse and Kaufmann. The creature seemed to react to his appearance. From the tangled mass of tentacles came a great claw, six eyes on the body all blinking simultaneously, looking directly at him.

"It's from the base. Must have followed us out through the underground tunnel before the sonics hit," he stated, nodding in amazement.

They were all entranced at the almost angelic grace before them. The six eyes that once carried immense despair within them were now full of brightness, the claw extended forwards, a display of tranquillity. Schumann placed his hand on the toughened glass. The squid man, torso now visible, luminous from the bathing Haunebu lights, tapped gently with its claw in response.

Von Getz came up to join him. "Sir, to allow this to remain in the ecosystem could be very dangerous," he whispered.

"I know, Klaus."

They had their own genetics programme back in New Swabia, heavily monitored and restricted. Nothing was ever given the chance to become airborne or to find its way into the river system. The slightest interference with nature in the wrong way could result in the extinction of species essential for the survival of mankind.

The constant struggle that the Terrans were unaware of as the Swabians tried to rectify the environmental damage created by ignorance, the fragile natural balance that hung by a thread that Schumann and the others had attempted to restore, could all be upset in one motion.

He weighed it up, looking at the great creation; how, despite the odds, it had survived everything. Was it his right to make that sort of decision? Maybe that was the way it had always been. Maybe man had evolved because of the same set of freak circumstances.

But man was not a laboratory creation.

As far as he could tell.

What floated before him was the last remaining experiment.

Through all of that was the nagging doubt that had stopped his usual decisiveness from destroying the creature.

The eyes looked down on him with kindness. There was clearly a trust in coming so close. He would be as evil as those he had just removed, to carry out such an act.

He brought up his right hand away from the glass, slowly returning it to his side. The creature responded, the claw still aloft as the tentacles pulsated, drifting away in retreat.

There was one last look from the squid man before tilting horizontally and shooting off into the ocean expanse.

Schumann stood for a short while, staring at the ocean space before ordering von Getz and Kaufmann over to the Haunebu. He watched them swim over and enter the other craft on the seabed.

"Hope I do not regret this." He turned to look at the Chancellor who was smiling.

"I think you made the right decision, Herr Schumann. I think it's time we went home."

END OF PART I

Coming in

The Rise
Part II
Protohuman

The lower levels of Dulce base have been destroyed.

While inspecting the caverns, Derek Mills and his team discover a lost city of ancient technology. Within the warrens of stone buildings they find a chamber, the interior walls covered in undecipherable writing.

The text could hold clues to support his controversial theories. It could be the greatest discovery of all time.

Sinister organisation MJ-12 have regrouped. They have a new research facility, more advanced than before where they are on the threshold of perfecting a terrifying organic product so powerful it could alter the path of human destiny forever.

New Swabia has survived a military coup. The people are living in tranquillity and isolation from the rest of the world. Hans Schumann has returned a hero after leading the assault on the Dulce base and rescuing the Chancellor. But there is a problem. During the assault, the location of New Swabia was disclosed to the leader of MJ-12. Now, he has demanded that Schumann hand himself over to troubleshoot their latest project. With the threat of military action against his country, Schumann has no choice but to co-operate.

Hypnotherapist Marius has been indoctrinated into the ranks

of the Templars. He has been exposed to a world of top secret conspiracy that he bitterly resents. His whole world has been turned upside down by revelations that many people would kill to know. Some are doing precisely that.

Then events take an even bigger twist leaving him questioning his sanity and even his own survival.